For D ~~
in F

Bear

M E Fuller

Also by Graham E. Fuller

Breaking Faith: a Novel of Espionage and an American's Crisis of Conscience in Pakistan
Bozorg Press, 2015

Turkey and the Arab Spring: Leadership in the Middle East
Bozorg Press, 2014

Three Truths and a Lie: a Memoir
Bozorg Press, 2012

A World Without Islam
Little Brown, 2010

The New Turkish Republic: Turkey's Pivotal Role in the Middle East
US Institute of Peace, 2008

The Future of Political Islam
Palgrave, 2003

The Arab Shi'a: The Forgotten Muslims (with Rend Francke)
St. Martin's, 1999

Turkey's Kurdish Question (with Henri Barkey)
Rowman and Littlefield, 1997

A Sense of Siege: The Geopolitics of Islam and the West (with Ian Lesser)
Westview, 1994

The New Foreign Policy of Turkey: From the Balkans to Western China
(with Ian Lesser) Westview, 1993

The Democracy Trap: Perils of the Post-Cold War World
Dutton, 1992

The Center of the Universe: The Geopolitics of Iran
Westview, 1991

How to Learn a Foreign Language
Storm King Press, 1987

Bear

A Novel of

the Great Bear Rainforest and

Eco-Violence

Graham E. Fuller

Bozorg Press

Copyright © 2018 by Graham E. Fuller

All rights reserved. No part of this publication may be reproduced, distributed, or transmitted in any form or by any means, or stored in a database or retrieval system without the prior written permission of the publisher.

ISBN: 978-1-9840-3594-3

Published by Bozorg Press
www.grahamefuller.com

This book is dedicated to the First Nations of British Columbia, Canada whose arts and wisdom have brought special richness and awareness to my life.

And to Bears, always a source of beauty, awe and inspiration.

Prologue

I am a particle drifting in the cosmos. A seed in a whirl of atoms whose dancing particles slowly converge. And then fuse. And then fuse again into a unique form of creation. My form took shape fifteen million years ago—when my purpose and mission were established. Solitary, I wandered the Asian tundra, slowly, ever eastwards, ever northwards, until I came to that swath of land that connected the old Asian landform with the new landform of the North American continent. I made my way across the great land bridge, merging with the living flow of all other creatures embarked on the great trek to the new continent. We roamed the land, part of a grand movement of diverse species fanning across the earth, finding our space.

And then, hundreds of thousands of years later, we first encountered two-legged creatures, latecomers who had struggled so recently across the land bridge behind us. The two-leggeds, unlike us, were out of their element. They were frightened, awestruck in the world, unable to make sense of the terrifying, primal, elemental forces of Nature in motion around them. They could not understand the Natural Order. As helpless diminutive creatures they showed fear, they cast about for comfort, for explanations of the natural forces on display. A few of the wise among them came to understand that through us, creatures of eternal wisdom, they could perhaps make some sense of Nature's daunting power and incomprehensible ways.

Thus early on the two-leggeds came to recognize my powers, my strength, vision, wisdom, my sense of order, propriety and justice—all that they craved in their threatened, helpless and exposed existence. Among myriad creatures I took primacy of place, mediating between the two-leggeds and the Great Forces.

That is my calling—the bearer of wisdom and insight. Even now those two-leggeds who do possess vision still seek me out to help navigate the medium between my world of Natural Forces, and theirs. They know they require me—if they are to make sense of Creation. If they are to perceive their own place and fulfill their own destiny.

But I, Bear, require no human perception to fulfill my own eternal destiny.

Chapter 1

The brown bear moves slowly up along the ridge, massive and heavy-set with a solid hump across its upper back. It grazes in the early spring grass, oblivious to the dot of a laser beam now playing across its body. "He's a beauty," the first man says. "Do we want to take him? We ain't seen nothing like him back home."

"Hell yeah, that massive head, make a great trophy. That's the finest grizz we've seen in a long time."

"Let's see if he's gonna move any closer, so's I can squeeze off a better shot."

Their adrenalin rising, the two men watch the bear amble slightly closer in their direction, still some quarter-mile off on the ridge perpendicular to where they are standing. It takes its time, and does not sense the hunters' presence on the ridge spur. Then suddenly it stops, raises its head and looks around.

"Shit, wind's changed, looks like he's caught our scent."

"OK, hold on a sec, let's see if he's going to move out any closer. There's not many places for him to run to. That stone ridge behind won't give him much protection. Worst, he might try to head down the snow scree. But that just gives us a better follow-on shot."

The bear now clearly senses the hunters even if it cannot see them. It makes a light huffing noise, and gazes all around. "I say go for it now. He could take off easy. Then it'd be a lot harder to get in a kill shot."

"Right. I got him right in the scope. Here goes." He squeezes the trigger. The great bear starts, trembles a moment, twists around, issues a bellowing noise. Suddenly, out of the trees behind, two yearling cubs head towards it, running.

"Shit, man, it's a fucking sow, she's got two cubs coming up to her."

"Jesus, we didn't even see 'em. How was we supposed to know she's a sow? We're not supposed to take a female with cubs. What in hell we do now?"

"Look, you already shot her. I say we follow through now, no point in leaving a dead bear here. We didn't see any damn cubs around her before we fired."

"I'm gonna get off another shot before she tries to run down the snow field, it'll be hard as hell to get to her if she goes down that steep slope."

The first man fires again, and a third time. The bear spins, stunned by the impact. She moves to the edge of the snow slope, a mixture of melting spring snow and bare rock scree. Traces of bright red begin to show up in the snow around her. She half falls down the steep slope, half sliding, still moving fast, undeterred. She turns to see that her cubs are following.

"Gimme a shot at her," the other hunter says. "She's not going down easy. We don't want her getting too far down that slope, be hell to get down there and get her back up."

He steps in and fires two shots in a row. The bear staggers in confusion, but still remains on her feet.

"You got her now, look at the blood on the snow, she's bleeding pretty hard."

But she still continues down the slope, stumbling, losing her balance here and there, the trail of blood growing behind her, mixing into the snow as the cubs follow. They can hear the cubs crying in fear as they try to follow the mother's erratic plunge down the slope. She loses her footing again, slips and rolls much farther down, no longer in control, emitting strange bellows. Her head begins to waver and sink, even as she struggles to get away.

"You got her, man, she can't stand up no more." The bear trips, unable to rise to her feet again. Her cubs, half rolling, half slipping, try to follow, giving small cries.

The sow now begins to roll down the hill out of control, leaving a long red wake in the white snow behind her. Her slide finally comes to a halt. She lies on the ground, gasping and bellowing. She raises her head up, blood pouring out of her mouth, and looks around to find her still unseen assailants. The cubs finally catch up and run up in fear to their mother's body, seeking protection. The mother still thrashes around on the spot, legs moving but unable to gain purchase in her death throes.

"Christ, that was messy," the other hunter said. "We got a long way down to go before we can get to her body."

"What are we gonna do about the cubs? This is goddam illegal. Think they would attack us? Do we need to take them out too?"

"No man, we didn't know she had cubs. Besides, they'll run away by the time we get down there."

"Shit, this is going to be a hell of a pull back up here with that monster."

"Minimum, we need the head and the skin, maybe the paws. That's plenty heavy right there. We can't carry the whole damn carcass back to camp anyway. Maybe tell some of the local Natives here. They might want to go and get the meat."

"No way, they're already way pissed off about us hunting their bears. Some damn sacred something to 'em."

"Well, we won't tell 'em then. Just leave it here. What about the cubs?"

"Just leave 'em. They're not too big but we'll need to chase them off before we skin the mother."

They set off, slipping and sliding down the scree. "Christ, it's gonna be a huge damn effort, but it's worth it. She's a real beauty."

"Damn right. That head'll look great over the fireplace. Or even get a bear skin rug out of it in your den."

The descent down the slope takes them half an hour before they finally bisect the blood-soaked snow path from where the bear had started her death descent. The two cubs are still with their mother, cowering beside her body, giving pathetic growls.

"Go on, get away," the first hunter shouts, waving his gun. The cubs don't budge from their mother's body. The other hunter finds a big stick nearby and comes back, threatening the cubs. But they don't move until he begins to deliver some solid blows. They pull back, cowering, snarling, as the hunters chase after them to scare them away. They finally take off, running down the slope and eventually into the underbrush.

"OK, let's get to work, it's gonna get dark soon. Last thing we need is to be out here with the blood and the meat. We'll skin as much of it as we can now, come back in the light to drag it up the slope. Maybe we can get some local guy to help us carry the skin out. Gonna be damn heavy."

They work their knives into the powerful neck of the mother, struggling to cut through the thick skin and fur, and to cut through the base of the skull and the vertebrae. Their hands are soaked with gore up to their elbows, but they finally detach the head from the carcass and loosen much of the skin around it.

"Let's leave the skin for now, we'll get it tomorrow, it's gonna be too damn dark to find our way back," the second hunter says.

They struggle back up the steep slope to the trail at the top where they first spotted the bear.

As they get back near the Native village where they had left their pickup a group of men confronts them. "You killed a goddam grizzly!" one of the men says. "Did you kill that sow that's out on that bluff?"

"We didn't know it was a sow," the first hunter says.

"Killing any of our bears is illegal! Get the hell out, this is our land and the bears are in our trust!" a man with some authority speaks out.

"We got permits, we paid for the hunt, we're legal here," the first hunter says.

"There's no legal, it's our land. Get out! Haven't you seen the signs saying no bear hunting here?"

"That's not an official sign. Nobody in Victoria told us we couldn't hunt in this area. This license overrides any regs you guys got here. Take it up with your government."

"The government don't represent us here, or our control over our land. And you killed a sow. We're reporting you guys, trespassing here on our land and killing our animals."

"Sorry, Jack, but we've got our license."

"We're gonna get your goddam license plate. This ain't over. You're gonna hear about this."

They spend the night in their pickup. Next morning they leave early to work their way down the icy slope to strip the skin from the carcass and haul it back up. "Probably the locals will go out and get the rest of the bear for meat, who knows."

As they struggle up the slope half-carrying, half dragging the heavy weight of the bearskin, they finally reach the top. They drag it towards a hunting gurney they had left farther down the trail to carry the bear skin out to their pickup. They finally manage to roll the gurney right up to the back of the vehicle.

A shot rings out. The first hunter totters and falls to the ground, blood coming out of a hole in his forehead. His friend ducks down for cover and to see what he can do, but the first hunter is already dead. The second hunter makes a run for the truck door. He fumbles in his clothes trying to find the keys to the truck. Another shot rings out. He claps his hand to his chest and then drops heavily to the ground.

"That should teach them sons-a-bitches," a voice in the woods says, as a white man emerges from behind the trees with a rifle in his hand, accompanied by another white man.

"Jesus, you shot them, you killed them!" a third man with them says. "I thought you were just going to take the skin off them, chase 'em off."

"What the hell you think we came all the way up here across the border for in the first place," the first man says. "These guys have been killing grizzlies for a good couple years. We know 'em from back home in Montana, they had it coming, sons-a-bitches."

"We better get the hell out of here fast, though," a second man said. "No telling who might have heard the shots. Natives'll be here in a flash."

"Let's get back to your truck, Joseph," the first man says. "We gotta move."

"Yeah, but Jesus, man, you've created a hell of a situation," the man named Joseph says. Cops are going to be onto us for sure. I wouldn't of come if I thought this was what you guys were planning."

"I think we done your Natives here a big favor, offing these damn poachers," the second man says.

They reach Joseph's pickup, clamber in and are soon out of sight. Behind them they leave the hunters' pickup, the two dead hunters on the ground and a trophy bear skin lying in the dirt.

Chapter 2

One dark fall afternoon as rain showers descended from the clouds clinging to the tops of the mountains of North Vancouver, Bjorn had to stay inside. He was playing on the dining room floor with a train set that he had recently been given on his fourth birthday. He made train noises as he pushed the engine along the tracks. He thought about the great distances that trains traveled and all the things that they carried. He had seen freight trains in the city, car after countless car loaded with goods. And he connected bridges to his wooden tracks so that the train could cross the waterways and mountains that were all around him. He concentrated on the shape of tracks as they wound around under the kitchen table.

Suddenly his older brother Malcolm, then six, stormed into the room. Bjorn was pushing the engine along the network of wooden tracks spread out on the floor.

"That's my engine, give it back!" Malcolm commanded. Bjorn refused so his brother tried to twist it out of his hand. Bjorn hurled it against the wall where it fell upon the floor with the wheel mechanism broken off.

"Now look what you did, you little rat! You wrecked my engine! I wish we had never adopted you!"

Senses moved into high alert. "What do you mean, adopted?"

"It means you're not part of this family. Your own mom didn't want you, so she gave you to our mom. And I can see why!"

"That's not true, you made that up!"

"I did not! Go ask Mom!"

The train went off the tracks. Bjorn fell silent, his mind flying off into orbit as he now absent-mindedly pushed his train out onto the red rug, onto new terrain. He rolled this dark information around in his head for days, trying to digest its meaning.

But as early as age three Bjorn had sensed he was somehow different from the rest of the Fisher family. His mother Claire often found him peering into the mirror, examining his features. He saw eyes that were black and almond-shaped instead of blue and rounded like his siblings. Hair dark instead of blonde. Skin swarthier than his older siblings. The difference disquieted him, but Bjorn kept it to himself.

Now it did explain why he looked different. He suddenly felt alone. But he wasn't ready to go ask his mother right away. He wasn't sure he understood what it really meant, or the biology of it all. But he did sense a snapping of some kind of bonds.

Over the next few days his mother Claire seemed to notice something was wrong. "What is the matter, Bjorn?" his mom asked. "You aren't feeling well? You seem angry about something."

"You know why." He stared down into his plate, scowling at it.

"No, honey, we don't. Is something bothering you?"

Bjorn looked up. "You don't care. You aren't my mother anyways."

His father Ralf exchanged glances with his mother, pursing his lips and shaking his head. "I knew this was coming," he muttered.

"Who told you that, Bjorn?" his mother asked, leaning over and putting her hand on his arm.

"Malcolm."

His mother looked sharply over at Malcolm.

"Well, he needs to know sometime," Malcolm muttered, looking down into his plate.

"You are very much part of this family, Bjorn," his mother said. "Yes, you are adopted, when you were only one. You were in a foster home and you didn't have your own mother to take care of you. But we chose you to be in our family. We were planning to tell you soon, when you could understand it better. But you have grown up here for four years in this house, just like Malcolm and Erica. You're no different. And we love you just as much."

That evening after his mother finished reading him a bed-time story he turned to her again. "Why didn't I have a mother?"

His mother folded the book closed in her lap. "You did have a mother, Bjorn, but we don't know what happened to her. We don't know why she couldn't keep you, she may have been very poor or sick, or maybe had too many other kids and couldn't take care of them all. She wanted to put you with a family that would be able to take care of you and love you. And we do."

"Dad doesn't."

"Of course he does, he's just a little stressed with problems at work at the moment, that's all. It's not about you."

"Well, he never smiles at me."

"Bjorn, he does. I don't know why you say that."

Bjorn had noticed that Ralf was a big and gregarious man with others, but not much with him.

Life in the family went on as normal although his father was often away. But for Bjorn nothing was normal any more. With the revelation of his adoption, a glass partition had slid down and clicked into place between himself and the rest of the family. Differences between him and the others grew more apparent. He was a little large for his age, solidly-built compared to his thinner siblings. Even though he was two years younger than his older brother, they were nearly the same size. Bjorn could tell that Malcolm was sometimes a little intimidated by him, by his unexpected outbursts. Malcolm never wanted Bjorn to forget that Malcolm was the oldest. And Bjorn knew Malcolm generally had their father's support when fights broke out between them.

Bjorn wasn't much interested in classical music, while the rest of the family all took piano lessons. When his parents started him on piano lessons Bjorn resisted. He hated sitting down for so long and trying to figure out the black keys from the white. He finally refused to take lessons anymore. He had little interest in team sports or going to matches where his siblings were competing. The only sports he was at all interested in were boxing or wrestling, individual sports that represented a test of strength and where he relied on himself, not on others. And the family all talked too much, analyzing this or debating that or trying to show who was smarter or who knew more, every night at supper his siblings telling about how well they had done at school that day. Bjorn just sat and listened distantly without a shred of desire to compete in the talk.

He also began to throw tantrums about seemingly little things, like demanding meat instead of the frequent vegetarian dishes that his mother made. Or about what television programs the family would watch. He liked nature programs, while Malcolm liked hockey games. Bjorn didn't like competing with others because it often ended up with him losing. That made him feel he wasn't as good as others. "Why don't you ever want to play board games along with the rest of us, Bjorn?" his mother asked. This was the last thing Bjorn wanted, competing openly at the table and trying to score points over others. He began to view the other members of the family with different eyes, watching like an outside observer taking mental notes. But he kept his silence, not daring to probe.

One day his mother found a brown teddy bear in Bjorn's closet she'd never seen before. "Where did this come from?" she asked Bjorn. He just shrugged, "I saw it Jason's house the other day."

"You just took it?"

Bjorn shrugged again. "I just wanted him, that's all. Jason doesn't care."

He had been alone in his cousin Jason's playroom for a few minutes and suddenly discovered this bear perched high up on a dresser, peering out. It had piercing black eyes and Bjorn was sure the bear was staring right at him; he could feel some kind of waves moving out towards him. He knew it was offering itself to Bjorn. It was meant for him. He stuck it inside his coat and snuck it back home where he hid it. He visited the bear in his closet sometimes to talk about things in his life. The bear was a good listener and offered reassurances to Bjorn. The bear's existence remained a secret between the bear and himself for a few weeks until his mother found it.

"Well, I don't know if you should keep it, Bjorn, if it belongs to Jason. If you'd like a teddy bear of your own you should just ask."

"No, I don't want another bear, I want this bear! He always looks at me. He wants to take care of me!"

"Well, why don't you maybe ask Jason, see if he'd let you have it?" His mother smiled. A few days later Jason told Bjorn he could have the teddy bear if he wanted. "Anyway I have a tiger that's better."

After the bear came out of hiding in his closet he always went to sleep with Bjorn. Jason had called it "Brownie", but Malcolm knew that wasn't the bear's real name. He gave it a new name, Ears. Ears had prominent rounded ears on top of his head and was always listening, watching, looking out for Bjorn. Malcolm sometimes grabbed Ears and ran off with him, enjoying Bjorn's outraged reaction of piling into him fists flailing.

"Jeesh, Bjorn, chill out, it's just a toy."

But it wasn't a toy. Bjorn and Ears became inseparable. He listened to Ears. And Ears listened to him. "We will always take care of each other," Ears told him. And Ears was always there for Bjorn when things got bad. He would listen to Bjorn's problems when family pressures grew too uncomfortable. Ears understood Bjorn when others did not.

The Fishers' house in North Vancouver looked out over the city from the base of mountains. Residents of the North Shore were accustomed to regular visits by black bears wandering down from the mountains in search of food. Like all residents of the area, they had to make sure they did not put out their garbage bin for collection until garbage collection day. "We don't want to attract the bears, do we Bjorn?" his mother said.

"But maybe we should give them something to eat," Bjorn said.

"No, then they'll get used to it and become nuisance bears. The rangers have to get rid of nuisance bears."

"A nuisance bear?" What was that? How could a bear be a "nuisance," and be killed because of it? They didn't see any bears around their house, but one day when Bjorn was helping his mother put their garbage bin out on the street for collection their neighbor came by and talked about a bear that had tried to get into his house while they were away. "What did the bear do?" Bjorn asked, his attention riveted.

"Well, it tore open the window screen and crawled inside our house looking for food in the kitchen. But I guess it didn't find any and it left."

The bear got inside the house! Bjorn found the story thrilling, terrifying. "Will a bear try to get into our house?" Bjorn asked his mother. "Would you like that?" his mother asked teasingly. Bjorn didn't know whether he would like it or not. But now he knew that a bear presence was out there.

When they went on walks in the local forest he sometimes used to watch the beavers in a nearby creek paddling around building their dams. "They may be interesting to watch," his father said, "but the environmentalists don't like them. The beavers need to be removed to let the water flow freely so that salmon can swim farther upstream to spawn. They're going to get rid of these beavers soon." Bjorn wept bitterly when he found the beavers were gone the next week and the dams had been destroyed. "People shouldn't be allowed to kill animals," he told his mother.

"I know," his mother said, stroking his hair.

Some evenings in bed he found it hard to get to sleep. He felt sad, isolated, and would sometimes cry. But he felt better when his mother held him on her lap and sang folk songs to him. "Sing the one about the bear."

"*Oh, the bear came over the mountain…to see what he could see… And the other side of the mountain was all that he could see.*"

"What was on the other side of the mountain?" Bjorn asked.

"I don't know, it's just a song."

"Well, was it something good for the bear, or maybe something bad?"

"Well, that's just it, we don't know what it was on the other side of the mountain, do we?"

"Was that bear like Ears?"

"Could be. But there are lots of bears who are looking to come over the mountain."

"Over our mountain, behind the house?"

"Sure, could be."

Bjorn fell silent, absorbing this reality so close to his own house. After a few moments Bjorn asked, "What was her name, then?"

"Who?"

"My mother."

His mother was taken aback at the sudden change of topic, revealing something deeper lying on Bjorn's mind.

"We don't know Bjorn, they didn't give us that information."

"So how did you find me?" He stared at her inquiringly.

His mother sighed. "Well, I've told you the story before. I used to visit the foster home regularly when I was a nurse for the health department. And I met you and fell in love with you. You were quite sick at the time. I wanted to take you home to be my own little boy."

"You already had a little boy. You had Malcolm."

"Malcolm isn't my little boy, he and Erica were part of Ralf's family before I married him. So they're my stepchildren."

Even though he had heard it before, this recitation of this whole complex family story was discomfiting for Bjorn. It suggested uncertainty, transience, instability of relationships.

Bjorn looked inquiringly at his mother.

"Bjorn, it's complicated, as I've told you before. My first husband John died of a bad disease shortly after I adopted you. I hadn't met your step-father, Ralf, then. And I had wanted you. You were different, you were special."

"How was I different?" he persisted.

"Well, your mother was First Nations, and they are a special part of British Columbia. And you needed a home. And you were sick for a while, with tuberculosis, until we could get you better."

One question threw the door open to another and to an endless series of chambers to explore, but for now Bjorn fell silent, needing to digest these new realities.

Story time seemed to lead inevitably to more questions about Bjorn's own story. His own life and background; that was a story too but nobody knew it all. He usually absorbed the additional nuggets of information about his background in silence each time, unsure of how to integrate them. But at night these facts perched over the backboard of his bed like a black raven. They dominated his thoughts as he tried to picture the past events that had brought him to the Fisher family. But he couldn't recall them. Sometimes he thought maybe he had a memory—some image of a dock next to some dark water, a small motor launch coming up as he was held in someone's arms? He couldn't be sure. He really couldn't access any memory earlier than living with this family. He was sure his new mother Claire loved him but he wasn't sure about his step-father Ralf. His step-father seemed to transfer some anger towards his mother every time he was angry at Bjorn, as if he blamed her for him. When Bjorn got into fights with his brother or sister his father took their side. Still, when all his cousins came for over for Thanksgiving dinner they all seemed to treat Bjorn no differently than the rest of their cousins.

Except Bjorn had now eaten from the tree of knowledge about his past life, and that had changed things for him. He sometimes felt like he was a guest among his family, or playing a role. He confided in Ears. *They all know I'm not really part of the family. They don't say anything. They're nice to me, but they know I'm from the outside.*

You are not outside. I am with you, and you are with me, Ears said.

One Saturday night after his parents had had some friends over to celebrate his mother's birthday, Bjorn woke up in the middle of the night feeling sick to his stomach. He left his room and struggled his way down the hall; it was dark but there was a faint light coming out of his parents' room. He heard strange noises. He came quietly up to the door that was slightly ajar. The sounds disturbed him. His mother seemed to be crying, as if in some pain. He peered around the door and saw his mother on the bed in the glow of the bedside lamp; she had no clothes on and was on her back and writhing in some kind of pain with his father on top of her. And his father was also big and naked against the lamp glow. His father seemed transformed into an animal. He heard him uttering a growling sound as he moved against his mother's body. Bjorn was frightened. He did not dare open the door or to call out. He knew his father was hurting his mother, but he didn't understand. He watched in mixed horror and fascination for a few moments before he retreated back down the hallway, trembling.

He went into his bathroom and knelt down by the toilet and vomited. A few minutes later his mother came down the hall into the bathroom, dressed in a bathrobe. "Is something the matter, Bjorn? Did you try to come into our room?" she asked. He shook his head but remained staring at the floor, unmoving. She stroked his head.

"Why was Daddy hurting you?" he asked after a minute.

"Why, Bjorn, no one was hurting anyone. We were just…playing a kind of grown-up game, cuddling."

Bjorn remained silent and allowed himself to be led back to bed. But as he lay there he knew he had witnessed something important, his father, doing things he found frightening, his father being like an animal. He had made animal sounds. He knew he hated his father. Bjorn could never rid his mind of the image again. He had gotten a glimpse into another world, a world of passions and drives he was not supposed to witness. But he now knew that a mysterious, wild, untamed, disturbing world existed out there. A sense of animals beneath the surface of human life, animals seemingly possessing people. He never asked his mother again about what he had witnessed, and nothing more was ever said. But something had changed. He had felt the animal presence in human life. *Yes*, Ears said, *Animals. We are all animals. We are all around.*

Then came the incident with the shovel. He and Malcolm had been quarreling over toys, again. When Bjorn was out of the room, Malcolm grabbed up Ears and snuck out back and stuffed him in the garbage can in the shed. Later in the afternoon Bjorn was smitten when he found Ears missing, distraught that he couldn't find him anywhere. Malcolm smirked at him for some minutes. Bjorn starting yelling at the top of his lungs. "OK," Malcolm finally said. "You want to know where your precious Ears is? Where he belongs, in the garbage!"

Bjorn rushed out into the shed and tore the lid off the garbage can, revealing Ears, lying among coffee grounds, egg shells and leftover food scraps. Malcolm then grabbed up Ears and danced around the yard with him, taunting Bjorn to try to get him. Too late he seemed to recognize that he had pushed Bjorn beyond the breaking point. Bjorn ran over to the shed, picked up a spade and rushed after Malcolm and swung it at him. Malcolm tried to dodge the spade, but it struck him a glancing blow in the face and cut a gash in his cheek and jaw. Blood poured out. He screamed and his parents came running. They witnessed the blood all over Malcolm's face and shirt. His mother yelled out at Bjorn who was standing there with the spade still in his hands, grabbed Malcolm and rushed him to the car. His father stalked Bjorn in the garden and in cold fury slugged him in the face. Bjorn fell to the ground, dazed.

His brother came home from the hospital late the following day with a huge bandage over the side of his face covering twenty-four stitches. "That was very ugly, what you did to Malcolm," his mother said. "You may have been angry at him, but that kind of violence is unacceptable. You were out of control. He could have been really seriously hurt. He is going to have a scar on his face for the rest of his life."

Bjorn took Ears and went off to his room and locked the door. "I'll never let them take you away again," he told Ears. The bear understood Bjorn had tried to protect him. Bjorn refused to come out for dinner. The next morning he refused to come out for breakfast. "If you don't come out, young man," his father threatened, "I'm going to break down your goddam door." Bjorn refused.

"Please, Ralf, let him be," his mother said. "Just everyone cool down!"

But the door latch shattered and his father burst into his room. Bjorn cowered in the corner. His mother rushed in. "Ralf, leave him alone!"

His father glared at him fixedly for a few moments, breathing heavily, and then stomped out. "I told you we're going to have to do something about this kid! It's getting dangerous!"

"Look, I know there's a problem," his mother later said to his father. "But just try to stay off his back, OK? I'm not defending what he did to Malcolm, but it does look like it was Malcolm who started it. Let's just try to avoid confrontation. It hurts us all."

The tension hung in the air for days, but nothing more was said.

Feeling more isolated, Bjorn's thoughts turned to his real mother. His imagination outran his knowledge. He often made up his own answers to his questions, especially when he was in bed, in the dark. Who was she, what did she look like? He was sure she had long black hair and a long braid. And rounded silver earrings. But why had she given him away? What had he done that had caused her to do that? He was reluctant to ask any more questions now, fearful of answers he might get. Any new facts would have to be integrated, any new revelations would have to find a place like bricks in the wall of his mind's story. Each new brick of information required slight restructuring of the wall again. He could feel his parents, his brother and sister around him, were now all beginning to look at him warily. They avoided dealing with him out of fear of his volatile temper. *They knew was not one of them.*

Chapter 3

"Hey, are you adopted?" Jimmy, Bjorn's friend in second grade asked him one day while he was hanging by his knees on the jungle gym. "I don't know," Bjorn answered sullenly, swinging down to the ground to cover his anxiety. How had Jimmy heard? Probably from Malcolm. Bjorn saw now he would always be a little bit different from everybody else even in the schoolyard. Nobody else actually asked him about it, but he knew they all knew. He felt sidelined, diminished.

He began to pick fights in school whenever any other kid looked at him askance; he knew why they looked at him like that. He started hanging out with other kids who knew their parents didn't understand them, who were often in trouble, or rebellious, or who challenged their teachers' authority. Bjorn felt they all belonged to part of a group he felt more comfortable with.

It took more than a year for Bjorn to feel he had mostly digested the raw lumps of information about the circumstances of his adoption. He wondered whether he was ready to pry the door open just a crack farther. One Saturday morning as Claire was driving him to his taekwondo class, he turned and asked, "Who was she, my real mother?"

"Well, first of all, Bjorn, I'm your real mother in most ways. I'm the one who is raising you, and feeding you and taking care of you and loving you. Isn't that real?" She looked at him in the rear view mirror and smiled.

"Yes, but I mean my *real* mother."

"Your birth mother is what they call her, Bjorn, the one who actually gave birth to you, even if she didn't raise you." When the car came to a halt at the stoplight she looked back at him. He was staring down absently at the floor.

"So who was she, then?"

"Bjorn, I really I think we've talked about all this before. All we know is she was probably from somewhere on the BC coast. We knew almost nothing about her. We never met her. But they told us she had been poor and in bad health and couldn't take care of you. That was before my first husband died. We didn't think we could have any kids and so I had wanted to adopt you. And I was happy to get you, the child I fell in love with in the foster home."

They arrived at the taekwondo studio and his mother waited for Bjorn to get out of the car. But he was still caught up in his line of thought.

"Well, do you know why she was sick?"

"Bjorn, we don't know. She was poor."

"So how did you know my name if you didn't meet her?"

His mother smiled. "We didn't know your name. You were less than one year old. We gave you your name ourselves—Bjorn—it's an old name in my family, and it's popular in Norway. And it's a nice name, it means "bear.""

Bear.

Eager for reassurance he wanted to hear his mother tell him again why she had chosen him.

"I fell in love with you when I first saw you at the foster home. You had black hair and dark eyes, like a deep pool of water, with a serious face. I knew you were the one when I first saw you."

"But what did Dad say?"

"My first husband died not long after we adopted you. Then I married your stepfather. You know about that, he already had two kids when you and I joined his family...OK, enough of that for now, I think you better get to your class."

This whole account was supposed to be reassuring, but it wasn't. Mothers dying, changing, disappearing, remarrying, fathers coming and going. And none of them really had anything to do with him. He felt angry. How could he not know where he came from? There were so many other things to consider now. Who was his real mother and where was she from? What had really happened? Where was she now?

These questions popped up in his mind, so often they kept him up at night thinking. They churned under his pillow in bed. A Native woman, Indian woman? He had some books about American Indians. Maybe he was born in a teepee out on the plains with the winds whistling through the grass and the beating of drums and the smell of smoke fires. People on horseback with feathers in their hair, carrying bows and arrows chasing herds of charging buffaloes on the prairie, with whoops and yells and the smell of sweaty horses. Was that him? Where he had been taken away from?

He now began to imagine himself differently, as a secretive and mysterious figure among his friends, bearing a secret identity unknown to everyone else. And "Bear" was his name. The name excited him, it sounded right. He had told Ears about the meaning of his name as soon as he found out. Ears was immediately delighted at the information. To Bjorn the name suggested power. He would smile inwardly to himself at his secret that set him apart, giving him special character among these unsuspecting ordinary white kids.

You are right. You are special. You are not alone. We will protect you. Bjorn heard Ears speaking to him.

After several months Bjorn had extracted all the nourishment he could out of the few additional crumbs that had been shared with him about his past. He never turned to his step-father to seek answers. He knew he hadn't even been on the scene when his mother chose him at the foster home; Ralf seemed uncomfortable with the whole matter. And Bjorn hadn't yet really thought much about who his own real father might have been either. Bjorn didn't yet know enough of the biological facts of life that would make a father just as important as a mother. All he knew was that a father was just a normal part of any family, but more distant than a mother. If he'd had another mother then he must have had another father as well, everybody did. But a father figure was someone who was more a kind of head of the family, stricter, and away much of the time, like his step-father on his periodic engineering trips.

Bjorn got along with his father best when they were out in the forest on family hikes. One Sunday afternoon in the springtime after the snow had melted away on the lower slopes of the North Shore, they were working their way along the trail when his father called out, "Look, kids, there's a bear!" Bjorn spun around and looked up the side of the mountain forest where his father pointed. There it was, a black shape loping up the hill away from them. And then he saw another bear alongside the first. Bjorn was surprised that the bears seemed to be running away from them. "They look like they're young bears, they're probably frightened of us," his mother said. *Frightened of us?* It was the first time Bjorn had seen bears out in the forest. He was thrilled. They were up there, in the woods, in the forests above their house. But he knew he did not need protection from them.

The very absence of any more information about his past continued to expand like an empty galaxy in his mind, leaving huge space to be filled. The few details that he had learned, the more his questions multiplied. He started ornamenting his imagination with vivid thoughts about what might have been. Alternative stories that insinuated themselves into his mind depending on his mood. His mother gave him books about First Nations people living in British Columbia. They didn't have horses and they didn't have teepees. They lived in the forest, and built long wooden houses and carved totem poles and caught fish and ate seaweed. He began to draw his own totem poles in his notebook. And the next Christmas he opened a package and found a colouring book all about totem poles, just what he had been pestering his mother about for months.

The totem poles seized his imagination. Huge logs were transformed into a column of amazing creatures all fighting for space high up on the pole—bears and beavers and ravens and sea wolves and sea snakes and salmon and orcas. And all sitting, crowded, piled one on top of the other. Did the smartest or the strongest animal get to sit on top? Or at the bottom? Columns of animal power. Animals unsure about all the other animals they had to share the pole with.

But he saw something else too. On some poles there were a few small human figures as well, but some looked worried sitting in among all the fierce creatures. He noticed a few of the humans were being held in the arms of some of the larger creatures, like they were being protected and comforted. Bjorn saw one bear that was protecting a human in his arms, just like he did with Ears. The creatures didn't seem to fight even though many of them had sharp teeth. They accepted their place on the pole, like one big family. Maybe they were more together than his own family. "Why are there so many different creatures on the pole?" he asked his mother.

"Well, I guess different tribes felt closer to different creatures. They're all supposed to tell a story."

All these animals—what were their stories? What were they all doing with each other? Were they pets to the First Nations peoples, or just decorations, or art like paintings? Or protectors like Ears? He especially loved the twin bear cubs on many of the poles, with their little round ears sticking up. You could always recognize a bear on a totem pole by its ears. But the bears looked more serious than Ears. He knew from the stories about them that the two bears had had a human for a mother and a bear for a father. Maybe there were real bears in the world that had mixed human and bear parents. Nobody knew a thing about who his real mother was. Could it have been the other way around with him, with a bear for a birth mother? He didn't dare ask his mother about that.

He watched programs on the Adventure Channel about bears, sometimes with Ears sitting with him. Bjorn even started asking for books about bears, and how they lived and what they did, books that might tell him more about who he was. "I think you wish you were a bear instead of a boy," his mother joked one evening as she stepped over Bjorn lying on the living room rug in his pajamas looking at one of his books on bears.

Ears was always there for him. He understood Bjorn's worries and concerns. Bjorn confided in him. Ears sometimes spoke to him, encouraged him, told him that he would be strong and learn about the real world.

One evening after he came home from a birthday party and was going to bed, he looked at his mother. "A boy at school told me that a hiker was killed last week by bears up in the North Shore mountains behind us. Didn't we walk up there once?"

"Yes, we did," she replied. "I heard about that poor woman. I'm afraid it's true. It can happen. But one reason is that the forests are the bears' home. Sometimes when people push too far into the bears' own areas the bears get upset and afraid and fight back."

"If I went into the forest, like even up the mountain behind us, is it dangerous for me? Could a bear attack me?"

"Mmm, it's possible if you aren't careful and alert to where they might be. But Bjorn, you shouldn't worry about this, it is very unlikely that you would be attacked by a bear. It happens only rarely, and usually when people aren't being careful, or walk by themselves."

You shouldn't walk by yourself in the forest? Bjorn reflected for a moment. "Well, how come this woman was attacked?"

"These things happen sometimes. I don't know what the bear was feeling—maybe scared or threatened, or it was a mother bear protecting her cubs."

And although Bjorn could tell Ears his secrets, Ears didn't always fully reassure Bjorn in the way that he wanted. The idea of dying in the forest presented a disturbing new reality to him. Mystery in the forest, yes, dangerous creatures, perhaps. But the idea that bears might also be killers introduced a new element of anxiety. Bjorn asked Ears about dying. *I am with you no matter what,* Ears said. "But will you protect me?" *I will be with you.* "Could I die in the forest?" Bjorn persisted. *We all die in the forest,* Ears seemed to say. *Do not worry. We will always be with you to the end,* Ears reassured him. "What end?" Ears said nothing more.

He began to resist family outings with his family. They all wanted to go and ride bicycles or play hockey and he didn't. He was known for having a short fuse in school and tore into anyone who dissed him. He especially hated Benedict, the boy that lived a few houses away down the street in a much bigger house than Bjorn's. Whenever he saw Bjorn, Benedict would ask him where his feather was, or to make whooping noises with his hand over his mouth and prance around like an Indian around a bonfire. One day when they were all out playing baseball in the park and Benedict started making sounds like an Indian chant again, Bjorn picked up the baseball bat and ran at Benedict with bat raised. Benedict raised his arm to protect his head and took the blow on the arm. There was a sound of a bone snapping. Benedict's parents said they didn't want Bjorn to come near their house again.

Bjorn was now on the lookout for indications that his parents might not really love him, that they preferred his siblings. His father certainly did. Any time his parents were angry at him Bjorn took it as evidence of different treatment. Sometimes he would make scenes or demand special privileges, just to test them, to prove to himself he was not truly loved. And then he grew angry that he was in this situation at all, that nobody would talk to him about it except Ears, that everyone had tried to conceal it all, that they didn't care. And finally he felt loneliness and anxiety: if there was trouble, could he be sure whether his family would really be there to take care of him? Or would he be viewed as in a different category than every other family member? Could he then be passed on to some other family?

He felt his father particularly found fault with him. At breakfast one Sunday morning while the children were squabbling at the table over who got the last pancake his father said, "It belongs to Malcolm. He asked first."

"He did not, I asked first," yelled Bjorn.

His father turned, looked down and slapped Bjorn's hand. "Stop playing with your food, Bjorn, I'm tired of this, you're getting syrup all over the damn table."

Bjorn stared at him coldly for a moment. "You can't tell me what to do! You aren't my real father. I'm not part of this family."

"This kid!" his father muttered, shaking his head. He rose up impatiently. "I'm off," he announced, "I'm late for a golf game."

"I thought you were going to spend more time with the family on Sundays," his mother said.

"I need a break."

"Yeah, and who with?" she snapped. His father glared at her and walked out.

Claire was growing more troubled that Bjorn's presence seemed to be creating deeper family tensions. And Ralf was away more often on business trips. She worried he had a roving eye.

That evening when Bjorn was coming downstairs to say goodnight he overheard them talking. "This is the kind of stuff I was afraid of. I know you've worked with him, Claire, but with a kid like this from a different background, he just doesn't seem ever to fit in."

"He just needs reassurance Ralf, cut him a little slack, he's still trying to find his place."

"OK. But it could be much more than that. We don't know a thing about his background, whether his mother could have been an alcoholic or something, he could have brain damage. It's asking for trouble when you adopt a kid with no knowledge of his background."

"We've been over this many times, Ralf, and I'm not going to go there again. It's all in how we bring him up that counts. And I think it's cruel to suggest there's some kind of genetic issue here, like some curse or something…and besides, I think you just…"

"Just what?" Ralf demanded.

"I just think you might resent him because I brought him from my first marriage. And that John had supported his adoption."

"Look, I never even knew John, he died before we even met. It's just I feel like I can't get through to Bjorn—he's not like Malcolm and Erica."

"That's just because they're your own biological children. Well, I feel like Bjorn is my biological child and I want him treated with love and respect!"

When a Parent-Teacher meeting came up, Claire Fisher went with mixed feelings. She hoped to gain greater insight into Bjorn's behavior from an independent, professional's view, but she also feared she might not like what she would hear. The fifth grade home room teacher expressed hope that both parents could be present for the meeting, but Ralf was away. Claire knew he was all too happy to miss the meeting.

Claire had to scrunch down a bit to sit in the too-small student desk opposite the teacher behind her own desk. "We're concerned, Mrs. Fisher, about Bjorn's general conduct in school. He seems distracted, has poor attention span, shows little interest in school work. I'm afraid he has a negative attitude, and spends a lot of his time with kids who aren't so well-adjusted to school. May I ask, are there any particular problems at home that we should be aware of?"

Claire shifted in her seat. "No, nothing special…well, first, I'm sure you know that Bjorn is an adopted child. He seems to think a lot these days about that, wondering about where he really comes from and where he belongs."

The teacher nodded with a seeming sense of recognition. "Well, I get the feeling he thinks a passive-aggressive approach towards his teachers will look "cool" in the eyes of the other students, maybe gain him greater acceptance."

"Do you think some kind of acceptance is that much on his mind?" Claire asked.

"Well, he seems to spend most of his time with other kids who are minorities, like Asians and Sikhs and First Nations. It's as if he feels that is where he belongs, not with the broader classroom of students. And sometimes it's with kids with similar negative attitudes. He can also be impulsive on the playground, he gets into fist-fights easily, as if he has a really short temper. I just mention this so you can keep an eye out for possible motivations behind his actions."

Claire hoped the teacher might herself possess some deeper insights into the situation, but she offered little more on this topic and limited herself to discussing Bjorn's grades which were fairly mediocre. "He does seem to be somewhat interested in animals. This comes out in biology classes when he talks with interest about how animals might view things."

"Yes, he's always had a lot of interest in bears. But I'm not sure how to tie it into anything else."

In the end Claire gained little new insight except that Bjorn's behavior at school seemed fairly consistent with what she had seen at home. She left the school, surrounded by the sounds of children laughing and yelling in the school-yard. She spotted Bjorn over in the corner with two other boys, not participating in the games. Where was he in this sea of swirling juvenile emotions, a storm of waves that could move in any direction? She didn't know where these impulses were sending him, and she was daunted by the reality that she had quite limited control over them.

On a rainy Saturday afternoon in the fall the family went off to the zoo as part of Malcolm's birthday celebration. Once inside, Malcolm dragged the family straight to the reptile house. But Bjorn's attention had been seized by a sign pointing to "Bear House" to where he headed off on his own. He approached the dark hall of the building and, upon entering, an intense odour flooded his nostrils, animal, raw, elemental. He entered slowly. In the gloom he perceived two cages. The first contained two young black bears draped intimately over each other in sleep right next to a big red ball and a small pool. Next to it was a second and larger cage. As Bjorn approached he saw that it contained a much bigger bear. "Ursus arctos horribilis, Canadian Grizzly Bear" the sign read. The grizzly was not only much bigger and brown, but bore a notable hump on its shoulder. He wasn't sure what *ursus arctos* meant, but the word *horribilis* caused the hairs on his neck to stand up.

The grizzly seemed to have been dozing as people watched it, but as Bjorn approached the cage it opened an eye and then quickly rose to its feet and stared at Bjorn and swayed its head. "Wow, what did you say to him?" a woman standing next to Bjorn asked jokingly. Bjorn recoiled. The bear was staring him right in the eyes. Its fur was rough and dirty, matted with straw and feces. The smell was overpowering, penetrating. *Turn me loose, let me go.* The unspoken message registered with absolute clarity in Bjorn's mind. He didn't dare look at the fixed eyes of the bear any longer because he knew he could do nothing to help. This was the first live grizzly bear Bjorn had ever seen and its presence overwhelmed him. The grizzly stood up on its hind legs, emphasizing its mass. A sense of latent power, dominance and majesty, all repressed behind bars, left among cage filth and gawking tourists— all these feelings emanated from its dark hulk. It stirred deep within Bjorn a sense of awe as well as fear. Was it malevolence? Or simply raw emotion, intensity of presence?

The cave is my place, my refuge, my nurturing womb, the home of hibernation where I belong. To hibernate is not to sleep. It is to reflect, to gain deeper perspective. To perceive, to bear witness to events. My cave.

Transfixed, Bjorn stood there for a long time. He received a flow of emotions, almost like words. But he did not fully understand the concepts emanating from the bear's presence. He just knew that certain thoughts were being transmitted to him. Bjorn retreated slowly to the darker shadows of the back wall of the Bear House, the bear following his motions intently. Minutes later his father came in. "Bjorn, damn it, you're not to go off on your own like this! We couldn't find you for ages."

Bjorn said nothing to his parents right away about the bear. But he knew something had passed between the two of them, he felt it in the pit of his stomach. Sensations that were not fully clear, concepts that he could not quite understand, but that were products of the bear's mind. It thrilled him. And frightened him. "That bear really wanted to get out of his cage, Mom, like he needed to go to his den," Bjorn told his mother as they stood in the aquarium section later on, eating soft ice cream. "Yes, I'm afraid most of these animals want to get out of their cages," his mother said.

"No, Mom, this bear really wants to escape. He's angry. He told me."

"So what did he say to you?"

Bjorn thought for a minute, trying to provide words and clarity to a series of powerful mental impressions. "He said this isn't his home. Like his home is in a cave. That is where he can hibernate and think. He can't hibernate in the cage."

Claire smiled.

Ears too also changed as Bjorn grew older. He seemed to age, his eyes grew deeper, more intense. The friendly smile stitched on Ears's face had grown faded and worn and a little crooked. He looked more serious. Ears told Bjorn that Bjorn was alone in this world except for him, but that he would find his own world outside, in the forest. Bjorn had the feeling that Ears had some special power inside, more than his fuzzy fur let on. Ears also was growing wilder in his thoughts, a little less comforting, less of a toy and more of a living force or part of the forest now, with feelings that Bjorn had not sensed before. He said that Bjorn should find other bears in the forest who could also be his friends. Bigger bears than Ears. Bjorn sometimes found it harder to know where Ears really belonged or whether he could trust him anymore.

At night when Bjorn was in bed, he could see Ears on the shelf nearby. His eyes were more alive in the faint light of the room and he seemed to be staring at Bjorn. Once he made Bjorn feel so uncomfortable that he got up and turned Ears around so that he no longer stared at him; he didn't know what Ears wanted and it kept him awake. He wasn't fully sure any more what Ears really thought about him now. He just knew that things were shifting towards something new.

Chapter 4

That summer when Bjorn was twelve the family set off again on the ferry over to Vancouver Island, to the vast stretch of land that runs hundreds of miles north, parallel to the coast of the BC mainland. They liked to go to a campground at the edge of the massive wilderness reserve of Strathcona Provincial Park. The trip was one thing Bjorn actually enjoyed doing with his family. His eagerness to set off on longer hikes in the forest caused his father to warm to Bjorn's more adventuresome character; the mountain hikes created virtually the only occasion when Bjorn felt he had any real relationship with his father.

His father mentioned he wanted to try climbing in the Elk River Mountains, located within the park. Bjorn showed immediate interest in the hike, more than his siblings did. His father seemed to appreciate his companionship on the trail. "It's funny how Bjorn responds to the wilderness," Ralf told Claire. "Maybe here's the First Nations coming out in him." The mountains towered over the plain below, patches of snow still dotting the green expanse, even in summer. As the sun went down the angular light revealed fissures in the face of the mountains lending them mystery, as if they were secret openings into some other world.

They camped at Forbidden Plateau campground. "Why is it forbidden?" Bjorn asked his father, enthralled. "Well, there's some old Indian legend from around here. Supposedly some of the Natives used to flee to this area away from the coast when enemies invaded from the sea. The women and children of the Comox tribe once came here to hide from the raiders, but when the men came back later, their families had disappeared, no trace. And there's a lot of red lichens on the rocks here; the Natives believed it was the blood of the women and children who had disappeared. So they thought maybe it was a dangerous and haunted place and nobody should come here anymore. They say that's why it became the Forbidden Plateau."

Bjorn felt a shiver down his spine at the story. Yet he was thrilled to hear of these First Nations' legends. He knew there were things in the woods, in the lichens, animals, stones, blood—scary things, stories, and he wanted to explore them. "Are there many bears there?" Bjorn asked. "You bet," his father replied. "We need to be prepared if we head off on some of the trails."

"Prepared? Like how?"

"Well, at least carry some bear spray, pepper spray in case we come across a bear that looks aggressive."

The only grizzly bear Bjorn had ever seen was the one in the zoo, the one that had stared right at him, eyes drilling into his soul. He remembered he had been sure of some kind of communication that he had received that he couldn't fully understand except that the bear was a prisoner denied his habitat. In earlier years Bjorn brought Ears on camping trips like this, but lately Ears seemed to have less and less to impart to him about bear matters. He regretted that Ears maybe couldn't be part of his communications with bears in the wilderness any longer.

After dinner at the campground he watched in awe as his father carried the remnants of the meal and the food supplies a hundred meters away and put them in a big plastic bag and hoisted it up into a branch way into the air, "so the bears won't get it." This whole complex ritual was centered entirely around the presence of bears; they were real, even to his father, even way up in the tree.

"Why are our tents so far from our fire?"

"We don't want bears coming near our tent site—if they smell food anywhere, even where we've been cooking, they might try to come into the tent."

Into the tent! Bjorn didn't know whether he was terrified, or thrilled. So close to them! Late the next afternoon as the family started to prepare dinner over the fire at their campground Bjorn felt a strong urge to look into the forest a little more deeply, to see if there were any signs that bears were really there. He wandered off on a side trail away from the camp. He walked for about ten minutes and then came to a hollow by a large boulder. He knew at once that it belonged to a bear. He didn't know why or how, but it felt like bear. It smelled liked bear, the kind of place a bear would want to be. He squatted nearby, looking around quietly, alternately hoping that he might see more signs, and yet hoping that he wouldn't.

Half an hour later he heard voices down the trail calling out his name—his parents, brother and sister. At first he did not want to respond, he wanted to preserve the special remote quality of this place, not be called away. But his family plunged up the trail continuing to call his name. Finally, around the bend of a tree, they found him squatting under the boulder. His father grabbed him and shook him. "What in hell are you doing out here alone, Bjorn? I told you, you're never to run off like this!"

"What were you doing out here?" his mother asked, her voice trembling. Bjorn scowled and gave no response.

"Answer your mother!"

"Nothing…just listening."

"Listening? To what?" his father said. "You're not allowed to wander off like that!"

"Yes, Bjorn," his mother said, "You could get lost—and there are lots of wild animals here."

"So?"

"It's dangerous! All kinds of animals. Bears, coyotes, maybe cougars."

"I'm not afraid of bears."

"Well, you should be!" his father said. But Bjorn wasn't sure whether he should be or not.

And early the next evening Bjorn went off again to the edge of the forest. He saw the trails disappearing into the dark, leading deeper into the forest. The fir trees were thick, the branches lightly swaying in the wind. He was not sure what he would hear, but he listened. He heard only a faint whistling of the pine branches as the wind blew softly through them. An inviting murmur. But he didn't go into the forest.

As they sat at the camp table eating their hamburgers, Bjorn asked, "Are the bears really that close to us in the forest here, Mom?"

"Probably not too close to here, they like to stay away from people. They're afraid of them."

"Why should the bears be afraid of people if they are so strong? They kill people sometimes, right?"

"Yeah, Bjorn, they could kill you," Malcolm said with delight.

"Well, yes, but the bears have learned that people sometimes hunt them. And bears like to be by themselves."

Bjorn put down his hamburger. "Why do people want to hunt them? Why don't they just leave them alone?" he persisted.

"Some people go hunting," his father said, "to feed their families in the winter with the bear meat. And some people want the skins."

"Have you ever gone hunting for bears?" Bjorn asked him.

"Yes, when I was younger. I shot a black bear once when I was out with a friend and his father."

Bjorn did not respond, but felt anger welling up inside him.

"I'm afraid some people just seem to like to shoot things," his mother added. "But it's illegal to kill a grizzly bear unless you have a special license."

"That's not right!"

"You're a freak, you know that, with all this bear stuff?" his brother said. Bjorn glowered. He refused to play frisbee with the rest of them that evening and stayed at the picnic table, listening and daydreaming, the forest tugging him away from family activities.

With each year Bjorn had less to say to his parents and grew secretive. At home he still avoided family occasions. Bjorn was quick to anger, and his brother generally stayed away from him, still remembering the incident with the spade, forever emblazoned in red across Malcolm's cheek. And Bjorn learned to avoid his turn at family chores, and seemed resentful when his parents or his siblings called him on it, especially if he felt he was being treated unfairly. His sister often just rolled her eyes at him. "Weirdo." At home he drifted, unsure of what to do with himself. "Can't you ever find something to do?" his father would say to him.

Sunday church had always been a pillar of family life, and much of their social life revolved around the church community. But with each passing year, Bjorn began to resist. He announced to his family one week that he didn't want to go to church any more on Sundays. "It's boring, and I just don't believe all that stuff," he announced. "All these stories from the olden days, they have nothing to do with me." His father was angered, his mother hurt. But they opted not to fight this one, given other behavioral concerns they had.

He got caught smoking at school. He and his friends tried to steal a blowtorch kit one time from the local hardware store, and got caught. The police were brought in and Bjorn was suspended from school. He was close now only to a few friends where he was also known for his trigger temper. "Hey, Indian," a kid yelled at him one time after school. Bjorn tore into him and gave the kid a bloody nose and black eye. From a friend he got a knife on a chain which he carried to school for a few days until it got confiscated. Most other tough kids chose not to mess with him.

Then a friend introduced him to pot. He found he could simply drift off from reality, letting anxieties leach out of his body. But the habit was expensive and eventually he learned he had to start selling it to friends in high school if he wanted to be able to pay for his own. He was expelled after two violations and the local police had begun developing a dossier on him. One time he took off with two friends in a car. The driver was underage, and they had beer in the back. They planned to drive over the US border into Washington state, but their joyride was abruptly terminated when they were apprehended at the Peace Arch at the US border checkpoint and were sent back to the RCMP on the Canadian side. Although Bjorn wasn't the driver, his police file grew. He had started to drift, often didn't come home till very late, or wouldn't show up at all. As he got a little older he got odd McJobs here and there but his mother was distraught and felt she had lost control. "I knew this was coming," Ralf said to Claire. "You'd find it a lot less painful if you just drop your expectations for him." And

Ralf would not engage in participating in any positive counsel to Bjorn. Claire felt she was carrying the burden alone. Bjorn's siblings had contempt for him, mixed with fear for his volatility. And he knew his future life would not be determined by this family.

He stands at the edge of a trail entrance. Verdant undergrowth lies just ahead of him, carpeting the ground. The wispy shimmering green of moss suspended from the trees and clinging to tree-bark lend a strange other-worldly light filtering through into the clearing. He is drawn forward in tentative steps, summoned, compelled. He pauses, looks back to reassure himself about the return path out, then steps deeper into the emerald gloom, unsure of his direction. The spruces and firs sway softly and soothingly in the light breeze that sweeps through the needles—the soughing reaching his ears as he stands and listens. But as he slowly advances more deeply into the structure of green, the soft sound of the wind is slowly overtaken by the sound of the fast-moving stream rushing down the embankment to his right. It soon camouflages all other sound as the water, in its downward encounter with each stone, generates its own white noise. Bjorn stands there silently, absorbed in the scene, captivated. He can only wait.

What does one wait for in the forest? Small events, furtive movements linked to animal life large and small, constantly unfold. But then, there it is, very distinct, over there, maybe fifty meters away—a heavy brown form silhouetted on a ridge, its snout testing the air. Then its bulky form begins to move, ambling slowly down the embankment towards the water, eyes intent upon the stream. Mottled light reflects off its rough tawny fur. Then the bear stops. It rears up upon its hind legs, alert, questioning. It turns its head, and then, unmistakably, fixes its eyes upon him.

I lumber, swaying on my four broad paws, in sure contact with the earth beneath me. My gait hugs the earth with each step, my belly grazing the plants just beneath me, directly sensing the ground.

I move slowly and deliberately—knowledgeably. I am close to the Earth.

I stand on two feet and I see far, as sentinel of the earth. I mimic your stance but you cannot mimic mine. You are condemned to two legs; you have no other option. But I am master of both modes.

My claws rend, yet I also lick gently, to gain knowledge through my tongue. I smell the world around me, its range of scents offering me more information than any other creature can sense.

The message is vague, he cannot put exact words to it, but it surges up into Bjorn's belly, mesmerizing him. As he stands there, neither of them moving, his fear gradually subsides, giving way to elation in the presence. The rush is heightened by a sense of discovery, that fearful and exquisite moment on the verge of some form of communication. An indefinable sensation of power resides in the Bear's knowing eyes. A current passes through Bjorn. He inches his way closer, hypnotically, against his better judgment, by magnetic force, his sense of fear ebbing as he advances. A barrier of large fallen nurse logs lie before him, blocking further easy passage towards the stream bank. Mesmerized, he trips over a root, slips backwards onto the ground helpless, exposed…and awakens.

Bjorn found himself bathed in sweat, charged with tension, disappointed at the abrupt dissipation of this vivid moment in his consciousness, yet relieved at his deliverance. He struggled to focus on the details of his room around him, to reestablish a grounded reality in the here and now, in the overwhelming transition from one reality to another. The image remained in his mind, transcending in power and lure the impulses of his juvenile joyrides.

Adolescence brought greater intensity to Bjorn's day- and night-dreams of the wild. He no longer mentioned these dreams to his parents anymore; they dismissed them as the product of an overactive adolescent imagination.

In his fifteenth year Bjorn began skipping school more regularly. His parents found out only when they got a call from the principal recounting the missing days. When they challenged Bjorn on it he shrugged. "Just didn't feel like going, that's all."

"Well, that means you probably won't graduate, you know that?"

Bjorn shrugged again, a gesture he knew infuriated his father. And then he started hanging out till late with friends, and always returning with his clothes reeking of tobacco—or pot.

"You're late, Bjorn! You're grounded!" his father barked.

"You can't make me stay home," he said defiantly. And he took to climbing out his window on occasion. His parents knew there was little they could do to control his behavior. "Bjorn, these friends you're hanging out with, I just feel uncomfortable about them," his mother said.

"They're losers, Bjorn!" his father added. "They're just getting you into more trouble, and deeper into drugs."

"They're my friends, not yours," Bjorn retorted. "And anyway you're not my real parents, why should I have to listen to you?" He understood well the cutting power of his words. He was directly challenging his father's authority, although he regretted the pain that this brought to his mother.

"Anyway, I'm sick of school, I want to drop out."

"Drop out?" his mother asked. "What kind of a future can you have as a high school dropout?"

"I'm just wasting my time at school, it doesn't mean anything, and you guys...I don't know, you've all got different plans for me. I need to get away, maybe learn something more about where I came from."

"There's probably not a whole lot you want to find out, Bjorn," his father warned. "It's going to be the same old sad tale—some dysfunctional Indian family that wasn't taking care of you. You should let it go."

Bjorn flared. "How in hell do you know they're dysfunctional? No more than you all here! And why should you give a shit?"

"You're out of line, young man! Now apologize to your mother. She's given her heart and soul to you to take you out of that orphan environment."

His mother stiffened and looked away. In his own heart Bjorn was angry at himself for hurting his mother. And he was angry that his father might actually be right about what he might uncover if he did dig into his background.

His uncle Bart from his mother's side came for his Thanksgiving visit. Claire told him about their problems with Bjorn. "That's a damn shame, I've always liked him," Bart said.

"Do you think you could go out camping with him again and see if he'll talk to you about what's on his mind?" Claire asked.

"Sure, it's been a while. Let me talk to him." And Bart took Bjorn out for a weekend expedition.

Bjorn liked Bart. He was a no-nonsense guy, a cop, a touch on the scruffy side. He had spent a year in the war in Afghanistan and had stories to tell of his confrontations with the Taliban and night raids in the hills. Bjorn was impressed. Bart brought along a cooler of beer on the trip and offered one to Bjorn who took it. "Don't tell your Mom, but I'm guessing this isn't your first beer, am I right?"

Bjorn smiled.

Over the campfire Bart took him on. "So what's eating you, Bjorn? You know you've got your Mom worried sick. And your Dad, well, between us, I don't think your Dad cares that much about it anymore. I'm afraid I've never gotten along with him much myself. He can be hard to take, lot of rough edges and I don't think it's been easy for your Mom...but don't tell him I said so," he said as he drained his second can. They watched the flames dancing in the fire pit in silence after they had finished cooking their pan-fried fish. "So what's going on?"

Bjorn shrugged. "Nothin' much."

"Don't give me that shit, Bjorn. You know damn well something isn't right. Why would you be getting in all this trouble otherwise?"

"It's just, I don't know, people are on my case all the time. I just want them off my back. They don't understand me."

"Is that any surprise? Your mom says you always distance yourself from the family, don't take part in anything. You don't tell them anything. You're the one's shutting them out."

"I don't feel like I belong at home. I'm not really one of them. They just do different stuff than I do."

"Well, who are you one of, then?"

"I don't know...Indian I guess, First Nations they told me."

"Hmm. So what in hell does that mean anyway, even if it's true? How much do you really know about Indian life?"

"Nothing. That's just it. I don't know a damn thing about where I came from, who my real parents are."

"Does it make that big of a difference to you?"

Bjorn turned and looked at him. "Sure, what do you think?"

"I think it makes sense. You know what? I think you should go off and see what you can find out about all of this. It's probably gonna haunt you for the rest of your life until you do. God knows what you'll find out, but I think you gotta try. And I damn well think you need to finish high school, yeah and even go to university. I see enough adolescent losers in my line of work, and a lot of them end up on welfare or in jail. You need to finish your education if you want any options in your life other than flipping burgers and snorting angel dust in the back alleys." Bart's message was not all that different from his parents in some ways, but Bjorn respected Bart, liked his straight shooting.

Nonetheless, early in the winter semester of eleventh grade he confirmed to his parents that he was quitting high school. "And just what do you propose to do with your life, young man?" his father asked. "If you think we're going to support you while you lounge around, you can forget about it."

His mother was indeed hurt by Bjorn's diminishing attachment to the family. But she understood the urgency Bjorn felt to undertake his own quest. And she knew it wasn't really about her.

"If you really want to pursue this, we can try writing to the Child Welfare centre and see if more detailed records are available," she said. But when the answer came back it was disappointing; it was just a form letter stating that there was no further information available. All that was known was that Child Welfare officers had brought Bjorn to foster care home from the Ministry's regional office in Bella Bella on the northern coast when he was eight months old. They knew that already. Where could he take his quest now?

Chapter 5

The idea of a quest introduced more focus into Bjorn's life. He had been growing tired of hanging out with his smoking buddies. Many had graduated on from pot to stronger stuff. And none of them even showed enough interest or concern to ask about Bjorn's own feelings whenever he talked about his situation. "It's cool man, don't fight it, that's the way parents are. Just chill, it's all good." Except it wasn't all good for Bjorn, and over time he was less drawn to just chilling with them. "Go with the flow, man, don't sweat it." But he didn't want the clichéd flow. His friends didn't really understand, or want to understand what was driving him. These issues struck deep at the heart of his very self and identity and would not leave him alone.

And in the absence of any substantive information from the Child Welfare office Bjorn knew he had run into a brick wall. And then one evening his buddies persuaded him to come along with them to a big party up the Sea to Sky highway to the ski resort of Whistler. Bjorn really didn't want to go, and already felt half zonked out on pot but he finally crawled into the corner in the back seat to chill out while his friends were talking about partying. Somehow he had put on his seat belt, one of his mother's major nags, and he fell into a doze. At one point he felt the car lurch around a corner. Then he heard the brakes squeal. The car was moving too fast for the driver's dulled reflexes to make the sharp curve and it rolled over the median into an oncoming logging truck. He recalled being thrown hard against the seat belt, rolling over, then hanging upside down, a sense of massive impact. And nothing more. The highway was shut down to traffic in both directions for several hours as the police and ambulances dealt with the wreckage and the casualties.

Bjorn slowly regained consciousness, gradually realizing that he lay bound in the grip of some kind of restraint that immobilized him. His seat belt seemed now to be strangling him. His body was one deep throbbing pulse of generalized numbing pain. It was quite dark, until he realized that he actually could not see at all. He panicked, tried to thrash around to liberate himself from the restricted space but stabbing pain in multiple parts of his body forced him back into passivity. As he struggled to gain awareness, images of red lights flashed by, swerving vehicles in erratic motion suddenly terminating in terrifying silence and darkness. He lay in a chill isolation, overcome by a sense of desperation and helplessness. His consciousness was slipping away, his very vital energy leaking out of his body as he faced intimations of extinction. His body was enveloped by cold and slow-flowing stickiness. He lay helpless, resigned, now only waiting for the blackness to envelop his consciousness and bring relief from the overwhelming shroud of pain.

But his consciousness did not yet fully recede. Slowly Bjorn grew aware of a source of warmth near him, some kind of massive comforting presence that now filled in the space immediately next to his body. He tried to speak, to communicate, but received no response. He only felt the presence. It radiated a huge sense of all-encompassing warmth, like a massive blanket, a huge swath of rough fur protecting him from the penetrating cold, reducing his shuddering convulsions in the chill night air and easing the pain that shot through his body. He felt a rough piece of flesh scrubbing his face, removing the still wet blood. Bjorn's existential terror gave way to a kind of reassurance from the shielding, nurturing presence. He realized he did not have to yield to the blackness of extinction. He faintly began to believe that he might survive whatever terrible cataclysm he had undergone. Warmth and animal embrace were the last sensations he could recall.

Daylight. Noise. People attending him as he lay in bed. "Good to see you awake, Bjorn. It was a miracle you made it out of the wreck alive. You came within an inch of bleeding to death," the doctor offered. While he had lost huge amounts of blood, his body was shattered in many places too. Various tubes penetrated his body. His left thigh was broken, and a rib had penetrated a lung. He was without sensation in his lower body. How could this have happened to him? He asked after his friends but got no clear answer until a few days later when a nurse broke the news to him that none of his friends in the car had survived the massive collision. The unthinkable—the possibility of youthful death—had just taken on reality. And the implications of long painful months in the hospital were beyond comprehension.

Bjorn lay in a body cast for six weeks, and then had to face a long process of rehab. But to his immense relief he gradually regained feelings and control over his lower body. "You're a very lucky young man," the doctor told him. And sitting in rehab for three more months gave him plenty of chances to think things over, revisit the night of the accident. His precise recollections of details from the fatal crash were few, his mind blocking out its horrors. But he had a persistent and powerful recollection of some kind of external intervention, of psychological support and protection, from a creature whose presence he was sure could only have been a bear. His mind had no concrete image of the circumstances, but he could smell the presence in his mind, feel the massive warm bulk of it pressed up against his shivering pain-racked body as his vital life force ebbed away. It was not logical, but it was utterly real to him. It was not the kind of comfort a small bear like Ears could provide—who had once eased his aches of childhood loneliness. It was rather a creature of massive bulk, power, and warmth, capable of standing guard at the gateway to death. A powerful symbol had engraved itself in his mind. More than ever before he realized his own destiny was in some way linked with these powerful and fearsome creatures.

The accident also brought him closer to his mother, his regular visitor, his main source of support. One evening as he lay in his hospital bed after the nurse had removed some tubes from his body Bjorn felt new emotions welling up inside him. He turned to her. "You know, Mom, I know it sounds kind of crazy, but I felt a bear was there in the car with me at the accident."

"Oh?" She turned her attention to him. "What was it like?"

"I don't know exactly. I mean, it was just freezing cold, I was shivering all over and in deep pain. I could feel I was bleeding heavily, I knew I was dying, kind of just drifting off. And then this huge presence next to me inside the car, a huge source of warmth, furry. I felt like it was licking the blood off my face. It was an unbelievable comfort." He shook his head. "What do you think all that was about?"

"Wow, Bjorn, I don't know. Sometimes there are events or feelings we have that we can't explain. Why do you think the creature, the bear, was there?"

"To protect me. To save me. I didn't see anything, but I felt it, I just felt this powerful presence."

"Well, who knows, it could have been that presence, whatever it was, that gave you the will to live, to survive the crash—that nothing else could."

"It's hard for me not to believe this. This feeling, it just keeps coming back to me, all the time."

"What you felt has been very real for you, Bjorn. It suggests powerful external forces providing a will to live when life is ebbing away. You should cherish that force, some force of Nature, even an animal force that supports the will to live. You don't have to explain it or justify it to anybody. For you it is the reality that sustained you. Don't dismiss it. You may have some special gift for communication with certain animals. Respect that." He felt greatly comforted. She understood him. She bent over him and hugged him, very gently.

Over the weeks and months Bjorn gradually got back on his feet, first to a walker, then eventually to dispense even with crutches. "You're good to go, Bjorn," the doctor finally said. "But I'm afraid that from now on you're going to have to watch out for any sudden impacts to your back. It's permanently vulnerable." He knew he had just moved into a new phase of his life in which life limitations had made their appearance. He was not invulnerable. And he had to lead his life within that awareness, perhaps demanding a greater sense of purpose in his allotted time, whatever that was.

His mother had been a constant visitor throughout the ordeal. He also received a few visits from his father and his siblings. But they seemed like visits of obligation. Everyone felt awkward and did not really know what to say to each other. His father and siblings now seemed to view Bjorn, the sole survivor, in a new light, perhaps now with a touch of respect. Few other of Bjorn's remaining friends visited him, apparently not up to coping with the realities of youthful death and its implications for their lifestyle.

His mother began a campaign of gentle persuasion to get him to reconsider where his life choices were taking him. He realized that the daily inanities of the TV screen in his room had begun to bug him; even the enforced locker room chumminess of the non-stop hockey broadcasts grew wearing. Apart from listening to his MP-3 player, he discovered a greater desire in himself to read. His mother brought him some thrillers and also brought along more books about First Nations in which he had expressed an interest.

A new Bjorn came home, softer, quieter, more pensive. He came to realize how life sometimes has a way of writing itself; his months in rehab had worked a change of perspective. The same old empty path from earlier days clearly had been going nowhere. His few remaining friends seemed to be spending more of their time in juvie court. He was tired of empty drifting, pointless arguments with his parents, absence of direction. The death of his friends made him realize that there were no guarantees in life about anything. That he had been given a new chance in life suddenly dawned on him with new meaning. He decided he wanted to finish high school after all. He attended a tutoring school and quickly got his high school diploma. He knew now that he wanted to go on to university. He could explore First Nations culture there.

His mother arranged for Bjorn to take an entry examination to the University of British Columbia. There was a box on his application where he had marked that he was of First Nations background. And four months later a thick envelope in the mail informed him he had been accepted into the University of British Columbia. Rather than a great sense of elation about it, he felt his life was moving onto a new track. Even his father offered his congratulations.

Bjorn went off to university, but the question of his origins never left his mind. Nor did the recurring images of the bear. His father had hoped Bjorn might follow in his own footsteps to pursue a career in engineering—"good access to the job market"—and for the first six months that is what Bjorn actually tried to do. But he quickly felt bored with the precision, the math and physics, the rigidity of the discipline that he now knew he wasn't cut out for. He associated it with his father's long absences and boring hours over boring plans and absence of human interaction. One day talking to a classmate he reached a decision on his direction; he would focus on anthropology. And there were courses on sociology and North American history. That was what spoke to him, indeed compelled him like nothing else.

Driven by a new thirst he enrolled in a course in First Nations/Native American aboriginal studies for the following fall. He didn't dare tell his father for many months about his decision to change his concentration; when he finally did, he immediately remembered why he had hesitated to do so earlier. His father exploded. "How do you think you're ever going to earn a living with all this touchy-feely anthropology crap? Who's ever going to hire you? You need some practical discipline, like engineering. You think you can just go off to some goddam tropical island and make a living studying native sex rituals?"

"Don't tell me what to do!" he lashed back. "It's my life, at least what little I get to control. You don't know me, you don't know jack shit about me!"

"Yeah, well just remember it's my buck you're living on. It may not be around for you much longer!"

A spark was ignited in Bjorn's mind as he sat in on his first course, First Nations Anthropology: History and Culture. It came as an epiphany to him: the first time he had ever been able to seriously learn about so many issues on his mind. This wasn't academic stuff, it was about him, his own background and life. He read about animal totems and their place in traditional cultures. How for tens of thousands of years humans often had personal totems that spoke to them and protected them, still a living tradition in the hands of Native artists. The impact of Ears on his early years, the compulsive attraction of bears for him—it all began to make some sense. He no longer was stuck alone with his own feelings in his white family, he was connected to part of a broader tradition. He trembled at the power of even belated recognition of these elements in his life.

He had met Julie, an older student who was finishing her last year. She had sat down beside him in the lecture hall a few times and they had begun talking. Bjorn was fascinated to learn that Julie had already done some field work in anthropology and in particular, about the meaning of animal totems. After the lecture they went for coffee at the student lounge and she talked more about her work. For the first time Bjorn found himself volunteering information about himself and his background rather than concealing it from others as he had so often done before. With her he felt a new confidence to express how much the revelations of this course had addressed him directly.

"Trust me, that is the real stuff," she told him. "Don't think of all of this just as some ancient wisdom of old shamans or something. The shamans of most of these early societies—some are still around—they had real psychological insight into people. A shaman could establish that this man or that woman carried inside themselves the traits of specific totem creatures. They could see how an animal totem could enter the personality of individuals."

"You mean, like animals taking over their minds?"

"Well, I don't mean take them over," Julie replied. "But sure, some people's personalities might reflect the characteristics of certain animals, their weaknesses and strengths. That might make this person an "orca person" or that one a "wolf" person. It's a little like signs of the zodiac, only way more deeply grounded."

"Wow," Bjorn exclaimed, "I just thought these animals were just some kind of personal mascots. I didn't think about how they might tell us a lot about a person."

"Absolutely. You know, Freud may have dreamed up some new German names for psychological conditions some people have. But early shamans also recognized these same psychological conditions, only gave them animal names."

Bjorn was reluctant to mention it right away, but he finally told Julie about his vivid sense of the presence of a Bear in his life starting from childhood. "I just knew a Bear meant something special to me, protecting me, telling me who I am." He shared with her the powerful image of an unmistakable presence of a bear as he lay near death in the carnage of the night highway.

"That's powerful stuff, Bjorn," she said. "It's not just all myth and legend. There are good reasons why peoples from the dawn of human memory have attached strong emotions to certain animals, creatures. They offer different ways to understand reality. We just need to open ourselves up to it. We're so uptight in our culture."

The next day she dropped a small box on his desk in the lecture hall. "A little present," she said. He opened it and found a set of animal cards and a book that discussed how to understand the characteristics and meaning of each animal on its own. "You may have a special affiliation for bears," she said. "But that doesn't mean that you should ignore the power and insights of other animals as well. That's what makes us more well-rounded. Check these out."

Later that day he looked the animal cards over. At first he thought they were New Agey from the way Julie talked about it, but he began to see there was something more to it. The cards gave him more information about the significance of the bear symbol in the world, only he just wasn't sure what it all meant for him. Ears as his childhood companion had certainly provided an opening glimpse. And then the Bear that gave him the will to survive the blood and carnage on the highway.

"You doing anything tonight?" Julie asked one Friday afternoon at the end of an exam. "How about coming over for some beer and pizza at my place? I'll show you some of the field photos I have from last summer."

"Great, but can I still get a bus back from your place later in the evening?"

"Sure. But then, you don't necessarily have to go back."

Her words sent a pang of anxiety through him. He had had very little experience with women, and here clearly was the suggestion that he might be welcome to stay the night. Girls had never shown much of an interest in him before, and Bjorn felt inhibited, even a little threatened by his lack of experience.

They had a few beers and sat on the couch together to look at some of her field pictures of animal carvings and totems projected onto her flat screen TV. Half way through the slides she put an arm around Bjorn and leaned over and gently kissed him on the ear. Bjorn was unsure how to react. She then stood up, removed her blouse and sat down next Bjorn again, took off his shirt and began to stroke Bjorn's body. She pressed herself up against him. But Bjorn was nervous, unsure whether he was capable of performing. "Just relax," she murmured in his ear, and she worked to stimulate him. But Bjorn felt under pressure. After some minutes he knew he could not perform. "I'm sorry," Bjorn said, "I just haven't had much experience."

Julie sat back on the couch. "Don't worry about it, Bjorn. It happens, maybe it's just not the right day," she said. They lay together in silence for a while and then she stood up and started to get dressed.

"I guess I had better get the bus back to my place. I'm sorry Julie." She kissed him lightly on the cheek again as he departed. "Don't worry about it Bjorn, it doesn't mean anything. You're welcome anytime."

But for weeks thereafter Bjorn found himself reviewing the encounter in his mind and reproaching himself for his timidity—the lost opportunity to lose his virginity. He could feel the animal instincts within himself. How could he release them? He thought of the power of a bear's sexuality.

Chapter 6

As a petroleum engineer Mason Surrey had not expected to find himself in such a god-forsaken region as southern Nigeria. But his orientation towards the greater world abroad had been foreordained from his childhood, starting with meals at the dinner table with his family. There his father's tales of traditions, rivalries, and periodic communal conflict in the Middle East provided the backdrop to the family's rich Levantine table: stuffed grape leaves, baba ghannouj, tabbouleh, fried halloumi cheese, falafel, chicken kebabs, and rich crisp pastries filled with pistachio nuts and drowned in sugar and rose water, along with thick Arab coffee or small glasses of mahogany-coloured tea. Food, regularly shared with outsiders, was an essential lubricant of social and even professional life.

Mason's father had grown up in Lebanon in an Eastern Orthodox Christian Arab community. He had brought his family to America when Mason was seven, just young enough to become thoroughly Americanized. The family name had been Sûri, reflecting its Syrian roots, but which his family promptly anglicized to Surrey upon arrival. His father maintained his knowledge of Arabic and French, the languages of his education in Lebanon. His father was an economist, and later a university professor of economics. And his father's stories about growing up in the shifting and treacherous sands of political and social culture of Lebanon left its profound imprint upon Mason. To grow up and make one's way in such an environment required early mastery of maneuver among different cultures, languages and traditions.

In his business life in America Mason's father had always emphasized these survival skills to his son. "Most Americans don't have much feel for foreign societies and cultures. They are lucky, they live in a big country like this where you don't need a lot of cross-cultural skills to survive. But believe me, if you're ever going to operate outside this country, knowledge and insights like that are crucial." Mason had heard enough about recent conflicts back in the old country to lose any desire to visit his father's conflicted homeland. But at the same time he was never allowed to remain ignorant of ongoing foreign events and the foreign powers that affected the life of most people in the Middle East—even if they hardly affected anybody directly in the US. Mason was sure he wanted to work overseas, though he wasn't yet fully aware how much his mind had already been stamped with a consciousness of cultural differences in the world.

As a new American, his father had also been introduced by friends to the outdoors, to going camping in the Rockies. "I can feel at total peace in a setting like this," his father exclaimed, broadening his arms in homage to real wilderness, "not like our feuding mountain villages in Lebanon. This wilderness is a gift from God—and it looks like it is vanishing." Mason learned from his father about the efforts of conservationists to try to protect the wilderness. "You know, the whole Middle East once used to be forested. But over thousands of years the forests have almost all disappeared. They need to be cherished, protected."

Mason learned of another side of the wilderness, listening with big eyes to the forest ranger as he instructed them about keeping all their food closed up in containers and hoisted up into the air on a rope over a branch to store it away from meandering bears. On one family trip to Jackson Hole, Wyoming, Mason, now about twelve, was out on a hike with his father accompanied by Tar, the family's ever eager black Lab. At one point Tar's hackles rose, he braced, growled and then tore off into the bushes and trees some distance away. They heard frantic barking and then a high-pitched yelp and a heart-rending cry of the dog, and then silence. They knew that something terrible had happened to Tar. Taking their hearts in their mouths they ran after him in the direction of the sound. A few minutes later, making noise as they went, they eventually found a spot where the underbrush had been crushed down. Signs of blood lay soaked into the ground, but they could find no trace of any animal, or of Tar. They found drops of blood leading off deeper into the forest, but they did not dare pursue whatever larger creature had taken Tar. Quite possibly a bear, the ranger suggested; dogs were enemies of bears and could be at risk. Or more likely could be a cougar. Either way, the wilderness had now taken on visceral personal reality.

So the trips to the Rockies were both wonderful and worrisome. Mason loved the mountains and the smell of the pines and cedars, and the clear running streams, and the swathes of grasses along the river valleys that would bend and shift colour as the wind stroked them into patterns. He loved the crisp air and the slight smell of smoke that signaled mountain communities. But he was made uneasy by its wildness as well. After each long hike he was always relieved when they finally got back to camp without encountering bears or cougars. He wished he had a brother or a sister to share his anxiety with.

From early on Mason loved to play in the cold mountain streams, building dams and trying to divert the water in new directions. His father had urged Mason over the years to follow in his own footsteps to become an economist, but Mason knew that was not what he wanted. When he got to college it was engineering that held the deepest fascination for him, especially in the face of challenges of construction in remote areas requiring special skills and knowledge. He sought out an engineering firm with overseas branches where he thought his skills would be useful.

As Mason began his own professional life as an engineer he was struck by how much he had unconsciously internalized from his father's dinner-table talks about enlightened business practices. "America is a rich and fat country, it can afford to be wasteful—for now. But wise use of resources is an obligation upon us all." His father saw no need for the interests of private enterprise to clash with the welfare of the people, and even of the planet. "The world is likely to run out of energy in the next half century," he predicted. "The oil left in the ground is getting more and more expensive to extract, and the costs are rising. When you add new demand for energy in developing countries, there's going to be a lot of pressure on prices. It's eventually going to run out. There will be great pressure to look for it in costly and difficult places, and at greater cost to the environment."

With a degree in engineering and a solid background in economics, along with his interest in foreign countries and cultures, Mason was quickly snapped up by a major European-based oil conglomerate, Royal Petroleum.

And while spending time in training at Royal's headquarters in the Hague, Mason wooed and married a Dutch girl, Melanie, a specialist in public health. They happily accepted early assignments in Venezuela, Iran and then Indonesia, greatly enriching their awareness of foreign cultures, attitudes, and, above all, the treacherous politics of oil in the hands of greedy leaders. They also believed their two children's exposure to foreign cultures living overseas would be a vital part of their kids' education and outlook.

As a result of his demonstrable political skills related to the oil business, the company gradually shifted him into areas of responsibility that included preparing political assessments of local situations. Mason was eventually offered a significant job, and promotion, to work as policy counsellor for Royal's operation in the Niger River delta area of Ogoniland. Melanie had been an enthusiastic partner in all their other postings, but Mason feared she would baulk at this one. She had easily found work with the UN or other health organizations in Venezuela, Iran and Indonesia, but it didn't seem very likely in Ogoniland, Nigeria.

Mason began to read reports on life in Port Harcourt, the city located in the huge southern delta of the Niger River in southern Nigeria and the centre of Royal's oil operations for Ogoniland. The reports were dismaying. They detailed great heat and humidity, and life confined within the company compound. The streets of the city were dangerous; brutal robberies and killings were commonplace. Expats were frequently kidnapped for ransom. It was dangerous to venture outside the compound; travel by car in the area required armed escort due to rampant banditry and dangerous road conditions.

Despite the highly negative conditions, for Mason the job would be an important promotion. It posed political challenges that were seriously demanding: resistance to oil operations by local populations; and serious environmental damage from the oil operations that required delicate negotiations between the company, local chiefs, and Nigerian officials in Lagos and Abuja. "I just don't think I can say no to this job, Melanie, it's a really important opportunity. It's not just about engineering any more, but the politics of the oil business and dealing with local people. I know I'm good at that. But I'm afraid it's going to mean separation for a couple of years, and there's no way we can bring the family to Port Harcourt. At least the hardship pay is really good. And I can get back on regular visits to Holland." So Melanie took their two children to her parents's home in Holland to wait out the end of Mason's term of duty in Port Harcourt.

The reality of the delta region was even worse than Mason had expected. It was wracked by a vicious insurrection of the native peoples of the Ogoni region in protest against the deteriorating conditions within the Delta. Topping the grievances were the devastating problems of pollution from oil operations that were destroying arable land, forcing farmers out. Chemicals associated with the drilling and the constant oil spills contaminated the water, decimating rich fishing grounds. Disease was rife.

Mason wasn't sure how long he wanted to work under such conditions. "Please come away from there as soon as possible," Melanie wrote to Mason, "I worry about your safety all the time."

Common wisdom within the company was that it was only going to get worse.

Chapter 7

It was clear from the format of the letter Bjorn had received from the Records Centre that this was a standard form letter designed to discourage further inquiries. "I think we can do better than this," his mother said as she looked over the brief contents. "Why don't you go to the Records Centre in person, you might get a more sympathetic hearing, maybe persuade somebody there to stretch the privacy rules a bit." Bjorn was pleased that his mother was taking an active interest in his search for his birth mother.

But for Bjorn the issue was cosmic, like a Big Bang. At the moment of adoption his past had vanished and anything that happened before that event could never be known. He didn't even know what his original name was at birth. His search held a mystical allure for him, including the effort to learn what his "real" name had been. For sure, Claire had given him the name Bjorn—a name he liked, now even cherished—but it still didn't link him to any blood ties. Or did it possess perhaps some deeper meaning? Was it just a coincidence that his mother had named him "Bear?"

This yawning gap in his basic life story felt like some black hole that would suck away all the rest of his identity and existence into it if he couldn't fill it with concrete facts. But how? Who knew what might really have happened? Nearly everybody else knew who they were and where they came from. It was cruel that he should be deprived of his very self-identity through ignorance of his biological heritage.

As Bjorn had expected, his father reacted poorly. "I think this search is a bad idea, Bjorn, it can only lead to more frustration or unhappiness for you. Don't look back, look forward. Why do you want to pursue this woman whose life of misery you escaped?"

His words infuriated Bjorn. "What do you mean, escaped! This woman gave me life!"

"And what if you find out isn't what you wanted to find out? There were bound to be unpleasant circumstances surrounding her life, her relationships—that's why she gave you up. Don't you think that will make you more uncomfortable?"

"At least I'll know!" Bjorn stormed.

"Are you sure you wouldn't like me to come with you to the Child Welfare Agency?" his mother asked the next morning.

"Thanks, Mom, but this is something I've got to do on my own."

Walking the streets of Vancouver to the Child Welfare Agency he felt he was setting out on a new path in his life. The snippy woman at the Agency seemed annoyed at having to do a more complex file search. "You're lucky government policy has recently opened up part of these files and is willing to let you see them, young man. You couldn't do that before." She didn't approve of the policy; she knew from experience that new background information didn't necessarily make adoptees any happier, often raising more questions than answers and revealing sad tales of struggles by disadvantaged mothers. "This may take some time. All we have is your adoptive mother's name, Claire Parreau, the date you were adopted, and the name of the temporary foster home you were living in. But we don't have any earlier name you might have gone by. We may have to match intake dates which could take some time."

Bjorn sat waiting in the visitor's lounge of the agency surrounded by posters of happy rainbow babies—Asian, black, First Nations, East Indian and other ethnicities—beaming over their new adopted lives. At noon they told Bjorn he might as well go to lunch, they wouldn't have anything for him till later in the afternoon. He walked around the back streets, too hopped up with anticipation to eat anything. Who knows what town might he have been wandering in at this point if he had never been adopted?

At mid-afternoon an archivist approached him. "Bjorn Fisher? This is the only information we can find right now that might relate to you, and there are major gaps. But take a look, maybe there's something you can follow up with on your own." She handed him a thin file.

Bjorn paused, then took it, almost as if he had just been granted access to a forbidden world. Or a heavenly revelation. Or a dark police record. He hesitated, fingering it, his stomach queasy, and then opened it. The Book of Life, his life, and there it was. Only a short paragraph, but a shred of new information nonetheless. Alice Martin. But it was marked only as the "reported name" of the mother. She was from Bella Bella, a significant Native town at the mouth of a fjord several hundred miles north. It was where, according to the file, she had reportedly given birth to "male child #335". The child was approximately eight months old as of the date of intake by Child Welfare. No further information was available. The clerk told him that the child in question at that time would likely have gone on to a foster home in Vancouver, but they lacked any further information since a fire had destroyed many of the records. A record from a foster care home in Vancouver indicated that a male child in normal health had been under provincial government care briefly at a foster home, and was adopted shortly thereafter by a Claire Parreau, his mother's name from her first marriage. The dates seemed to coincide, but the spotty records provided no precise linkage to his being the same child that Alice Martin had given birth to in Bella Bella. A few other Native male infants had also been inducted in that same period.

When he got home he immediately reported the information to his mother. Claire smiled warmly. "It's not a lot to go on, Bjorn, but it's something. It's a little more than we knew before." And they both decided it would only irritate his father to hear more about the investigation details at this point. They searched in telephone directories in the public library but nothing came up about an Alice Martin or anything linked to Bella Bella. Nor did an online search of this very common name yield anything meaningful. "I don't want to give up on this, Mom," he said. "I really want to go up to Bella Bella this summer and see what more I can find."

That June his mother gave him five hundred dollars—"but don't tell your father, he doesn't approve of any of this"—to augment what Bjorn had saved from part time work at the university. And so in mid-June Bjorn set off on his journey north from Vancouver, his first along the northern BC coast, entailing several ferry rides and water taxis along the jagged coastline. He had never been on a small ferry before; they were far cheaper than an air ticket and much more adventuresome. He loved standing on the front deck as the boats chugged up the coast, salt breeze blowing in his hair as he scanned the coast line, making him feel like an adventurer exploring new lands.

Bella Bella was located on Campbell Island at the very mouth of a fjord that knifed its way several hundred kilometers into the interior of British Columbia. As the water taxi rounded a promontory in the late afternoon on the final leg of Bjorn's journey he spotted the row of low-set houses of Bella Bella in the distance. A thrill passed through him, that he had reached this place on his own in pursuit of his quest. "Any idea where I can find some cheap lodging here?" he asked one of the Native passengers at the dock. "Sure, I'd start at the post office, they got a big notice board just next to it." Bjorn walked through the streets and realized Bella Bella was a relatively small place, with houses and shops interspersed. There was not a lot of traffic along the road that paralleled the water. Most of the inhabitants appeared Native. At the post office notice board he found a flyer for a small boarding house. He went on foot for half a kilometer, carrying his light bag, sometimes asking for directions. He found the people on the street warm and helpful. The boarding house—really just a large old two-story house with seven bedrooms—had a room available. "Lucky you arrived before the main tourist season," the proprietor commented, a stooped elderly Native man with white hair. "From Vancouver, eh? What brings you here?" Bjorn soon told him about his search for his family roots. "But I don't have a lot to go on," Bjorn added. "I'm not sure what band or tribe or people she might have been from."

"Well, that makes it a bit tough," the proprietor said. "I mean there's lots of different groups here." And he proceeded to give Bjorn a long account about the Native peoples of the area. It was almost more information than Bjorn could cope with at the moment, and he gradually grew impatient as the man seemed to hold forth on everything he knew about all First Nations peoples in the area.

"Yeah, most of the Natives here in Bella Bella, they're Heiltsuk Nation. And you might want to know how to pronounce the real names of these places, like our name for Bella Bella was Waglisla." He laughed at Bjorn's problems in trying to string together the multiplicity of consonant-rich sounds. "But then it's likely your ma was linked to the local people here in Bella Bella, which could make her from the Kwakwak'awak people. Or she could be part of the Kitasoo Nation just north of here, they speak Tsimshian up there." The flurry of complex names caused Bjorn's head to swim. Leads to his mother seemed to be splitting off in complex directions, involving names he was hearing for the first time.

After settling in he decided to check in first with the local RCMP office in Bella Bella. "I'm here trying to locate my birth mother," he told the sergeant at the desk.

"Well, we don't usually assist in searches for individuals in non-criminal cases," the Native officer told him, "but I'll make a quick check for you. Come back tomorrow." He seemed sympathetic to Bjorn, the kid who had come all the way up to this place from Vancouver on his own. The next day he told Bjorn he had checked and their files showed only one record, that one Alice Martin had resided in Bella Bella in 1989. "I'm sorry to say, but that record relates to an intoxication charge, and there's nothing more on that name. That doesn't mean she might not still be here now, or somewhere in this area, but we have no specific record of her," the officer offered. "Might even be a different person. It's tough, but she could have come from anywhere, gone anywhere. I doubt she died here because we don't have any record of death of a person with this name. And we're not allowed to search for private citizens unless it relates to a specific police investigation."

Bjorn's funds were limited and he hadn't prepared for a long stay in Bella Bella, but having got here he knew he had to persist. That evening he was struck with a vivid feeling that his mother had probably trodden these very streets herself at some point. It brought him a fleeting sense of greater closeness to her that helped overcome the physical emptiness inside him. What had been the trajectory of his mother's life that had brought her here, if indeed that was her?

Bjorn was meanwhile able to find some temporary work washing dishes in a dock cantina kitchen that would help cover his modest expenses. Over meals at the cantina he began to meet a few local people and mentioned his quest.

Early on he'd met Joseph, a tall, lean, wiry young man with long black hair in a braid and Native features, and wearing a blue plaid shirt and a wide pleated belt on his jeans. Joseph ran a charter boat service for fishermen and tourists. Bjorn found him friendly, chatty. They shared a few beers. "You're adopted, you say. How'd that happen?" Bjorn filled him in on his parents' story. He found Joseph shaking his head during the telling. "You know what, Bjorn? It pisses me off, that story. We struggle enough as it is to keep our community together here over the years. These goddam white people, they weren't satisfied with coming to our lands, bringing plague and conquest. They're still destroying our culture. Here they're taking our kids out of our own community so they end up losing contact with their own people and their ways. Just like you."

Bjorn found himself rising to the defense. "Look, my adoptive mom is a good person, she's sympathetic to Native peoples, she really raised me with a lot of care."

"I'm not saying she didn't," Joseph responded. "But they're still killing our culture, deliberately or not. Let 'em adopt their own damn white kids." Bjorn felt upset. But he realized a key source of his own anger wasn't because his parents had adopted him. It was because he had been put in a situation where he had had to be adopted.

Joseph stared at him a moment in silence, watching him as he stared out over the swirling waters of the inlet. "Bet you don't even know much about your own culture, do you?" Joseph said.

Bjorn flared. "Are you trying to rub it in? That's why I'm here, for chrissake. I want to learn! I don't even know if my mother is still around here. Fuck you!" Bjorn got up to leave.

"Calm down, man, calm down. I didn't mean anything by it. Just that you have been cut off. Even if your mother isn't around here anymore, don't you still have blood in your veins from this community?"

If it really is my community, Bjorn thought. His few short weeks of inquiry had brought no clear results, leaving him frustrated. He had trouble expanding contacts in the town and things moved slowly. A lot of people offered to help but little came of it. Some even viewed him with suspicion as an outsider. Joseph himself had not delivered much of the help he promised. "Look, I'm sorry I haven't been much of a help on this, Bjorn," Joseph said a few weeks later. "But if you're serious about it, you might think about coming up here again later. Once the tourist season is over I'll have more time, and I'll try to ask around among some of the old people in town. Maybe I can dig something more up for you. Also, now that some people at least know you a bit, they may be more helpful next time."

Bjorn decided he would be willing to come back next summer if there was any promise. He found it gratifying just being there. The place was exercising some pull over him, particularly as a sheltered city kid. Here he felt the draw of the different environment: the smell of the harbour, the salt air mixed with the putt-putt and the exhaust of the small water taxis coming and going, the occasional huge passenger ferries stopping off for a few hours on the way up to Prince Rupert and Alaska, fishing boats unloading their catch, the smell of fried fish in shops near the water, the green forests beckoning him up into the fjords, and the slow, relaxed and friendly pace of the Native townspeople. As a key coastal town Bella Bella promised more leads that any other place he could think of. He felt a hunger to immerse himself more deeply in the local culture.

His mother hugged him at the door when he returned to Vancouver. "Tell me all about what happened." They sat alone in the kitchen as Bjorn recounted his time in Bella Bella. Her heart went out to him when she heard that he had not been successful in coming up with anything firmer. "But I do want to go back, Mom," he said. "I've got a few contacts. There are some older people that might know more. And I really like being there."

His father came home in the evening and over dinner he probed Bjorn's account of his trip. Bjorn didn't want to discuss it much. His father's negativity predictably angered him, eventually pushing Bjorn into a deliberately provocative effort to throw it back at him. In a flare of anger Bjorn finally described almost tauntingly how some Natives viewed adoption of Native kids by white families as some kind of genocide. "Well, screw 'em!" his father retorted. "Someone tries to do something out of the kindness of their hearts they just get it flung back in their faces. I don't think you should go back up there, Bjorn. You're not going to find anything out, you're just going to get knocked about and more upset. It's a wild goose chase. You got your whole life ahead of you here. Let it go."

Privately his mother continued to back him, seeing how much the quest meant to him. "Just don't pay any attention to your father, you know how he is. Don't give it up if you think you can get more leads, Bjorn," she said. "I'd do the same if I were in your shoes. This is about blood. You won't rest until you feel you've gotten to the bottom of it." Indeed, Bjorn knew he was going back.

Chapter 8

Bjorn continued at the university in the fall including taking another course on First Nations culture. And he sent word to Joseph that he would come up to Bella Bella again in the early summer. He said he hoped he could find a job so he could stay longer. Joseph welcomed him and said he might be able to help out by giving Bjorn a part time job out on his boat on the day charter trips.

When Bjorn returned to Bella Bella again the next summer it was no longer so foreign and exotic. He now felt some identification with the town, knew his way around, and a number of people greeted him. He got a room at the same boarding house, and the proprietor remembered him well. Bjorn met Joseph the next day as he was coming back from his run taking tourists out fishing.

"Well, you did make it back! Wasn't completely sure you'd follow up. You know, I been doing some asking around while you were gone. I think I may have located someone who maybe knew your mother," Joseph told him. *Knew his mother?* This was the first time he had ever heard these words, confirmation that she had left concrete traces as a physical identity. He felt almost sick with anticipation as to what he might learn.

The following afternoon they traveled out to the far end of the town, down to a house at the end of a road. There was a weathered trailer in the front yard with weeds around it. "Look, Bjorn, remember, I know you got a lot of questions on your mind, but take it easy, OK? I know Emma's son from town, he says she wasn't all that eager to talk about the old days. Most older generation aren't." Joseph knocked on the door a few times and eventually a woman came out. "Oh, it's you," she said, nodding to Joseph.

"Hi Emma, this is Bjorn, I told you about him." Emma looked in her sixties, weathered skin, worn clothing, a smell of cigarette smoke about her. She looked Bjorn up and down. "So you must be the young man looking for his mother, are you? Well, I can't say, maybe I knew her, maybe I didn't— if you're the kid she gave birth to," Emma said. "Joseph, maybe you can give me a hand here, I'll make some tea. Having trouble with the stove, one of the burners doesn't seem to work right."

"Sure, Emma, I'll take a look at it, but I can't stay too long, I've got to get back to the boat for some stuff, but I'll leave Bjorn here with you."

"Alright, come in, young man, I'll get the cups. Have you ever had nettle tea?"

"No."

"Well, keeps me going all these years, takes care of all kinds of ailments."

Bjorn followed her into the trailer. Emma lived in the front section next to the kitchen. There was living space at the back end as well, apparently where her son lived. A moldy odour hit Bjorn's nostrils. He looked up and saw water stains on the ceiling. "Here, take these cups," she said, rattling around in the cupboard. "What did you say your name was again?"

"Bjorn. It was the name my adopted parents gave me when I was a baby."

"Yeah, well, never heard of it. Now just take the cups outside and I'll bring out the tea."

They sat down on a raised platform outside the door to the trailer, where a couple of lawn chairs sat along with a bench where Emma placed the tea. The sun glared in Bjorn's face at first, but it gradually moved behind some trees.

"Don't like the tea?"

"No, it's just a little bitter. I'm not used to it yet."

"Well, you need to know about it, it's good for you."

Emma asked Bjorn more about his background, nodded at times, but didn't comment right away. "Well, I'd like to help you, young man, but I don't know as I got much to tell you that's useful. I don't know about any Alice Martin. My friend was Sarah, Sarah Martin, from around here. I knew Sarah pretty good, we both went to the same residential school, way back."

"I wonder if you could tell me anything about her, about Sarah Martin, then," Bjorn said, trying to conceal his disappointment. "She could be the same person even though the records said Alice Martin. Some little detail still might help me to find her."

Emma thought for a few moments and then began to talk slowly. "We was friends at school. We tried to run away one time together but we got caught, you know, and got sent back. They'd always catch you, they knew where you'd head for." She sighed, staring into the distance rather than looking at Bjorn as she talked. "Well, anyway, after we left school Sarah and I come back here to Bella Bella where her parents was supposed to be, but she had a hard time. Best I recall her father went off to work in the interior some years earlier, never came back. She didn't know him too good anyway. And then a year or so later after school her own mother passed too. Wasn't really nothing for her to come back to here anymore. She started seeing some logger in those days. Then she got pregnant. Best I recall she gave birth to a little boy here, but times was tough and she couldn't manage to take care of him, hard to get a job, no money. The government finally took him is what she said. That's what happened a lot back then. I don't know what became of the boy after."

Bjorn found the details grim, but was elated that it did sound like this Sarah Martin could have been his mother, especially given the story about giving up her child for adoption.

"So if she is alive, you don't think she'd be in Bella Bella anymore?" Bjorn asked.

"Don't think so. I think she moved away, following that logger. Couple years later I think we maybe heard that she died, some illness, I don't know what. But I can't be sure the story was reliable. I can't say, young man, if it was even her that you're looking for." Emma shook her head. "We thought the baby would be given to someone in the community here, but we found out later a lot of these babies was given to foster care down in the city, or to some family down there, probably white." She turned and looked at him directly for the first time. "I suppose that could be you, young man, though I don't know as you got much to go on in all this story. Could be any number of boys. Wasn't hardly the only case like that…"

Bjorn knew he was on sensitive turf and didn't want to press too hard right away, so he sat silently, waiting to hear more. The details were frustratingly sketchy. "Well, I'm sorry to tell you all this—what did you say your name was again?"

"Bjorn. But if she did die, does anybody know where it was, where she might have been buried?" Bjorn asked.

"Can't say as I know she actually did die, and I wouldn't know where. Don't even know if she was your mother."

If she was his mother. So many uncertainties. He was worried that Emma kept calling her Sarah and not Alice like the Welfare Agency had said, although the surname Martin was the same. But even then it was not an uncommon name. He considered that if she really was his mother she would have been from around here and that might mean Bjorn had been born into the Heiltsuk Nation. It was the first possible firm identity he might be able to cling on to.

As the sun went down Emma had begun nodding off in her chair. Bjorn waited a few minutes until she opened her eyes drowsily. "OK, Emma, thanks, it means a lot to me just hearing this much. I wonder if I could come again, soon maybe? I'd really like to learn a few more details about her life, and your lives in the residential school."

"Well, we don't talk much about times at school. It was painful."

"I'm sure it was. Still, if you wouldn't mind just telling me a little more, I'd like to know what experiences my mother might have had."

She looked at him questioningly. "Alright," she sighed, "I see this means a lot to you. Come back tomorrow afternoon, I'll see what I can recall for you."

Emma's comments left him unsettled. The various accounts Bjorn was getting were still so ambiguous. Same last name, different first name, but there was a clear coincidence of information about her having a child and giving him up for adoption around the same time that might match his age. In one sense Bjorn had craved these details, yet in another he almost felt he didn't want to find out more. His life still had the same gaping hole in the centre, and now he had come across a patch of unconnected chunks, hunks of raw information whose reliability he didn't even know. The picture that emerged was troubling, unsatisfying; a woman who had faced a hard life from childhood may have just been swallowed up in a sad end. The account left as many questions as it answered. It sat on his consciousness like a lump of raw dough on the stomach, defying digestion. Worse, he might even learn definitively that he could not track his mother.

The trouble with questing for this kind of information was that he couldn't just delete what he had learned earlier and start over on a new quest. He had been mulling, ingesting information for years, much of which might turn out not to be right. Wrong information was worse than no information. This was stuff he had partly absorbed, partly come to terms with, he couldn't just delete the emotional dent the information had already made upon his mind. All he could do was to follow up on alternate stories, and try to incorporate each turn of the account. But which one? Which version should he believe? Which version did he *want* to believe?

Bjorn rolled around on the lumpy mattress of his rooming house. Sounds of carousing outside drifted in through his window with people coming and going even late in the night. His mind worked overtime, poring over the possibilities of his life's tale as former certitudes vanished. Here he'd had a life with a settled family in his adopted home for nineteen years—virtually all of his life. For years growing up he had not given all that much thought to that early empty space in his life, but now it had taken on large proportions on the mental map of his timeline. This information right now had become the most important thing in his life, more important to him than the story of his adopted family and all the years with them. With each new revelation he was like a tree bending in contrary winds, constantly struggling to adapt to something new or different.

And what of his real father? "A logger" Emma had suggested, whether First Nations or white was unknown. Bjorn found that unsettling too. He assumed maybe that his father had been white since his own features seemed to be only partly Native in appearance compared to some of the others he saw around him. But then there were all kinds of faces. "If he was from around here, he might have been Norwegian too," Emma had offered. "There was a lot of Norwegians around here, going way back, fish cannery days."

Norwegian? Incredible coincidence if it was true, given his mother Claire's own Norwegian origins. And why had his adopted mother given him this particular Norwegian name of Bjorn?

But what Emma gave with one hand she took back with the other. "But I think that logger more likely might have been a Haida man, come to think of it, I know she took up with a Haida man for a while, went up to Haida Gwaii with him. Poor man had to give up logging, lost a hand to a snapped cable out in the forest." Considering the dates, he could well have been Bjorn's father too. A father roaming around the coast with just one hand?

And Haida? That put it in a whole different category. The Haida were from the large islands called Haida Gwaii, once officially named the "Queen Charlottes" by some fawning British sea captain currying favor with the royal family back home; large mysterious misted islands that lay over a hundred kilometers off the BC coast to the north. The Haida were renowned for the strength and vigor of their cultural and warrior traditions, their massive sea canoes carrying up to one hundred warriors that ranged up and down the coast marauding as they built a powerful culture on their home islands. Bjorn was thrilled that his father might have been Haida, it opened up proud new vistas about his identity. But how would he ever know?

Bjorn mentioned his confusion to Joseph about all the different tribes and clans and nations in the area. "There just seem to be so many Native groups."

"Yeah, and you know what the government called all of us? Indian! You know what, Bjorn? Actually there are no 'Indians.' And yet there are. The goddam government just saw us all as fucking red men—chucked us all into the same goddam basket. Like herds of animals out on the plains. Couldn't tell the difference—hell—didn't care about the huge differences of culture and language and way of life among us all. Just 'Injuns.' Well, guess what, a funny thing happened. We'd been fighting each other off and on and living alongside one another for long centuries. We sure as hell always knew who we were and what our tribes and clans were and our different languages and who our neighbors were. But you know what? After the white man laid all this shit on us, taking away our rights regardless of who we were, we suddenly woke up! Yes, goddam it, we *are* all red men! We are all "Indians" together, in the same kettle! And only if we stick together are we going to have a prayer of standing up to the power of the white man."

"So how did you learn about all this stuff then?"

"I hung out with Indians in the States working in the Seattle area a few years. A lot of them were angry guys, got into local Native politics, knew a lot about the past. Hell, I was young, naive, didn't know a lot of this stuff. But I got changed from hearing about some of what they were doing. Made me angry, made me want to do something if I could."

"Do? Like what?" Bjorn asked.

"What can we do? Should we do like Whitey tells us, 'just suck it up'? No, man, wake up. The shit they made our grandparents eat, it still affects us, affects me now. Whatever place, whatever land our ancestors had before the white man came, well, we lost all that. We hardly even know any more who we were back then, 'cause we don't have any society to fit into any more, we even lost the stories about who we were. We just fit into Whitey's little plan about who we should be now. Quiet, submissive. Sure, how could we even think about making trouble now—no culture any more, no identity, no traditions, no economy, no independence, no nothing!"

"Come on, Joseph, it doesn't seem to me everybody's that submissive. I mean, I get a strong feeling for local culture here. And people being pissed off about a lot of it."

"You know, Bjorn, if this pisses you off up here, you should go down and talk to some of the Natives down in the States. Now there's some pissed off people. Some of them were in the American Indian Movement, I knew a number of them. They got into some radical shit back then, stirred up a lot of trouble, really put their cause on the map."

Bjorn felt a little intimidated by Joseph's anger, and didn't want to push the issue any more for now. He needed to think.

A few days later Joseph took Bjorn to a ceremony on the beach at the mouth of the inlet to welcome the salmon's return. It was an overcast day, like so many, with a diffused light lending a moody quality to the beach. The elders had brought in a large newly-carved totem figure, twice as tall as a man. The group gathered around it, sprinkled water on it with spruce branches and sang some prayers before erecting it where it could look out over the incoming waters with outstretched hands. "It's for thanking the Salmon People for coming and helping keep us alive. We're offering thanks to the Creator for their annual run."

"What Creator?" Bjorn asked Joseph on the way back. "I've heard a lot of that stuff about Jesus and God and all in church and from my parents. Sorry, but that crap just doesn't mean anything to me."

"Crap? Where do you think this world we live in comes from anyway?" Joseph retorted. "Nature is powerful, man. We're just little creatures here, like worms on the ground, coming out of the sea and crawling around, trying to make sense of things. You owe your life to the Creator, man. You want to be Indian, you better be open to the Creator."

Chapter 9

Bjorn made his way back to Emma's house the next afternoon. He hoped she would still be willing to talk about the past with him. He hungered for more details—any details.

"Oh, it's you again, you came back." She didn't invite him in or offer him any nettle tea this time, just sat him down on an old settee on the porch while she took a seat in a rocking chair opposite. She remained silent, folding her robe around her, waiting for Bjorn to speak.

"Thanks for being willing to talk to me," he said. "You know it's hard, I'm just searching, just trying to understand, like where I come from, and what my mother went through."

She nodded. "I understand what you're looking for. But I'm not too happy to open that whole door again, school and such. It's a world where I closed the door. May not do you much good to open it again neither."

"But you know things that hardly anybody else does, about my mother's life. I really need to know about it."

"This may not even be about you, or your real mother." She shook her head. "I told you, none of it's certain. And it was all a long time ago." Emma looked away into distant years for a moment, took a long drag on her cigarette and sharply expelled a puff. "You don't smoke I guess." Bjorn shook his head. She removed a piece of tobacco from her tongue. The hand with the cigarette, trembling slightly, began to cut an arc through the air, summoning up the energy to go on. "The whole time back then, been laying on my mind like a hot stone. It's been a long time, and I can't forget it…but I feel old. Our memories get covered over, like mist off the sea covering the land. But it's a welcome mist. It cools, softens the pain. Mists my memory. There's a lot of bad things I don't want to remember. The wounds have sort of healed I guess, so there's mostly scars left now."

Emma's eyes were slightly almond-shaped, her skin a light brown, tightly drawn. Big-boned. Strong and seasoned face. He couldn't tell how old she was. If she went to school with his mother, she couldn't be much more than forty, but the lines etched on her face said more.

She looked Bjorn up and down. "Yeah, you might be Sarah's son, might not. Can't say's I see anything of her in you, but you never know."

"What can you tell me about Sarah."

"Well, she was tough. Had to be to get through school. Residential schools toughened us right up. And took away everything we had, everything we were. You had to pretty quick figure out who you were, to keep strong, to survive. We kept strong partly because of one another."

"Did you see her a lot?"

"Sarah? Sure. Her and me shared an upper and lower bunk, with a lot of other Native girls in the room…" Her voice trailed off as her eyes retreated into memories. Bjorn remained silent, waiting.

"It was…bad. First off was the loneliness. They just came, these government officials, took us away, seven-eight years of age, taken away just like that from our families, our homes. We were all real lonely, all the time, missing our families…it was cold, official, I mean, like the people there running things had no feelings, just rules, schedules, what you could do and couldn't. It was like being in the army or something. That made us real vulnerable. We got yelled at a lot, punished if we said anything in our own language. And it was so lonely without our parents. We just needed a little attention, some sympathy. A little affection. But there wasn't hardly any. That was maybe why we…" Her voice fell off again. Bjorn waited.

"I think that's what made us all more vulnerable, to the abuses." She fell silent for a moment, shook her head at some internal memory. "Some of them were teachers, help staff, even a few were priests. They took advantage of us. Young girls losing their innocence to these people…a few of the men came almost every night…and it wasn't just the men, some of the women were interested in young girls as well. And we couldn't do a thing about it…and sometimes it was the older boys in school even, preying on the younger ones, boys and girls when they could…

"Couldn't you report it to anyone?"

"And who would we report it to?" Emma turned her head to look fully at Bjorn. "The teachers? When a few of them was doing the same stuff to us? Mostly we just accepted it, we didn't dare speak up. We didn't see our parents for many long months at a time. You try and write a letter, the staff read everything we wrote before it ever got mailed, if they ever did get mailed. They never even sent them if we wrote anything bad. And we were too ashamed to tell our family about what was going on when we did get to get back to visit home. But they knew it anyway, pretty much. Everybody knew. That was the way it was."

Bjorn cringed at these lurid details, he didn't dare think about them, and didn't want to ask.

"It may seem strange, but I think for the young boys it maybe was worse. Because the number of men with access to the girls' part of the school was pretty limited. But the boys—all the men in the school had access to their dorm. Sarah knew about this…" Emma paused and her voice trembled.

"Cause she had a little brother in school as well, although she didn't get to see him very often. But sometimes he found his way to see her. He used to cry bitterly. He had been abused regular by some priest, and some teachers, older boys and everybody. I don't mean all the priests and teachers. It wasn't. A lot of them were decent people, some of them tried to protect us. Maybe it was only a small group of them doing it. But there was enough of them…"

"A brother? A little brother? Who was he?" Bjorn's antennae rose high.

"I don't know, Jimmy was it? Three years younger than Sarah, small boy, got picked on a lot. And he was miserable. He was one of the kids who tried to run away, tried to get home. But he never made it, got caught and sent back to school, whipped. I used to see him sometimes outside our dormitory waiting for his sister to come out. Dark circles around his eyes, eyes was often red. I've never seen a kid look so miserable…"

"What happened to him? Where is he?"

"He died. A few years after he left school, he died."

"Died, how? As a kid?"

"I don't know exactly how it happened. But Sarah told me. She was crushed…he killed himself—fifteen years old." Emma shook her head. "He wasn't the only one."

A spasm ran through Bjorn's body, his mind racing a hundred miles an hour. He'd had a young uncle?

Emma was now deep into her own mind. "You don't want to hear about this, young man. None of it's pretty."

"No, I do want to hear, I need to hear about what happened…to my mother. Where was all this?"

"Mission school, St. Agnes, not too far away from Victoria, small town up north near Eagle Rock Lake. It wasn't easy to run away from there, too far from the main roads. Didn't too many of us ever manage to run away and they usually caught us and brought us back. Punished us."

Emma stirred the boards of the porch with her toe, endless circles circumscribing the past. "Like I say, it was a cold system…we were frightened, hated the abuse when it happened. But sometimes…at least there was occasionally some little bit of affection, some warmth—or whatever you want to call it, for a little while. For short periods we felt maybe briefly loved—or at least we were wanted." Her voice trailed off.

Bjorn found his mind drifting away in red fury from her voice. It was too terrible to hear—all this happening to his mother. Emma glanced over at him and stopped her story. They both remained silent for a minute. "I think that's all you need to know, young man."

"I'm sorry," he gulped, "but thank you for telling me this. I know it's hard. You've helped me. I just needed to know what happened with my mother. It's a lot to think about."

Emma leaned over to him and patted his shoulder. "Sure. I understand. You led a pretty sheltered life down there in the city. This is a lot for a white boy to take in. But you can come again some time, if you want. I don't mind the company."

"Just one more question. My mother. Do you have any idea where she might be now? How I could find her?"

"I wish I could tell you. She just seems to have disappeared from around here, maybe ten years ago? I just don't know what happened. If she's alive or not. And I don't want to get your hopes up, she's just one story that I know. And there's lots of stories just like that."

As Bjorn departed he felt his mind reeling with anger, with dark images. He was entirely lost in his thoughts until he finally found himself back at his lodgings without having been conscious of getting there. He was surprised to find his mind now turning back to his adoptive mother in Vancouver. He felt a deep need to share this information, she was the only person in the world who could listen to this with understanding and sympathy. Share his birth mother with his adoptive mother...

He called her that night. She was alarmed at his emotional state, as his voice broke down into tears. "I'll come up to Bella Bella as soon as I can, in the next few days, my Bjorn. I know you're feeling a lot of pain over this."

Chapter 10

Bjorn turned up at the dock at 7 am as usual to go out in the "Sea Snake" and help Joseph on his charter fishing trips. "We got to get a move on, Bjorn," Joseph said. "Need to swab down this place fast before the tourists arrive."

"I had a hell of a talk with Emma about her life yesterday afternoon," Bjorn commented.

"OK, I want to hear about it, but not now. There's work to do."

Bjorn set to cleaning up the decks and helping get the fishing tackle in order and some early preparations for lunch on board. He hadn't done much fishing himself at all before, so he was interested in learning from Joseph and watching the fishermen. These were useful skills he might need himself at some point if he ever got into the business.

Although he was eager to tell Joseph about his talk with Emma, he had no chance to bring it up during the day. He needed to assist the tourists in getting settled in, offer them coffee or beer or something stronger, and get the boat ready for departure.

He loved going out in the boat, a voyage into a new world, a world that he did not really belong to, but that he aspired to. The perspectives of the rivers and bays, of the fjord entrances, all beckoned to the Great Bear Rainforest and its secrets. Bjorn often felt annoyed at the banter among the tourists who mainly seemed to want to talk shop about tackle and hooks and bait and stories of the ones that got away. He knew he was not part of that fishing crowd nor could he ever match them in fishing lingo or sailing tales. He didn't even want to. What really annoyed him was how little they seemed to appreciate the power of the place all around them. They often referred to the setting as "pretty." Pretty? Shit, it was goddam majestic. They seemed concerned with the catch, what they could take away, legal limits—not what experience the whole rainforest scene and its culture offered. It was all about comparing their charter boat experiences here with the Caribbean, or with Florida, or somewhere in Hawaii—all just marine supermarkets or adventure thrills for them, ticking off the boxes of places visited, fish caught. What in hell did these people know of the power of the forest and the wisdom and tales that it contained of creation? But he bit his tongue and swallowed his contempt.

"It's a little early in the season," Joseph told his guests, "but if we're lucky we might get some salmon, or large halibut, maybe even some lingcod closer in to the shore. Might even spot a pod of orcas."

By late afternoon the tourists had all departed with their catch in their ice chests, happy with their trip. Joseph knew how to deliver. Bjorn also sensed Joseph himself was pretty cynical about most of his passengers too. But it provided a good living.

"Time for a beer," Joseph announced. Bjorn felt tired and sticky after the day's work and welcomed the chance for some rest as he plopped down in a swivel chair. They cracked open two beers and took a few swigs.

"So you were going to tell me about Emma."

"Yeah," Bjorn looked up. "I really felt bummed out, kind of worn down by her story. She's pretty sure she knew my mother. Jesus, the story of what she and my mother went through in the residential school—some really bad shit."

"Yeah, I'm not surprised. You didn't know about residential schools?"

"I'd heard about them, yeah, vaguely, but it never came up in our family. I mean, why would it? It had nothing to do with us. I hardly knew a thing about all this, especially the details, like how much it affected the kids who went there."

"Yeah, well, welcome to the wonderful world of Whitey. They've been fucking us over for a long time. Now you're out of your lily-white family, you're learning something about the real world."

"All that abuse…" He shook his head. "And they got away with it. I mean, like nobody's been sent to jail for what they did."

"Nope. And these are all pretty common stories. My own Dad had been at one of the schools as well. He wouldn't talk about it. He said there were some very decent men there he owed a lot to. And some very bad men."

Bjorn shook his head in silent dismay. They sat quietly, swigging their beers, some kind of country song about unfaithful women playing on the radio in the background.

"And Joseph, listen, I may have even had an uncle, Jimmy, my mother's little brother—Emma said he committed suicide at age fifteen, after leaving school. Can you imagine that?"

"Damn right I can. My own Dad, the experience at the fucking school drove him to suicide later on in life. Sons of bitches!"

"Shit, Joseph, I didn't know about that. I'm really sorry."

"Yeah. And there's a lot more stories like that around here."

Bjorn let the breeze blow by him, cooling him as evening set in. They sat silently, contemplating what the world had brought to their families.

"So, did you learn anything more about where your Mom might be?"

"Emma doesn't know where she is, my mother. Even if she is my mother. I don't have anything else to go on right now. The documents said her name was Alice Martin, but Emma says her name was—is— Sarah Martin. I just don't know how I might find her...don't even know if she's alive." Bjorn's lips tightened with emotion.

"Well, good luck, man. But you're probably going to hear a whole lot more bad stuff in the process. And now maybe you understand a little better why I talk the way I do. Yeah, I'm angry. Our parents were made to suffer and eat shit in silence, they're too damaged to want to talk about it, or even do anything about it..."

"So how did the government let all this happen, just go by, when so many people knew?"

"Because this is colonialism, man—white colonialism, pure and simple. Get real! This is only the latest chapter of over a hundred years of exploitation, near extermination of our peoples. That smallpox they brought? Killed up to ninety percent of Native populations in most places. This has been a First Nations fucking Holocaust...don't forget it."

Bjorn squeezed his eyes tight shut and tightened his lips. "But isn't a whole lot of this out on the table now? Like I hear how the churches apologized for what happened in the schools?"

Joseph laughed. "Apology's cheap, small potatoes. This stuff is still going down. The government's still dragging its feet on honouring its treaties with us, or giving us our stolen land back. It's like pulling teeth. And the fat cat capitalists are out trying to exploit our lands even now, get access to them to drain our resources, pollute our streams." Joseph swiveled around in his chair to face him. 'Listen, Bjorn, do you realize we've lived here twelve thousand years? Living from the bounty of the land, respecting what we were given? And now, since Whitey came— and we're talking barely a hundred years here since they've been in BC—the fish stocks have dropped by ninety percent. Just think of that, *ninety fucking percent gone.* That's *our* fish, *our* forests. And in many cases they've bought us off, bought off the Natives on the cheap—barrels of beads and fucking trinkets in exchange."

Bjorn shook his head. "Unbelievable. I just wish I knew more about all that treaty stuff—all I know is just the little I've read about at university, and a little bit in the news. It's complicated."

"Complicated! Bullshit! It's not complicated, Bjorn!" Joseph stormed up out of his chair. "What's complicated about stealing land and resources? And that's not the half of it. Have you been up to Alberta? Heard of the tar sands?"

"Yeah, heard of them."

"Well, it's a fucking mess. It's the dirtiest oil in the world. And it's polluting our aquifers, and now they're planning to pump that stuff right over into our territories here in BC, in pipelines. And then put it in tankers, all out along our coasts. *Our* coasts, *our* communities along the coasts, not Whitey's."

Bjorn stared at him in silence.

"You look surprised. You haven't heard about this? The Tundra company? These are the guys sucking this dirty oil out of the ground, who want to run it in new supertankers through the Great Bear Rainforest. That's going to be the fucking end man, when one of those babies goes down and pollutes the whole damn area, hundreds of miles, for generations."

Bjorn stared at Joseph in astonishment. "Christ, Joseph, I didn't know half of all this…"

"Well, you're gonna hear a lot more. And it might make you mad. But don't get mad, get even, that's what I say."

The flow of revelations twisted Bjorn's mind. The landscape didn't look quite the same to him anymore.

Joseph thought he had more insight into what was going on in Bjorn's head than Bjorn knew himself. Joseph was observing him, guiding him in new ways of thinking as Bjorn began to learn first-hand more of the realities of the First Nations. Not the romantic pictures, the impressive totem poles and arts, not the academic articles and anthropological studies, but the dark history of what the First Nations peoples had been through. Right here on the ground. For sure it had been way worse down in the US where so many more of them were just exterminated deliberately like buffalo, but that didn't make it any easier here.

Joseph at least showed a touch of occasional sympathy for Bjorn's anguished quest, more than some of the other young Native men did. Most other Natives found Bjorn's experience—adoption into a white family—strange, outside their ken. Some of them mocked him, even resented him for it.

Joseph was shrewder, hungrier. He sensed in Bjorn malleable material, someone who might be drawn into his corner, open to Joseph's own views on the world they had inherited.

Joseph's family had produced hereditary chiefs over several generations. Joseph's grandfather had been possessed of a prodigious memory, had been a great raconteur and repository of tribal history and nature lore. He had been the tribe's major negotiator with the provincial government in defending Native land from logging interests in the past—a firebrand and respected orator in both his native language and in English. He had enjoyed deep Native respect for his outspoken and articulate leadership.

His son, Joseph's own father, was not so lucky. He had been caught up in the government's social planning dragnet and spirited off to residential school to be stripped of his Indian identity, "civilized," turned into something neither fish nor fowl, no longer really Indian but would never pass for white either. The spirited boy who went in proud came out wounded, gutted, wouldn't talk about the things that had happened at school. The fire and spirit gone out of him. He dropped out of community college, left behind the education his grandfather had wanted for him. He took to drinking away his bitterness, ended up never being much of a father to Joseph, who learned to look more to his grandfather and grandmother for guidance. But Joseph's grandfather had died before Joseph had reached manhood and he was left with no role models apart from his grandmother.

Indeed, the band had been uncomfortable with the idea of passing on one of the hereditary chiefs' positions to Joseph's father who had lost control over himself. Nor did his father even try to promote himself for the position, implicitly acknowledging the truth of the band's reservations about him. Instead he retreated inside himself, trying to find within his own fogged and anesthetized mind that vital Native spark that linked him to his land and his people. One afternoon when Joseph was fifteen he had found his father down by the river with his rifle, blood on the ground, his brains scattered back upon his native soil.

A shadow had fallen over Joseph's family and he wanted to put some distance between him and his Native town. With a friend Joseph went down to Seattle to work on the fishing boats there, to get a little more experience and see the world. While in Seattle he had run into a number of Native Americans who had connections with the American Indian Movement. Joseph attended some of their meetings, listened to their rhetoric, and gained a new radical perspective—one oriented towards political action and not just gentle protest. And he heard about the Animal Rights Movement and their efforts to stop experiments on animals and oppose grizzly hunting. Joseph took part in a number of demonstrations, one of which got violent and he was jailed. The US immigration authorities caught wind of his activities there and gave him forty-eight hours to leave the country.

After getting back to Canada Joseph went to work in the lucrative labor market in the oil fields of Alberta. He was separated from his cultural ties in Bella Bella for three years during which time his family scarcely knew where he was. But he worked hard, acquiring skills in how to operate the big machines, the monsters that ravished and devoured the earth. He made good money, and with his savings he came back and bought himself a fishing boat, the "Sea Snake," on which he set up a fishing charter business. He already knew he had no ambitions to enter tribal politics.

While he was away his favorite younger brother Luke, who had moved down to Vancouver, got caught up in a drunken altercation with the police. The police officer claimed that Luke had pulled a knife on him and the officer fired; Luke died in jail of his gunshot wounds. But Luke's friend, who had witnessed the incident, contradicted the details of the story, but got no real hearing. Joseph was grief-stricken and bitter over the incident which only reinforced his anger at the system.

Alberta had taught him where the power of the white man lay— Native aspirations for equitable commercial treatment were a pipe dream. Power and action were not compatible with Indian status. That was the only coinage the white man dealt in. At least with his boat he could be independent and earn his living relieving white tourists of their money.

Joseph found in Bjorn someone who would listen, who still was capable of a sense of outrage rather than passive fatalistic acceptance of what was.

"OK, Bjorn, you want to be Native, let's go the Native route. There's a Native guy here you ought to talk to. He's a thoughtful guy about our community. Been around. Sam Winters. Some people like to call him the Shaman."

"Shaman? Come on Joseph, I don't do all that mumbo jumbo crap. I've read about these guys, drinking psychedelic shit in the Amazon jungle and turning into panthers and all that stuff. That's not for me."

"Dammit Bjorn, I'm trying to help you! Don't give me all that Amazon stuff, you don't know what in hell you're talking about. You're bitching all the time to me about how lost you feel. I get it. That's why you should give some respect to people who know the old traditions. Sam's a savvy guy."

"How old is he?"

"I don't know, sixties maybe. But he knows the score. He's worked around the province, works with local authorities on youth cases, people really respect him."

"Well, I don't know…"

"Look, you're the one's thrashing around, don't have a clue as to what you're really doing, or what you want. You should talk to this guy. He's in tune with things, able to see into people and situations pretty well. He's helped me when I've been feeling confused, or when I was having trouble staying away from drugs."

"So what's he going to do, give me some potion?"

"Will you cut it out? He's going to try to figure out what's eating you. But let me tell you, he's not going to make you feel comfortable. It's sort of like being looked at without any clothes. Anyway, I can fix up a meeting."

Bjorn scowled. "So what's his name?"

"I told you, Sam Winters."

Chapter 11

Mason's time in the oil fields in Ogoniland grew increasingly depressing. With his responsibility for political reporting on the oil region, he had become appalled at the unfolding brutality and desperation in the Niger delta. The area was rich in oil, and Royal Petroleum dominated the exploration and production work. But Nigeria was also a country whose leadership was notorious for its reigning kleptocracy. Royal's presence was skillfully manipulated by the country's military junta to their own personal ends. Ever since the first discovery of oil in the region in the late 1950s the Nigerian government had routinely expelled farmers at gunpoint from their land to turn it over to the oil companies, offering little or no compensation to the farmers.

Mason, feeling increasingly lonely and isolated, had finally been able to persuade Melanie to leave the kids with their grandparents in Holland and come down on a special one-time week's visit half way through Mason's tour in Nigeria. She knew she wouldn't even be able to leave the compound out of security considerations. Melanie picked up on the vibes from the first moment. "Mason, this is bad. What is all this violence actually about?" she asked.

"It's really the fault of the bloody ruling elite in Lagos," Mason replied. "All of Ogoniland is rich in oil, but it's growing constantly poorer as the military junta sucks up all the profits for itself. And traditional agriculture here, it's just dying as the government takes more land for oil exploration. They offer virtually no compensation. I've been out on a few regional inspection trips, it's an ugly scene, chemical and oil spills are destroying the environment. It's basically become a toxic hell. You can smell it in the air."

He gave her a quick sketch about how local public outrage by 1992 had led to the start of demonstrations and even the creation of a resistance movement that called itself The Movement for the Survival of the Ogoni People. It called for the protection of their own native lands against the destruction and pollution at the hands of the oil companies. The movement quickly found charismatic leadership in its struggle for ethnic and environmental justice in the person of Ken Saro-Wiwa, a nationally known poet, playwright and activist.

Mason and Melanie were sitting in the compound in a featureless restaurant that passed for French. "Well, at least it has a credible French menu," Melanie commented. "Yeah, they did bring in some some French-trained cooks, but it sure as hell doesn't know anything about French charm," Mason replied. "Still, after a few months here even this begins to look pretty good to me."

"Well at least they have decent French wine to drown your sorrows in."

"Yeah, the hell of it is, the situation here just didn't have to be this bad," Mason replied, shaking his head. "This whole movement of Saro-Wiwa, the government totally mishandled it. By the end he'd even gone beyond talking just about Nigeria any more—he'd begun speaking in the name of all indigenous peoples everywhere, calling on people to gain control over their own resources. The final straw for the government was when he demanded a share in the oil royalties, compensation for all the environmental damage and a clean-up."

"So what did the government do?"

"Well it finally declared that any local protest, any resistance to Royal's oil operations constituted treason. I mean, it got really bad. Government troops struck back with vicious attacks on the people, killing hundreds, torching villages. And since Saro-Wiwa had become a hero to his people, he was put on trial for murder, and promptly hanged. Totally trumped-up case against him."

"Wow, sounds really ugly," Melanie said as she extracted the last mouthful out of her snail shell. "I think I did read about that in the international press."

"Yeah, well his execution sparked international outrage against the Nigerian government. And then we had international demonstrations breaking out against the company itself around the world. The company later admitted that it had paid money to the Nigerian military for protection. The company doesn't like to publicize it but it also ended up having to hire its own militias for protection. I've been up to my eyeballs in all this, and it's just getting worse. Just more wars among rival local militias, and really bad human rights violations. I just can't handle this mess much longer. I've asked for a transfer at the end of the year."

In his position as political counsellor on the scene, Mason had a strong premonition of the direction in which events were moving, and he knew the atmosphere was poisonous. He spoke out forcefully within the company on the need to open up some kind of negotiations with local people. "But I'm stuck between the company on the one hand and the goddam Nigerian government on the other."

A month after Melanie had gone back to The Hague, Mason finally created an opportunity to negotiate with some of the local tribal leaders about improving conditions in one area that had been particularly hard hit by oil spills and environmental degradation. He knew it wasn't all the company's fault; some of the worst of these spills came from local militias fighting for access to tap illegally into the crude oil pipe lines.

After much discussion within the company, Mason and a few colleagues finally arranged to meet with key village elders at a site where some of the worst local sabotage had occurred. They hoped that by going themselves to one of the troubled villages for direct discussions with local leaders, they could begin to create the foundation of greater mutual trust and the groundwork for some cooperation.

They headed out into the bush one morning in a sweltering Landrover with no air conditioning. As they moved away from their compound, they found the dirt track rapidly deteriorating, the distance intensified by the pervasive humidity. Ahead of them was the lead car with armed guards from one of the militias on contract to protect Royal facilities. They eventually came to a sharp bend where the road was partially flooded and the vehicles were forced to slow to a crawl as they lurched through the mud. Suddenly, out of the trees, shooting erupted. The tires of the lead car instantly collapsed with a loud hiss.

Automatic rifles maintained fire, riddling the guard vehicle; the guards inside scarcely had time to fire off more than a few return shots before they fell dead out of the vehicle. The driver of Mason's vehicle leapt out of the car and ran into the trees. Masked men then approached Mason's vehicle and shot out all the tires. "Hands up! Hands up!" they shouted hysterically. The gunmen seemed in some kind of terrifying hair-trigger mental state, high on something. One of Mason's colleagues in the car opened the door and tried to bolt for the woods himself. He was mowed down within five seconds. Mason knew too much about similar attacks elsewhere to have much hope that he could ever survive this assault.

He and two remaining colleagues were blindfolded and led off into what seemed an interminable march along foot paths in the forest laced with roots. The guards reacted nearly hysterically when one of them tripped along the path. Finally they all stopped and their blindfolds were pulled off. He stood in front of several crudely built wooden dwellings in a small clearing. Mason's companions were ordered by their armed captors to sit on the ground under a tree. Another man with an automatic rifle led Mason into one of the buildings with a single large room occupied by a lone desk and a dozen wooden chairs around it. At the desk was seated a man in a khaki combat shirt, with a goatee and wearing steel-rimmed glasses, suggesting that by local standards he was educated. His features indicated he was likely from the delta region himself.

"Take a seat, Mr. Surrey."

Mason was torn between fear and fury. "This is an outrage, kidnapping me and murdering my men like this! Who are you, and how do you know who I am?"

"We know very well who you are, we have full information on everything that goes on in the Royal offices. You may call me Samuel." He spoke in educated, lightly accented British English. He opened a drawer, pulled out a revolver, and placed it on the table in front of him.

"What do you expect to get out of this?" Mason demanded.

"Calm yourself. If our conversations are successful you will not be harmed. We are sorry for any personal inconvenience to you," he smiled ruefully, "...or to your company. But the fact is your company's operations have considerably inconvenienced us here in Ogoniland."

Mason listened in silence, unsure how to react. He reflected for a moment on how his own father might have reacted to all of this, he who had talked so much about cultural sensitivity in doing business abroad. And Samuel's apparent calm seemed mildly reassuring compared to the hopped-up soldiers with reddened eyes.

"The fact is, Mr. Surrey, it is hard to get your people's attention. I thought an interview in greater privacy might be more productive."

"Kidnapping me is not going to get you anywhere."

Samuel smiled. "My friend, we are not kidnapping you. We have no such intent. We wish only to deliver a message that does not seem to be reaching your company through other channels."

"And the message?"

Samuel pulled two sheets of paper out of the same desk drawer. "Here is our statement. You may have heard some of this before. But we hope you will take the message more seriously now that we have your attention."

Mason listened.

"You will take this statement back to your company. But I will explain it to you here in simple language. Our way of life here in Ogoniland—my home, my land—is being destroyed. How can you not see this before your very eyes? Vast areas of forest now dead. Gas flares from the ground burning day and night around us. Our rich delta land—the biggest delta in Africa—is now horribly polluted. The fish are dying in the rivers as the poison waters flow out into the gulf. It threatens our entire fishing industry, our way of life. Our traditional agriculture is becoming impossible as our fields are polluted; seeds shrivel and die in the earth and produce nothing. The government ruling junta has massacred our peoples."

"Surely you know..." Mason interrupted, but Samuel raised his hand to cut him off. "Be silent. Your company always does all the talking because you have had the power to silence us." His eyes narrowed into slits. "The arrogance of the white colonialists is endless...but now I possess the power over you at this moment. You will listen to me for once." He picked up and brandished the gun in Mason's direction.

"Your company has drilled into our native land to bring up your black poison. You have spilled it recklessly and without concern, making our lands unlivable. You have made billions of dollars in profit, but you have shared none of this with our Ogoni people. None of it. This is our land, not yours. It is our oil, not yours. You think you can own it because you pay off the Nigerian generals in Lagos. But it is our land, not the generals'. Yet, rather than deal with our grievances, you turn to the military butchers to protect you so you can keep on polluting and profiting."

Mason tried to respond, but Samuel waved him off again. "Now listen very clearly, Mr. Surrey. Our people, our movement will no longer tolerate this. When your company has drained all our natural resources, it will go take its money and go home. But what about us? We will be left behind here in our home, in our poor and poisoned land forever...we will not permit this to happen."

Mason heard the sound of shots firing outside, and the door suddenly opened as one of the soldiers burst in, shouting something in the native language. Samuel immediately snatched up his gun, leapt to his feet, and gestured to the soldier to stay and watch Mason. This is surely the end, thought Mason.

Several more shots were fired outside and cries were heard. Samuel came back into the room, angry and upset. "One of your colleagues was very stupid and tried to grab the rifle from one of my men. I am not responsible for his blood." He glared at Mason. Mason tried to rise to see what had happened outside but Samuel peremptorily waved his weapon for Mason to sit down.

"You had better listen carefully now. You may not believe it, but we in Ogoniland are not alone in the world. Our movement is linked to the struggle of all aboriginal peoples against white imperialism and exploitation by foreign companies."

Mason recognized the international left-wing rhetoric and felt he could no longer just sit and listen passively. "You may call it imperialism, Samuel, but it is also development. I agree that the resources should be better distributed. But my company has no power to make those decisions. It is your own government in Lagos that decides how much of its national oil revenues goes to you. And the pollution you refer to—most of that is not from our own operations which are careful and professional. It comes from illegal siphoning off of oil from our pipelines in the jungle. And of course these militias spill a lot of oil in the process of getting it to the black market."

Samuel stared at him with unblinking eyes. "But what gives you the right, Mr. Surrey, to come into our land—our land—and take its riches? Is that not robbery? You pay off those butchers in Lagos and Abuja, you think that makes it right? Where is your conscience? What if Nigerians were to come to Holland, or Britain and start drilling your local oil, destroying the land in the process, and gave you nothing? And if your government said it was all OK? What would you do?" Samuel looked Mason directly in the eyes.

"Fair enough, but you have to realize that our company has to deal with someone in authority, and they are the leaders of Nigeria. It is not our fault that your leaders have bad policies and are corrupt. We have to deal with them as they are. We can't come into any part of Nigeria without their permission."

"Don't give me your legalisms, Mr. Surrey." Samuel's eyes narrowed. "We are talking about human beings, human lives. We don't care how you deal with our rich fat generals. But if you come to our land, our homes, we expect you will treat us properly, to share the profits of our oil with us, right here. Your company is the most powerful force anywhere in Ogoniland. You can change what happens if you wish to. But you seem not to care about what happens to the people. Why do you think there is sabotage of your pipelines and siphoning off of oil for the black market? Because the people are desperate, they have no recourse, they are trying to take the situation into their own hands. Their own *lives* into their own hands!"

Samuel let his words sink in as Mason remained silent. "And now you will excuse me, I have some bodies to attend to. You will stay here tonight."

Samuel left and a soldier came in and escorted Mason to a small room next door with several cots, a washbowl and latrine. Mason was appalled to see the inert body of a colleague lying on the ground under the tree, the shifting light of the sun through the trees illuminating the blood on the ground. Mason was pushed into the small room, only to be joined minutes thereafter by Arno, his assistant, also shoved in as the door behind them locked. Arno's face was ashen.

"Are they going to kill us too?" Arno whispered.

"I don't think that's what they want. But we've got to be careful. These soldiers would shoot us in a second if we give them the excuse."

They lay down on their cots to calm their nerves. At sunset they were brought a black pot of indistinguishable meat hunks on bones with some kind of watery reddish hot sauce and stale country style bread and a pitcher of murky water. They ate without a lot of conversation, each engrossed in his own thoughts about their fate, wondering how all this would end, whether they would be released, or shot, in the morning. Mason wondered what turn of circumstances had brought him here. Perhaps this was the outcome that he might have anticipated in accepting a job which involved destruction of native culture and way of life, and generated huge amounts of hardship, violence and hatred. He thought of his family back in the Netherlands, and whether he would ever see them again. If he survived he would never again allow himself to be drawn again into such morally compromising circumstances.

In the middle of the night Mason and Arno were awakened by more gunfire, long drawn-out firing of automatic weapons. A pitched battle seemed to be underway outside that lasted for many minutes. They hunkered down on the floor as several bullets penetrated the thin walls of their shack. The acrid smell of gunpowder filled the air. Ten minutes later the firing ceased, and they then saw flashlights outside in the dark shining against their room. Mason feared the worst. The door was kicked open and several soldiers broke in all yelling excitedly. In the dim light Mason could make out that they were dressed in the Nigerian national army uniform. They shouted for Mason and Arno to get up, and gestured with their rifles. Mason thought they might be on their way to be executed, but outside, in the light of a jeep's headlights a Nigerian officer came up to them. "We have rescued you in the name of the Nigerian Army. You are now safe from these terrorist animals. We have killed them all."

They were brusquely hustled into the back of a big army truck without any further explanation. They set off standing in the back, swaying as the truck lurched over potholes on the long road back to Port Harcourt, the dust swirling up behind them, capturing the first pink rays of the dawn light.

Chapter 12

S am Winters figured out pretty early on in life that he was essentially alone in this world. Whether this was true of all men he could not say, but in his own world he felt alone. He was not a recluse, nor was he antisocial, nor was he lonely. He engaged with the world on many levels, but never quite as a regular member of an identifiable circle. He accepted this reality, although it did not spare him from experiencing periodic moments of isolation. But he also knew himself and knew that it could not be any other way.

Life experience had gradually taught him the essential value of the perspective of distance. Simple observation of the natural world around him revealed just how modest the place of human life was in the totality of Creation. And life gained meaning only through unsparing awareness of one's place in that Creation.

Now in his later years, Sam often rose early to watch from the window of his wood-shingled house the crowning of dawn's winter light on the distant mountains. It was a special time of day when his thoughts roamed at their freest, intent on the shifting faces of Nature before him. Whether by choice or not, he had the privilege of undisturbed silence and reflection in his now empty house. His wife had departed this world a decade earlier due to cancer, and his son was away working in Alberta. This winter morning, like so many, he watched the sun imperceptibly rise, casting its early eastern glow over the face of the snow-covered mountains to the west. Its beauty never lost its power. But more striking was how the shifting light yielded transitions, revealed new contours of physical reality. These features of the mountains were always present but each distinctive face was revealed only at a specific moment of passing time. The casual observer glimpses only the mountain's momentary face; yet that was not the face of minutes before nor would it be the face of minutes thereafter. It was merely one frame in the movie of existence.

This is the way of the world, he realized. We can't ever capture reality because it is constantly shifting. And now, as the strengthening morning light struck the mountain face more directly, the earlier contrasting shadows and contours were gradually bleached out as direct sunlight began to homogenize the scene. It erased the clarity of deeper fissures of the rock face that he had observed in the angular first light. What we thought we knew is no longer there.

Though Sam's own youth lay many decades in the past, his present work among Native youth brought new challenges. This younger generation of youths was often bold and impetuous—useful qualities but only at certain times and places. Youth assumed that what they saw right before them was the sole reality. They were often blind to the insights of constant shifts in the face of reality around them. Perhaps they needed the patience to watch more sunrises, and to learn to shift with changing reality.

Sam often took groups of Native youth out into the forest for study of traditional nature lore, to let them experience the healing impact of distance from civilization and its technologies. For these young people such trips often represented an initiation—an initiation into contemplating the power of Nature on their lives. A few generations ago they wouldn't have needed a guided tour into the forests. When Sam was young every youth would be required to make his spirit quest, to remain for a week in the forest, at the start deprived of all possessions, sometimes even of clothes on his back until he could improvise, make do, cope, understand, adapt, come to terms with unforgiving Nature. Such quests were an indelible life-altering experience. It had shaped Sam and he had never forgotten. Nor had his friends during their own solo stays.

For modern Native youth the abiding messages of Nature had to compete with the dazzling but transient messages of modern devices. Television, cell phones, internet, social media offered stunning distractions from the realities of Nature itself; technology was more addictive than narcotics. Their Native band possessed rich traditions but Sam felt so many of their youth had become cut off from it, lost, scarcely better off than their white contemporaries long since lost in the urban thrall of modern media.

And for Sam the ultimate irony was that all this unlimited media access to the world of the internet ended up actually narrowing rather than widening their consciousness. In Sam's experience only the forest offered the anti-toxin for a brain hopped up on hormones and technology. But it took time and patience to impart even glimmerings of that truth to the younger generation around him. Still, Sam had learned to harvest an alternative power—to awaken their latent youthful pride in their Native traditions. It lent them confidence. This was a stabilizing, orienting traditional legacy that white youth lacked.

As a child Sam had been visited by visions of hawks—personally experiencing in his mind the rush of the soaring uplift, the enchantment of gliding effortlessly over the winds, the expanse of limitless vistas below. But sometimes that recurring dream vision could give way to moments of sheer terror when he felt his feathers lose control, leading to a long screaming helpless plunge to earth.

But with age Sam recognized that the thrilling panopticon view of the hawk was still only one face of reality. He realized that even the magnificent vision of the hawk could not simultaneously possess insight into the world of small-scale realities, the ones that actually determine daily life on the ground. Sweeping vision could thrill, but real events worked themselves out on the ground, locally. Hawks may be noble, but these daily realities were more clearly perceived by modest creatures operating on the ground within limited and intimate space. Which was more important, the view of the hawk, or the perception of the mouse?

"He has a gift." People often said that about Sam when he was a boy. But to one who is gifted a "gift" is just part of one's ordinary daily reality, nothing special. It is only others who can alert you to something special in yourself.

Growing up in Haida Gwaii, Sam clearly showed an instinctive feeling for animals. He knew early on he understood dogs, for example, what they expressed and what motivated them. He was known to be able to "tame" dogs immediately, to quiet them when they seemed fierce or dangerous. A wild-looking half-starved mangy dog had once wandered into the family's section of their long-house dwelling looking for food as the family was sitting down to eat their noonday meal. His father tried to chase it away with a cudgel, but it bared its teeth, growled ferociously, and poised for attack. His father sought the help of others to bring sticks and chase the dog away, even to beat it. But Sam, who was only eight, approached the dog quietly and raised his hand half-way, whereupon it immediately ceased to growl and accepted him. He was able to slip a rope around the dog's neck and lead it out of the longhouse. He gained a reputation for being able to handle other creatures as well. He learned how to gain the confidence of ravens who would allow him to pick them up. He soon demonstrated a feel for exactly when oolikan and salmon and herring were about to enter the rivers and inlets when the People could go out and harvest them.

As he grew older, people in the community appreciated Sam as a well-spoken and open person. He also got along with other boys known for being rebellious. He knew how to speak to the ones who appeared sullen and engage them in conversation, to get them to share their fears and worries, even weaknesses that they would otherwise hide. And he was in turn respected by them. Despite his youth, Sam's help was sought out by many families to help with a troubled, difficult or withdrawn child. And as he got older, he showed insights into the motivations of adults around him, to understand what lay behind the actions of quarreling parties; he would offer to arbitrate and to try to effect reconciliation.

But the same gift of insight similarly enabled him to sense the qualities of weakness and insecurity in some of the Elders. Sam readily spotted those whose judgments he felt were flawed and lacked understanding. As a relatively young man he began to speak out on some of these issues of the clan, and in their dealings with other clans. This frankness was viewed as presumptuous by a number of the Elders who felt Sam failed to show sufficient deference. His insight into the character and weaknesses of others discomfited many who resented his ability to see into their hearts and intentions. These Elders soon urged his father to muzzle his son's outspokenness and to teach him his appropriate place before them.

As a student in the local school Sam came to the attention of his teachers as demonstrating qualities of an aspiring leader; they urged him to seek higher education. They saw his potential promise as a future leader within the community. Sam indeed did go to high school and finally received a scholarship to the University of British Columbia in Vancouver. He initially began to study law, but after one year grew disillusioned; the more he learned about the history of British rule in BC, especially in their dealings with Native peoples, the more negatively he viewed the BC legal order. The British-inherited legal system neither spoke to, nor understood, the situation of Native peoples. White policy was all part of a single-minded effort to "change" the Natives, to integrate them one way or another into a "modern" life, meaning "white life." But it was also clear that such "integration" also meant accepting what was clearly second class status on a daily basis. Even those Natives who made the effort to fully integrate into the white order learned that they were never truly socially accepted as individuals, even if they were granted a degree of honorary respect by the authorities. Such honorary respect had little value in the coin of the realm.

Sam's increasing nonconformity began to represent a problem for his parents; they grew reluctant to have him return to Haida Gwaii. His frank assessments of others made him no longer welcome there. He decided to move to Prince Rupert, the largest town along the northern coast of the mainland and the terminus of the eight-hour ferry crossing to Haida Gwaii. He worked there in the grain elevators, quickly graduating out of physical labor and into the lower managerial ranks. But he continued to speak out against the conditions of the workers, especially for those from a First Nations background.

Many First Nations members came to him with grievances asking him to represent them. Although he had no formal law degree he had absorbed a considerable amount about practical law and was able to act in many cases as a kind of counsel to Natives having troubles with the labour system. As a result his employers came to perceive him as a dangerous element within the labour force, a potential agitator crystalizing grievances among workers. Soon he was no longer welcome in the work place and lost his job.

His developing reputation as a "trouble-maker" did little to help his employment capabilities elsewhere in the town.

Like so many other workers in BC and other parts of Canada, Sam was eventually lured to the tar sands of Alberta, where huge underground deposits of "dirty oil," the tar-sands or oil-saturated shale, offered massive productive reserves. Yet as the economic value of the tar-sands gained prominence across the country, so did a growing awareness of the environmental damage that the recovery and processing of the tar sands created. Sam worked in Alberta for two years, learning how to operate more sophisticated types of machinery. But, as earlier in Prince Rupert, he found himself again counseling workers, especially First Nations, about how to stand up for their rights. And as he grew more knowledgeable about the scope and environmental implications of tar sands oil production, he grew hostile to the project, especially when it came to the industry's plans to ship the noxious liquid through pipelines across pristine lands and then ultimately along the treacherous coastal waters alongside the sacred Great Bear Rainforest.

Eventually blackballed by most of the tar sands industry, Sam gradually drifted south down the coast and ended up in Bella Bella where he worked in the canneries for some years. This time, however, he found himself losing interest in specific labour agitation. In the cannery he met many disillusioned and even angry Native youth who seemed to be lost souls. Sam developed an interest in working with the conditions of troubled First Nations youth. He again demonstrated his sensitivities in dealing with their troubles, and in helping intervene on their behalf when there was trouble with the authorities.

Sam knew that without psychological health, no amount of organization could bring these youths strength and resilience. He regularly attended youth circles and began to offer counseling sessions within the old traditions. Because he was not from the Bella Bella area, and was neither Heiltsuk nor Kitasoo, he was not perceived as much of a political threat to the status of the local Elders. He was rather a useful outsider, able to help the community without threatening its power hierarchy.

To most people in Bella Bella Sam's own background remained murky. He learned to communicate in the Heiltsuk language, but clearly as an outsider. Many people knew he came from Haida Gwaii, but he was not known to keep company with other Haida and over time the matter of his precise origins became ever less clear, or even of interest. Only his marriage into a Heiltsuk family gave him some limited status within the group. But Sam was never allowed to forget his status as an outsider. And he remained instinctively a loner.

As Sam lay in bed at night he could glimpse the clear points of light from Venus and Mars, projecting their light into the starry void. The face of the moon wheeled in the sky, sometimes reflecting its light in through his window over several hours. The night sky awed him. What an infinitesimal speck his being constituted in the cosmos! How insignificant his daily sphere of activities was that made up his "world." We are all no more than faint-hearted and frail creatures clinging on to a hunk of astral rock revolving in the void, hurtling through dark space. How tiny we are in the Creator's order! How can we speak of the place of justice and truth in such a vast orbit? Yet we must still find the path to justice even within the tiny context we are afforded.

The cosmos had served to teach him humility. Sam quickly gained respect as someone free of self-promoting ego. He found himself being approached by other Natives, who had sensed even in his reserved manner some flashes of deeper sources of Native wisdom, people who hoped he might offer them some perspective on their lives and troubles. Sam knew too, that the momentary face of any one human represents only a brief interval in a shifting kaleidoscope. Sam needed only to look inside himself to perceive this complex pattern of weave in others.

Sam expected a visitor that afternoon. Joseph had asked Sam if he would meet with a kid named Bjorn. A young guy from the city of

Native background who had been adopted into a white family. Sam had had no experience in helping anyone socialized in the white world and who was unaware of his own Native traditions. Sam was curious, but decided he wanted to start out in a low key approach. He was aware that this young man might nourish romantic aspirations of gaining instant enlightenment through a one-time forest immersion course. He had seen them before. He would first take the boy's measure.

Chapter 13

Bjorn wasn't even sure he wanted to go through with it. But Joseph had talked him into seeing Sam Winters. During his time in Bella Bella Bjorn realized that, other than Joseph, he had found few other people in the town among the Native people with whom he felt he could share his concerns. His mother Claire was clearly sympathetic to what Bjorn was trying to do, but she wasn't there. Joseph had suggested Sam Winters might be open and sensitive to Bjorn's concerns. Bjorn's sense of isolation, even loneliness now overcame his skepticism and reluctance to meet the so-called "Shaman".

Bjorn worked his way through the back streets of Bella Bella only a short remove from the road that ran along the seafront and the wharfs with arriving sea taxis from other Native villages and from the neighboring town of Shearwater. The houses along the street varied greatly, from the inviting to those in poor shape or even abandoned. But everyone he passed in the street nodded pleasantly to him. Many still took him for an outsider and some people asked if they could help. When Bjorn finally mentioned Sam Winters, people smiled, nodded in recognition and pointed the way.

He was looking for a small single-story pale blue house with a green metal roof. It stood a bit away from other houses in the neighborhood. A rickety wooden fence surrounded the yard. And, just as Joseph had described it to him, there was a large sculpture in the yard of a breaching orca carved from cedar in traditional First Nations style. Bjorn had to lift the gate up from the ground to get it to scrape open. It didn't seem like Sam had very many visitors. He probably shouldn't have come.

He went up to a weathered blue door, knocked, but heard no sound from inside. Perhaps Winters was out. Perhaps the time of his visit was only meant to be approximate. He knocked again, and hearing

nothing, finally turned to walk back to the gate, half relieved. Just then
he heard the door open and a man stood there whom Bjorn presumed
to be Sam, a faint smile on his face. He nodded as Bjorn gave his
name; he obviously had been expecting him. He gestured for Bjorn to
enter. He did not give his name or offer his hand, and Bjorn didn't
know whether to extend his own. Winters was dressed quite simply in
brown slacks and brown sandals, a green shirt with open neck—
nothing at all unusual except for a woven Native shawl around his neck
and shoulders. No wild eyes, no long hair, no bear tooth necklace, no
furry hat—none of the usual stereotypes that Bjorn had heard about
spiritual mediums in other cultures. Winters may have been in his
sixties, but his body movements were lithe and youthful.

Bjorn followed him into the next room, apparently where Winters
received visitors. The interior was modest, with a low ceiling, furnished
with a mix of what seemed to be hand-made tables and chairs, all well-
used. Bjorn observed the many objects lying around that seemed
related to the forest—twisted pieces of wood, pieces of grey and brown
fur here and there, a few jars filled with some kind of substances, a
mirror, a carving of an eagle. A tooth that must have been from a bear,
or perhaps a cougar. The room smelled of must and smoke. Winters
gestured for Bjorn to sit down on a couch of stretched skin over a
shellacked wooden frame that sat at one side of the room. Winters sat
down only five feet away in a straight-backed wooden chair directly
opposite him. Bjorn started to speak, but Winters put his finger to his
lips in a request for silence. He sat with a slight smile on his face,
staring intently at Bjorn, making him uncomfortable.

After what seemed to be several minutes Winters broke the silence
softly. "Yes," he said, "welcome. I am Sam. Can you tell me who you
are?" Bjorn gave his full name and briefly described his background,
and how he had come to be adopted. Winters nodded, closed his eyes
for a few moments. "But *who* are you?" he repeated.

"I told you," Bjorn said, and added, "I believe that my mother was
a First Nations woman, possibly Heiltsuk from the Bella Bella area. But
I don't know any of that for sure, or who she is, or even if she is still
alive and where she would be."

Winters nodded, pinched the skin between his eyes. Bjorn waited.

"What is your story?" Winters then asked.

"My story?" Bjorn repeated. "I told you everything I know about who I am, and where I come from. That's what bothers me—that's all I know about it."

The Shaman paused and then said again gently, "Yes, but what is your *story*? What is its path? Where do you see your story going?"

"You mean what will I do, in the future? My plans? How should I know now? I have no idea."

"But you have a story, we all have a story, starting in the past and moving into the future. How you see your story is a guide to your thinking…"

"I'm sorry, I'm still not sure I understand what you are asking."

The sound of a cell phone rang and it was not Bjorn's. Winters picked it up from under some papers, listened, said a few words, and then hung up. Bjorn was slightly surprised that he even had a cell phone, he had given such an impression of withdrawal from daily life.

"When I talk about story, I mean the account in your own mind of where you are coming from and where you are going. Your personal path. Those events in your life that *you* decide will direct you. Which events. How you *see* your story. What matters to you and what doesn't."

Bjorn stared at Winters in some degree of confusion. "I'm still not sure I understand what you're getting at."

"Look, that may be part of the problem. You don't have a clear picture of the direction of your life, past or present. You've mentioned a lot of events here and there. But you have a unique story that puts it all together, you just need to find it, see its shape. I am not able to see your story, or tell it for you. No one else can know it or tell it. Knowing your story gives you direction, purpose."

This was the longest Winters had yet spoken, and he finally seemed to be making greater sense than his initial probes which Bjorn found verging on the mysterious, not the real world.

Bjorn paused. "Well, I guess my adoption is the most important part of my story. I was taken away from my original mother and brought up by others."

"But which part of that story matters the most? Your lost Native family, or your second white family? Or your own future family? Which one will direct your life?"

"My lost family can't very well direct my life when I know almost nothing about them, can it?"

"It sounds to me like that is already the most important part of your story for you. That is why you are here."

"Yes." Bjorn felt irritated that it was taking so long to get to the point. "That is what I want to know about. You keep asking me about things that I can't answer. They are the things I want to ask *you* about. Like, who am I? What should I do?"

"I cannot tell you who you are. You are who you are. Only you can know. Only you can decide."

Bjorn, squirming in his seat, felt a flush of impatience again with this circularity, indirection, evasiveness.

"Look, I don't know. I can't answer those questions. That's why I'm here. I need help."

"You do know. You just have not opened up to yourself, allowed yourself to discover your spirit."

"And just how do I discover my spirit?"

"It is already there in your heart. It will reveal itself. You must let it out into your consciousness."

"But how? Are you talking about taking some drugs or shrooms or something? Mind drugs that will reveal things to me?"

"Have you taken drugs?"

"A little. I've smoked marijuana, snorted some cocaine a few times, nothing regular. And I'm not hooked if that's what you're asking."

"Drugs are not good. They do not bring clarity. They conceal rather than reveal. They can only provide escape to the troubled mind, not clarity. Too many of our youth think they can find truth there, but they only lose sight of truth."

Bjorn fell silent and looked at Winters in helplessness and irritation. "Look, I need help. That's why I'm here. You don't seem to be able to offer much advice. Perhaps I shouldn't take any more of your time." He stood up.

Winters motioned for him to sit again. He reached out to the table behind him. "I want to establish your feeling for different animal spirits. I will give you five stones in this leather pouch. I want you to keep the pouch on your person all day every day. At the end of each day you will feel around in the pouch among the stones until you feel strongly that there is one that you wish to take out. Take it out and note the symbol. Then put it back for the end of another day with the same process. When you are ready, bring the stones back to me and tell me which stones you have felt you wished to select over the period."

Winters set down the five rounded stones, not fully equal in shape, with slightly flattened surfaces. Each bore a simple symbol, but nothing that Bjorn recognized. It also seemed far from what was on Bjorn's mind.

"So just what are these stones supposed to be?"

"They represent different spirits, spirits to which we feel drawn, which can influence our lives at different times. There is no one spirit, you may feel different ones. But do not think too much about it. Just remove from the pouch the stone that feels right to you at that particular moment. Then we will see." Winters nodded abruptly to him and stood up, indicating that the discussion was over.

Bjorn stiffened at what he felt was verging on some magical practice. "Look, I'm sorry, but I'm not interested in these stones. You're not listening to me. I have questions. Things I'm worried about. We're not even going to discuss that? That's what I came for. You've just been talking around in circles. You haven't given me any answers for what I need!"

Winters remained silent for some moments, then smiled. "I have no answers. You have the answers. And the answers alone are not important. If you do not ask the right question you will never get the right answer…"

"But we haven't talked about the main things on my mind..."

"We have spoken today about the most important questions of all." And he gestured Bjorn to the door. "When you are ready to come back," he said.

Bjorn flared at this continuous run-around. "Well, I'm not sure there is anything to come back for. And I'm afraid I just don't feel like messing with these stones." He stood up impatiently and tossed the pouch back onto the table. He walked to the door and opened it. Neither he nor Winters made any parting comments.

And then Bjorn was back outside, walking the dark back streets of early dusk, noises of daily life emanating from the houses around him. He was angry, frustrated, and disappointed. What had Joseph set him up with here? He wasn't even sure Winters was for real. The Natives maybe thought of him as a wise man, but he had offered Bjorn nothing other than throwing a lot of the same open-ended questions back in his face. It all felt like meaningless spiritual claptrap. Was it worth even bothering to come back?

As evening drew close, after working on some sketches that he did as part of a daily discipline, Sam reflected on the visit from this young man from Vancouver, Bjorn Fisher. He had been moved by his brief recount of his story, the frustrated passion of his quest. It was heartening to find a boy of submerged Native ancestry who was passionate about his roots and their meaning.

In Bjorn, Sam recognized a few glimpses of his own restlessness in his youth. But Bjorn was different; he had clearly been uprooted from his tradition early and came of age in a white community. Bjorn's emotions were clearly unfocused, without direction; he was not sure how easily they could be positively channeled. He lacked elementary self-awareness.

Who are we at any one given moment? We are not, we cannot be the same person all the time. Reality is not something to be spotted, identified, stuck on a wall-board with a pin, captured for all time. It is a journey of exploration. Bjorn cannot cling to the momentary reality he thinks he sees, some single fact from the past as something permanent.

Sam knew Bjorn wanted quick answers—something that reflected the impatient culture of his white upbringing. But he had to realize too that there was no glib response from just one meeting that would resolve his concerns.

Chapter 14

Bjorn sat at the table at the small fish place down by the dock that he often frequented early in the morning, absent-mindedly munching on his fish filet sandwich before he joined Joseph on the boat for another charter trip. Joseph came in ten minutes later and sat down and ordered bacon and eggs and fries. Bjorn looked up at him. "That shaman buddy of yours you sent me to? Sam Winters? It's hard to believe that guy is for real. He didn't answer a single damn question I had, just asked me a lot of questions. Tried to give me some little sack of magic stones to carry around for a week. He told me to come back. You know, I'm not sure I'm going to go back. I think it's a waste of time."

Joseph stared at him without showing any reaction. "OK. Fill me in."

Bjorn recounted the detail of the encounter as Joseph worked on his fries.

"I'm sorry to hear that, man," he responded, wiping his fingers on his pants. "Sounds like you were too wound up to even get something useful out of it. What can I say? He's a very wise old guy. Most people have great respect for him. He does a lot for the people, and the community, especially young people. He may be just testing you out. Seriously man, you shouldn't give up."

"I don't know. I just don't think I'm into all this old Native wisdom stuff."

"Hey, call it what you want. You're the one's hurting. And by the way, if you're serious about your heritage, you should check out a cool ceremony tomorrow night, a transformation dance. I'll take you if you want. But you damn well better not tell me it's another waste of time."

The next evening Bjorn went with Joseph by water taxi to a village across the bay where the dance ceremony was taking place.

They entered a classic Native longhouse, a large structure built of single logs, its great length illuminated only by torches, which cast ghostly shadows upon the walls and ceiling, and undulated in the flickering light. Bjorn had entered a different world. "This story we're going to watch tonight, it belongs to this clan, it's about their origins and the events in their story. Nobody else has the right to tell it," Joseph explained.

All around the room sat members of the clan who were offering the dance ceremony in honour of a new addition to the ranks of the chiefs. Children sat on the ground in the front row, quiet and sober in the dark setting, excited at anticipation of the dance. Flames flickered in the ring of stones in the centre of the room, heightening a sense of anticipation and drama. There wasn't much sense of schedule, things seemed to happen when they happened, preparations unfolding within their own rhythm. After a long period of waiting they heard a shuffling from behind a screen and several drums began to tap out a steady beat. And then the drummers appeared, dressed in black clan robes decorated with white buttons and the outline of a raven on the back; on their heads were round woven cedar bark hats. Their drums took up a solid rhythm as they sang a welcoming song. Then a dancer appeared as if out of nowhere, in a crouching pose, wearing a fearsome mask of a wild bird with great eyes and a huge long red beak, only partially illuminated by the ghostly flickering light. The children shrunk back in awe and fear in the presence of this shimmering and powerful figure, crouched and radiating energy and intensity.

The human medium entirely vanished in the drama as the masked creature took on reality, moving in jerky motions forward and backward in birdlike motion, its great beak bobbing upward and downward as it circled. After many minutes the great bird retreated back from the fire. Suddenly its long beak swung open sideways into two hinged pieces to reveal in the light of the fire the mask of a human face deep inside the bird's beak. The face bore an intense expression, fearlessly observing reality. Bjorn felt the hairs on the back of his neck rise at the emotional power of the glaring face emerging out from inside the great bird.

"We all come from spirits and animals," Joseph whispered to Bjorn between the dances. "They came first, and we are descended from them, we're all different kinds of animals with different qualities. They are our connection with the spirit world."

"So where is this spirit world?" Bjorn asked.

"Well, who knows exactly? The Elders say the spirit world is the true world, the world lying beyond that exists forever. And we are all in a state of constant transformation. It's the world we come from and where we will all return. Unless our world is destroyed."

New figures now emerged into the dance, wearing different masks; they moved to the forefront, representing the unfolding of the clan tale. Bjorn was transfixed by the spectacle. *We are all transformed.* Could he himself be in the process of transformation? Some vague, inchoate emotion was awakening in his mind, intensified by the dramatic setting and the flickering shadows. He didn't understand what exactly was happening, but he felt a presence. Joseph had told him that the exact animal origins of humans were hidden, not readily revealed—and were different for each person. But they were there. That was part of the quest.

And finally the climax of the ceremony was approaching. A new figure leapt out, covered in a long furry skin, a mask with a snout, and unmistakable long claws on the hands. Bjorn instantly felt the connection.

"That's the grizzly bear. He's the most powerful figure of all," Joseph whispered. But Bjorn didn't need to be told. The grizzly stood on his hind legs and swayed, his powerful arms moving back and forth, claws exposed. "The grizzly keeps order, enforces the rules."

Bjorn was transfixed, feeling an electric current run through his body. Was this spectacle connected to his many dreams of bears? Was this his figure? He felt a simultaneous sense of awe, and then some vague identification with it. Its eyes stared fixedly at him. The staccato drum beat was mesmerizing, it penetrated into his head and mind. He felt drawn to this being, his own body swayed imperceptibly with the lumbering motion of the bear as it moved against the background of the fire. By the time the last dancer finally withdrew behind the screen

Bjorn had been drawn in completely. He felt drained, emotionally absorbed by another entity. The dances had come to an end.

My mind feels like it's coming loose, I'm not fully in control of it. He experienced a mysterious exhilaration, a sense of yearning. *Something has entered me, some force, but I cannot see it or identify it.*

With the end of the performance Bjorn sat in silence for a few minutes without rising, his mind and body recomposing itself, absorbing it all before he finally got to his feet. He walked out silently into the night air just behind Joseph as they left, plunged into his own thoughts as they headed for the house nearby where friends of Joseph had offered Bjorn a place for the night. They gave Bjorn some skins to sleep on and he was startled to note that they were almost surely bear skins.

As he thought about it, he realized that the bird mask of the first dancer was only half a creature. And when the mask opened up, it wasn't just another creature inside, it was a person who was the other half. They were part of the same whole, different faces of the same thing. Maybe Bjorn knew only half of his own face and had been unaware of the other half.

He lay down upon the skins on the floor, noting their roughness and faint muskiness, intensifying his awareness of how the grizzly dance still lay heavy upon his senses—the intense staccato character of its powerful unchanging rhythm. He recognized the same emotional attraction that Ears had once exerted upon him, only this was far more intense. Ears now seemed to be a child's version of an adult reality. This was the real thing, its dimensions huge, its arms equipped with lethal claws. It was Ears evolving too, transforming.

The transformation dance that evening had revealed the passage from creature to human and back. A connection had been forged between himself and the Bear figure.

A vision opened up to him as he lay in the darkness. He thought he heard multiple overlapping voices in his head that he could not at first make out.

I am among you. I mix with you. I lurk in your mind.
I am the world in ways you cannot see.

I emerge, I walk the earth, alone. I feed on the world, all it offers, from green shoots of grass and plants, to sweet honey of the meadow's bees, to the leaping salmon of the spring freshets, to the dead deer lying gutted on the forest floor. I partake of its body before I leave its remaining flesh to continue its journey back to nourish mother earth in the cycle of creation.

I guard the land, the forest. My spirit wanders abroad. You see me only in my fur. My fur is merely the outward covering of a world of instincts and knowledge.

I am righteous. I am the conscience of the forest and the Great Spirit.

The message that came upon him was not really in words. He somehow sensed words, but it was more like emotions, latent impulses of meaning. Even if he could not fully understand the meaning of all that it said, its impact remained powerful. He was sure the Bear's message was addressed to him even if it was not all fully clear.

Was any of this linked to the dim past of his own early life, of which no one, not even his adoptive parents knew anything? Had he finally made a connection with the world beyond through the medium of this dance?

Bjorn felt his destiny, some kind of unknown but clear destiny, was waiting. He realized now he did have something more to tell Sam Winters.

Chapter 15

"Hey, Bjorn, tomorrow's open, I don't have any clients. A bunch of us are going out in my boat on our own. You should meet them. You might find a couple of them interesting. We're going to check on some crab traps, cook up some crabs, catch a few fish, crack some beers. Come on along."

"Mmm, OK, but I'm not sure I'm into big party scenes, Joseph. Who are they?"

"No big party. Native guys, originally from around here. But some of them been working down in Vancouver. One of them, Carl, says he wants to meet you. He likes to play it cool, but he's basically a good guy."

Next morning when they arrived at the boat four other young men were already on board, sitting around a table in the stern with a head start on the beers and eating fries along with salsa and chips out of a big bag. Fishing equipment lay around on the deck.

"So, Joseph, you brought along our Indian wannabe! I heard about you," said a tall thin guy, long black hair, with a slight scar on his left cheek. He stuck out his hand to Bjorn. "I'm Carl." He then handed him a beer.

"Carl and me first worked up in Alberta together," Joseph said. "He bought some fancy-ass house down in the city with his money but he's up here summers working with tourists. Also part-time artist. Check out his stuff sometime."

"That's right, tourism's big now," Carl said. "White people have gotten all interested in First Nations culture—maybe partly some guilt trip, whatever. Lot of local guys already making some good money selling Native art, like me. It's mostly good stuff. But these days even if some of it's crap, if it's 'Native', people will pay big bucks for it. They like 'authentic.'"

"OK Carl, if it works for you," Joseph replied. "But don't think I'm going to go out in some fucking grass skirt and deer antlers and prance around and whoop for a bunch of tourists. I've got more pride than to sell out for a bunch of glass beads."

"Who's selling out, man? I'm a good carver. Proud of it."

Bjorn was taken aback by the some of the cynical commercial nature of these comments. He didn't let himself get drawn into the conversation.

A short guy with a buzz cut, camouflage vest, and dark glasses turned to Joseph. "Look, we play the hand we got dealt, man. If it means selling our traditions on the stage, then why shouldn't we? It helps keep the traditions alive, it's good for our kids to see that other people in other cultures appreciate it, are even willing to pay money for it. Hell, all kinds of other cultures do the same thing, peddle their folklore. Europeans come over here, they really eat up this Indian stuff."

The short guy turned to Bjorn who was standing at the edge of the boat and hadn't said a word so far. "What did you say your name was?"

"Bjorn."

"So what kind of a name is that?"

"It's Norwegian, I was adopted into a white family."

"One of those, eh?"

They loosened the line to the dock while Joseph went up top and started the engine. They moved slowly out of the harbour and he set the boat out on a course that wandered first right and then left, weaving around a constellation of small islands, a route that Bjorn didn't recognize from the charter trips. The day was warm, with mixed clouds. Green spruce trees sloped down the sides of the islands leaning out over the water. The waters quickly took on a pure blue colour offering incredible visibility deep down into the depths. A few sandy beaches lay within sight in a number of inlets, although most were rocky. A few had dark pebbles on the beach. The vistas were wide open and the inlets undisturbed by any visitors.

"We're gonna pick up some of my crab traps first," Carl explained. Nobody said much as they stood along the edge of the deck holding their beers and scanning the water with their binoculars. "There's one of them," Carl called up to Joseph, pointing off to starboard. They pulled deeper into an isolated inlet where Bjorn could see a number of small floating buoys where crab traps had been set. They pulled alongside the first one and slowly hauled up the rope. Soon a cage-like box broke the surface and Bjorn could see about eight large crabs inside the cage. They hauled it dripping aboard, opened the top, and dumped the crabs out into a container. One of the young men separated out a few crabs to keep and threw the rest back overboard. "Too small." Bjorn watched the lucky crabs sink back down into the blue-green depths. Somebody thrust another can of beer into his hand.

They moved from buoy to buoy hauling up the crab traps and emptying them out. After they had assembled about three dozen crabs they pulled into a small inlet and anchored. "Looks like a good spot," Joseph said. They carried the crabs into the galley where they turned on a gas fire under two large metal cauldrons. Within a few minutes steam started to rise out of them. Bjorn winced as the crabs were dumped live into the boiling water, flailing for a brief moment. "What's the matter, city boy?" one of them asked who had been watching Bjorn. "Haven't seen crabs cooked before?"

"Not really, most of this is pretty new to me," Bjorn admitted.

"Well, if you want to know about our life out here, you better learn about cooking crabs pretty quick."

A few minutes later the boiled crabs were hauled out of the water and they all sat down around the large fold-down table. Bjorn had never eaten whole fresh-cooked crabs before and was at a loss as to how to proceed. Carl showed him how to use a mallet to break open the crabs, especially the legs where the shell was harder. Bjorn was not very adept at the process, and one or two of the young men laughed at his attempts. Meanwhile they were bantering about their night on the town last time they were down in Vancouver.

The sun poured down on them and the beer flowed. The inlet they were in had a sandy beach, unlike many of the more rocky shores elsewhere. Bjorn was captivated by the setting—the mountains all around, the blue-green water, the quiet and isolation, the trees beckoning onshore, Nature's bounty in full display, providing them with an instant delicious meal right out of the sea around them. The alcohol intensified his sense of emotional attachment. This was where he truly belonged.

They also fried up some filets from a small halibut they had caught earlier in the day to add to their meal. "So Bjorn, tell us why you're here. What you doing messing around in Bella Bella?"

Bjorn told them about his search for his mother and his Native roots. "But I haven't had a lot of luck finding out much so far."

One of them, Roy, an older man in a sleeveless vest, smirked during much of Bjorn's tale. "So why would you want to give up what you've got, living with a nice white family in the city to come up here and search out a bunch of Indians who are struggling to make it?"

"Maybe he's looking to get Indian status up here like some others, get the bennies from the government," another commented.

"Yeah, sounds a bit lame to me," Carl said. "You think you're Indian? That you can find your roots here? You even talk white." He winked at the others.

Bjorn felt suddenly threatened. "Look, guys come on. I didn't ask to be raised in the city. Everybody wants to know where they come from." He looked in appeal to Joseph but he only grinned back at him.

Bjorn found his speech beginning to slur with the many beers and the hot sun. "I want to be part of some place like this, someplace where I can belong."

"Yup, looks like we got a genuine bleedin' wannabe on our hands here," Carl said. "How many white people you think want to come up here and actually live like us?"

His friends laughed and took up the theme. "I mean, come on, man. What do you actually know about being Indian?"

"I don't know a lot, but my Native mother makes me Indian. Maybe my father too... Just as much as you," he added.

Joseph had pulled up anchor and they were now heading back in the opposite direction, out towards the open sea, where they hoped to catch a few more halibut. The boat began to rock more as they began hitting some swells. Bjorn was starting to feel uncomfortable with the whole situation. The boat felt narrow and constricting.

Roy, who now seemed to be feeling no pain, turned to Bjorn. "You know, I don't think you're going to find a whole lot of sympathy here. Frankly I don't even give a shit who you think your mother was. You've grown up pampered by rich white folks in a pretty suburban house. You're lucky you never had to take a shitload of hardship off Whitey like some of us!"

Bjorn flared. "I've got a right to find where I come from as much as anybody else. Even if it does mean giving up a lot..."

"Oh, so you're giving up a lot just to hang with us Indian boys, is that it? We see enough of these wannabes like you, these white folk tourists who come here to take our pictures, our houses and crafts and shit. They think it's spiritual to be poor. You think you can just come in here and watch our ceremonies and act like you're an Indian? You're just a radish, my friend. You may look red on the outside, but you're all white on the inside." Bjorn bridled at the accusations.

"Yeah, you talk just like one, even smell white to me," the short guy growled. He'd been drinking the hardest during the trip.

Bjorn felt a surge of fury. He lurched to his feet and took a swing at the guy, who, not expecting it, took it glancing on the jaw. He hesitated, smiled for a second and then tore into Bjorn who lost his balance and fell back against the railing hitting his head and ending up on the deck floor.

Everyone around the table jumped up. "Cool it, guys!," Joseph yelled. But Bjorn's head was swimming with the boat's movements and the booze and the sun and the confrontation. A small trickle of blood ran down the edge of his mouth where he had been struck. Nausea washed over him. He tipped his head sideways and vomited heavily in three great heaves onto the deck.

"Oh, for shit's sake," Roy growled. He went for a bucket to swab down the deck. Bjorn remained on the floor, back against the rail.

"You can't just *decide* you're Indian!" the guy with the scar said, massaging his chin and looking down at Bjorn. "This isn't about choosing, my friend. You can consider yourself fucking Zulu if you want, but it's not going to cut any ice with anyone here. *We'll* tell you whether you are goddam Indian or not, and so far it doesn't look very damn likely that you'd ever fit in up here."

"Come on, guys, leave him alone," Joseph yelled out. "Stop giving him a hard time. Bjorn's a decent guy. He cares about where he comes from. He just wants to figure out where he belongs."

Carl surveyed the scene coolly. "Figure it out?" He expanded his arms outward. "Man, they told us right off who we were. From day one it was Whitey's world. We were just in their way, not even real people, or real citizens. And on our own fucking land!"

Roy chimed in. "Bjorn, think about it. What do you know about discrimination? Have you ever had anybody call you 'Injun'?"

Bjorn had by now managed to sit up with his back against the boat. "Yes, I goddam well have! I've been called Injun on the playground too, kids whooping and dancing around me!

"Oh, he's been called Injun on the playground, boys, hear that? That's white man's world. Listen, you ever been denied a job because they didn't like that you come from Bella Bella? Had trouble at the bank because of your address? You don't know shit about what this means." He looked to Joseph. "If it was up to me, I'd just give the kid a feather to stick into his hair and send him home!"

"Listen, I said leave the kid alone," Joseph said. "He works with me on the boat and he's our guest here after all." Bjorn crawled off to the corner on the other side of the deck, in the hopes of calming his delicate stomach, to cool his temper and nurse his wounded pride. He had come here in all good faith and eagerness. He felt profoundly betrayed at this rejection and the anger directed against him—as if he were the symbol of white dominance. The place he thought might be a refuge, he could identify with, had turned on him. He felt in utter isolation.

Bjorn thought they would never get back to the harbour. He stayed away from the whole bunch until they docked and then he walked off the boat without a word to anyone. He turned angrily to Joseph as he caught up with him on the dock.

"What right do these bastards have to tell me if I'm Indian or not?" Bjorn railed. "Just because they're pissed at what they've been through in the city? They want to keep their own little private club to themselves? I know who I am and I goddam well don't need others to tell me who I am! And thanks for standing up for me!"

"Take it easy Bjorn. It's just a sensitive topic for everybody. You need to hear some of this shit. We're not just talking about stuff that went down a long time ago. This is now."

"Yeah, well I'm not going to be fucking dissed over my background, not by anyone! Especially by your loser friends!" Bjorn stalked off from Joseph who, shaking his head, watched him go before turning back to the boat.

Chapter 16

Bjorn pointedly skipped work on the boat with Joseph over the next two days, leading Joseph to come by Bjorn's room on the third day.

"Come on, Bjorn, I'm sorry at the way things went on the boat. I didn't expect it. But you need to hear how things are. Anyway, I need you on the boat now. How about it?"

Bjorn grudgingly got his stuff together and climbed in Joseph's SUV. On the way to their charter trip for that day, Bjorn and Joseph stopped off at a local supermarket to pick up a few additional items. The woman with the shopping cart just ahead of them caught Bjorn's attention. She was overweight, puffing slightly in her exertions. The cart was loaded with food for the family: five loaves of squishy soft white Wonderbread, packages of white hot dog buns, three packs of hot dogs and sausages, four packages of frozen french fries, several six-packs of soda pop, boxes of sugar-coated cereals in various shapes and colours, bags of potato and corn chips, soft cheese dips, packages of Twinkies.

The cartful of items immediately provoked a flood of childhood warnings from his mother back into Bjorn's mind. Life in the Fisher family routinely involved his mother lecturing about nutrition. Junk food was the forbidden fruit of their Lutheran family. As he opened his lunch box during noon-hour at school, revealing his little plastic bags of carrots and celery and cheese and raisins and nuts, he would look longingly at what his friends were eating: peanut butter and jelly sandwiches, bologna sandwiches, little bags of potato chips, Froot Loops. Sometimes he would scrounge half a peanut butter and jelly sandwich from a sympathetic friend. Sometimes he'd go off after school to a local convenience store and pig out on potato chips and corn crisps and cans of Coke or Dr. Pepper. It tasted so wonderful, and all the more for being illicit. That was a few years before he discovered beer—not the taste, but the kick, which made the bitter taste worthwhile. And later on a friend introduced him to pot, BC's best bud. He smiled—junk food as a path to pot.

Yet he was also annoyed with himself at his judgmental reaction to this woman's cartful of junk food for her family. He felt ashamed that his Native culture, the one he had returned to embrace, had fallen into this enticing and self-destructive trap of the modern North American bad diet—its cunning mixture, developed by taste chemists, of sugar, salt, fat and spice to make it almost as addictive as a narcotic.

As they left the store he mentioned it to Joseph. "You've just noticed? This is all part of the corruption that we've fallen into. You think we were goddam waddling around in the forest with diabetes for ten thousand years? No, we were healthy and proud. The food was perfect, and good for us. Salmon, the wealth of the sea, sea vegetables, game, berries, the bounty of the land. It was civilization that brought us all this industrial food, this sugar and fat shit for us to mainline on. That's why we're sick all the time now, it's on this diet."

"Then why can't we just resist it now?" Bjorn asked. He noticed that he had just used the word "we."

"Because that's what happens when a people gets beaten down, they lose their way, they fall into despair, the old traditions go down the drain. They get drawn to all the worst parts of white culture. We're fucking weak, man. That's from eating all this shit...and killing ourselves."

"Well you're not fat. Or most of your friends I've seen."

"Cause I know how bad it is. All of us younger brothers, we know about this, we take pride in staying away from the white man's shit, we don't let them get to us. The only thing we got going for us is our salmon, the ultimate gift from the Creator. They've kept us alive and healthy for ten thousand years, and still will. That's why our salmon ceremonies mean so much. Only way we're ever going to fuckin' survive, man."

Bjorn had never thought of this before. He now saw the endless lectures from Claire about good nutrition in a brand new light. And for

Joseph, "eating healthy" was part of an expression of identity for him—even an act of resistance. Bjorn could see now why eating wild salmon right from the sea was not just about health and tradition, it was incorporated into ceremony, sacred celebration.

The day's charter run brought together a lot of fishermen, mainly for the salmon. Joseph had provided Bjorn with a crash course on fishing in the previous weeks; he'd listened carefully as Joseph talked to his clients, and observed their experiences. On this trip there were about eight fishermen, most of whom had signed up as first timers at salmon fishing; they listened intently as Joseph briefed them on the use of various kinds of bait and lures, as well as how to choose from among the variety of rods and reels available.

Bjorn was by now fairly adept at knowing how to filet the salmon to be put on ice, and taken back to Bella Bella to be vacuum packed for the fishermen to take home.

This time the "Sea Snake" headed out to some new spots.

"By the way, folks, we're gonna pass a fish farm in a few minutes," Joseph announced to the group as they swept out into broader waters. "I suggest you all take a good look, and learn about this serious threat to our wild salmon." About ten minutes later, as the boat sliced through the water, Joseph pointed off to starboard. "There's one of 'em. Can't see much from here, it's mostly under water. But see all those things that look like floating docks? Kind of like huge wooden frames with water or a pool in the middle? Each one contains a huge deep underwater net with half to three quarters of a million small fish in them. These new fish farming projects are growing up all around our waters of the British Columbia coast. We're now the fourth biggest producer of salmon in the world. You can see some of these farms out here, dozens of them staked out—guess where? Right along the major wild salmon runs from the inlets out into the open sea."

One of the fishermen turned to Joseph. "Sounds to me like they should be good news for the salmon industry. I mean, if there's a lot of salmon being produced in the fish farms, should ease the pressure on the wild ones from overfishing."

"Wish it was that that simple," Joseph replied. "These farms, they're huge enclosed pens in the water, half a million fish or more, but they pollute badly. The whole thing was started by these giant Norwegian fish farm corporations. They'd already gone a long way towards destroying their own wild salmon up in Norway by setting up these aqua-culture farms as they call them. Then they decided to move to Scotland and then Chile, where they also devastated the wild salmon population. Now they're doing their number here in BC."

"Can we get closer?" a younger fisherman asked. "Can't see much from here."

"I'll try," Joseph said. "They don't like it though." He swung the boat more towards the floating pens. When he got within about fifty meters he saw some man in a yellow Mackintosh come running out of a shack on the edge of the pens. He waved his hands and put a bullhorn to his mouth.

"You are trespassing on private property. I order you to leave immediately or I will photograph your boat and file charges!"

"Jesus Christ," Bjorn said. "Maybe somebody could explain how you can get away with making sections of the ocean private property." The group all leaned over the deck to look at the farm as they passed. One fisherman gave the guy the finger.

"Actually it doesn't look like that much from the surface," another fisherman commented as Joseph turned the boat away.

"Yeah, might look that way, but below the surface it's bad news. The young fingerlings are all penned up in tight quarters and so they get diseases. Then they routinely have to feed them doses of antibiotics in their fish food. And then guess who gets to eat the salmon with a lot of antibiotics in them?"

"What's this I heard about something called sea lice?" another fisherman asked.

"Yeah, well we could spend all day talking about this and we need to move on to our fishing spot. But in a word, this is a big-time debate here. I don't mind telling you how I see it, along with most other Native peoples and fishermen, and of course the environmentalists. There are lots and lots of problems. Some of the sick fish escape into the wild carrying their salmon diseases. And then a whole lot of the salmon in the pens end up developing sea-lice on their bodies as well, kind of like suckers. And here these farms are, lying right on the natural migration channels of the young wild salmon and a lot of them pass close by the farm. These damn sea lice on the farm fish swim out and attach themselves to the young wild salmon swimming by. All it takes is just a few sea lice attaching themselves onto the young salmon bodies, they start sucking their blood and that usually means death fairly soon for them. The pictures of it are pretty ugly. They cause about a billion dollars' worth of damage to the salmon industry each year."

"Well, where's the Canadian government, how come it doesn't do something about controlling all this?" another fisherman asked. "You guys are supposed to be all gung-ho environmentalists up here."

"Long story," Joseph said. "Short of it is, our so-called Liberal party government here in BC basically never saw a business venture it didn't like. It has no serious interest in the environment. And guess what, money talks. I think you know a thing or two about that down in the US too. Pretty sickening if you ask me."

"So your scientists, where are they?" a young fisherman asked. "The environmentalists? How come nobody's speaking up? Back in the US the environmentalists have a big voice."

"Well, I don't want to harp on this a lot more. We do have environmentalists. It's kind of inspiring the way a number of private environmentalists have done their own scientific testing, they've showed how these commercial farms in the fish channels were responsible for a drastic drop in the amount of wild salmon returning back three or four years later. But the damn government here, and the Conservative government in Ottawa, they've been trying to suppress the research and the findings. They muzzle the scientists from commenting publicly on the situation. So if any of you are wondering why salmon catches are down, that's one big reason. OK, enough of that. But frankly it pisses me off."

Joseph turned the prow to port and throttled up moving away towards their fishing destination.

They spent the rest of the day cruising around a few key spots that Joseph liked and a couple fishermen were having some luck.

"Jesus Christ, what is this?" a fisherman suddenly asked, pointing to a middle-sized salmon dangling from the line he had just pulled out of the sea. "Are these some of those goddam sea lice you were talking about?" The other fisherman moved over to the side where the fisherman was displaying his catch. On the body of the fish there were three large brownish lice, maybe three inches long and many smaller ones that had implanted themselves along the body of the salmon. "That is disgusting!" one of the fishermen said. "They look like small horseshoe crabs or leeches, with that shell and those feelers. There's a hole in the flesh of the fish all around where they are attached. Gross!"

"Yeah, well you can imagine what it's like filleting your beautiful salmon and finding these brown spots inside the flesh where lice had got to them. Turn you off eating salmon for good," Joseph said. The lice had eaten away a portion of the salmon's scales and revealed an open suppurating sore on its flank. The fish looked emaciated. "One of them mothers works its way up to the eye of the fish, they'll eat the eyeball clean away."

"God yeah, I can see why somebody's got to do something about this," the fisherman said.

"Well," said Joseph, "we're working on it, but these damn fish farm bastards got great lobbying power with the government. Like I say, money talks."

A few minutes later another fisherman pulled in a beautiful 30 pounder. He asked Bjorn to snap a picture of him holding up his catch. Bjorn felt a wave of contempt about playing a supporting role in glamourizing this "sport" of pillaging nature, but he bit his tongue. He didn't want to damage Joseph's charter business.

The fishing was slow that day, but they stayed out long enough to ensure that everyone caught at least one salmon.

After they got back to Bella Bella and the fishermen had departed, Bjorn started to clean up the boat.

"All that stuff you were telling about the fish farms, Joseph? Some of that I hadn't heard before. That's really bad!"

"Damn right it's bad. But I can't come off too preachy to tourists or they'll get turned off. But most fishermen have an interest in the story. I mean, they don't want the fish to die out either. For them it's not just catching a fish to eat, it's the whole experience. I could have gone on a lot longer about all that if I'd wanted."

"But I can't believe nobody's doing anything about all this," cried Bjorn.

"You don't know the half of it," Joseph said. "It's not just about the health of the salmon. It's all these chemicals and pollution sinking down to the bottom that destroys the clam and abalone beds. They're dying. Nobody seems to care that they're destroying the very idea of the natural bounty of our seas."

"Well, there must be some way to have better farms," Bjorn said.

Joseph threw down his mop he was using to mop up the deck and turned to him. "You know what this really is? It's the fucking industrialization of sacred food. And the goddam government is denying that anything at all is happening. They're protecting the fish farms, not the salmon. Really pisses me off. Ain't nothing the white man won't exploit to the max—till it's gone."

Chapter 17

Bjorn had been on Claire's mind a good bit during his periodic silences that she alternatively imagined to be days of smooth sailing for Bjorn, or the silence of troubled darkness. When the phone rang one evening as she was finishing dinner alone at home she was delighted to hear Bjorn on the other end.

"Hey Mom, how are you?"

"I'm good, Bjorn. It's great to hear your voice. More to the point, though, how are you making out up there?"

There was a pause. "I'm OK...well, not so good actually. I'm feeling kind of depressed."

"What's the trouble, Bjorn?"

"I don't know, it's just...I just don't feel like I fit in up here so well. The local people are mostly friendly, but they kind of view me as an outsider."

"I'm sorry to hear that, that must be hard."

"Yeah, I'm just finding it tough to really settle in here, and I don't have too many friends. I'm not really getting anywhere with finding my birth mother, either." He paused. "I think I'm just having trouble finding my place."

Claire was deeply touched, even gratified, that Bjorn was reaching out to her in emotional need, to his mother. This was not the more confident Bjorn that Claire had observed on previous occasions. He had then maintained an independent air as if he wanted to keep his distance from the family and establish his own life.

"Is there any kind of trouble?"

"No, no trouble. But I was just wondering if you'd like to come up and visit me for a few days."

Her heart flooded with feeling. "Bjorn, I'd be delighted to come, it would be my first visit. I just wasn't sure how much you wanted me to come. "

A week later Bjorn watched her Pacific Coastal Airlines flight land at Bella Bella's small airport. When she came into the waiting area she hugged him in a long warm embrace that seemed partly to embarrass him, but also to comfort him. He appeared really glad to see her, to have someone who would listen sympathetically to him. He found her a place in a small nearby guest house. "My own place is too small and too much of a mess for visiting."

That evening when Bjorn came by to pick her up for dinner she got a whiff of pot off his clothes but chose not to comment. He took her to one of the waterside fish places. "It's kind of simple, but they have good fish." The decor was modest, decorated with typical maritime objects, a few anchors, nets, glass bubbles. They took a table overlooking the water.

Claire noted in him a new intensity. On the one hand she observed his growing sense of identification and commitment to the area. He spoke with special fervor about what he had learned about the First Nations peoples in Bella Bella. He held forth on all the various leads he had pursued to try to find his birth mother and father, and how nearly all of them had come up dry. He described in somewhat emotional detail his meetings with Emma. "Christ, Mom, before I came up here I just didn't know about most of what the Natives were put through here, especially related to the schools." She found in him a new sense of indignation, a desire to do something, to act. And he also told her with scarcely concealed anger about being mocked by some Native youths for not really being Native at all, just an Indian "wannabe."

"Oh Bjorn, I'm sorry. That must have been really painful, especially when you've made so many efforts for deeper contacts with Native peoples up here," she said. "You know, I had hoped to come up here earlier actually, to see you in your 'Native setting'," she said with a smile, "but I wasn't sure you wanted me to come."

"No, I'm really happy you've come," he said with a big smile.

"My own main big news will interest you, Bjorn. I've been tying up final papers of divorce from your stepfather."

"Really? I hadn't known about that." He put down his bread stick while taking it in. "Well, frankly I think that's great. I hated him, and he didn't do you any good either."

"I'm sorry you hated him, but I understand. He could be a hard man."

"Hard man? He was a cold fish. He never made me feel like I was part of the family. And he was really insulting about First Nations and my background." And there flashed through his mind the recurring image from his childhood— his father's heaving nakedness on top of his mother in their darkened bedroom, growling like an animal.

"I know," Claire sighed. "I feel guilty about all of that. I tried to soften his attitude."

"Mom, he was the one that drove me away from the family." Tears of emotion welled up in Bjorn's eyes that tore Claire's heart. "I never felt like I belonged there…and now I'm not sure I belong here either."

"Bjorn, I'm so sorry. I knew you were unhappy growing up but…"

He wiped his eyes. "Well, you stood by me, Mom, that's what's important. I appreciated that. And I'm so glad you've come up here."

A moment of silence passed between them as they watched a yacht move by in the harbour, its lights probing the night sky.

"It's been a bit of a rough year for me, actually," his mother went on. "I didn't want to trouble you or drag you into the details, but the divorce was messy. But it had to come." Claire glanced around looking for words. "I felt increasingly isolated, Ralf was rarely home, and I knew he was having at least one affair. Actually he was the one who asked me for the divorce, saying he wanted to marry some other woman. I didn't know her, and by then didn't really care who she was. I was happy enough to agree, but my lawyer advised me to hold out for better terms before granting it. Your father's company has been quite successful and I was finally able to get a good settlement out of him, including funds for you. Your brother and sister are going to go with him, by the way."

"Good riddance. Malcolm always had it in for me, and Erica just treated me as if I was some idiot."

"Ralf is a very self-centered man. He hasn't been that close even to his own biological children," she replied. "It just goes to show a successful businessman doesn't necessarily translate into a successful parent. The more his engineering business grew the less interest he had in any aspect of his family."

"I'm not shedding any tears."

"Well, thank God it's over now, and we're well enough out of it. And," she said, her face lighting up, "you have a decent piece of the settlement which will help give you a little independence in deciding where you want to take your life. That's the good news."

"Well, at least that's something, Mom, thanks. That could make my life up here a lot easier."

Claire ordered a bottle of wine, "to celebrate."

"I just hope time and life will help heal some of these wounds for you. It's wonderful that you can be up here in First Nations territory, and explore your roots even if it's painful. I know you've been thinking about it a long time."

"Yeah, bottom line, I do like being here, mostly. But it's also made me feel more pissed off about things. The Natives have really gotten the shaft here in BC, Mom. You don't know the half of it," he said, looking at her pointedly.

"I'm aware of some of it, and I'm learning. I hope you'll feel free to tell me about more of it. I just don't want you to feel despondent, or lonely. Or feel a need to retreat to drugs."

"No drugs, just a little weed now and then. Don't worry. And I want to try to get a more permanent job up here, maybe related to the environment in the Great Bear Rainforest."

"Bjorn, that's great! I really hope you can find something. You've always wanted a chance to work with the environment, and maybe even bears. It should be easier now with this new financial cushion. Being here is bound to help you find yourself."

"And I've met this guy, he's kind of a youth counselor, First Nations guy, they call him 'The Shaman.'"

"Shaman? That does sound unusual."

"Well, he's not really a shaman, no magic formulas. Sam Winters. He's just a savvy guy, supposed to have good insights into people. He works with a lot of Native kids, giving advice to young people on their problems. I've just had one meeting with him so far and I'll have to see how it goes. But it's probably good for me to have somebody to go to." Claire nodded, uncertain about where all this was going.

Over the next two days Bjorn showed her around Bella Bella, and on the last afternoon took her out on one of Joseph's tourist water tours to see the local sights. Joseph had little to say to her during the trip, but as they began their return Claire came up to Joseph. "I want to thank you, Joseph, for being a friend to Bjorn. I think he's found it a little hard to make many friends here in Bella Bella while he's been searching for his birth mother."

"Well, thanks, but I'm sorry to say, it's not easy for a kid who's brought up in a wealthy white family and isolated from Native life. He's having to adapt to different conditions up here. Local people just don't identify with that kind of city life."

Claire stiffened. "Well, I'm not sure I'd call us a 'wealthy' family. Yes, we're comfortable, but I don't think we were isolating. After all, I've done a lot of social work in the city, including with First Nations."

"Mrs. Fisher, it's not Bjorn's fault, but fact is he has grown up without a clue about his traditions. Of course he's finding it hard. That's the problem when Native kids are given up to white families."

"Look, Joseph..." Claire had to suddenly grab for the rail as the boat hit a wave. "Bjorn didn't have a choice about whether to grow up in a white family or a Native one. He was an orphan. It's that simple. He was given to me because he had no other options at the time, and I wanted to give him a home. Do you think he would have been better off living in some foster home for his whole childhood?"

"I can't answer that, Mrs Fisher. All I'm saying is, no matter how nice the white parents the kids still grow up deprived of their own culture. I can see what pain it's caused Bjorn now. And his isn't the only case."

Joseph's blunt words offended Claire even as it brought some pain of recognition as well. "Well, we're just going to have to agree to disagree on that. We've done the best we could in raising him. Nobody offered him anything better."

"I hear you," Joseph said. "Let's let it go at that."

Claire had no desire to continue the conversation and went back to her seat. She said no more than "thank you" to Joseph as they left the boat.

"I'd have to say I found Joseph a bit hostile, Bjorn. Our discussion wasn't very pleasant."

"Don't take it too seriously, Mom, that's just his way. But he's not the only one. A number of Natives feel strongly about this adoption issue."

Claire suppressed some pangs of guilt. "Bjorn, I certainly hope you don't share Joseph's views, especially as it has to do with us. You got dealt a bad hand with your birth mother not being able to care for you. We did the best we could."

"I know that Mom," and he squeezed her hand. "It means a lot to me that you brought me up. But just so you know it's a sensitive issue."

Claire decided not to pursue the topic any further. On the afternoon of her departure she hugged Bjorn at the ferry dock. "I love you, Bjorn. I always have. And I've always felt a connection with First Nations people. I fell in love with you when I first saw you at the foster home…please take care of yourself. I appreciate that Joseph might be angry about a lot that's happened up here in the past. But try to resist falling into anger. Anger is always corrosive…and try not to get hooked on drugs. That can't help you either."

"Mom, I can't help feeling angry about some of the stuff that's gone down here with the Natives. It's not really about adoption. Maybe it's about whether adoption should ever have been necessary in the first place. Anyway, don't worry, I'm not on drugs or anything, things are OK, I know what I'm doing. And you were always there for me from the start."

"OK, stay positive about your great chance to explore your roots up here," she added as she started down the walkway to the large ferry.

But she left with an awareness of some darker and unresolved issues in Bjorn's mind and she wasn't sure where it would take him. She knew she wanted to stay in closer touch with her son.

Chapter 18

Mason's experience of being kidnapped by the Ogoni Liberation Front had riveted his attention like nothing else. His brief captivity and exchange with Samuel brought home to him the powerful case Samuel had made for the plight of the local people in the face of foreign oil exploitation. Indeed, Samuel had put a human face onto a broader political and economic struggle. It was clear the rebels were far more than mere "terrorist militias" as the Nigerian authorities liked to call them; they personified a *cri de coeur* of a desperate people whose culture and livelihood was drowning in a tidal wave of unbridled international oil markets.

And it was clear the crisis did not belong solely to the Ogoni people. Samuel had spoken emotionally about how they identified with other peoples in the developing world caught up in the toils of global corporations operating on their lands. A terrible question begged response: were there any governments anywhere *not* so corrupted by the process? Massive oil reserves invariably enriched the power of any state—and spawned systemic corruption everywhere. While the local people sought to preserve their own way of life, the major corporations had no vested interest in preserving the way of life of people. It came down to human lives against market forces.

Sobered by his experience and insights gained, just before he left Nigeria Mason penned a memo narrowly circulated within the upper reaches of the company in Nigeria: "Long term global implications of the Ogoniland experience." With the rising flow of information across the globe the oil business could not avoid becoming ensnared into internal domestic politics everywhere. If they failed to foresee these conflicts early on the repercussions for their companies could be highly damaging. Ogoniland was only the latest and ugliest example.

Mason's own father's background in the Middle East had given Mason an instinctive grasp of how volatile these identity issues could become in the world. Large corporations involved in resource extraction inevitably trespassed upon peoples whose traditional lands possessed a near sacred character. Yet, for all the importance of Mason's insights he had encountered little awareness of them in the ranks of senior people in the energy industry. Globalization and production were the sole mantras; let the local anthropologists work out the details of community accommodation.

Mason's memo stirred controversy at the top and he was called before several senior managers. "Mason, we understand the emotional impact of your encounter in the bush with the Liberation Front. And your insights are important as regards to our operations. But basically we feel it is beyond your call to chart the international strategy of the company. The reality is that almost all oil companies are caught in a no-win situation either way. When all the pros and cons of the moral debates are said and done we still have to keep an eye on the bottom line. You know how much ruthless competition there is out there from other companies who might be even less fastidious about the deals they cut than we are. I've circulated your memo around, and to our headquarters, but it's got to be treated as a strictly internal memo."

Mason's own family, meanwhile, was still in Holland. He initially concealed from Melanie the whole kidnapping saga so as not to upset her, but the story soon appeared in the international press. "I always felt from the start that the Ogoniland scene was bad news, Mason, really ugly vibes. I'm not remotely surprised it came to this. The sooner you come back the better." Mason was more than ready for reassignment out of Ogoniland. His kidnapping and his memo had made him too controversial a figure within the company to remain in regular operations. He was assigned to a Liaison Office within the company back in Holland, responsible for contacts with other oil companies.

When he got back to Holland he sensed that his relationship with Melanie had suffered from his two year absence. He told her of his concerns. "OK, but you can't be away for over two years and expect that everything will be back to normal upon your return, Mason. The kids are older, we're not living in developing countries like we used to any more, our family's life has taken on a new rhythm." He found that his distance from his children too had taken its toll. They had moved into teen years and were now less open to talking with him about the details of their daily lives.

A few weeks after his return he received a call from a man named Jim Moore, a craggy and intense but soft-spoken, Canadian businessman, and a senior figure from Mason's former company, Tundra Oil. Moore was aware, he said, of the memo that Mason had written in Ogoniland. The paper had surreptitiously made its way around to a number of oil company executives who realized that Mason had made explicit what was often only reluctantly perceived, generally ignored, or hushed up in the volatile field of petroleum politics. No one had ever forgotten, least of all the Iranian people, how British Petroleum's policies in Iran in the early 1950s had led to its collusion with MI-6 and the CIA to overthrow Iran's first elected Prime Minister Mossadegh, and put the Shah back on the throne. Iran's hostility to the West had never receded since then.

Moore launched into a discussion about how Canada was now deeply involved developing the tar sands—he called them "oil sands"—of Alberta, a massive source of oil but plagued with multiple problems—technical, economic, political and environmental. Indeed, the project was already running into significant problems with environmentalists as well as First Nations peoples of British Columbia due to its potentially spectacular environmental threat. Would Mason consider taking on the task of political chief for the operations in British Colombia, given his experience and sensitivity to the concerns of working with environmentalists and local cultures?

And so, to his considerable surprise, Mason soon found himself offered a job as Tundra's COO, Chief Operating Officer for political relations on local operations in BC, working out of Calgary, Alberta and reporting to Tundra's CEO based in Toronto. Unlike the environmental hell of Ogoniland, British Columbia presented an image of a coastal and mountain paradise. But the emotionalism of the issues surrounding the exploitation of the tar sands was no less environmentally explosive in BC. It entailed a likely pipeline from Alberta hundreds of miles to the Pacific coast, integrally linked to plans to employ huge modern supertankers to wend their way through the narrow and treacherous waters of the Great Bear Rainforest on the way to Asian markets. Both were bitterly contested issues in British Columbia. Mason was drawn to the challenge and accepted the job offer with alacrity. The tasks were considerable: liaison with First Nations communities, dealing with environmental groups in BC, and liaison with the provincial government of British Columbia in Victoria.

Melanie was reluctant to give up her job in Holland, but she agreed she would probably be able to find a similar job in Calgary, Alberta. Mason and his family would depart shortly to Calgary to take up his new job. He looked forward eagerly to assuming the political challenges and emotional confrontations that, if not as violent, in their own way were as complicated as in Nigeria.

Chapter 19

Bjorn still hadn't seen one—a grizzly in the wild. They had pervaded his dreams over the years, and he sensed some kind of psychic communication there that he couldn't quite define. But he'd had no chance yet to penetrate overland into their inner sanctum, the sacred lands of the Great Bear Rainforest.

He knew he wasn't equipped simply to set out on his own into the forest. After work on the boat in the evening Bjorn tried to persuade Joseph several times to take him. "Come on, Joseph, do something for me. Take me with you when you go out deer hunting. I really want to see if I can see a grizzly in the forest."

"Bjorn, you know, you're half-crazy with this bear stuff. All this business about some sort of communication with them and all. That's pretty far out."

"Well, I'll goddam well find somebody else to take me then, if you won't," Bjorn snapped back.

Joseph put down the coiled rope he was stowing. "Chill out man! It's not so simple. I don't know that much about where the bears hang out this time of year anyway. You should check it out with some local hunters here who could take you."

"Come on, Joseph, I'm sure as hell not going out with any goddam bear hunters!" Bjorn hurled the wiping-up rag into the corner of the boat as they finished up.

"I don't mean bear hunters," Joseph said. "I'm talking about hunters out for deer or elk. Look, our people have respect for the bears. Not like the trophy hunters coming up here from the US. Our local guys know the terrain better than me. I'll ask around, see what we can do. I may actually go out next week and scout out some deer hunting areas, myself. I guess you could come along. But it's kind of crazy going out and just looking for griz, they're problem enough when you're not looking for 'em."

"You're scared of an attack?"

"No, probably not an attack. Most bears aren't looking for a run-in with people. But you never know. We'd need to be pretty damn cautious."

The following Friday Joseph came through. "OK, Bjorn, it's against my better judgment, but tours are slack here for a few days, I'll take you out tomorrow for two days, while I check out one area I haven't been to for some deer hunting later in the season."

Early the next morning Bjorn threw his pack into the back of Joseph's Ford pickup along with Joseph's gear. Joseph also gave him a canister of bear pepper spray to keep with him. Bjorn noted a hunting rifle in the back as well. "A rifle? You're hunting?"

"No, we just need some basic protection, man, just in case."

"So have you ever actually had a close-up encounter with a grizzly?"

"As close as I would ever want. Been out with some of our own people hunting black bear couple years ago. They took a few for their winter's meat supply. One time we did see a grizzly, stood right up on its hind legs and watched us not too far off. Big guy. That was all I needed. We didn't try to shoot it—out of respect."

"You really think we need the rifle?" Bjorn asked.

Joseph stashed it behind the seat. "Yeah, you got to be prepared. Biggest problem with griz, they're unpredictable. When you run into one, you can't know what's in his head. Especially if he's guarding some kind of carcass he's killed and wants to keep control over it. That can be one dangerous bear if he's guarding some kill. Or a mother with cubs. Or if you startle a bear it can react violently too. There's a lot of bad stuff can happen."

Bjorn wasn't sure what to expect as they set out. For some time he was immersed in his thoughts as he watched the asphalt road give way to a roughening dirt track as they finally began to ascend an old logging road deeper into the forest. He felt an emotional exhilaration at setting out onto his first real road trip into the rainforest, a feeling that competed with nervousness at what they might encounter. But this was a trip he knew he had to take to test himself, learn his reactions.

A few hours out they followed the dirt road up to a ridge which they followed. Bjorn could peer down the steep ravine into green glens below. Joseph took note of a few deer here and there, but nothing bigger. It was hard to see what lay further into the forest where verdant undergrowth and waving ferns camouflaged many of the animals that might be lurking there. "Sound of the truck will probably scare off a lot of animals, too."

They eventually came to a place where the forest opened out revealing a vista below. "Yeah, this is right. This guy told me about a look-out point some ways down this ridge road." They got out and walked out onto a rock outcropping with an open view down into the expanse of forested valley below. Beyond the wooded area the sun caught a lazy-flowing river wandering like a silver ribbon over a flat sandy delta area. The river then split off into multiple channels. They pulled out their sandwiches and ate in silence before the spectacle. Bjorn was captivated and spent a long time using Joseph's binoculars to survey up and down the valley and the surrounding mountains. "Don't see anything moving."

"Well, you probably wouldn't from here. But there's a lot of animals down there. Bound to be grizzlies as well."

They drove another two hours looking for a spot where Joseph said there should be a decent place to set up camp in a clearing, not too far off from a bend in the dirt track. "I sort of remember this from a couple years ago." They encountered no vehicles on the track the whole day, though Joseph thought there could be some hunters in the area. They set up a small tent near a fire pit of stones not too far from the road. Most of their supplies they left locked inside the truck so as not to attract bears to their tent and fire pit area. Joseph heated some cans of pork and beans over a camping stove near the truck and later washed out the pot and their dishes in the nearby stream, trying to leave nothing to broadcast their presence to a hungry forest. Joseph pulled out his stash of pot and offered to share a joint but Bjorn knew he didn't much like the way pot curdled his mind anymore. They gazed silently into the coals of the small campfire, each reading his own visions into the flickering flames.

"So how did you get into all this bear shit anyway?" Joseph asked.

"I don't know. Ever since I was a kid they kind of grabbed me. I sort of felt some kind of communication, like they were looking out for me, even then. And then I got really shook up one time when I was around eight and saw a huge grizzly in a zoo. I swear the thing jumped up when he saw me, looked me up and down, kind of expectant. I had this strong feeling about how it wanted help in escaping."

"Yeah, damn sure."

"No, I mean I felt like it said something to me, just not in so many words. And then, it's kind of crazy, but I was in a bad road accident when I was sixteen, smashed the hell out of myself, in the hospital and rehab for months. But when I was lying out there in the cold in the wrecked car that night, busted up and bleeding bad and couldn't get out, I just had this powerful feeling that a bear was with me in the wrecked car, like this big thing lying next to me, heavy weight and a lot of fur keeping me warm, almost like a hug. Right till the ambulance came."

"You don't really believe that, do you, bear in the vehicle with you?"

"It felt goddam real to me, Joseph, that's all I can say. Like it gave me the strength to hold on and survive."

"OK, if you say so. But you know what, you're a little weird, Bjorn, anybody ever tell you that?"

"You're not the first."

Joseph got up and stretched. "Well, we might not see any griz this time out. But you better know what to do if we do. Main thing is, never try to run away. They move fast. Try to look big, tough, and keep your ground, they often bluff charge. If it really looks like it's going to attack, then play dead, lie on your stomach, cover your neck. They often go for the neck."

"What about climbing a tree?"

"With griz it's possible. But black bears, they really know how to climb and they'd follow you right up into the tree. But if you can get high enough, a griz probably won't follow. And make sure you got the bear spray. Aim for the eyes."

The discussion heightened Bjorn's nervousness. He just didn't believe that the bears were automatically a threat to humans. And he had some confidence in himself.

Joseph yawned. "OK, man, I'm going to hit the hay. We need to get up early."

The night passed interminably for Bjorn. He felt excitement at his first serious overnight trip into the forest since camping with his parents. The fulfillment of a long-held desire. And there was a touch of fear still crawling in his gut. He lay in a fetal position in his sleeping bag, heart beating at every sound in the forest just outside the thin wall of the tent, his ears at the alert for potential sounds of twigs cracking under a heavy weight, his mind now set to the same frequency of forest sounds. The slight soughing of cool air through the firs. The awareness of the presence of raw power brooding somewhere outside in the forest near them. In the darkness of night the power of imagination outran his rational mind. At one point, after restless hours in his sleeping bag, he almost thought he would be relieved if they decided to abort the trip and head back home. But that was flirting with self-betrayal. He had to be willing to open himself to the bears, this had to be his destiny.

The first glimmers of dawn brought heightened awareness of the cold. He shivered in his sleeping bag and pulled the hood over his head. Finally the dark phantasms of the unknown receded with the morning light. Bjorn reproached himself for his earlier flickers of timidity and fear. He felt a sense of pleasure and awe in the presence of the forest morning. The surroundings were still silent as they struggled up out of their sleeping bags, few sounds of animals or birds yet to be heard. They relit their gas stove tripod, warmed their hands over it, and put some coffee on to brew. As the morning rays began to penetrate through the trees, casting a green pall over the scene, Bjorn began to feel less exposed, his existential angst receding. The environment became more familiar, less threatening.

"We're heading up to some falls in the river, good two hours from here. They told me if we're lucky we might see some bears there.

Hopefully we can see them from a distance, and they should be intent on searching for fish, not us."

"I don't see a trail."

"No, it's not well marked but we need to head due east from here to hit the river. Should be some paths we can follow with the compass."

They left their camping equipment in the truck and took only their smaller packs. "Make sure you got the canister of pepper spray," Joseph said.

Bjorn's face showed an ambivalence. The mere act of carrying bear spray signaled to him a presumption of hostility in any encounter he might have. "Come on, jerk," Joseph growled, "you may be goddam glad you got it at hand. These aren't teddy bears you know." An image of Ears flashed through Bjorn's mind. Ears would be glad to know that Bjorn was out here. Meanwhile Joseph carried his large rifle. "Big enough gun you brought," Bjorn muttered to Joseph.

"Goddam right. If we have to stop a bear, I'm sure as hell gonna fire something more than a popgun. This is a .338 calibre, Browning Win Mag, big kick but my hunter friends say it will stop a griz if we have to. But we're not here to hunt anyway, this is just smart backup. Bears can move fast when you least expect it."

The forest was still and silent as they moved along a rudimentary path, scrambling over big nurse logs and other fallen trees in their way. "Are you sure we're still on some trail?" Bjorn asked.

"Near enough. I recall there are a few old paths here if you know where to look, and we're heading in the right direction according to my compass."

They stopped periodically and stood in silence, alert to any sounds or motion. A large deer with fine antlers made an appearance on a nearby knoll at the top of a small cliff and stared at them for some moments before bounding off. "Would have made a good shot if I was hunting for deer now."

They pushed on through the underbrush for over an hour, and Bjorn found it harder work than he had anticipated. He couldn't see any real trail, but Joseph was consulting his compass often. Bjorn had to be constantly alert for roots and branches under foot that could trip him up. They maintained a reasonable silence but they could not avoid signaling their presence to the forest.

Eventually they came within sight of the river and slowed their pace. The sound of the river masked their presence to possible bears and they did not want to surprise them. They crept forward towards the bank and peered up and down the milky-gray glacial river but saw no sign of bears around the falls where they frequently caught fish in-season. They stood in near silence for half an hour but nothing rewarded their wait. Finally Joseph nodded. "I don't think we're going to see anything right here today. I recall there are a few smaller salmon streams on the way back. But the salmon may not be running up these streams right now."

They turned around to begin the two hour hike back to the camp. Joseph swore softly to himself as he searched around to find the faint trail by which they had come. He said he knew they had to return due west to get back to the fire road but could not be certain exactly where they would come out on it. After one hour they rested, sitting on a fallen tree in a glen and drank from their canteens, savoring the cool for a few moments before moving on. Suddenly Joseph gestured. Bjorn turned and then saw it. A large bear was clearly observing them from no more than fifty meters away. It stood up on its hind legs to get a better view of them. "It's a griz, sure as hell," Joseph whispered. They heard a whuffing noise issue from its jowls. "That's a bad sign," Joseph said. "That's a sign of aggression."

Bjorn was seized by an icy fear. "But we're not bothering it, we're staying away from it, shouldn't that be okay?" he whispered back in hope.

"Actually we shouldn't be whispering," Joseph said, "we should be talking loud, like this, like we're dangerous," and his voice rose accordingly as he shouted at the bear. Bjorn joined him in yelling.

The bear began to move down the hillside towards them with some determination in its pace. "Quick, give me the spray canister," Joseph ordered. Bjorn felt a sickly fear as the large animal continued in their direction, undeterred. He dug around in his backpack for the spray as the bear gained ground on them. "No time, find a tree to climb, now!"

he yelled. But Bjorn stood transfixed, fascination and fear together inducing a paralysis of will. The power of the primal moment, long fantasized about, now overwhelmed any survival instinct. He was face to face with his destiny.

Joseph pulled out his rifle. The bear was moving slowly but steadily in the underbrush, a moving target. As the bear moved ever closer, Joseph raised the barrel and took aim. Suddenly Bjorn slammed his hand down on the rifle barrel in Joseph's hand, causing him to drop it. "What in hell are you doing, you asshole!" he yelled. And Joseph moved to a tree a few steps away that afforded some purchase in lower branches that enabled him to begin to climb.

"Don't mess with the spray! Quick, up a tree!" Joseph yelled. Bjorn finally got out the spray and searched for the spray release. The bear slowed and began to survey them, and then moved to the tree where Joseph was now four meters up. It rose up onto its hind legs, began to reach up for the first few branches. Joseph moved higher up the tree, yelling at Bjorn to spray the bear. But Bjorn remained paralyzed. He just stood transfixed at the base of a tree as the bear scratched around, reaching up into the tree where Joseph clung, only six meters away from him. Surely the bear wouldn't continue to pursue them if their presence didn't seem threatening.

The bear then paused, and dropped back down on four legs to the ground. Bjorn felt his moment of truth had come. The bear turned towards him, its ears back, uttering a terrifying whoofing sound out of the deep bellows of its lungs. It stared at Bjorn for what seemed like ages, its eyes black, penetrating, unwavering. "Spray it, spray it!," Joseph yelled. But Bjorn was paralyzed, no longer even aware of what Joseph was saying. He retreated, transfixed, and then stumbled backward onto the ground. The bear looked at him, sniffed the air, and pawed the ground. After an eternity, it looked at Bjorn again, made some snuffling noises, turned and slowly ambled off in the direction from which it came.

"You fucking fool!" Joseph yelled as he worked his way down the tree. "Why didn't you spray it? You almost got us both killed. It was a goddam miracle that it gave up on its attack."

And then Bjorn began to tremble, rose onto his knees, and broke into unquenchable sobs. He could not process the moment of terror and possible salvation, even redemption that had passed between himself and the bear. *Miracle?*

Joseph too had been thoroughly unnerved. They began their long walk back to the pickup, alert to any other sounds of animals in the underbrush. Joseph was so furious at Bjorn he could hardly speak. "What in hell did you think you were doing batting that rifle out of my hand?"

"I don't know, it was just instinct. I didn't want you to kill the bear."

"So you'd rather have us both dead?"

"I didn't think it was going to kill us."

"So what was it going to do then?"

"I don't know, check us out. I don't know, I just felt like it wasn't looking to kill me. I know it could have. I think maybe there was some kind of message there for me."

"What bullshit," Joseph muttered, and they continued their wary way back to the vehicle.

As they drove back Bjorn replayed the scene over and over again in his mind, trying to extract some greater meaning out of the encounter. It had terrified him beyond his expectations. The reality of the bear's presence in the wild was far more overwhelming, primal, than he would have expected. The size, the sheer bulk of the creature, its noises, its penetrating *smell*, like something from another world. Was it a positive sign that in the end it had chosen not to kill him? Did that signal some degree of acceptance of him by the bear? The Bear People?

He finally mentioned some of these thoughts to Joseph on the long drive back. "Will you stop trying to find some goddam meaning in what happened, Bjorn?" Joseph snapped, glaring at him. "It was a goddam bear in the goddam forest and you were goddam stupid and goddam lucky! Got it? People run into situations in the woods, it doesn't mean that every one of them has to be sent by God, or meant to carry some personal message. It was what it was. There are lots of bears in the forest. The bear in the end didn't try to kill me either, it left us both alone and went off. Does that mean I'm somehow blessed in all this too? Or how do you know it didn't just want to chase us off from some carcass it was guarding? How in hell do we know? Not everything that happens in life has special meaning! Give it a rest for chrissakes!"

Bjorn remained silent the rest of the way back, sullen in Joseph's rebuke. Joseph didn't get it. And that night back in his room, in his mind, in his sleep, Bjorn again replayed the scene, tried to recreate the moment of possible communication with the bear. Was it linked at all to Bjorn's presence in Bella Bella, his search for his parents, for traces of his past? Was it designed to encourage him in his quest, that it had spared him? Or to discourage him? No answer felt fully right.

Before dawn, in a half-awake dream he felt a moment of clarity descend upon him once again. A flash of awareness of wordless communication inside his head.

You people fear my power. My beauty, my soft, shining fur and my powerful arms overwhelm you. My teeth are long and my jaws can crush a skull. My shoulders are powerful and my claws gut a torso in one swipe. You fear my vision of the reality that you do not wish to perceive.

You seek to deny my power. You rush to belittle me in images of pets, toys, cartoons and mascots. In your fear you shrink from knowing anything of my mind. But you will know of it.

This dream, this hallucination deeply disturbed him. It seemed to address him again, address his questions about the Bear. He realized that this event marked a final transition from his "practice bear" Ears, to a living, awe-inspiring wild creature that roamed the forest with a mission.

The most shocking thing for him was a new loss of confidence in himself, after standing in the presence of a bear. That long felt sympathy, warmth, good-will and closeness towards bears had now given way to a sense of overwhelming awe at their sheer presence. The bears might be speaking to him, but it was on their terms. He would admire them, be in their thrall, but would also keep a distance. No more warm, affirmative or cuddly messages. It was an apparition of awe, power, raw Nature. Yes, the bear had spared him, an incident he now accepted as an affirmative event but utterly beyond Bjorn's control.

He was certain that future events would offer him further decisive signs as to his purpose and quest. But he could no longer consider his relationship to the Bear as fully benign; it was too powerful, too straight out of raw Nature.

He must ask Sam Winters about the experience.

Chapter 20

"Hey, Bear Man, you heard about this "bear seminar" they're holding in the city next week?" Joseph asked. "Guy here was telling me it's got hunters all riled up, maybe could lead to some kind of hunting ban. Given all your attachment to bears, you might want to check it out." Bjorn went online to learn more about it. The seminar was sponsored by green groups to raise environmental consciousness about hunting in the province. He knew right away it would benefit him to gain more knowledge on the subject.

"May I?" He'd noticed the young woman earlier as seminar participants had filed in to the hotel conference room, but she took a seat right next to Bjorn at the opening reception. She almost looked like a caricature of an American cheerleader—blonde, perky, slightly snub nose, long legs, bouncy bust. Also yesteryear's cheerleader—she looked a little over thirty. Bjorn used to be instinctively wary of girls like this—he knew they would look down on him as gauche, a nerd, a "Native" and he knew he stood no chance. And when they stirred his groin it frustrated him, making him feel more humiliated.

She turned to him. "Hi, I'm Dawn—as you can see," she laughed, pointing at her name-tag stuck on her sweater with her name written on it in green felt-tip. "Are you part of the Rainforest protest?"

"Not officially," Bjorn replied. "But I'm interested in seeing what's going on with it."

"Yeah, me too. Are you from around here?" she asked.

"Kind of. I'm First Nations, from the coastal area."

"Cool! First Nations! And what's your name?"

"Bjorn."

"Great to meet you, Bjorn. I think this is an awesome protest project. It's about time people got their shit together on these bear hunting—and oil issues."

"You follow these issues here?"

"Not here in Canada so much, or only recently. But I've been interested in Native American issues for some time."

"So you're from the States then?"

"Yeah. My first time up in Canada. But I've been involved in some Indian politics—Native American stuff—in the US."

"Really?" Bjorn asked. "Like what?"

"Well, all over the map—restoration of lands, treaty rights, water issues, oil and mineral exploitation, animal rights—you name it. I'm sure a lot of the same issues as here."

He could see she was more serious than he had first assumed from her appearance.

"So what are you doing up here?" Bjorn asked.

"Finding out about grizzly hunting, the tar sands, tankers…and the Great Bear Rainforest. This is just some fabulous country! All these incredible mountains and waters—and misty forests. Very mysterious. We don't really have anything like this in the States, at least where I come from, in New Mexico. It's beautiful there, but bone dry. I'd love to get involved in some of the issues here if I could."

"Yeah, the Rainforest is awesome, it's supposed to be as big as Ireland. But a lot of this is just really starting to get rolling here now in Canada. We're a little more cautious in our approach here than in the States I guess. But it's great you're interested, especially coming up from the States."

"Been in organizational politics before?"

"Not really. You?"

"Yeah, I worked with AIM for a while. You heard of it?"

"Don't think so."

"Beer?" She walked Bjorn over to the bar and ordered two bottles of beer and paid for them both.

"Yeah, AIM, the American Indian Movement. It's been a serious kick-ass organization some years back, totally laying it out in public about how Indians have gotten screwed over in the past. Demands for change. You guys in Canada here could maybe benefit from their experiences. They've been outspoken, really gotten down in the weeds on the details of issues, carried out some illegal actions, taken some hard lumps, even serious trouble with the police."

"Sounds interesting."

"So what are you doing here tonight?" Dawn asked, looking around. There doesn't seem to be a lot more going on till tomorrow. If you're not doing anything, I'd love to go out and grab a bite and I can tell you about it. I don't know my way around here."

"Sure. There's a fair number of Asian places right around here."

She picked up her backpack from a corner table and they pushed open the back door from the hotel. It was drizzling; she stopped and pulled a yellow windbreaker out of her pack. "Not weather I'm used to."

"Well, hang around here for very long, you'll get used to it. Why do you think we call it the rainforest?"

They wandered along the street until they found an Asian noodle place. They sat down in a booth and ordered two beers.

"So tell me about AIM."

"Ever heard of the occupation of Alcatraz Island, in San Francisco?"

"Like the prison?"

"Yeah, but it was abandoned as a prison, some time ago. Then a whole bunch of Indians, a lot of them linked to AIM, occupied the whole damn island around 1970. It was a big deal, lots of Indians from all over went there, maybe 400 people at some point. It got a lot of publicity. They proclaimed the "discovery" of the island, just like white people earlier claimed they had "discovered" America. The occupation lasted, I don't know, like nineteen months before they were finally forced out, can you believe it!"

Bjorn was surprised at her eagerness. "Wow, I'd barely heard about anything going on at Alcatraz. That sounds pretty bold."

"Yeah, and that wasn't the half of it. Later on Movement members organized a huge march on Washington, ended up seizing and occupying the building of the Bureau of Indian Affairs right in downtown DC, got big time TV coverage, all around the time of presidential elections. The word really got out to the public about Indian issues."

"Amazing!" Bjorn felt himself being drawn into her world.

"OK, but it got really rough later, there were even some shoot-outs with the FBI on reservation lands out in the West. There was the huge standoff at Wounded Knee around then too. You know Wounded Knee?"

"Wasn't there some massacre or something there?"

"Yeah, well a long time ago it was the place where white army troops massacred over 200 Native Americans—sometime in the late 1800's, you know, when they tried to force them off their land? That place. Well, in '73 the American Indian Movement occupied the town for 70 damn days—incredible!—before the FBI attacked them and finally took back the place. Those sons of bitches...lot of people got killed. Some real bad vigilante action by whites against Indians too, man, really bad scene. White power just unloaded on them at the end. A few Feds got killed too. Lot of Indians ended up in jail, including Leonard Peltier, you know him?"

Bjorn nodded.

"Yeah, thought you might have heard of him, he was Canadian, Native activist. He managed to escape back to Canada but the chicken-shit Canadian government shipped him back to the US where they tried him for murder of a Fed. He's still in jail, well it's been more than forty years now!"

Bjorn nodded. "Yeah, I heard something about that. But things don't usually get so violent around here, although we've had demonstrations. Native people here are a lot more cautious."

"Yeah, well, Canadians at least didn't kill off so many of their own Indians either, compared to the slaughter in the US. But you know how it is with Indians, they get fucked everywhere."

They finished off two beers apiece, more than Bjorn was used to, before ordering some Thai noodles. Bjorn found himself intrigued by this woman, she radiated a kind of energy and commitment he wasn't used to.

"So tell me about yourself, Bjorn," Dawn said, and she placed her hand lightly on Bjorn's wrist.

"Not a lot to tell. Actually I'm adopted, into a white family, good enough people, but I just didn't really feel I was part of it, is all. I've been finding out about my own biological parents, my heritage. My mom was a Native from Bella Bella, and my dad's from Haida Gwaii, a huge Native island up in the north." He surprised himself, uttering these assertions to her as if they were firm.

"Must have been difficult, being adopted and all."

"Yeah, well it is, but still, I've learned a lot. It's only lately I've kind of gotten drawn into this oil thing which is a big deal on our coast now."

"This is a beautiful land, Bjorn. I love the atmosphere, so different from the desert of the southwest."

They talked about the coastal region and the Great Bear Rainforest. "You should see it, Dawn, just beautiful unspoiled lands, and the home of a very special bear, the Spirit Bear, all white."

"I'd love to go there, it must be amazing." And she told him about her life in New Mexico. "I was married one time to a Navajo there, you know. Gorgeous guy, but he began to drink hard, and things finally got rough. Broke my heart. And it was really tough for an outsider like me to get into Navajo life, to be accepted." She laughed. "I guess I found out what it's like to be a minority, when I was among Navajos." Bjorn thought about his own problems in being accepted, as white or Native.

He found himself laughing too at some of her tales, and starting to relax. He began to tell Dawn about his experiences in school, and how he found his identity changing from being part of a white family to being a Native. "For one thing, whites often drink big time, but me, two beers, and you've already pushed me to my limit."

"Yeah, I guess that proves you're Native, I can see you're flushed already," she laughed. "Kind of familiar."

"Yeah, and then my dad—my adopted one—he got all bent out of shape about my searching for my biological family. He felt threatened or some damn thing. So relations were bad. My mom's been supportive though. And I've also been interested in bears ever since I was a kid," he confided.

"Bears, wow, that's cool! What about them?"

"Well, it's kind of a coincidence, but that's what my name means in Norwegian, my adopted mom's family was from Norway. I guess it's a common name there. But bears have always fascinated me." And he began to open up to her about the symbolism of bears in Native tradition. Dawn stared into his eyes as she listened, fascinated. She seemed to sense his youth, inexperience, and was charmed by his hesitation and shyness as well.

"I'd love to go to the southwest sometime," Bjorn said. "I've seen pictures, it's fantastic with all those red cliffs and adobe buildings and stuff."

"Yeah, really different world. Well, you got an invitation to come down any time." She paused and looked at her watch. "Wow, we've been here over two hours. What are you going to do?"

"Well, I'm going to some of the sessions at the conference tomorrow."

"No, I mean right now."

"I don't know, just going back to my room in the hotel."

"Do you want to come up to my room for a nightcap?"

Bjorn hesitated. He could see where this was going, and found his emotions swirling. He remembered his inability to perform with Julie at her apartment at UBC when he was back in school two years ago. He wasn't confident he could manage.

Dawn sensed his hesitation. "Bjorn, look, don't worry about it. Just come on up. We can just chill."

Bjorn felt like clay in her hands. He was not the pursuer, not even the eagerly pursued. When they got to her room Dawn kissed him and then went into the bathroom and came out in a bathrobe that was half open. She reached to unbutton his shirt, embarrassing him a little and causing him to resist slightly. She drew him towards the bed.

Finally Bjorn lay on the bed, naked, one knee cocked to diminish the sense of his nakedness. He watched as her body swayed before him. He remained hesitant, torn both by lust and a fear that he was still not ready. He closed his eyes as she sought to stimulate him. An image of the Bear came into his mind. He could picture a large male bear, huffing, mounting a female. Its balls were large and swayed. Its phallus emerged from its sheath as it moved to penetrate the sow. Bjorn felt a sudden surge of desire in himself and found himself beginning to take the lead with Dawn. He clasped her hungrily, but then found himself exploding into a fast climax with her. But Dawn seemed to accept it as natural, just an opening round of their relationship that evening. Half an hour later they moved towards each other again and this time Bjorn felt strong; he had been able to satisfy her. Later, as they lay in bed, Bjorn luxuriated in his new experience, an incredible state of mind and body that he had never known before, his first successful sexual encounter. To Dawn it seemed almost a routine part of the evening.

"You should come with me down to New Mexico sometime," she said. "You should see how other Indians live, in their own world so different than here. Maybe the arid plains make us tougher people down there. Indians in the US are clearer about the rougher realities of how the white world screws them. You Native BC'ers here have it all from what I can see. Just open your mouth and a fish jumps in, big trees that protect you, give you everything you need, a plentiful sea and rich forests. Moderate government. Down my way we got harsh sun, it beats down on us, we have to seek the coolness of the shadows for relief. We're lucky if we can grow a bean in the dry soil. Government down our throats half the time. But maybe it makes us tougher, more realistic about what life has brought us…and we're not going to take it anymore." Dawn lit a cigarette and took a long drag on it. "Ever heard of Johnny Cash?"

"Sure, who hasn't?"

"Well you should listen to his classic album, from the sixties, "Bitter Tears: Ballads of the American Indians." It's awesome, really tells it like it is. And there's Buffy St. Marie."

"Yeah, she's Canadian, I know of her. I think she's Cree. She has sung some really angry songs about the treatment of Indians. I wish we had more singers like that here. We got this one guy, Bruce Cockburn, got a few great songs about Indians, but he mostly sings about injustices in other parts of the world."

They lay in bed for a while more. "I'm leaving day after tomorrow, but you should come down with me to the US for a few days, maybe just as far as Denver, meet some of my friends."

"Well, I'm supposed to be working next week, but…" This new relationship had assumed a bigger place in his mind and he didn't want to give it up right away. Joseph could probably do without him a few days. He sensed the start of new doors opening. He couldn't say no.

Chapter 21

Two days later Bjorn crossed over the US border and was on his way to Colorado in Dawn's old red Corolla that looked like it had seen many desert roads in its day. "I still know a number of these Native guys," she said. "A bunch hang out in Colorado these days. And a lot of them are pissed, they've taken a lot of shit off the police. They're just trying to stay out of trouble right now. But they haven't lost the faith. But you know, I think some of them might be interesting to you guys up there in Canada—activists there seem to be a little less violent than down here from what I've heard."

"Yeah, I guess we're more law-abiding," Bjorn said with a smirk.

After cutting through Washington State and Idaho, Bjorn found himself entering a different world as they plunged into the dramatic dryscapes of Wyoming. Wherever he looked it felt parched, abandoned, desolate, desert. "Wow, I've never been outside the rain forests of BC before. This is bleak."

"Yeah, it is bleak, but it has its power. We call it the Big Sky. It's actually much nicer down our way in New Mexico, we got all these desert monuments out of red sands. But yeah, no moss growing on fir trees here."

They reached Denver the afternoon of the following day. Dawn took Bjorn to her apartment and gave him a place on the couch. Bjorn had hoped he might share her bed again, but she yawned and stretched, "I'm tired, see you in the morning." He worried whether he had proved disappointing to her in bed that first night. He wondered how aggressive he should be in coming on to Dawn.

Next morning they got back in the Corolla and crossed town to an apartment in a northern suburb of Denver. The place looked more like a crash pad for transient visitors than a lived-in apartment. Furniture was old and shabby, venetian blinds on two windows were broken and hanging down skewed. It smelled like nobody had taken the garbage out for days. There were two guys there, seemed in their forties; one looked white, wearing a red bandanna over the top of his head, a work shirt and worn jeans. The other guy was stockier, had a slightly pock-marked face, darker complexion, looked Indian. They introduced themselves as Carl and Ray. "Good to get a Canuck down here," Carl commented. "Don't seen them down this way much."

"Too pussy," Ray commented. "Beer?"

Bjorn didn't feel he could say no, even though it was still morning. Ray cracked him open a Coors, and gave one to Dawn too.

"So what you guys doing up there about all this pipeline shit we been hearing about?" Carl asked.

"Not too much so far from what I can see," Bjorn said. "Mainly meetings, discussions. But I think it's coming along. This oil company is trying to shove it down our throats, ship their damn tar sands oil down through the waters of the Great Bear Rainforest, it's just asking for a bad accident. I don't know how much of a say the First Nations are going to have in the end."

"Like maybe, none?"

"Well these big companies, they've got big backing from the federal and provincial governments—and the governments are in the pocket of the big energy companies."

"Talk's no damn good," Ray offered. "You can talk till you're blue in the face, don't mean shit. Action's where it's at. That's what you guys need to think about. Speeches and petitions won't ever cut it. You need something to get attention to your cause. Incidents that'll get you into the headlines, TV, make people think about it who didn't think nothing about it before. Raise the stakes."

Bjorn felt inexperienced, naive and a bit intimidated in their presence, but he was fascinated in hearing about their experiences. As far as he knew it went well beyond the things that had been going on so far in Canada. Carl told him about the sit-in and takeover movements that had gained them international attention, creating public awareness and discussion. Bjorn had never thought much about political action before, or what its impact could be. And he wasn't certain just how much dramatic illegal protest would take place along the coast. But he was beginning to realize that tanker issues in BC were actually just part of something much bigger. He began to see how this American Indian Movement wasn't just about politics, it was about their identity too. He felt his own sense of broader identity, even pride, grow with his exposure to them.

"Yep, in a way you can say the white man taught us to be Indian," Carl commented. "Before then we was all different nations and peoples. We traded, fought, made alliances, but we all knew we had different languages and customs. Along comes the white man. To them we were all the same scum, "red men," "Injuns," all that. Equal opportunity discrimination. And they started calling us "Indians" officially. Can you imagine that shit? Just because Columbus couldn't figure out he was in the goddam Caribbean, thought he'd maybe landed in India, and started calling all the natives "Indians"? What kind of screwed-up shit is that?"

Bjorn shook his head in sympathy.

"Well, next thing you know, we decided, OK, if you're going to treat us as all the same, then alright, goddam it, we *are* gonna be Indians. And we're gonna stick together for strength, the power to fight Whitey. And so we even accepted the word, yeah, Indian for ourselves, and among ourselves. It's our mark of unity. "

"Honey, can you bring us some chips and salsa from the fridge?" Ray asked Dawn. Dawn came back with a big bag of corn chips and opened a container of salsa she found in the fridge. Bjorn took a break, went out on the balcony for a few minutes, trying to take it all in. As he looked out over the busy traffic below him on the nearby freeway, talk of Native Americans and reservations and protests all seemed a bit unreal. Like utterly different worlds were playing out their separate lives.

When he came back in, Dawn asked Carl about how he viewed where the whole identity thing was now.

"Yeah, well, OK, identity, it's not that simple anymore. They killed our identity. It's not just like, okay, I'm Iroquois or Sioux or Cherokee or whatever. Our real identity was the *place*, the sacred land we were on. That's what the white man never understood. Or maybe he did understand and that's why he drove us off of our land. Once we've lost our land, our sacred places and names, then we've lost most of our identity. We can't take our land with us. So good luck trying to keep the language up, that's the last shred. They tried to destroy that as well. Just leave us drunk, stupid, unemployed without any identity, on some shit-hole of a reservation."

"Shit, we can't even decide if we want to be Indian," Ray said. "One day we're out celebrating our powwows doing our Indian thing, next day we're trying to pretend we're not Indian so we can get a goddam job without being discriminated."

Carl turned on Bjorn. "Yeah, Bjorn, that's you too! You think you can just "pass" cause of your white boy education? Well I can "pass" too. I'm like a fucking chameleon, I can play in Whitey's game, do pretty well at it, as a matter of fact. I can talk all that talk about belonging to American culture and all. But I also have to have my contacts with my people, my culture, my roots, it's like air to me, to breathe. I'm like an actor on the stage—I play the role pretty good. Hell, I'm good at my mason's job too, and I get all this respect and shit for being a "good Indian" or a "smart Indian" or "good worker." You got to roll with the punches man, play in the white man's movie and on their stage—that's how you live. And you keep your roots to yourself— that's your own dirty little secret. But you got to get back to breathe that Native air every once in a while before you go back into the white man's arena. You got to keep something authentic in your life."

"Whaddya mean, 'authentic' Carl?" Ray countered. "That's bullshit! Sure, some of our leaders talk about going back to 'authentic' ways. Well, how in hell are you gonna do that? What was 'authentic' a hundred years ago sure as hell ain't now! The conditions are gone. We're just gonna go out and build some goddam Indian museum and dress up and put on shows for white folks with our chanting and tomahawks and loin cloths? That's bullshit, man!"

They fell silent and ate some more chips and salsa. "Yeah, well, ain't nothin' much gonna happen now," Carl added. "Most Indians just want to keep a low profile. We want to get some action going again at some point, but it's not easy. Fucking FBI all over our necks."

They finally broke up after another round of beers. "Keep the faith, man," Ray said to Bjorn as they left, and they high-fived him. "Lot a work to be done up there." Bjorn left with his head swirling in the face of these new attitudes that went beyond what Joseph had talked about. They had perspectives on action that he hadn't thought about before. But he also felt very foreign as a Canadian in this environment. A little more cautious, a little less bitter about the Canadian past that had not been as violent as the American past, a little more hopeful about the future.

That night at Dawn's apartment she pulled Bjorn into her bedroom. He was gaining in confidence, and felt empowered that she wanted him again. He reveled in it, and later slept solidly.

"Mornin', lover," were the first words he heard as Dawn came into the bedroom nude the next morning bearing a cup of coffee. She kissed him on his head and slipped back into bed. "I slept great. Judging by that big grin on your face I'd say you did too."

Waking up in the same bed in the morning with Dawn gave Bjorn a wonderful feeling of belonging. He stretched luxuriously, feeling a secret pride in his ability to perform in this ongoing intimate relationship, one that he had never experienced before. It gave him a new sense of confidence quite unrelated to his work.

"I know you've got to be heading back to Canada tomorrow, but there's one more person I'd like you to meet," Dawn said. "Just to give you a bigger picture of stuff that's been going down around here over the last ten years."

"Who's that?"

"Guy named Ricky Shawn. Used to be with the Animal Liberation Front till he got arrested after an arson attack on an animal research laboratory in Wisconsin. I'll let him tell you about it."

They drove some ways south on the freeway and turned off into a modest residential community and into a suburban driveway cluttered with tricycles and plastic basketball hoops and other signs of children at play. Ricky came out to greet them, a fairly short man, small goatee, mid-forties. He carried in his arms a smiling girl in a yellow sundress who looked to be about five. "Glad to meet you, Bjorn. We don't see many people from Canada these days, or hear much about 'em neither."

He ushered them into a cluttered living room with brown upholstered furniture that smelled of tobacco smoke. "Honey, come say hello to a real Canadian," he shouted. His wife came out of the kitchen. "Nice to see a fellow Canuck," she said. "Where're you from?"

"Vancouver area," Bjorn responded. "And up along the coast a bit, Bella Bella."

"Beautiful territory. I'm from Saskatchewan, the prairies, so we don't see too many mountains. Coffee?"

After delivering the cup she took the girl and went back into the kitchen and closed the door. "You don't have to close the door, hon," Ricky called. "We're not talking nothing secret here."

"Well, you better not," she replied. "We know where that leads."

Dawn took the initiative. "I think Bjorn would benefit a lot from hearing about some of the stuff that you guys used to do in the ALF," she said. "There's animal problems up in Canada too, especially with griz hunting for trophies."

"Yeah, well we know a thing or two about the damn US griz hunters going up there." Ricky turned to Bjorn and sized him up for a moment. "You know about the ALF, Bjorn? Animal Liberation Front? Kind of fallen on hard times now. Got so that by the end probably half our members were undercover FBI agents. Still we gave 'em a hell of a run for their money. But they caught up with me. Served seven years in the goddam pen."

"I heard of the ALF, but that's about it, I'm afraid," Bjorn responded.

Ricky stretched his feet out onto the coffee table. "Well, I'll tell you, it was quite a movement. Still is, but it's got to act different now, times change and the Feds want to call everybody terrorists these days. But 9/11 at least sort of helped turn the heat away from us and onto the Ayrabs."

"Weren't you guys freeing a lot of lab animals who were being experimented on?" Bjorn asked.

"Damn right. Still a goddam scandal what these so-called scientists are doing. Experiments like something out of Nazi concentration camp. Back in the day we ran a lot of operations, breaking into labs and cages for test animals, letting them loose in many cases. We set some of those labs on fire as well and the scientists lost all their records on the experiments they'd been conducting. Now warn't that a shame! But it was pretty horrible what they were doing, operations on the brains of monkeys, testing levels of pain, animals tied up to god-awful machines and sending electricity into their bodies to make their muscles twitch. It kind of makes me angrier than if they were doing experiments on humans. Hell, humans at least can do something more to protect themselves. More than that though, I think humans can just be goddam evil. Animals won't be practicing cruelty on other animals just for experiment. Sure they'll kill you and eat you, but run experiments on you? No way. They're creatures of nature, kind of innocent, not like people. So no, I've got no tears to shed for these fucking scientists and their labs—torturers is a better name. But, you know, I got a family now, got to get out of the business. Some of you guys up in Canada, though, you might think about stepping up the action some."

Ricky went on to tell Bjorn of the many operations that the ALF had engaged in over the years. "Beauty part was, it wasn't a centralized movement. Was hard for the Feds to bust us. All kinds of people joined in with us, and yeah, some of it was maybe not good, some people threatening researchers and scientists with violence and all that, destroyed a good bit of property. But the message got through to the general public in the end, you know? You got to take dramatic, even violent steps sometimes to drive the point home to people who'd just as soon sit home fat and sassy and ignorant about what's going on out there. After a couple of operations, we made it into the news and a lot more people knew about these things. And in the end some of the labs and research centres got investigated. Some people got prosecuted for violation of research ethics. Some places even got closed down. Lot of big corporations had been backing up some of this so-called research as well. But when all this negative publicity came out they began backing off too"

"Yeah, well our problem is a little different," Bjorn commented. "We're trying to protect large endangered species from hunters, most of 'em coming up from the States. Like ibex, long-horned sheep, grizzly bears especially. Our damn provincial government in British Columbia is still happy to sell these permits for people to come up and kill the grizzlies, make rugs out of them or hang the heads in their den. And a lot of it is illegal, under the radar."

"Well," Ricky went on, "you got to collect the evidence so you can force the government into facing what's going on. I know some guys have been up there in Canada to try to stop the US griz hunters—actually killed a couple of them I heard. I'm afraid you guys up there in Canada kinda got the reputation down here of being too law-abiding, not willing to take much illegal action. But might be one or two people around here that could come up your way sometime, help finding out who these US guys are with their assault rifles, maybe get photographic evidence on the killing."

Bjorn was surprised to hear of the extent of ALF action, and people acting on their own locally. He hadn't thought a lot before about the possibility of taking action, especially illegal action.

"Illegal's the way to go, my friend. Playing by the rules won't get you nowhere, not when the people who are raping the system is also the ones making the rules."

Bjorn got back to Dawn's apartment with his head spinning. Even though the hour was late he wanted to sit down and talk about his powerful impressions with Dawn—about what it all meant, where to go with it, and the implications for Bjorn's own life. But he was disappointed that Dawn was yawning after the long day and didn't seem to have the energy to join him for a discussion. Nor did she ask him to join her in bed again. "Time for bed, love. I got a lot of driving tomorrow, and you need to get to the airport." And she pecked Bjorn on the cheek, a disappointing coda to the tumultuous day.

Lying on the couch, watching the lights of passing cars flash by on the ceiling, Bjorn was too hopped up to sleep, still mulling over all he had heard from Ricky and the AIM people about taking action. His most overwhelming impression was about the common experiences of so many Native peoples and the raw deal they had received everywhere. He felt a sense of anger, an immense sympathy for how they had gone out to take action on environmental issues, often working in tandem with non-Natives. This wasn't just about one region, it embraced all Native peoples facing common problems. Passivity was not an option. But what could he do as just one person?

And maybe for him the most important part of his time with Dawn was losing his virginity and gaining some experience in bed. It empowered him in new ways for the first time in his life.

When Bjorn came through immigration at the Vancouver airport the next afternoon an officer asked him to step aside into an office. "What was the purpose of your trip to the United States, sir?" the immigration officer asked.

"Tourism, visiting some friends."

"Who did you travel with?"

"Just a friend."

"Name?"

"Dawn Robertson."

"And who did you visit in the States?"

"Just some of her friends."

"Can you give me their names, please?"

"Look, I only met them briefly for coffee or a beer. I'm not sure I even know their last names. One was Ricky Shawn, I think. And Carl somebody. Ray somebody, I'm not sure I got their last names."

The officer typed a few things into his computer out of Bjorn's vision.

"OK, did they give you any messages for anybody here in Canada?"

"No, no messages."

"Any instructions to be passed along?"

"Instructions?" Bjorn's voice quavered. "What do you mean, what kind of instructions?"

"I'm asking you. Anything about conducting any environmental activism here?"

"No, I just heard a little about what had gone on down there in the States, ten years ago."

"Did they suggest anything to you?"

"No," Bjorn answered firmly.

The officer stared at him a few moments and then stepped into another room for a few minutes before returning.

"OK sir, just so you know, at least two of those gentlemen are on a watch list in the US—for engaging in violence in environmental activism. I would advise you to avoid further contact with them, just for your own sake. Based on information from the United States they are barred from entering Canada."

Bjorn felt intimidated and a little angry. This seemed like an extension of some of the shit he had heard about from them. He was disturbed to see security people keeping watch over some of these guys and that authorities in the US had perhaps been aware of his meetings.

"OK. But I wasn't planning on going back anyway."

The officer flipped over a few pieces of paper. "Now, do you know a person named Joseph George, in Bella Bella?"

Bjorn flinched. "Yes."

"What is your association with him?"

"Look, he's a friend, why shouldn't I know him? I help him out on his tour boat."

"Have you ever heard him talk about bear hunting?"

"Bear hunting? No, nothing in particular. I mean, he's against it, so am I, so are a lot of people. What is this all about, anyway?"

"Please just answer the questions, sir. Have you heard him talk about any US hunters coming to Canada where they were killed?"

"Killed?" Bjorn's voice rose. "No, I never heard anything about that."

The officer nodded, stepped out of the room again. Bjorn felt unnerved, angry at the interrogation, unsure what he was getting into.

The officer returned. "OK, Mr. Fisher. You can go now."

Bjorn caught a direct flight back to Bella Bella to be there in time
for the next day's charter trip with Joseph. "Jesus, Joseph, listen, I got
into a whole lot of shit with the RCMP yesterday, at the airport
coming in."

"About what?" Joseph quickly raised his glance.

"About some Native American guys I met down in Denver. Some
of them had been with the AIM movement, and some animal rights
guys."

"What did the police ask about?"

"Just about these guys in Denver, what they had told me about,
whether they were talking about any operations here, or sent any
messages to anybody here, about environmental protests."

"Did they send any?"

"No, for chrissakes, Joseph, what do you think? What is this all
about? But, yeah, they did ask about you."

Joseph spun around. "About me? What did they ask?"

"How I knew you. And they asked about bear hunting, and about
some American hunters who came up here and got killed or
something."

"What did you tell them?"

"What do you think I told them? I told them the goddam truth, that
I'd never heard about anything like that."

Joseph shook his head.

"So what's going on, Joseph?"

"Nothing. Just some bad stuff went down a couple years ago. Some
crazy guys from the States."

"Crazy guys? What crazy guys?"

"Look, I shouldn't be telling you about this. I don't want to get into
it all again. Just some hunters came up here, Americans, wanted to
take a grizzly for a trophy. I knew the local guide here who was going
to take them out on the hunt."

"Yeah, and?"

"Some animal activists came up here from the States around the same time. They told me they were fighting to stop grizzly hunts. They knew the hunters who had come to take a trophy, apparently they had been up here before. Wanted me to help them, stop them from taking any trophies. I knew one of the guys from when I was down in Seattle some years back. Animal activists. They wanted me to take them to the hunting camp site where the US hunters were."

Bjorn waited but Joseph didn't say anything more. "So what happened, Joseph? How did these guys get killed?"

"Look, Bjorn, you got to keep your mouth shut on this. I just took these two activists out to the hunting lodge, just kind of a shack. I didn't know what they were going to do, I thought they were going to take the bear carcass away from the hunters, at gunpoint."

"So?"

"We were waiting back in the woods near where the hunters were coming out, they had a big grizzly on a roller gurney, dead, carrying it to their pickup." Joseph shook his head in memory. "Then before I knew it one these guys with me lifted his rifle, stared down the sight, and dropped one of the hunters right where he stood. They hadn't suspected a thing. The other hunter panicked, tried to run to the truck. Then the other guy with me aimed and took out the other hunter. They just dropped like a stone, didn't know what hit them."

"What happened then?"

"Nothing. I couldn't believe what had happened. We took off and the US guys soon split for somewhere, I guess back to the States. It hit the papers a day or two later about two US bear hunters getting killed. RCMP asked all around town, didn't get any info I guess. I sure as hell didn't say anything."

"Jesus, Joseph, that's bad!"

"Yeah, it is. I had no idea these two guys were going to take these hunters out like that. Can't say I feel sorry for 'em, though. They had it coming."

"Does anyone else know about this in town?"

"Just a buddy who I trust, I told him about it."

"Well, how did the RCMP know these activists knew you?"

"Cause the guys went out in the boat with me one time before any of this happened. That's where they asked me to help them find the hunting lodge. One of them knew me from before, Seattle days when I was doing some protesting. I had no idea what they were up to, except maybe to rob the bear carcass. Their alibi, if anyone asked, was they were out in the boat with me. I could vouch for that. RCMP asked if I knew anything about them. I just said I met them on the boat fishing, twice."

"Christ, Joseph, that's some really dangerous stuff."

"You're telling me. So you got to keep your mouth shut on it. And let me know right away if the RCMP talks to you again."

Bjorn was deeply disturbed at the violent tale and the implications of some of this environmental activism coming up from the States. It brought home what some of the men in Denver had been telling him about. Yet he had to admit, as nasty as the incident was, he also found the story satisfying in some way. These trophy hunter bastards really had it coming. Deep down he was glad it had happened. But the event sure as hell wasn't what Bjorn had figured on the way to handle these issues. It was much more in line with his talks with the Animal Rights people in Denver. And now he had come onto the RCMP radar.

Chapter 22

Mason Surrey thumbed through the in-flight magazine, weary of reading the oil market reports his staff had stuffed into his briefcase. As COO he found himself gravitating more towards the politics of the project than the marketing reports. He checked his watch. Less than half an hour before touchdown back home in Calgary. As he flipped the pages, a picture of a magnificent snow-capped mountain vista with an azure-tinted finger-lake lying at the foot of the range caught his attention. He looked to see where the picture was from. Sure enough, it was in the coastal mountain ranges of British Columbia. The article was entitled "Unknown BC Treasures Feed the Soul." And in a box at the bottom of the page he noticed a quote from the poet David Whyte:

"When I look at everything
growing so wild and faithfully beneath the sky,
I wonder why we are the one terrible part of creation
privileged to refuse our flowering."

The final phrase struck him, at first take annoying him. "Privileged to refuse our flowering"? What in hell was the poet saying? Mason believed mankind was indeed flowering over time, slowly perhaps, but with growing awareness of the environment. That was the whole nature of human progress—finding that delicate compromise between development and preserving the environment. That was precisely the balance that he was trying to attain.

The experience of Ogoniland was never far from Mason's mind. Yes, it had been terrifying to be kidnapped and he had barely made it out alive. But even more he was haunted by the man who had captured him—Samuel. Ogoniland had indeed been turned into an oil-drilling hell, and Mason and so many of his colleagues knew it. They hadn't wanted to dwell on it—after all, that's the downside of progress that also needs a little attention. But Mason could not forget how Samuel's eyes had blazed, his passion incandescent. Samuel put a human face on environmental destruction, a desperate, bitter and haunted face of a man who deep in his heart knew he was losing the game against the great economic and industrial forces of the world.

And now Mason's new job as COO of Tundra oil for BC was proving challenging beyond his expectations. The whole business of extracting oil from the Albertan tar-sands was growing more politically heated. And the problems only began with extraction. Then the task of transporting the oil from landlocked Alberta to the Pacific Coast raised even more controversial issues—hundreds of miles of pipelines would cross native lands and sensitive environmental terrain. And finally, there was the most controversial task of all, moving the oil by tanker through the jagged and twisting fjords of the BC coast out into a turbulent open ocean headed for Asian markets. First Nations and environmentalists were starting to raise hell about it.

Ironically for Mason, it had been the hellfire of Ogoniland and his reporting on it that was mostly responsible for bringing him here to Alberta. He had ended up appointed COO of Tundra operations in BC precisely because of his insight and handling of that political experience. He had acquired skills—how to deal with volatile energy production issues in the face of Native and environmentalist concerns about ecological damage.

He resented the fact that he was often portrayed as an opponent of the environment. His task here required real skills that he knew he possessed—technical, political, social, and cultural—to smooth the path to peaceful solutions.

Mason's absence from his family for two and a half years, sequestered off in the compound in Port Harcourt, had been difficult. But even though he was back with his family now, his new job was creating unanticipated new tensions. He felt new pressures from his wife with her strong environmentalist instincts, and from his children who were now old enough to know about green protests against the tar sands and to challenge him on it.

As he emerged from the airport in Calgary he wished for a moment that Melanie might have decided to meet him. It was, after all, the day before Thanksgiving; he was looking forward to a warm family celebration. But he knew she would be busy, and his company driver, as usual, would be the one to take him home. Understandable, but disappointing.

Yet Mason was worried to note that even the complexities of the office in recent months sometimes felt like a welcome refuge from problems at home. He worried he might be more capable at managing the challenges of the job than his own family and teenage kids. Melanie often accused him of "falling short in emotional intelligence;" he feared she might be right. And Melanie raised the usual concerns—he was always at the office or always away on trips, he didn't know his kids, or his kids didn't know him, that he wasn't a presence in their lives. She had even raised the possibility a few days ago that if things didn't change, she wasn't sure how long their marriage might last. His last effort before his previous trip to get the family together for dinner at the table had fizzled out dismally.

"Really, is it too much to hope that at least once a week you guys could make it to a family dinner all at the same time? Why is it such a big deal to sit down together?"

Teen eyes rolled, sure-fire triggers. "Yeah, Dad, why is it such a big deal?" his daughter Shelley said. "You're not here half the time yourself. We're busy, and it's boring to sit down for a whole hour just to eat dinner. Anyway, we've already eaten a big snack after getting home from school, nobody's hungry."

They sat around a sculpted wooden French-style blond dining table in their home in one of the plusher suburbs on the outskirts of Calgary. The soft, late summer light was still filtering in through high windows that rose up from the floor, with hydrangeas waving their lush blue flowers just outside the window, which revealed the expansive lawn behind and the set of lawn furniture that would likely be used only a few more weeks before colder weather set in. It had actually been many years since the family had really shared a home together.

"Dad, this just seems like some command performance for you. Why can't we do our own thing like we used to?" his son Jason chimed in.

"Look, is it too much to ask? It means a lot to me at least, I missed you guys in Nigeria. We should at least once in a while sit down together as a family, talk about what we're all doing."

"OK Dad, but this isn't like some meeting in a board room. You can't just order people to sit down at some formal dinner." His daughter's words were painful, and she could be skilled at wielding them. He wondered what it might take to forge some kind of family togetherness again.

"I think your Dad's right, guys," Melanie said. "I think some sense of family is something worth preserving, and easily lost these days. Think of it as a once-a-week ceremony in the middle of all our busy lives."

"OK, you want to know what we did in geography class today?" His daughter broke into in an edgy tone. "We talked about the pipeline. Everybody, even our teacher said, like the whole idea sucked and was bad for the environment. Nobody said anything directly to me about you—I don't know how many of them even know about you being COO and all. But I was embarrassed. Don't you realize how angry people are about this idea?"

"Shelley, I'm not sure your class has all the facts on this. You might want to find out a little more about it before you make up your mind. For starters, I'm personally very concerned myself about the environment and protecting it. That's a key part of my job. Really, it is. You know how I watched the nightmare of what happened to the people in Nigeria? How I nearly got killed? And here we've got a huge staff devoted just to safety issues, to make sure accidents don't happen."

Shelley shifted in her seat, preparing her next assault. "OK, but it's not just accidents, the whole thing is...like polluted. One guy's report in class talked about how all this pollution is produced from getting this tar sand out of the earth and having to inject it with chemicals and all to get the oil out. She said there are huge pools of these chemicals all around polluting the underground water."

"That's not always the case. Sometimes it can be dug up from the surface and the oil extracted by steam processes. There's different kinds of production."

"Dad, don't get all technical, it's all harmful to the environment!" Jason broke in.

The whole conversation had drifted too far into confrontational mode. Mason decided to just let it go. He noted he even felt relief to let the kids finally leave the table for their iPhones. The frequent undertone of challenge in their voices depleted him. How had he caused this state of affairs to come about?

After supper in the kitchen Melanie had said, "Mason, you shouldn't get technical with the kids. You know Shelley's right on this. Don't try to avoid it. There are big-time environmental issues involved."

Mason smouldered. "Dammit, Melanie, why are you always taking sides against me on this! We've talked about it many times before, and you know about the range of technical safeguards we're implementing. I resent being cast as just some ignorant heavy on all this stuff." He put down his dishtowel. "Or maybe you're too busy running around with your environmentalist friend Jan to bother to hear the facts!" He then bit his tongue, regretting he had gone too far.

Melanie had been out a number of evenings attending "environmental discussions," with a new Dutch environmentalist friend, and hadn't gotten back till late. Mason had overheard her on the phone once or twice and her relationship with Jan had sounded a bit too cozy for his liking.

Later that evening when they were going to bed, Mason felt compelled to raise the question about Jan again. "Melanie, look, I'm frankly bothered by something, and I'm just going to have to say it right out. I'm uncomfortable that you're spending so much time with Jan. Is there something going on between you two?"

"Going on? I enjoy his company, Mason, when your company is scarce. You're at meetings all the time, or seem distracted. You know you can't just walk back in after years apart and expect us all to show up at a family dinner together when you happen to come home early some evening."

Mason put down his magazine. "Look, I know I've been spending a lot of time away. I get that. But it bothers me that my own family seems to be taking sides against me on my whole professional project, as if I were some evil person with the pipeline negotiations." He turned his gaze towards her. "And you don't help me much, Melanie. There are a lot of trade-offs in this whole thing. I wish you could see the complexities I'm having to deal with in this instead of just holding a one-sided view." He stretched out his hand to her across the covers. Melanie patted his hand and then withdrew her own.

"You know I can't pretend to be in favor of the project Tundra is doing here," she said. "Fossil fuels in general are bad enough, but the tar sands? You know there's so much wrong with it—and too many businessmen and politicians with dollar signs in their eyes who don't seem to give a damn about the environment."

"Come on, Melanie, that's an ideological caricature. You know I care a lot about the environment. Why do you think I got promoted to become political head of this project here? It was because I called a spade a spade in Nigeria. I understand the environmental element."

Melanie put down her iPhone and turned to him "Mason, look, I know you do care, personally. You're also trying to make the best out of a bad situation. But this is a 20th century fossil fuels industry. You can't make it better."

"I can certainly mitigate the downsides of it. This is going to be some of the highest tech planning there is out there. Look, I took the job partly because if I don't do it, and do it well, someone else will come and do it—with a whole lot less care. And because this pipeline project *is* coming, like it or not. People's thirst for oil is insatiable, right here in Canada alone. You don't like it, I may not like it, but that's what it is."

"But you surely can't feel comfortable with all this. The environmental aspects are screamingly obvious. And the habitat issue, the symbolism, especially when a place like the Great Bear Rainforest is involved."

"OK, and you know what, Melanie? I'm specifically focused on that very thing—where the pipelines and tankers might go. It totally involves understanding the Rainforest. And I really want to look at this bear issue more closely and see what can be done to protect the habitat. I'm actually planning to visit the area myself soon."

Melanie smiled. "You know what the irony is here, Mason? I'd almost rather Tundra hadn't hired you. Because unfortunately you can put a more caring face on the whole operation than most. You have one of the greenest faces in the whole energy business. You're sincere. But it's still putting lipstick on a pig. Your skills are being used in the wrong direction." She turned back to her phone. "I think you sort of know that yourself, deep down."

He winced. "Look, I'm the first one to admit it, Melanie. You do have a lot of truth on your side on this. We've all been hostages to these goddam oil monarchs of the Middle East for decades, tiptoeing around so we don't offend them. That's one reason this oil sands pipeline is a really a big deal. It offers the US and Canada total energy independence. One that gets the damn oil sheikhs out of the picture! It's a game changer!"

Melanie got out of bed, walked over to the window and stared out into the darkness. Then she turned around. "You just don't get it, do you? We're not talking oil sheikhs, we're talking fossil fuels. From anywhere. And this Alberta stuff happens to be the worst of it! Oil money corrupts. It corrupts everybody everywhere, right here in Alberta, in Victoria, not just in the Niger Delta!"

"I suppose that's the line that Jan has been feeding you," he muttered, angrily backing into more emotional waters.

"Yeah, Mason, that's right. As a matter of fact, Jan's the one who has helped educate me on this. You could stand to hear a little more of this yourself." She got back into bed, switched off her light and turned her back to him.

The few times Mason had met him, Jan had really irritated him—his smugness, his relative youth, his European air of moral superiority, his condescending refusal to engage seriously with Mason, fully shielded in his own righteousness. And it wasn't just the intellectual thing that bugged him. Jan had a kind of male magnetism that Mason instinctively found threatening, making him feel that he was somehow wanting as an attractive male figure. It was a feeling in the gut, visceral and sexual, that crowded his emotions. He knew those feelings contributed to his hostility towards Jan, and even transferred towards Melanie—the unspoken hormonal backdrop to their more rational surface discussions about their marriage and her career and the oil sands. They were ganging up on him in a battle he could not win. Work indeed became an almost welcome refuge.

Chapter 23

The world of the forest provided his mental refuge, a soothing cocoon of soft sound and undulating shade. The cedars and spruce formed a canopy overhead, offering a phalanx of tree trunks to protect him from the caprices of the outside world, a source of solitude and solace. People often warned about the dangers of the forest. Yes, it contained unknowns. But why should the unknown be a source of fear? On the contrary, the known dangers of the "real world" were a far greater source of worry.

Bjorn knew from childhood that bears are essentially benign. He was aware of course they could turn deadly dangerous if cornered. But they were not malign in spirit. Theirs was rather a spirit of nobility, of order, of wisdom, of things-as-the-way-they-should be. Bears were direct and honest. They were not furtive or stealthy. They did not creep up on unsuspecting prey or lie in wait to ambush like the treacherous big cats did. Bears roamed through the forest at will, their own hearts free of fear, without natural enemies. Humans were their only enemies, humans who profaned the forest. The older Bjorn grew, the more he realized that it was people and not animals who were the primary source of ugliness, fear, cruelty, danger and destruction in the world. Animals did not gratuitously kill.

And he knew the bears were aware of *him* in some special way. His recent close encounter with a grizzly in the forest, where he thought his life might have been coming to an end, had been harrowing. Yet he had been inexplicably spared. Joseph said it had been a "miracle" that Bjorn wasn't killed. But Bjorn knew it was not a miracle. A *purpose* lay hidden behind the encounter.

And now a new option opened up. For some time Bjorn had been aware of The Great Bear Adventure Company in Bella Bella. It had piqued his curiosity. And then he heard the Adventure Company was looking for guides. Why not? There was every good reason for him to seek a professional job which could bring him closer to the Rainforest and to the bears. He would develop knowledge and experience on a professional level, build his credentials.

Since he had arrived in Bella Bella his mental map of the Great Bear Rainforest had gradually expanded, giving him a sense of its range and mini-environmental zones; heights were drier, the trees and underbrush distinct from the lower-lying areas. Alpine pastures offered green swards where bears would visit in the spring to graze among the newly sprouted grasses. In the wooded areas, especially in the bottom lands, there were dead trees that contained termites or grubs that fed on the decaying wood, or even the thawed corpses of animals that had not survived the winter—all this provided elements of bears' surprising variety of diet.

At the job interview Bjorn mentioned his First Nations connections; he stated flat out that his mother was a Native from Bella Bella and his father Haida. No one challenged him. That he had attended university and would be working towards a BA, with some background in First Nations studies—all this worked heavily in his favor. A week later he got a call offering him a job. He would undertake two month's training on boat tours with other guides and then be qualified to go out as a guide on his own. He was now no longer a loner, an outsider, but working within the system. And after some twenty trips as an apprentice he was going out today on his maiden tour as the chief guide.

The Adventure Company touted Bjorn as a "Native guide." The visitors were mostly retired people, well-traveled, still spry and active, possessed of a sense of adventure and predisposed to environmental sympathies. They were willing to pay generously for a unique nature adventure of this sort. He'd even spent a week in a special course taught by a zoologist where he'd studied up on flora and fauna of the Rainforest as part of the training for the tour boat guides. "And to think I get paid for learning about all this stuff!" he told Joseph.

The tour boat slipped into the inlet and its engines stilled. The water around it grew calm, the craft gently rocking, now afforded serenity from the open sea. The craft was surrounded on nearly three sides by spruce and cedar rising up in green palisades against the gray skies. Mists drifted across the face of the mountains and forest, lending a mystical quality to the scene. Bjorn had always loved the mists. They hinted at concealed mysteries, they enveloped him, helped cushion and protect him, soften blunter exposure to the world. Here before him lay a quiet, remote rain forest paradise. A hush fell over the passengers as they leaned toward the edge of the boat with their cameras poised, trying in vain to compress the vastness and mood of the panorama before them into one impoverished frame. Many tourists yielded to the immediacy of the moment, abandoning their cameras to simply absorb the scene into their consciousness.

And as he looked out from the deck he was struck again as always by the relative silence of the forest. Song birds were few, although the occasional raucous caw of crows or ravens punctuated the quietness. He had been told that ravens had special knowledge of the world, paths between this world and that. But ravens were also tricksters and humans could not trust them. They were also said to foretell death.

Even though he loved his job, Bjorn found it hard to suppress a slight sense of contempt towards the tourists. These were *his* forests, *his* bears. These people had no deep appreciation, no personal connection to what they were looking at. They were simply hunting with their cameras, capturing their trophies for display later on, on their flat screen TVs—although certainly better for sure than an armed hunting expedition. But he often found tourist banter irritating and annoyingly similar on each trip.

"Do Natives come out here to get inspiration for their carvings?" one woman asked him. He found himself flattered to be at last addressed as a Native, and an expert at that. "Yes, I think we feel a special connection with Nature, it almost comes with our genes," he replied.

Nonetheless, he thought of these tourists as essentially invaders onto his own territory, a presence he had to put up with as part of the realities of his job. He was sometimes curt with the tourists, prompting his supervisor to tell him to improve his attitude towards the visitors if he wanted a future with the company. He worked to keep his condescension out of his voice as he shepherded his groups on the tour.

"You are about to move into the inland waterways, ladies and gentlemen, inside the Great Bear Rainforest," Bjorn announced. "The Rainforest extends for thousands of square kilometers, 21 million acres. It is sometimes referred to as the "Amazon of the North." We are situated in just one small part of it here. But even from our limited perspective you can get a great sense of the place—a rare preserve of animals and nature almost unmatched anywhere else in the world." The passengers then clambered carefully off the boat down into the waiting Zodiac boats, each one to carry twelve passengers. They kept the electric motors on the Zodiacs on low throttle to move as quietly as possible up the inlet and into the still waters.

"Don't see any bears yet!" one of the passengers called out.

"Is that the bad news, or the good?" another one laughed.

"Sorry, we don't have a contract with them," Bjorn said. "But if you quiet down and are patient you should probably be able to see some grizzlies around the bend of the inlet."

"How dangerous are they?"

"Well, they prefer to leave humans alone, unless you threaten them, or corner them. Or if you're unlucky enough to come across some animal carcass they've stashed away—they'll guard it fiercely. Or if they have cubs—mother bears don't like strangers coming onto their cubs."

"Would they attack us then?" someone inquired.

"Sure, they might. But the good news is that even if they kill you they're not necessarily likely to eat you. It's more black bears do that."

"Whew, that's a load off my mind," someone else countered.

"In any case, we're not going to get out of the Zodiacs. And when we see some grizzlies, we're going to do everything we can not to disturb them. Please keep your voices down. They'll certainly note our presence, but if we're far out enough in the water, they should ignore us. It's important that we not violate their habitat or affect their daily habits and feeding patterns."

As they moved forward the inlet opened out to reveal a broad flat expanse rich with bright green grassy plants covering the area between the beach and the rising rocks and looming forest behind. And there, off to the left, they saw five bears in the middle of a grassy area. Their heads were down and they were clearly busy eating grass. "They almost look like cattle grazing in a pasture," one woman whispered.

"Grass?" Someone else whispered. "I thought they ate salmon."

"They're omnivores," Bjorn replied in low voice. "They eat anything, depending on the season. In the spring, like now, when they come out of hibernation they eat a lot of grass, several dozen kilos a day. The spring grass is super rich in protein, and it helps to fill them out early on. They'll eat other things later, including insects, grubs, carrion, and salmon, but it's not salmon season yet right here."

"I don't see any white Kermode bears in there," one passenger complained. "I thought we were supposed to see one."

"It's pronounced *Kermodee*, not *Kermoad*," Bjorn replied. "And sorry, I can't order them up out of the woods for you like fast food."

"No, but they might order you up for fast food," another man quipped.

On the one hand Bjorn was delighted to be the repository of knowledge, to play the expert to impart information to the tourists. And they held him in special respect when they were told that he was "a Native guide" and bear expert, a title he found quite satisfying. On the other hand, he felt he was demeaning himself, prostituting himself, playing "Native" to these white people. He was exploiting the bears, bringing transient tourists out for a day or two of thrills on their vacation so they could go home and say they saw bears. But at least they weren't killing them. Still, these city people didn't really deserve to see the bears in their own setting. They were just paying big money to buy the privilege of invading the bears' own remote habitat. Even if they weren't really disturbing them very much they were profaning this sacred ground and the bears' sacred ways, all for a photo, for another notch on their touristic rifle, some place else they had traveled to, been-there-done-that, and could tick off on their list of tourist accomplishments and here's the picture to prove it. But he worked to conceal any contempt he felt for them.

In the foreground there was a mother and two young cubs, and just behind them two other adolescent bears, all feeding. They looked up briefly to note the presence of the Zodiacs in the distance, but basically ignored them. Bjorn made sure the Zodiacs kept their distance from shore.

The passengers looked on in silence, in awe at the spectacle of these huge creatures, feeding in their Spring silence. Every so often the bear cubs would decide to play and rolled around in the grass in a wrestling match, delighting the watchers.

With each expedition Bjorn felt himself grow more comfortable with the Rainforest. He knew if he had been away from his tedious tourists, on foot alone, he would have spotted a few hollows, caves and shelters in among the rocks which he was sure were dwelling places of bears. Like the granite bluff and overhang he often visited not far from Bella Bella. There he had come across the small plateau at the top where low-lying salal bushes with their purple berries grew in profusion, offering something of a bed to lie in at this high point in the immediate forest area. Bjorn would sometimes go there, lie down, close his eyes and review the passage of his life, his concerns. He would listen to the silence, broken only by slight sounds in the undergrowth, or the few birds singing, perhaps a stray querulous squirrel. He was at peace here and nobody could know where he was.

He knew too, that if he possessed a bear's sense of smell he would have detected a bear's presence. By now his nose was in fact growing more attuned to the musky, often intense scent of a grizzly, sometimes like a wet dog that had rolled in black earth. He soon sensed that he shared this space with a bear. He had not seen the bear there, but he knew it was there, that it was the bear's place even if the bear was not there. And he knew for sure that the bear would at some point appear. But it would ignore Bjorn's presence, knowing that Bjorn's presence was in the right order of things, requiring no interaction.

Back in the Zodiac his mind still wandered deeper into the scene. He could feel the lacy arms of the cedars and spruce close in around him, in the moist but chilly Pacific air currents, beckoning, summoning. He should be there on the ground with them on his own, right in among the bears, and not tethered to a bunch of superficial city tourists. He thought back to the electrifying fear and later transformative insight of his encounter with the grizzly bear some months ago with Joseph. He was sure he had overreacted, that he was in the process of moving closer into the bears' world; he was determined he would never allow that sense of alienating terror to possess him again.

I'm in my element here. I understand the patterns of the bears' behavior. They know I am here. But am I exploiting the Bear People?

As much as he hated dragging tourists into the bears' territory, he also knew he was teaching them about the bears that might serve to protect them as tourism increasingly took precedence over trophy butchering. But this contribution was just a drop in the bucket, only a tiny environmental operation that paled next to the size of the vast land, its unprotected character, and the forces of commercialism and huge oil companies and massive capital combining with greed lurking, ready to ravage the earth. Those were the people who should pay.

And then, on another tour, an incident took place that sickened him. Only a week later he took a tour group by bus to a special raised bear-viewing deck along a small river where bears were catching fish, eating them on the spot, or sometimes delivering the silvery-red salmon still flopping in their mouths to eager but inexperienced cubs waiting on the bank. An armed forest ranger was on duty at the site, helping direct tourists and to prevent incidents. As the group watched the bear scene, enthralled, the next thing Bjorn knew, a heavy-set red-haired tourist had climbed over the railing of the deck and dropped down to the bank by the stream with his camera, right in front of a bear cub to capture it up-close at ground level as it chewed on a big salmon in its paws. Within seconds one of the grizzlies in the stream, presumably the mother, snarled and rushed out of the water, up the bank and hurled herself towards the man. The man stumbled backward, dropped his camera, and lay helpless as the bear moved onto him. "You damn fool!" the ranger yelled who had not initially seen the tourist jump the railing. He leveled his rife and fired at the mother bear who fell heavily, struggling unsuccessfully to get back onto her feet. At that moment a second large grizzly came charging out of the water as well. The cub rushed to the second bear who headed straight for the tourist, who had finally managed to get back up to his feet in order to clamber back over the railing with the help of another tourist on the deck. But the second bear, with the cub right next to it, had caught the man's jacket and pulled him back down to the ground. The ranger fired again but the bear absorbed the shot, and the ranger had to fire several more times to stop the bear before it could move in for the kill. In the scramble the bear cub was also hit by a bullet and fell to the ground, crying out to its mother as blood gushed from its mouth. The ranger, deeply angered at the situation, was finally able to get the tourist back to safety and onto the deck just in time as more bears began to move onto the scene.

Bjorn was livid. Two adult grizzlies and a cub now lay dead at the scene. He trembled with rage as the ranger ordered the group to leave the deck immediately and get back onto their bus. "My camera," the man said, "it's still down there." "Fuck your camera!" Bjorn yelled. He glared at the man responsible for the incident. "You're going to fucking pay for this," Bjorn snarled. "Just wait till you see the fines we're going to hit you with, you asshole! You don't belong out here in the wilderness."

"You can't talk to me like that!" the man said. "It was an accident."

"The ranger should have fucking shot you instead of three innocent bears!"

"You're way out of line, man!" the tourist shouted back. "I'm reporting you." Bjorn saw red, clenched his fist and moved upon the man who was bigger than he was, but several of the group rushed to separate them before blows were struck. They got into the bus and Bjorn, seething, said not one word to anyone on their way back to the company tour office. He pointedly thrust away the few hands that tried to offer him a tip.

His boss later sharply reprimanded Bjorn for his unprofessional behavior and loss of control over his emotions. "Fine, take me out of the picture," Bjorn responded. "I got better things to do than drag around a bunch of assholes with cameras!" His boss removed him from leadership of any more tourist excursions until he could show he could conduct himself professionally again. Bjorn remained in sullen isolation in his room for two days before he decided he would not quit. He told his boss he had learned his lesson. He vowed to himself he would bite his tongue in order to stay in close touch with Rainforest projects. They represented an important part of his professional credentials. He resentfully accepted his demotion to assistant guide status again.

Your heart possesses right understanding. You are working to protect the Bear People and the Rainforest. Do not shrink from approaching those who seek to destroy our lands. Work with them, divine their intentions. That is the way you can best serve the Bear People and the Rainforest.

They are powerful, you are not. The farther away you are from them, the weaker you become. The closer you get to them, the more you can gain power and influence.

The precise words were not always clear, but Bjorn had not the slightest doubt that he had received the full sense of the message.

Chapter 24

"Well, it looks like Tundra Energy has decided to mix with us Natives," Joseph remarked, having his second beer with chaser with Bjorn after work at the Coho. "They're sending a delegation over here tomorrow to consult with us. They want to see how willing we are to spread our legs wide enough for these tankers to come down through here with their dirty oil."

"Sounds like a waste of time," Bjorn responded. "Don't those bastards know people around here have no time for Tundra's money-grubbing?"

"Tundra fucking Energy, what an outfit! You see, now they're holding some kind of meeting with us ignorant Natives from the town, to explain to us what a safe and wonderful project it all is."

"Is this the first time you've heard this pitch from Tundra here?"

"Nope," Joseph replied, "they've been around before with their advertising and flyers and shit. All their beautiful posters of happy beaming Natives joining together in what they call 'Our Project.' So now its 'our state of the art technology, our tested fail-safe procedures, our scrupulous attention to preserving the pristine beauty that is the heritage of all of us.' Yada yada. We've heard all that bullshit before."

"Why you want to go the meeting then?"

Well, we need to hear their latest line if we want to stay ahead of them. But they're likely to get quite an earful from the community tomorrow night."

They headed over to the meeting hall the next evening. The place was crowded and already smoky in what was officially a no-smoking hall. Three representatives from Tundra Energy sat at three tables shoved together at the front of the hall. They seemed to glance around a little nervously, trying to gauge the mood of the room. They conferred with each other out of the sides of their mouths as the room filled up. They looked expectant, waiting for the crowd to quiet down. Finally the moderator banged his spoon against a coffee cup and brought some silence to the room. A figure stepped forward dressed in a leather vest decorated with an orca, and with a bandanna on his head.

"We welcome you to our Native lands where this meeting is taking place," he said. "We want to open this meeting with a song of thanks for the beautiful lands in which we live, that was given to us by the Creator. This song was written by my grandfather on another occasion when we welcomed government officials who came to visit us from Victoria."

"And you can imagine what we got out of that visit," Joseph whispered to Bjorn.

Three Native men and two women stepped out to the centre of the room, each carrying a small open-ended drum, a skin stretched tight across a wooden circle and decorated with a stylized orca in the Native tradition. They began their steady beat and soon their voices joined in: "heya ho, heya ho." It was followed by words in what Bjorn thought he could recognize as the local Heiltsuk language, but that were not translated. The voices rose and fell, and the beat of the drums shifted, now soft, now loud again, with an unvarying hypnotic rhythmic power. Then the song came to an end and the audience raised their arms in front of their bodies, bent up from the elbow in a gesture of thanks.

The chief took a long pause and glanced around the room. "We welcome you to this beautiful place, and we thank the Creator for giving it to us. We've been here for a long time, many thousands of years before any white man set foot in this part of the world. We expect to be here for many thousands more...I don't need to speak in sugary words. It is good you came from your company to speak directly to us. We all share a deep concern for what these tar sands and pipelines and tanker proposals may do to affect this land that was given to us to preserve and protect. So we await your words with interest and concern."

A tall but solidly-built man with a receding hairline who had been seated in the middle of the Tundra group then stood up. He was dressed in a dark suit with a blue dress shirt without a tie. A murmur arose. "My name is Mason Surrey, I'm the Chief Operating Officer for Tundra's operations in BC, based out of Calgary. And I bring you greetings from Tundra's CEO Martin Forthright at our headquarters in Toronto."

Joseph smirked and turned to Bjorn. "I can't believe this, this guy's seen too many cowboy movies. What a fucking typical way to start—'I bring greetings from the Great White Father in Washington.'"

"And these are my colleagues," Surrey continued, "John Pritchett who is chief engineer, and Amos Waldorf who is the chief logistics planner for the project."

"Can't hear you!" several people shouted to the speaker from the back.

"I'm sorry, we don't have a microphone," Surrey said, "We'll just try to speak louder."

"Louder doesn't make it any better!" someone shouted and the crowd laughed.

Mason Surrey looked back at his two colleagues as they sensed the developing mood of the room.

"This is your meeting," Surrey said, "Let's get right to your questions and concerns. That's what we're here for."

A young woman with a bandanna and an embroidered leather vest stepped forward. "You all talk about how you need the full community's support for this project. But what if we don't want to give it to you? We've got concerns, at lots of levels. Pumping that oil out of the tar sands is a bad idea—it's the dirtiest oil in the world. Here in Canada we're supposed to be moving away from fossil fuels. So I just see Tundra as increasing fossil fuel production—of the worst kind. And then you're going to pipe that poison across the most beautiful land in the world? We don't want that."

The second Tundra rep, Pritchett, stood up, a portly balding man with a big smile that seemed forced and could not completely conceal his nervousness. "Thanks for bringing up your concerns. That's what we're here for, to listen and learn from you all. Now we all know that fossil fuels have not had a great environmental history in the past, especially with coal. I think we all look forward to the day when we can move to some other technologies in the future. But that day's not here yet, folks. We are all consumers of oil in our homes and businesses and cars, all day long, you and me. If I'm not mistaken I don't think any of us are quite ready to give it up in it our daily lives yet." He smiled broadly at the crowd as if he felt he had just delivered the clinching argument. "So even if it's not the actual oil we're using, we all still need the electricity produced by the oil. That's why we believe oil drilling and refining will be around a bit longer even as new technology is under development, including at Tundra."

Muttering was to be heard around the hall. "We've got all the electricity we need from our rivers, we don't want oil!" someone shouted. Another woman raised her hand to speak.

"Let me make one comment here before we take more questions," Surrey said. "Now on safety and problems of oil spills, these are real issues. But I'm happy to say that technology has already been moving forward by leaps and bounds in the last few years. We now know how to drill and transport, and yes, even consume oil in far more efficient, responsible and cleaner ways than ever before. Our pipes are now electronically and digitally monitored. In the highly unlikely event of an oil spill, our computers can spot even the slightest variation in pressure, and furthermore immediately identify the location of a leak. With our company choppers we can be out at the site of any leak within hours. So I think you'll find we're pretty responsible on that end."

The woman stood up again. "With all due respect, I'm glad to hear about the technology, but the fact is we've been hearing that line for years, and there have been more spills all over North America, from Tundra and other companies. I just don't think we believe all these reassurances you people have been giving us over the years. Accidents happen. Big ones happen. Just read the papers. It's not if, but when."

Many in the audience nodded vigorously at these remarks, and a few applauded.

A middle aged man waved his hand and stood up, eyeglasses perched up on his forehead. "Look, we can all argue all day about how clean it is to extract all this dirty oil and pipe it over our province down to the ocean terminal. But that's not the half of it. What happens to the oil then? You guys are planning to ship it out from the terminal in super tankers down the BC coast, on to Asia. Seems to me like you guys have just been sitting around in your Tundra offices too long. How many of you have ever gotten out of the office, traveled in a boat down the inlet from the spot where you're planning to load all this oil onto the huge tankers? These are some of the narrowest, rockiest, twisting waterways anywhere. And as you get through the long twisting journey to the sea you're hitting some of the most treacherous open waters in the world. Now come on, folks, how smart do you have to be to know this is an accident waiting to happen. A terrible accident. There's no way that you can avoid it. And now with these new tankers, massive ones, an accident is certain. Nobody remembers what happened up in Alaska with the Exxon Valdez about twenty years ago?"

"That was a terrible spill," Surrey said. "I know they're still cleaning up. I've personally been up there to look at it. We have studied that disaster very carefully, believe me. We think we have identified most of the key mistakes they made, and we think we can avoid committing them again down the road."

"OK," the man with the eyeglasses continued, "but do you have any idea what a spill like that would involve if it happened here? It would destroy the livelihood for a century for the communities exposed to the spill. You don't have to be a rocket scientist to see that. Just look at the channels through the fjords that you guys are proposing. Look at the fierce and unpredictable weather we have all along the BC coast. This is crazy! And it's our communities that are the first to suffer. And for what? A few jobs at the loading terminal, half of which are specialists brought in from the outside? We don't want to pay the price of a bad idea and bad planning."

A large wave of applause followed as he sat down. Someone shouted out, "Twenty years later and the community is still messed up by Exxon Valdez. And you're talking tankers twice the size or more than that."

"OK, you're right to be asking these questions," the second Tundra rep responded, adopting a more conciliatory style in the face of the emotion in the hall. "I'm glad to see the level of community interest, it shows that you're taking this seriously and doing the research on the issues. An informed citizenry is a great asset for everybody. But I want to assure you that we at Tundra take these issues very, very seriously as well. We are determined to follow the strictest procedures to ensure that any accident of any kind becomes highly unlikely."

An elderly man with a gray pigtail stood up, clutching onto the chair in front of him, seeming to have trouble keeping his balance. "Well, for most of us here, you know, frankly this all comes down to jobs. Our welfare. Putting food on our family's table. That's why some of us do favor the project, it'll bring more work."

"What jobs?" someone else leaped to his feet shouting. "You think you'll sell coffee and donuts to the passing tankers? How many jobs will there really be up there at the terminals? The only certain jobs we can look forward to are cleaning up the oil spills. Now there's steady work for you!" Ripples of scornful laughter and murmuring swept across the hall.

"Christ," whispered Bjorn to Joseph. "These Tundra guys don't seem to be catching the mood here."

An older woman with glasses, gray hair and a dress of loose robes stood up. "I want to ask about the process of all these government permits for the pipeline and tankers. We're angry about being kept in the dark on these issues. We hear reports that government scientists have been muzzled and prevented from speaking out on their knowledge and experience, they're afraid of losing their jobs. The process has been anything but transparent. And we asked some environmental groups like Sierra Club from the States to come up to offer advice, they have a lot of background and knowledge on these issues. But as soon as they came to share their knowledge and experience with us up here, the government branded them as foreign agents. We're not even allowed to hear their voices here. You can talk all you want, but this is not an open process." Loud murmurings and applause broke out. The speaker had to wait for a moment before the room quieted down. "You all at Tundra have not been honest with us and have not been held accountable in public meetings with informed experts…we got a bad taste in our mouths about all of this, we're being railroaded!"

"Hear, hear," someone shouted.

The third Tundra spokesman sighed. "Look, we fully appreciate the need of the public to be informed on all aspects of these issues. We at Tundra try to stay out of the politics of the issue. We know that just pits political parties against each other. We welcome full debate among political parties, but we can't take sides on this issue. All I can say is that we are deeply committed to a process of safe, environmentally-friendly extraction of the oil and its shipment to consumers, especially in Asia. It's good for Canadian business. And the livelihood of citizens in countries like China depend on us for a steady supply of oil as well. We see this as a long-term partnership with Asia."

"Yeah, and how about a long-term partnership with Canadians, and our livelihoods, our environment?" some shouted. Other people stood up and began shouting questions at the Tundra staff. The three men looked at each other nervously. Mason Surrey tried to quiet the crowd.

"Look, I know there's some skepticism among a lot of you about this project. Given the past, I think that's quite legitimate. I don't blame you, it's a big project. It offers a lot to your community. But it also needs to be done right. Together we need to make sure that everyone's interests are taken into account. We can't do this alone. It's the project of all of us."

A hefty man leaped to his feet. "Don't dare tell us that! It's your damn project, not ours, and you're tryin' to shove it down our throats! But you know what? We're gonna eat you." And he turned around and pointed proudly at his big blue t-shirt that swelled out over his belly. It showed the huge face of a bear drawn in Native style, its huge mouth wide open with the image of a huge oil tanker sailing into right into its waiting jaws. Everybody cheered.

"So thank you all for coming," Surrey said over the hubbub. "That's all we have time for tonight. But let me tell you this. Tonight has been a learning experience for me as well. Frankly I did not fully anticipate quite the level of concern in this community over the whole project. That tells me we haven't done our homework sufficiently. We are going to go back and come up with some more convincing details for you on all these matters. And I look forward to more discussions on these issues in the months ahead."

"Boy, this is cut and run if I ever saw it," Bjorn said to Joseph. "These guys look scared."

"And by the way," Surrey continued, "if there are any interested people from among the community here who might want to work with us and help represent Native views to the company, we need that, big-time. There's got to be two-way dialogue the whole length of the project. Now is the time to start. Come on up and talk to us afterward."

As people began to get to their feet, Joseph turned to Bjorn. "Why don't you go up and talk to them, tell them you're interested in being one of the Native representatives?"

"Are you kidding? This is bullshit. They're the goddam enemy."

"Well, all the more. You know, have you ever thought about getting a job with them? Getting close in with them?" he smiled.

Bjorn raised his eyebrows. "Close to them?"

"Yeah, you know, if they get to trust you, who knows, it could get interesting. You're the one's got an interest in all this bear stuff. Here's a chance to talk right to power first hand. It might present some opportunities." Joseph flashed a smile, patted him on the shoulder, and turned away.

As various groups around the room fell into debate among themselves, Bjorn rapidly turned over in his mind the crazy nature of Joseph's proposal. He had never remotely thought about such an approach. Then he realized the idea might be bold and daring, approaching the cause in a new way. Maybe he should get involved. Maybe he could have some influence. He did care about the bears, and Tundra should be thinking about how to handle that issue. Bjorn thought for a few more minutes and then finally sauntered up to

Mason Surrey as they were putting their papers away in their briefcases, people shrinking away.

"Hey, I was interested in your talk. I think I might have some ideas that will help you guys, in helping sell the project and appeal to our public."

Surrey looked up in surprise from his briefcase. "Well, great! What kind of things do you have in mind?"

"Well, first off I'm First Nations myself, from the Bella Bella area. I've got a university degree. And I work as a Native guide with fishing charters in the Rainforest area. So I think I can speak with some authenticity."

Surrey stuck out his hand. "Mason Surrey. What did you say your name was?"

"Bjorn, Bjorn Fisher."

"Good to meet you, Bjorn. Now what impressions did you get from all this tonight?"

"Well, frankly, I think you guys aren't thinking creatively enough about the Rainforest. The symbol of the white bear, the so-called spirit bear, is a fantastic tool for the environmentalists. Everybody loves bears, and especially a white one. Right now the Rainforest is being presented by your opponents as the symbol of what you are going to destroy. You guys need to embrace the bear, make it your symbol. And not just a symbol. Something you want to help save. You got to do something positive, make some seriously big contributions to it."

Surrey smiled and seemed to noticeably warm to Bjorn. "Those seem like some very interesting ideas, my friend. Tell me more."

"Well, just think about it. The bear is a symbol of vision, of seeing into the future, of wisdom. Aren't those the qualities your company wants to identify with?"

"Absolutely. Look Bjorn, we've got a plane to catch, but I'd really like to hear more from you, especially as someone from the younger generation. Can you give me your info? I'll want to get back to you."

"Up to you," Bjorn said as he jotted down his name and info on a napkin. "Just a few thoughts." And he sauntered out and away into the night.

Chapter 25

Bjorn had argued back and forth with himself—was it worth going back to see Sam Winters again? It had been over two months since his first frustrating meeting and he hadn't been sure he wanted to subject himself to any more psychological scrutiny about who he really was and what he was really doing. On the other hand, Sam had peered into his mind and soul in probing ways and asked some very pointed questions. Bjorn now realized that he did have more to say to Sam, and questions to ask, as a result of his recent experiences with the bear in the forest and his meetings with the environmental activists in the US. And he felt a growing need to talk to someone who might understand him more deeply.

By now Bjorn knew his way through the back streets and down to the gate that had to be lifted to swing open. It was late afternoon and Sam was home. He smiled slightly when he saw Bjorn at the door, simply nodded in silent greeting and gestured for him to come in and sit down. Again there appeared to be no one else in the house. Bjorn sat down on the same animal skin sofa with Sam sitting opposite him in a straight-back chair.

"I wasn't sure you would come back," Sam said after a moment.

"Well, I wasn't sure I wanted to come back. Frankly I just didn't feel like I got much out of our first meeting. But I've been thinking. Some things have been happening. I feel I'm a little clearer about some of my feelings, the things that affect me. You told me I needed to know more about who I am. Maybe I'm getting there, slowly."

Sam nodded. "What new feelings have you experienced?"

"Well, I know now that I often feel negative, angry with people. Mainly because I don't feel like I belong to any of the groups around me. I feel like, I don't know, like I'm sort of an outsider everywhere."

Sam raised his eyebrows. "An outsider to what? We're all outsiders to something."

"That's just it, I don't know for sure. But to other people, to groups here. And they don't seem to feel that I am naturally part of them."

"Do you want to be part of them? Do you think you belong to them?"

Bjorn hesitated. He felt Sam zeroing in on him with his uncomfortable questions again. He knew he had come to Bella Bella in the hopes of establishing real ties with the community, a place of belonging. He wanted to believe that the ties of blood and culture ran deeper among people here, unlike much of normal white urban life where relationships seemed less rooted, more transient, and where bonds and ties were often briefly and casually formed, only to be casually dissolved again. "Well, yes, I had hoped I would find some acceptance. But so far," and his voice wavered a bit," I don't feel like I have been accepted. And it's strange…"

Sam looked at him silently, waiting.

"Sometimes I think I almost feel closer to animals than people. I feel like I understand them better."

"Hmm. What animals exactly?"

"Well, dogs I've always liked. And…bears."

Sam's attention seemed to be sparked. "Bears? In what way do you feel close to bears?"

"It's hard to say, I just feel like I can sometimes understand something about what they are thinking. I see them in my dreams, and I'm not even sure if they are dreams. Sometimes I feel like they speak to me. Like they have an interest in me."

"Do you have any clear sense of what the bears say?"

"No, nothing very specific. Just that they are out there, aware of me, aware of realities around us. They are communicating thoughts to me. They are angry about the Rainforest. That they have great knowledge that I don't."

Sam nodded. "Can you tell me how you have felt the presence of bears?"

Bjorn was concerned that they seemed to be treading the same ground as last time, cryptic questions from Sam, with little feedback. Bjorn was unwilling to go through that all over again. But he decided to offer a bit more. "Well, it's a little strange, but I had a strong impression that a bear helped me to survive a very bad car accident a few years ago, kept me alive, kept me warm when I was nearly bleeding to death. And I feel like bears are watching me. They seem to know something."

Sam nodded again and actually looked pleased. "You are right. The bears do know. They represent the wisest of the animals. They protect us…you are fortunate that you feel this connection. Your feeling that a bear protected you earlier in an accident—that's a thought you should pursue. It can be understood in many ways."

This was Sam's first actual voluntary offering to Bjorn, a welcome shift.

"And then I had a big moment in the forest with a friend a few weeks ago. We were out in the woods when a bear charged us. All of a sudden I found myself knocking the gun out of my friend's hands when he was about to shoot, to defend himself. He then climbed up a tree. Then the bear charged me, stopped short, and finally left me alone."

"So what do you feel that means?"

"I don't know. I've puzzled over it. I felt somehow that it was something extraordinary, like a miracle. That the bear clearly wanted to spare me."

"Hmm, at the least it probably means you have a strong sense that the killing of a bear in the forest is an unjust act," Sam said. "That you felt some kind of exchange with the bear *is* a kind of miracle, or a profound moment. We can experience daily miracles if we are open to them."

"So how do I follow up on these feelings?" Bjorn asked.

"That is for you to decide. If you feel some communication, pay close attention, they may help you know what you are, where you should go."

Here was Sam's evasiveness kicking in again. Bjorn wanted to talk about concrete things in his life, issues on his mind like his quest for his parents, his job, his frustrations in trying to win acceptance in Native circles, a possible future association with Tundra.

"Listen. I need help. I feel you are not helping me enough. There are things on my mind that are troubling me. Please help me."

Sam smiled. For the first time Bjorn detected a note of sympathy in Sam's expression that he had not seen previously when they were talking in frustratingly abstract terms. With Sam's sympathetic smile Bjorn suddenly felt like an emotional dam had broken inside him. He desperately wanted to be understood. To understand. Tears came to his eyes as his emotions simply burst forth.

"Look, I feel like I am half a person. Maybe even less. You tell me to learn who I am. But I can't. I come from a Native background I know almost nothing about. The roots of the real me—I can't get back to them. I don't know what they are. I'm officially a member of another family, the white family where I was adopted. They are basically good people, they wanted to take care of me, bring me up, especially my adopted mother. But I don't belong there. I can see it in their faces when they look at me sometimes, even my mother, as if she was looking at an outsider—somebody she loves, but still an outsider who she's trying to understand. I'm just different than they are in most things."

"Different how?" Sam peered at him intently in that same discomfiting way.

"I don't know, just even physical things. Like I run much better than any of them, my body swings differently. When I get sweaty I smell different than they do. I don't like the music they do, and I don't like music lessons that they all enjoy. I don't laugh at the same things they do. I feel like I'm a guest, a visitor. I told them that I listen to animals, but they just smile. They don't hear anything. They aren't interested in animals."

Sam nodded sympathetically and paused, waiting for Bjorn to say more. "Go on," he urged.

"Look, it's even simple things. Like we celebrate my birthday, right? Just like my brother's and sister's—but what birthday? I have no date of birth, it's supposed to be March 27, but it's all phony, all made up by bureaucrats, nobody has a clue what my real birthday is. I think about that when I go to birthday parties of friends. People ask me when's my birthday—and what can I say? It pains me that I don't know what my real birthday is, they wouldn't understand. So it's just easier to say 'March 27.' It's part of a bigger lie."

Sam nodded and paused. "But does a white man's birth-date make a difference to who you are? You are who you are."

"It's not just the date. Like my name, Bjorn. I like the name, I really do, it means bear in Norwegian. But I must have had a Native name when I was born, or the name my birth mother gave me. I don't know what it was. I probably never will know what my real name is!"

"A name doesn't have to come from a First Nations people to be real. Don't you think maybe your adopted mother had some sense of something about you, that she gave you that name? You say you like it. Would you like to give it up for something else? Would you be happier if you found out that your birth mother named you Frank?"

Bjorn was taken aback at the thought. "No, I wouldn't," he answered slowly. "I wouldn't want to change. But still, it's an amazing coincidence, isn't it, that having that name I ended up feeling close to bears?"

"Nothing is a coincidence. We can have many names. Some of our names are known, but some are not. Give your adopted mother credit that maybe she knew what she was doing in giving you that name. You are lucky to have it. Accept it, and don't worry about what you might have been called originally. First Nations people aren't the only ones to feel a connection to something in nature."

Bjorn paused to reflect. "OK, but I'm still living a phony story. I came up here from the city hoping to find my roots. Yet when I go to First Nations groups I am basically treated like an outsider. Young people, some of them anyway, they make fun of me, they reject me as a wannabe, they don't understand my life, where I grew up. And I don't fully understand theirs." His voice trembled again and he was embarrassed that he had to wipe his eyes with his sleeves. "Have I just fallen into a crack in the world?"

Sam waited patiently. "But you say you feel connections to bears."

"Yes, I realized that, especially when I went to a transformation dance. And even more when I have encountered bears in the forest. Or in my dreams. I know there is another side of me, that no one sees. I hadn't really seen it myself for a long time. But now I know that I am not alone. There is another world—bears and other animals. I feel comfortable with that. Bears speak to me, even if the message isn't fully clear."

Sam nodded. "You mentioned a crack in the world you have fallen into. That is important. Yes, there is a crack, an opening into another world that we do not fully see. You are not lost if you fall into this crack. The crack is a passage. The crack will help you find your place in the world, or maybe in both worlds. This is a good thing, a gift."

Bjorn raised his eyes in surprise. "And I want to learn more about the traditions. I'd like to try to learn something of the Haida language. I think it might be my father's language. I feel drawn to it, even if I have to struggle to learn. I've heard about the power of the Haida people, their culture."

Sam smiled and nodded. "That is interesting. I am Haida. I have not been back for many years, but that is my native place. That is my language."

"Well, I would like to learn some, to get closer to First Nations languages and understand something about them."

"It's valuable to learn a Native language. Language is a unique space to explore, it's kind of a living creature," Sam continued. "When you learn a Native language you are discovering the bones of the past, the thoughts and feelings and views of people who lived in ancient times. They created these words and strung them together in a unique way, unlike any other language does. They gave names to things in the world tens of thousands of years ago, and passed those names down to us. They perceived the world in a certain way, and they created word-pictures of how the world works."

"But it's not just about pictures from the past, is it? I mean people still speak these languages."

"Yes, so these bones from the past are part of a living skeleton, and new flesh and clothes are put on it all the time. A language is a creature that is always growing and evolving. Through these languages we are privileged to see how the world fits together in the eyes of the ancients, how they organized reality. And how it continues down to today. To learn one of these languages gives us a window into the realm of the sacred."

This topic really seemed to open Sam up in an entirely new way, lent power to his tongue. Bjorn had never seen him so continually expressive before.

Sam smiled a bit at his own spontaneous enthusiasm and then fell back into momentary silence, signaling that their session was drawing to a close for the day. "I am glad we have had this talk, Bjorn. I think our words are coming closer together than last time. I hope you will come again. And if you will now excuse me." Sam rose and ushered Bjorn out through the door.

As he walked away, Bjorn felt much more gratified than before. On the one hand he was almost exhilarated. He had had some real communication with Sam this time. Sam had given validity to Bjorn's feelings of communications with bears. He had grasped the nature of Bjorn's painful quest. He had also acknowledged that there can be passages to other worlds that we are not fully aware of. Sam understood. He was encouraging Bjorn to proceed.

Chapter 26

S ince her first visit with Bjorn in Bella Bella some six months ago, Claire had had only a few brief exchanges with her son. He rarely answered his phone. He apparently had abandoned any idea of going back to university. After her last visit she had been concerned about his state of mind in Bella Bella, whether he still felt alone, and how he was managing some of the anger he had expressed about the First Nations experience. She had been surprised and pleased last time that Bjorn had actually reached out to her when he had called her. She heard his frustrations at his inability to find any traces of his birth mother and his feeling that he was not truly accepted into the local Native community either. She dropped him a line. "Bjorn, you're on my mind. I'd love to come up and see you again. I'll try to get away soon, very shortly."

A week later Claire flew in to Bella Bella. Bjorn greeted her warmly at the airport and seemed filled with things on his mind he wanted to tell her about. At dinner Bjorn launched into a passionate description of the recent incident of the tourist jumping the railing to photograph the bear cub up close. "That bastard was responsible for the death of three bears because of his stupidity." Claire grimaced and scrunched up her napkin. "That's a terrible story, Bjorn, I can imagine how painful it was to witness all that. There's always some crazy person in groups like that."

"Yeah, Mom, but it's part of a bigger exploitation of the whole bear thing. Stupid tourists on boats is one thing. But did you know BC allows people to come up here to pay big bucks to kill grizzlies for trophies to put on their damn walls? That's a scandal!" Claire shook her head in agreement.

He then told her at length about his trip to the US and his encounters with the AIM people. He didn't mention his transformational sexual encounter with Dawn. Claire's face betrayed some concern as she heard about the violent actions of some of the radical environmentalists. "I think it's complicated. Some activism is probably good as long it doesn't drift too far into violence," she commented. "But some of those people you met sound pretty radical and maybe on the edge of the law. I hope you'll stay out of trouble with the authorities. That can't do you any good."

Bjorn also did not tell her about his brief interview with the RCMP at the airport upon his return to Canada.

"OK, but I can't just sit around and talk about these issues, Mom. I've got to get involved, do something. This is a bad situation. All this discrimination against Native people and no concern for the environment. These companies, just pillaging the earth, and all these tar sands and pipelines and tankers." His anger grew as he spoke, kindling his own emotions that were beginning to turn into a lecture to his mother. She listened quietly, just observing him as he grew more carried away. She looked around to the other tables out of concern that other people might be listening to his vehemence. Then Bjorn concluded, "Somebody has got to make these bastards pay."

Claire was disturbed at his choice of words but she decided at this point not to respond, fearful of the anger it seemed to generate in him. As a white person, the issue made her especially uncomfortable. She didn't want to find herself among the enemy, and yet it wasn't clear how much Bjorn was drawing lines that were too sharp between white and Native peoples. She felt it might be an oversimplification, but she didn't dare make the point for fear of heightening his wrath. Above all she would not let ideological issues stand between herself and her son.

Towards the end of the evening she finally expressed a little more about what was on her mind. "Bjorn, I'm very happy that you seem to have found your way, doing things with bears and with the Rainforest. I think you've always known your roots were among First Nations, and this seems to be a good way to work into that environment. But again, I do find you more angry than I've ever seen you before and I'm concerned about that. I just don't think anger is a healthy emotion, or a constructive one to help the environmental cause. You seem to harbour feelings of hatred in your heart against others. I'm worried it could eat you out from the inside."

"Dammit, Mom, somebody's got to do something. These Natives down in the States, they took action, changed things, shook up the country. We can't just be passive here against this system. It's rigged against us, against nature."

"I hear you. I just think you need to find healthy and constructive ways to try to bring change. Your adventure tours are surely helping spread the word about bears and the Rainforest. There may be one or two crazies like you told me about, but I'm sure for most people it is a really moving experience, letting them experience the environment first hand."

"Well, I'm afraid these eco tours are just a drop in the bucket. We need something bolder...and the bears sort of send me messages about some of this."

His mother paused. The conversation had just crossed a threshold, into a different mental world and state of mind that bothered her. "How do you mean, Bjorn, they speak to you?"

"Come on, Mom. You know bears have always spoken to me. Well, not so much speak, but communicate their feelings to me. You must remember that when I was a kid."

"Yes, but that was just child's talk, children's creative fantasies. You still feel you are in touch with bears?"

Bjorn stared at this mother fixedly. "I know I can understand a lot of what they are thinking, Mom, what their concerns are. My task is becoming clearer as I receive these ideas."

Claire grew more dismayed with this line of conversation and was not sure how to handle it. "Excuse me for just a minute, Bjorn, while I use the washroom." She stood up and walked to the back of the restaurant, seeking a few minutes to reflect.

When she came back she felt she had to pin down as much as she could Bjorn's state of mind.

"Bjorn, I'm sure these communications you feel with bears are really important in helping you gain insights...but what do you think they are really trying to tell you?"

"Look, Mom, they are telling me that things are wrong, that some action must be taken."

This was what Claire had feared. But she felt she couldn't push the conversation any further at this point and was unwilling to probe the mental state of her son more deeply for now. "Just be sensible, Bjorn," she said, again laying her hand on his arm across the table.

"I will."

Claire was also mildly disturbed that Bjorn seemed a little naive in his understanding of what was involved in taking on the authorities. He went on to tell her with some pride too, about his developing relationship with Sam Winters who was helping advise him. She wondered whether Sam was the one encouraging and contributing to these thoughts in Bjorn's head. For the first time she felt out of her depth. What was really going on here? Was it a sign of a loss of reality, fantasies, hallucinations? Or maybe it was a kind of spiritual insight. Bjorn had never been particularly spiritual before, apart from his near mystical feeling about bears.

Bjorn's accounts of his meetings with Sam did draw her attention. While her Christian views in earlier years might have raised concerns about "alternative religions," she had come to realize through her work with children in First Nations communities in more recent years that it was misleading to think of it all in terms of religion. First Nations traditional wisdom was something different, a world-view, a perspective on life that could offer important psychological insights to troubled people, especially within their own community. Towards the end of the evening Claire surprised herself when she told Bjorn that if he had no objections she would value an opportunity to meet Sam Winters herself. Bjorn was hesitant, feeling that his mother's parental perspective could crowd him in what was a private relationship with Sam.

She initially accepted his argument that Sam wasn't like just some doctor you could make an appointment to see. It had to be arranged through personal channels. But she told Bjorn about her work in recent years as a counselor to school kids and in foster homes including First Nations kids; she said she would value the opportunity to talk to Sam about the challenge of dealing with the special issues of First Nations kids in an urban environment.

As they parted that evening, Bjorn relented. He went to Sam's house alone the next morning to see about arranging a meeting with his mother later that day. When Claire arrived with Bjorn late the next afternoon, Sam met them—perhaps a bit stiffly—at the door. After showing her a seat, Sam left the initiative to Claire to direct the conversation. She told Sam of her work with children, including First Nations children in foster homes. And about identity issues that came up. She knew Bjorn had always had concerns about his own past and identity. She said she wondered how best to handle them in general. And she mentioned her awareness of Bjorn's interest in communications with other species. Sam nodded. To Bjorn's surprise Sam then turned to Bjorn and said, "I think I would prefer to talk professionally with your mother just between the two of us, if you don't mind."

"I don't see what difference it makes if I'm here or not when you're discussing these things," he replied.

"Bjorn, if you wouldn't mind, I'd just like a little time alone with Sam," Claire said.

Bjorn glowered, resenting the exclusion, but withdrew, muttering. He slammed the door as he left.

"I don't want this to affect your relationship with Bjorn," Claire said, "but I did want to speak to you privately, and about some of my concerns with Bjorn."

"You need to work that out with him."

"Well, I know, and I thank you for seeing me," Claire said. "I know Bjorn values his relationship with you—and I'm afraid he is going through a difficult period in his life. I think you may have some understanding for these issues, especially his search for his identity."

"Let me be frank," Sam said. "First, I am not in favor of these adoptions between white families and Native peoples. I believe it leads to confusion and makes it hard for the child to know his place. That is not your fault, and I know you are concerned for his best interests. He tells me how you have done a lot for him. But the situation in general has created problems for Bjorn as you know, removing him from his Native environment. He and I have talked about it."

She felt pained at the implied criticism, but persisted. "I understand that—may I call you Sam? I see Bjorn's new intensity in his quest for his roots. My husband unfortunately was never particularly sympathetic to that quest, whereas I always was. I was the one who first encouraged Bjorn to come to Bella Bella on the chance that he might find traces of his birth mother, or even father."

Sam nodded. "But his search has not been successful, Mrs. Fisher. I wonder if it has not been more upsetting in his mind than if he had not tried to find his roots at all."

Claire found Sam rather blunter than she had expected. "What can I say? Yes, I know it has been traumatic for him. And painful for me too. But he was already in the foster home when I first found him. This has been something difficult for me to acknowledge, I mean, that something that was a well-meaning and heartfelt desire on my part—to adopt him out of a foster home into a family—has created its own kind of difficulties for Bjorn. But I hope he has still gained something by being brought up in a home with a family where he was loved. I think that was better than staying in a foster home."

Sam tapped his fingers impatiently on his staff next to him. "I hear what you are saying, Mrs. Fisher. But what do you want me to tell you? I can't make this situation better. I do understand why you did what you did. I think your motivations were good."

"Sam, I'm not asking you to approve of what I did in adopting him. But I would value some advice."

"You know my position. I agree, I do not believe that the adoption has been entirely negative for Bjorn. Even if he had not been Native and had been adopted, he would still have questions about his origins as an orphan."

"That's right. But I am also concerned with his general state of mind. He may have told you about his belief that he has special communications with bears. That goes back to childhood."

Sam nodded. "He has mentioned that. And we First Nations people believe that some people possess certain channels to animals, to what we consider as animal totems. They help guide and protect—and offer orientation and insight into who we are. I do not see that there is any problem here. Bjorn does believe he has some communication and contact with bears."

"But do you think it is normal for people to feel these communications?" Claire persisted.

"Normal? The distance between the human world and the animal and spirit world can only be crossed by those who have the sensitivity to do so. It represents a gift. Bjorn may have that gift."

Claire remained silent for a few minutes considering this new perspective. She became aware of the ticking of a wall clock in the next room. "So you do think this is a gift that Bjorn has then, and not a source for concern?" She hesitated. "That it might not represent a kind of, a loss of touch with reality?"

"No." Sam tapped his stick on the floor. "The animal and spirit world *are* part of reality. It is open to those who do not close it off. Now, Bjorn may have other problems, perhaps a loss of reality in other aspects of his life, I cannot judge. But not in this."

Claire persisted. "Do you think Bjorn might…be unstable in any way, with his passion and anger about some Native issues?"

Sam shifted his position on his chair and seemed uncomfortable with the line of questioning. "It is not for me to judge, Mrs. Fisher. Nor can I even judge from the little that I know. But Bjorn's concerns about injustices are legitimate. They are appropriate for someone in quest of the roots from which he was taken away."

Claire saw that Sam was unyielding in his disapproval of the adoption, even if he did not personally blame her. She was relieved that Sam at least did not believe Bjorn was suffering from loss of touch with reality.

"But his anger. That does concern me," she continued. "When he speaks of the conditions of Native peoples, and the policies of the government in the past, he reveals a lot of anger."

Sam nodded. "There is much to be angry about, Mrs. Fisher. But I agree, I do not believe that anger is the most productive way to approach our current problems. We need to maintain cool and keen minds to make further progress."

"Well, I hope he listens to you on that."

"I say what I can say when I feel his mind is open to hearing certain arguments."

She sat in silence for a moment, glancing around the room, at the variety of objects related to animals, collecting her thoughts. "Well," she said, finally rising, "I thank you, Sam, for seeing me. I apologize for putting some of these questions to you so bluntly, but you can see where my concerns come from. You have a perspective on all of this that I cannot possibly have. It is very helpful and reassuring to me. I don't want to violate any confidences you have with Bjorn. And I know Bjorn values his contact with you. So do I."

Sam nodded. "I am happy to talk with him if it can bring him any clarity. He is an intelligent boy, and passionate in his concerns about First Nations, and about our environment. But his feelings must be guided in the right directions."

Sam saw her to the door. She bowed and went out.

When she got back to her rooming house she found Bjorn waiting there. "So why did you kick me out of the meeting with Sam?" he said with clear anger in his voice.

"I'm sorry, Bjorn, I didn't mean it to go that way." She reached out to hug him but he withdrew. "I just wanted to get his view on how you are doing under all this strain. I know it is hard on you, it would be hard on anyone. And I just value knowing there is someone here who can help keep a friendly eye over you. I don't know anybody else here. I just didn't want to embarrass you by raising some of these issues in front of you with Sam."

"So what did Sam say in your secret conversation about me?" Bjorn said with some petulance.

"You'll be happy to know he thinks a lot of you. He thinks that your feeling of communicating with bears is a gift, an ability to reach out. And I'm relieved, because in our white culture we don't seem to be able to understand communications with animals much except as some kind of weird thing. Sam has helped me understand that it isn't."

Bjorn listened silently.

"You know, I really respect Sam," Claire went on. "I think he has wisdom and experience to offer. It's clear he likes and respects you. And adoption across communities always has its own difficulties—as you know so well, my son," she said, hugging him. "I'm sure it will be helpful and supportive to maintain contact with him."

Claire left two days later to go back to Vancouver. "I'm glad I came. I just really wanted to see you, Bjorn, to see how you are doing. I know this is hard all that you're going through. But you have to pursue what you have to pursue. I really sympathize with your feelings about animals and the environment. It is good to be concerned, even maybe a little angry. I just hope that you don't let anger cloud your mind, or push you into unwise company."

He hugged her warmly as she departed for her flight. "I'm not sure when I'll be up here next," she said. "But please stay in touch and let me know how you're doing, how your feelings are on all of this. And please take care of yourself. And be proud of who you are, no matter what you can find out about your origins."

"I'm glad you came too, Mom, thanks."

"Well, you have helped me too, you know. To be more aware of First Nations traditions and lore and how it relates to the environment. I want to look into all this more myself. Meanwhile, you know I love you and you have my support. God be with you."

Chapter 27

He had already perceived the rush of the water from a distance. Moving water touched a deep chord in him. Water is a primal element, a vital substance. As it moves in its inexorable downward course we stand beguiled, watching it from our firm stance on land. Water connects the solid and the moving. Land is eternal and timeless; but water flows away into time.

Following the sound, Bjorn soon came upon the running stream. Its many stones stood like sentinels in the stream, forcing the water to swirl and shift path, cascading from pool to pool, intensifying its sound. Water could trick like that; given enough stones it could make itself sound more powerful and voluminous than it actually was. Its sense of direction and purpose offered reassurance to him.

Bjorn knew instinctively he wanted to proceed upward along the rough trail that paralleled the stream. Upwards meant moving towards sources, towards clear, precise origins, where things start. As opposed to descent where things come out and merge in muddier confluence.

He remembered too, the need for caution in the proximity of running water in the forest. He knew it masked the sounds of anything approaching. If a bear had been unable to smell his approach from downwind then it might feel surprised, angered, threatened at the sudden silent appearance of a human without warning. Bjorn thought about singing something aloud to signal his presence. He regretted he had no Native song to sing. What if he chose the song about the bear coming over the mountain, he thought with a smile.

He felt a sense of peace in the proximity of moving water and stood mesmerized by the patterns of the flow. He proceeded slowly upward for a few minutes, sometimes right at the stream's edge, sometimes forced to step back from the stream where it flowed too deeply, or offered no foothold. He noticed that the water appeared to be emerging out of a deep recess in one of the pools higher up, as if from an underground source. He sat down to rest on a dark stone to cool his brow. He cupped his hands to partake of the water, a meaningful gesture of received grace. And then a white stone caught his attention, just out of reach, between himself and the stream's edge. It seemed to possess an unusual shape for a stone. He leaned over to touch it, examine it. It lay partly buried in the wet earth, but his curiosity aroused, he stood up and worked around in the sandy soil with his hands to unearth it. Its irregular shape now emerged from the wet and sandy earth, the cold sand chilling his hands.

It was not a stone at all. It seemed to be some kind of whitened skull of a fairly large animal. He looked at the canine teeth, long jaws and lengthy nasal cavity. There could be little doubt. He was sure it was a bear.

How had he come to seat himself here, next to the skull of a bear? How had the skull gotten here? Where was the rest of the bear skeleton? He found a stick along the stream and used it to probe around in the wet sandy soil near the skull, but he found no immediate evidence of any other bones.

He picked the skull up again and brushed the dirt off the white platelets. He bent over and washed it in the cold rushing water, scraped some of the sand out of the sockets of the eyes, and dislodged the dirt from the nasal cavity and from between the large incisors of the jaw.

What was the skull doing here? He couldn't judge the animal's age, but it appeared older and larger than a bear cub. Had it come to die here? Old age? A bullet? No other predator could likely have killed it— except man. And why was just its head here?

He suddenly grew nervous, as if profaning a sacred object that he had unearthed and disturbed. He felt he was perhaps handling frivolously something that was not meant to be extracted from its place in Mother Earth. He looked around, almost in guilt, to see if he was being observed—by anything. His eyes swept the trees along both sides of the stream, but detected no motion other than the light swaying of branches and the speckled reflections in the moving water.

His anxiety gradually diminished. He turned his attention back to the skull. He turned it around in his palms at different angles as if trying to penetrate its meaning and content. But what content could a skull have? Contents it had once indeed possessed, but its living biological essence had long since intermingled with the soil of forest and the waters of the moving stream, returning to its source. He shook the skull, as if to awaken something latent within it. He found himself putting it up against his ear, like a conch at the seashore, not sure what he would hear, if anything. There was no evident sound within it. But he felt some strange sense in his hands, almost as if it emitted some kind of resonance, a kind of communication.

You lack the vision to perceive my vision. We are of different worlds. We have different roles on this earth. Mine is abiding, omniscient, protective, eternal. What is yours?

Learn from us. We are an ancient presence. There are secret worlds that we inhabit. You cannot yet perceive them, but you will discover your real nature there, the tasks to fulfill.

"But I am only one person."

Cherish your human form. It gives you freedom to act. You will understand this mission with time. Guard your thoughts as you create your place among people. They do not understand you.

What was this Bear? Was this skull a symbol for him that the Bear was in his presence? Or that he was in the Bear's presence?

He debated taking the skull back with him. But he had disturbed its resting place. And why should it be meant for him? Maybe he should he leave it where it was—where it belonged. He sat and contemplated the question, waiting for some kind of insight.

In the end the answer was obvious to him. The bear belonged where it was. He had no right, even meaningful purpose, to take it with him. To what end? Surely it had greater purpose right here where it was in its permanent natural locus, than to be dragged off demeaningly to adorn some coffee table as a novelty item. He dug down with his bare hands again into the depression in the sand and earth from where he had originally unearthed it to make room for it again. His hands were cold and raw from the effort. But it felt right that he had restored it to its proper resting place.

He climbed back up onto the bank to return the way he had come. He knew the discovery had not been an accident. He felt like some kind of communicant.

Chapter 28

B jorn's life had now begun to move in new directions. With his job as a Rainforest tour guide and his initial contacts with Tundra representatives, new horizons were opening up. Yet, all these developments felt spur-of-the-moment, impulsive, lacking plan. He needed clearer focus about where things were going. He found himself once again on the back streets and down to the sticky gate at Sam's house. Sam had shown greater empathy for Bjorn at their last meeting, as well as a willingness to talk about actual issues instead of merely throwing Delphic questions back in Bjorn's face. Maybe he was more willing to take Bjorn seriously now—one of the few people around who did so. Joseph was a friend, but he often seemed removed and insensitive to Bjorn's deeper worries.

"And so how is the search for your parents going?" Sam asked as soon as Bjorn had come in and sat down.

Bjorn looked down to the ground. "No luck at all. I've asked around but just haven't been able to find out anything more about them." His voice trembled inadvertently. "The trail seems dead. I feel—I don't know—like I've been left to drift on my own in the world." His eyes filled.

Sam looked at him in silence. The room struck Bjorn now as stuffy and close. A smell of old wood pervaded the room, steeped in timelessness. Various objects not readily identifiable around the room lent a touch of the distant or mysterious. Sam then sighed, a sign Bjorn took to represent some emotional acknowledgement of Bjorn's feelings. "We are all of us alone. And none of us are alone. It is how you choose to act in this world," he said, looking Bjorn in the eyes. "You are you. You have your own mission in life. That mission comes from you and no one else. You may actually find it easier to find yourself and your purpose if you search on your own. Other people can offer advice, but they have their own views and goals in this world that may not be yours. I know that being on one's own can be lonely. You may never avoid being alone. But it can also be a liberation if you accept it and are willing to open your eyes."

Bjorn found more empathy in these remarks from Sam than he had yet encountered from him. He decided to change the subject. "I often think about my close call with the grizzly in the forest a few months ago. I told you about that. I got the feeling that I had somehow been especially spared by the bear. Maybe a sign that the bear somehow even accepted me. Joseph laughs at my interpretations. And I can't be sure myself about how to understand the experience."

Sam stared at him. "You are not wrong to seek meaning in events. In reality every event has some kind of meaning. Nothing happens simply by pure chance. As human beings we need to derive meaning from all experiences we have. They are precious and should not be dismissed. But still, you cannot simply take this one confrontation with a bear in the forest as the chosen signal for your life."

"You're saying it was not a signal? That it meant nothing?"

"No, I am not saying that. But there is no little handbook that I can pull out and find the interpretation of a given event for you. This is your event, not mine. It is just one event. A big event in your eyes, certainly, but one event. You have to fit it in with all the other parts and events of your life to find meaning in the path you are on."

"But that's no help to me!" cried Bjorn. "That's exactly it, I don't know how to read the signal, about my quest, or my whole damn time here in Bella Bella! Or my dealings with Native peoples here!"

Sam nodded. "I see your frustrations, Bjorn. But your life is still young. Your life's journey contains signals every day that are there for you. Only you know the totality of those signals. No outsider could, or even should, give you a simple one-time interpretation. Any interpretations I gave would be molded by my life, not yours." Sam paused, sensing the impatience in Bjorn's face. "I am sorry if this is not satisfying, but it is the reality. That is why life presents such a mystery. But I do believe that time and further events will definitely help you understand your interpretation of your life path so far."

"But I have to make decisions, I can't simply wait for things to all fall into place before my eyes."

"I understand your impatience," Sam said. "But there are hundreds of ways to interpret your life so far. You can select them and link them together to mean one thing—or another. And there are different answers for us at different times and places in our lives."

Bjorn was encouraged that Sam at least was no longer simply throwing questions back in his face. But the meaning of Sam's words was still vague and he simply seemed unwilling to offer Bjorn clear advice. It was, at best, just advice about how to think about the events in his life, not how to proceed.

After a few moments of reflection Bjorn pressed on into new territory. "I'm doing some new things. I have a job now with the Great Bear Adventure Tours, as a guide taking tourists out in Zodiacs to see the bears."

"Really? That's good. And you like the job?"

Bjorn hesitated. "Yeah, I do, it brings me closer to the bears, to the Rainforest, I enjoy the work. But I also feel like I'm commercializing myself—and the bears."

"Which is better, that tourists have an appreciation of the bears? Or not have an appreciation of the bears?"

"Well, I suppose it does help to create awareness about them. It's certainly better than damn hunting expeditions."

"And what else are you doing?"

"I went to the big meeting the other week with the Tundra delegation at the main hall. Most of it was big company propaganda. But at the end I went up to them. I asked some questions, made some suggestions. They liked the fact I was from a Native background. They actually offered me a chance to work for the Tundra company, to work on promoting the pipeline among First Nations peoples."

"Given the way you feel I'm surprised you would have volunteered your help. Is that what you really wish to do?"

"Not at all. I'm not really sure why I did go up and speak to them. But—I don't know—it would offer me some more money, I could stay on the coast here. I want to stay in this environment. The company says all it is doing is providing energy to people, jobs that people need. They claim it can all be safe, that they'll do it carefully and properly." Bjorn paused, knowing what he said would bring a swift response.

"And you believe that?" Sam raised his eyebrows.

"No. I damn well don't believe it. I'm sure this pipeline project is a bad idea, maybe dangerous."

"Then why did you look interested in a job offer?"

Bjorn squirmed in his chair. "I don't know, I thought there might be some value in getting in close to the company, getting on the inside. Maybe influencing them."

Sam showed a flicker of emotion. "The company looks at our world with the eyes of profit. They do not see the land. Our responsibility is to the land. It was given to us by the Creator. It offers itself to meet our genuine needs, not for making profits off it. The land does not truly even belong to us—or to them. We are simply the custodians. And we are obligated to work with it responsibly and protect it."

"But the company says it will exercise new security practices." Bjorn knew this would goad Sam further.

Sam suddenly seized his staff and stamped it upon the floor. He'd never seen Sam demonstrate such a flash of personal emotion before.

"I am not ignorant, or a fool! I told you before, I have been to the tar-sands, I worked there for a while. My son works there now. It is an operation from hell. I am a man of patience, but these issues of the preservation of the land are not to be discussed in just some casual fashion or business terms. There is no compromise on the sanctity of our lands and of the Rainforest."

Bjorn remained silent, even pleased in the face of Sam's display of emotion, his sudden adoption of a strong stand. "I told my son he is not welcome in this house again as long as he is working there. He says he is just there working to earn money, he does not support the project. But by his work he is supporting the project and making it possible for these evil things to take place. I told him we will not speak again until he changes his mind and leaves his work at the tar sands."

"How do we know what should we should take out of the land then?" Bjorn wanted to push Sam into clearer policy views.

"Do you know the story about the King of the Oolikan?"

"Oolikan? The small, greasy fish they use to make oil from?"

"That is correct." And Sam settled into a new way of speech, a way of telling a story that was unfamiliar to Bjorn.

"Let me tell you the tale of Sharp-Eyes and the Oolikan. Sharp-Eyes was granted the gift of skill at fishing. When he was young he could already sense when the first Oolikan of the season would come up the river. He wanted to be the first to greet them and tell the People the good news so they could celebrate their nourishment for the season ahead. The early fishermen would set out into the river in their canoes to round up the newly-arrived Oolikan in their nets and bring them back into the village, the canoes overflowing with the small silvery fish. The People had deep respect for the Oolikan for they brought life. Their arrival formed part of the Spring Rituals of the renewal of the Earth's bounty for the People.

The Oolikan were intended to be a gift to all in need. The first canoe-loads were always given to those small or poorer families who lacked hunters or fishermen to provide for their nourishment. How can our bellies be comfortable when other bellies are uncomfortable? That is the way of our People.

The Oolikan are our truest and trusted friend. They are the first fish to give themselves to us after the cold winter. Their oil is our sustenance. Some call them candle-fish, for their oil is so rich that when they are dried in the sun for two days you can put a wick in their mouths and they will burn like a candle for long hours, providing light as well as food to our People.

We would catch them by the thousands and when we had more than we could eat we would put them into our "stink boxes." After many weeks they would melt into a thick liquid, powerful in smell, deep in flavor and rich in oil. We would then store it for eating with our other food during the rest of the year. It gave both flavor and health.

But as he grew older, Sharp-Eyes began to tell the People: Oh People, it is good that we have so much Oolikan oil. But we cannot use it all ourselves. We can become richer if we trade it to other peoples for beautiful robes and precious stones. And so Sharp-Eyes began to organize the People. We no longer thought about how much oil we needed for ourselves. We wanted to catch more and more Oolikan to make more oil to trade to other peoples. So we began to carry it in heavy wooden boxes up the steep trails into the high hills and over the far Snow Mountains to the dry prairies—many many days travel to far away. And our People were happy that we received in return woven robes and arrows and precious stones and furs that we took back home. Some of our men were offered beautiful women to take back as brides to our villages to become part of the People. Sharp-Eyes now told us how we could organize our fishing to catch still more Oolikan and get more robes and more precious stones. So our people began to spend even more of their time and energy processing as much Oolikan oil as they could. And their path up into the interior became so familiar it became known as the Grease Trail.

But then the Oolikan saw that their numbers were growing smaller each year and they became afraid of their future. One day the King of the Oolikan came to visit the chief of the People and said, "We have offered ourselves to your needs since the Sun and Moon came into the sky and the children of men began to walk on the earth, so that you could use our bounties and seek nourishment. This is our obligation. We are happy and fulfilled in offering ourselves as part of the greater wheel of life. Each creature has something to offer to other creatures. But Sharp-Eyes does not show gratefulness to us. He no longer seeks to find nourishment for himself and his people, but to acquire many riches and make his position great. We are not willing to sacrifice ourselves just so others may become rich. That is not our role in this existence."

But the People had grown greedy and were not content with what they had. Sharp-Eyes did not give up his plans for carrying more Oolikan oil to far places for more riches. Then the King of the Oolikan came to the Bears and told them of their problem. "We have been to the People, but they do not listen, O Bears. But you are aware how we feed so many creatures every year."

"Yes," said the Bears, "you do not feed us directly, but you nourish the salmon and other fish that are so important to our lives. Without the Oolikan we would not have the salmon that have fed us faithfully since the dawn of time, and long before two-legged creatures walked our land. You have been generous in giving to the salmon, and they have been generous to us, even leaping up the falls and into our mouths. They enable us to survive the hard winter so that we can sleep till spring and produce our babies. All creatures give to other creatures so that they may all live in balance together. We do not wish the fat mouths of greed to upset your lives and our lives."

"Then you must know, O Bears, of our problems with Sharp-Eyes," the King of the Oolikan continued. "He is using his greedy quest for our bodies and our oil to change the balance of Nature. He is passing this greed to his own people like a sickness."

But Sharp-Eyes still did not cease from his ways. Soon he had many followers. Some of the people said that Sharp-Eyes should become the new chief of the People. The People began to lose their way and forget their traditions of making things for their own livelihood. They began to forget their role of working for all the People. Their pile of treasures and possessions began to sit heavy on their hearts and cloud their minds.

So one day one of the great Bears went to Sharp-Eyes to tell him that the ways of the world were departing from their appointed path, and threatening the balance of all things. Sharp-Eyes laughed and said "Talking of balance is from the Old Ways. We the Human People are strong now and able to draw from the earth and the waters everything we want and as much as we want. We are simply making more of the oil available to the rest of the world. The way of the world changes. Go away, Bear, and do not interfere in what our people now want."

The Bears consulted among themselves. "We must restore respect to all our creatures and balance to the wheel of life," the chief of the Bears said. And so he instructed a younger bear to pull off his fur and turn himself into a fair young man. Then this young man went to Sharp-Eyes and told him, "You have made many of our people rich. I wish to join you. I can show you many places where you can find even more Oolikan for your trading." Sharp-Eyes's heart expanded, offering more room to greed. And so they went into the forest together and they walked a long way, passing many new rivers Sharp-Eyes had not seen before. "We have been traveling for a long time, how far are we going?" Sharp-Eyes asked the young man. "I will show you where you can find the greatest riches," the young man said.

Finally the sun began to drop below the mountains. "We must sleep, and tomorrow I will show you the best place. It is a secret known only to the Bears and where the salmon people come." And they lay down to sleep. But when it was dark in the forest the young man put his bear skin back on. And when the sun rose up into their world the next day, Sharp-Eyes found no young man at his side, but a great Bear that sat watching him. And he became frightened. "What have you done with my guide?" he asked. "I am your guide," he answered. "You are now living in the world of the Bears. And you have violated the order of our world. You have destroyed our balance. And now you must feed the Bears to help make things right."

Sharp-Eyes could not believe what his ears were hearing. "But I have done no wrong to the Bears," he cried. "I have only worked hard and organized the life of the People so that they can all have greater treasures."

"Yes, treasures to some of the people. But at the same time you are taking it away from all the rest of the world and its creatures and people." And the Bear advanced upon Sharp-Eyes. Sharp-Eyes now understood that his end was near. The Bear's powerful claws struck Sharp-Eyes knocking him unconscious, and his jaws sunk into the Sharp-Eye's neck. And Sharp-Eyes was never again seen by his people.

And when Sharp-Eyes did not come back to his village, the People asked themselves what had happened. And that night a Bear came and told them that Sharp-Eyes had destroyed the sacred balance of things and had paid with his life so that the world could come back into balance. The People now realized how all their activities had been twisted. They remembered how they could think of nothing except to catch more Oolikan and to produce more Oolikan oil, far more than they needed for their living. They now saw how they had damaged the rhythm of life. They knew in their hearts that the Bear's warning was right. And they returned to the path of balance in which all people shared in all the activities for the benefit of all the creatures. And the Oolikan came back each year, their numbers strong once again, and happily gave themselves, but only as much as the People actually needed. And the People no longer carried huge boxes of oil over the mountains again."

Sam ended his tale. He looked at Bjorn in silence as the truth of the story sunk in. He then put down his carved stick.

"And now, it is late. Go, and sleep upon this story."

Bjorn already was aware of the Bears' moral role in the workings of the world. The Oolikan tale only made it clearer. Surely this had to be a clear message about the nature of Tundra company operations. How should he handle it? And upon reflection, he also realized that his encounter with the Bear in the forest with Joseph also had significance. Although it had terrified him, he had understood that communications with Bears would now be a part of his future life. That prospect awed him, and thrilled him. And it terrified him, because he was not yet clear about how he would fit into the Bears' scheme of things.

Chapter 29

Mason still hoped to restore some sense of family cohesion after his years away in Nigeria, his absence from his children's lives, the worrisome deterioration of his relationship with Melanie, and her interest in the Dutch environmentalist Jan.

Three days later the children actually did join for dinner again in Calgary, this time with less grumbling.

"Guess what, guys?" Mason said. "I'm going to a conference in Alaska on bears next week. Specialists from all over the arctic world are going to be there!"

"Wow, bears! That's cool, Dad," his son said. "What about the bears?"

"I haven't seen the whole agenda yet. But discussions about how bears are doing, the numbers of bears, what kinds, where they are, what the outlook is for them, preserving their habitat, all that."

"Well, I don't think you have to go to the conference to understand that tankers through the Great Bear Rainforest isn't so great for their habitat," Shelley offered.

"Come on, Shelley, don't be snide. We've got to be informed about the issue if we're going to avoid problems. I'm serious about this. I want to protect the bears as much as anybody, and help promote their cause."

"Well, yeah, but what about global warming…and the polar bears? I saw on National Geographic they may be starting to drown out in the open ocean as the ice melts," his son said.

"Yeah, I do care about that. That's a far bigger issue than even the pipeline. What makes global warming and how to handle it, that's all still under research."

"Mason, it's still fossil fuels, above all else," Melanie broke in. That's the basic long-term problem. It's in the media all the time."

"Look, I know there's a problem with fossil fuels. But—"

"And the tar sands produce more carbon dioxide than anything."

"Melanie, the hard reality is that, whether you or I or anyone else likes it or not, this fracking and oil sands production are simply going to go ahead. It's driven by global market demand. It doesn't mean I like it. It's way bigger than me, or anybody else. I couldn't stop it if I wanted. Nearly all Canadian and American politicians agree. The problem for me, for Tundra, is how conscientious we can be in handling these issues until better energy sources come along."

They both knew by heart the well-trodden path to their old standoff positions and both decided that there was no point in going there again, especially at the family dinner table.

"Actually, I'm surprised," Melanie commented later after dinner. "The COO of pipelines and tankers going to a conference on bears? That might be kind of fun, actually."

"Yeah, it's not the usual COO pastime. But remember I'm trying to break out of the old mold."

"It's a tough course to follow, Mason."

"I know, but I really feel personally engaged. Tundra absolutely has got to be credible on the environment, and sympathetic to the issues of wildlife, otherwise we're just as bad as all the others. And we have to look at the bears especially. I'd really like to learn more about bears myself as a matter of fact. I remember them from when I was a kid back east going camping with my family. I'll never forget how a bear— or it might have been a cougar—killed our family dog out in the forest."

The conference was taking place in Juneau over four days. Mason had never been to Juneau before, but he had heard a lot about its beautiful setting. "I'd love it if you came along, Melanie. It's supposed to be a picturesque place." He put his hand on hers.

She looked away. "Mason, I'm sorry, I've just got too much to do here to go for that long."

Mason withdrew his hand. "I'm sure you've got pressing environmental business with Jan to attend to here while I'm gone," he snapped. Melanie didn't rise to the bait and Mason knew he shouldn't have said it.

Mason bounded into the board room for a strategy session the next day. He felt more and more ideas flooding into his head, an excitement about a new approach to the project that could drastically change the whole image of an oil company's responsibility to the environment.

As they got into the discussion, one of the senior board members spoke up. "Mason, I know we need to appear enlightened and all that on the environment. And I know a lot of the public will get all teary-eyed at pictures of a Kermode bear, but it's not enough to win the PR war. For the public the bottom line is still jobs and the economy. All the polls say that."

Mason looked at him. "First of all, Arthur, it's *Kermodee*, not *Kermoad*. Let's at least get the name right. Second, OK, I agree, pretty pictures aren't enough. But I'm talking about a far broader approach. And we can't aim it all just at white Canada. If we can get the First Nations on board the project will be unstoppable. White Canadians are all over the map on this issue right now—greens going head- to-head with the conservative and business types. They're a divided community. But if First Nations agree on the issue, they can deliver a unanimous vote of their whole community. This affects them as a *people*, and they'll vote as a community, not as individuals."

His executive officer turned his chair around to face Mason. "Yeah, but what makes you think you can win over the First Nations? We're seeing strong reactions from them so far. They see the pipeline and the tankers as a direct threat to their lands. They're really taking a tough line in public meetings."

"Listen Dan, I really get that. Don't forget I was presiding over that disastrous public meeting we had a few weeks ago in Bella Bella. Arthur, you were there. When we gave the usual talk about state-of-the-art technology and commitment to avoiding accidents they damn near rioted. It was very clear that was not the right approach to take."

"So how do we approach it then?"

"Look, the First Nations feel like the decisions are being made over their heads—just further victimization as their lands are exploited. I saw that in spades when I was in that nightmare in Ogoniland. We've got to make them partners in this. And not just the elders and the chiefs, but youth. Do you know who is actually already aware of this? China. China has already established direct contacts with First Nations groups in BC to discuss business in raw materials. And the Chinese are way ahead of us in showing respect for First Nations traditions as part of dealing with them. We've got to be more creative and sensitive on all this."

At the next staff meeting Mason pressed ahead further with his concepts.

"Look, I want to develop an entirely new image," he declared. "We're losing the PR game. We're just not projecting the right image—all this stuff about jobs and the economy. Yeah, sure, that matters, but it's not enough. We have to buy into the environment issue, show that we're a part of it, a project that will showcase Canada's natural wonders, one in which clean modern industry can coexist with nature. Tundra could actually put some its resources in to help heighten public awareness of the Great Bear Rainforest. There's no reason we can't be advocates for a broader green vision."

His executive officer looked skeptical. "So what do you propose in practical terms to sell this green vision as you call it? It's got to be persuasive back in the head office in Toronto."

Mason leaned forward. "OK, so rather than viewing the Rainforest as a problem, we need to make it our centre piece—as something we can sensitively develop in a spirit of responsible co-existence. The Rainforest needs funds, Tundra can be the key sponsor of the Rainforest, even assist in major funding for its expansion and preservation."

"Nice words, Mason, but as I say, it's going to be a hard sell back in Toronto."

Mason had already begun exploring the idea with some politicians in BC's parliament on his last trip to Victoria. He told them how he wanted Tundra to sponsor a major new centre for bear research in the region. With lavish and visible funding available for researchers to come to a beautiful facility in a stunning place on the coast he could build a strong cadre of support for Tundra and change its image dramatically. Sure, some might accuse him of just playing a cynical game or PR gimmick to buy public and scientific support. But he was convinced that done right it could be total win-win for everybody. Toronto might find it a little unusual for the COO to be going off to a bear conference in Juneau, Alaska for four days, but he knew he was onto something.

On the way out he turned to his secretary and dropped a piece of paper onto her desk. "Can you see if you can dig up this Native kid down in Bella Bella? He showed up at our public meeting down there a few weeks ago and seemed interested in working with Tundra on bear issues."

Chapter 30

Bjorn was determined to undertake the full journey to the islands by sea, traveling by boat in order to experience the sense of the distance—eight hours on a ferry heading straight out into the tumultuous Pacific seas to reach the mysterious isles of Haida Gwaii, one hundred kilometers off the coast of British Columbia. He'd heard about Haida Gwaii much of his life as a legendary place, a northwest Pacific Galapagos, its surrounding waters known for their extreme treacherousness, fierce unpredictable winds, high tides, rain storms and often colossal waves. A place in the world distinguished for its clashing sea currents that produce massive wave peaks and troughs that in a bad storm could snap a lengthy sea vessel in two.

Bjorn stood by the railing on the deck alone, peering out into the white misty gloom moving past. The rain was light, but it came at him sideways due to the movement of the ferry, bolstered by the unceasing wind. Yes, this was the kind of crossing that he wanted, water in his face, turbulent waves, in touch with the elements, bearing witness to his ritual passage to a different world. And it was thrilling to think that, according to Emma, it might be where his father was from. He had to learn about this place where he might even have blood ties.

The Haida were famed both for their warlike ways and their advanced artistic culture. A century earlier European visitors arriving by sailing ship into the coves of these seaside villages had been astonished at the works of the Haida on display: a row of symbolic waterfront sentinel carvings addressing the external world, a phalanx of high wooden totems each bearing the personal narrative of a specific clan standing between the sea and the long houses, the dwellings of the totems' creators.

Bjorn had been appalled to learn how the Haida had lost upwards of 90% of their people after their initial encounters with the white man.

Europeans had been the bearers, on occasion deliberately, of the smallpox holocaust that decimated Haida life and nearly swept the culture away in a firestorm of fever, death and destruction. Populations reduced to ten percent on the southern island were forced to move to a handful of shared new settlements in the northern island if they were to perpetuate a sustainable community. Here were the homes of the main Haida clans—the Raven and the Eagle. He knew the bear too figured importantly in Haida legends and their world view.

"I hope you are not thinking of jumping in." A voice arose behind him. Bjorn started, unaware that someone else had joined him in the harsh weather out on the deck. He turned to find a short man with a graying Lenin-style pointed goatee, dressed in a long faded green parka with the hood turned up against the intrusive elements.

"No, of course not," Bjorn responded, on guard.

"It is very stormy. Did you know one reason people are afraid of standing in front of great waves or on high cliffs is that they think of suicide? Do not ask me why they do, but it is well known."

"Are you a psychologist or something?"

"We must all be psychologists to survive in this world," the man replied, with a distinct foreign accent.

The remark seemed pretentious but Bjorn let it pass. "This is your first time to Haida Gwaii?" Bjorn asked.

"No, far from it. I feel like it is a home away from home. In fact, it was familiar to me even before I came the first time."

"How do you mean?"

"I mean this land is familiar to anyone who knows Russia. Far eastern Russia on the Pacific. Perhaps you know that these North American continents at one time were physically part of my country, Russia. Of course that was several hundred millions of years ago so do not be worried, we do not really claim it now."

Bjorn stared questioningly at the figure, unsure what to make of him.

"Do not look surprised. All the continents of the world were joined together in a single continent at one time. Then they gradually all pulled apart, in different directions, making new continents. Canada pulled away from eastern Siberia. But who knows, we actually still share a few flora and fauna, from when our continents were all joined."

"So you are Russian then?"

"Vladimir Medvedev, at your service," he said affecting a sweeping bow.

"And what brings you to Haida Gwaii?" Bjorn asked.

"What brings anyone? It is a remarkable place. And, among other things, the bears."

He had captured Bjorn's attention. "Why the bears, especially?"

"Why, bears are the supreme creatures of the earth. We honour them. Our natives in Siberia call them the "Bear Nation.""

"But what's your interest?"

"I am researching bears from all over the world. In fact I may say I am the number one specialist of bear life in the world—even though not everyone recognizes that yet but they will." He chortled.

"But why Haida Gwaii?" Bjorn sought a better grasp of this curious character before revealing his own interests.

"Because it has a rare species of black bear that no one else has, not even in Russia. I presume you do not know Latin. But if you did, its species is called "*Ursus americanus carlottae.*"

Bjorn frowned. "Doesn't that mean 'American bear' or something?"

"Good, yes, but '*carlottae*,' that means Charlotte. She was the idiot English queen the British explorers named these magical islands after. The 'Queen Charlottes.' Can you imagine such a pathetic pampered aristocratic name for a majestic, raw and powerful native land like this? It is really quite reprehensible, you know. All these English explorers, buttering up the Queen by giving her name to unknown places in which she had no knowledge of or even interest in. As if these places had no names until the English came along. But never mind, the Haida are not fooled by these imperial names. They know it is their country and keep their own names." Vladimir assumed the self-satisfied expression of someone revealing a great truth to the uninformed.

Bjorn decided not to respond to the multiple provocative remarks that Vladimir seemed capable of weaving into any single statement. But he was intrigued, uncertain about the strange personality.

"Shall we go inside?" Vladimir proposed. "It is getting dark and the fog is getting less interesting to look at. Come, we will order a bottle of vodka." He fairly bounced back through the heavy sea doors into the cabin.

They sat down at a table in the ship's bar, fairly well populated. Most of the people looked to be tourists, although there were a fair number of men who looked like they might be native to Haida Gwaii, everyone drinking beer at the tables.

"I'm not sure they will have vodka," Bjorn suggested.

"No fear. They will have it. It is the number one drink of the civilized world. Bring a bottle of cold vodka," Vladimir told the waiter, without asking if it was available. The waiter hesitated a second, looked at Bjorn, and soon came back with a bottle. "This is not Russian vodka!" Vladimir protested. "Finlandia! This is some Finnish imitation. Is this all you have?"

"That's all we have," the waiter said.

"It is Finnish piss! And it is not even cold!" Vladimir felt the bottle and shot a glance at the waiter, who simply shrugged. "I'll bring ice," he said and walked away. "Cretins, these people. They do not know even how to drink vodka. Ice ruins the taste." The waiter returned with the ice and put it down on the table. "We do not want ice, it ruins the drink, take it away," Vladimir commanded. The waiter exchanged glances with Bjorn again. Vladimir sighed and opened the bottle of Finlandia. He sniffed at the mouth of the bottle, shrugged his shoulders and proceeded to fill each tumbler half way.

"*Na zdorovie*, as we say. To your health." He lifted his glass and downed the contents at one go. He then slammed down the glass with gusto. Bjorn made no attempt to mimic him, and confined himself to a cautious sip. He immediately felt the pure vodka burn its way down his throat and then cut through his brain like a scalpel. He shook his head inadvertently.

"Not used to our vodka, I see."

"No, it's just I don't drink that much…and it's very strong."

"If you do not mind my asking, I see you might be of aboriginal origin?"

"Yes, but I'm not fully sure which people."

"Well, I can see that in your face, you're already turning red. You need to be careful, some aboriginal peoples lack a gene for processing alcohol. It goes to their heads very easily."

Bjorn was not sure how to respond to all these assumptions that almost invaded his sense of privacy. They sat in silence for a few minutes, looking around at the bar scene, feeling the roll of the ship in the waves.

"So," Bjorn said, "you say you are a specialist on bears?"

"Yes, member of the Academy of Sciences of the former USSR, at your service...but the fools later expelled me from the Academy."

"Why?"

"I knew too much. I embarrassed them. They did not like my theories. In fact, I had experience on the ground with bears that all these other academics with their precious degrees and scientific laboratories did not have. And they were all zoologists who talked about zoology in terms of Marxist-Leninist theory. I had no time for such stupid theories. I was in touch with the bears directly. Nor had the bears heard of Marx or Lenin you see."

Bjorn wasn't sure he followed and kept his silence.

"*Da*, that was the way it was. My way was not the way of Soviet science." He sighed.

"How do you mean, you were in touch with the bears?"

"Simple, my dear. I was in touch with the bears. I went to the Kamchatka peninsula. You have heard of it, yes?"

Bjorn shook his head. "Not really."

"It is a huge long peninsula in Russia. Stretches down along the northern Pacific coast of Siberia. It is approximately where Haida Gwaii is, if you would match up the Russian and Canadian coasts across the ocean. It is a nature paradise, and the home of wonderful bears. I lived among them."

"What do you mean, lived among them?"

"I mean I lived among them. I refused to work out of the official government stations there. They were all just a herd of academicians who would come out in the daytime in their jeeps to inspect the bears, collect bear hairs and droppings and then go back at night...but I lived there, in a tent, among them."

"Wasn't it dangerous?"

"For ordinary people perhaps. But not for me. The bears knew me, they knew I understood them. They got used to me over several years when I stayed for the summers and studied them."

Bjorn wasn't sure what to believe of this. "They didn't bother you?"

"No. But the other scientists did. They kept telling me it was dangerous. They also said it was "unprofessional," the fools. As if to live among the bears and to study them first hand is unprofessional for a zoologist. They said that my presence disturbed the bears, that I would not get normal readings...you know the Heisenberg Principle?"

Bjorn shook his head.

"The Heisenberg Principle. It means that when you are present and take measurements of a phenomenon, your mere act of measuring will change the nature of what you are observing...well, that may be true for atoms, but not for bears." Vladimir reached for the bottle and poured himself another half tumbler of vodka. He waved the bottle toward Bjorn who just shook his head, and continued to nurse his own glass with tiny sips.

"I got to know the bears well. The same group always came each summer to the same place. I even gave them names. Not professional, said the other academicians. You are anthropomorphizing them, they claimed. Such bullshit, that's what you say, yes? What a long word they accuse me of—anthropomorphism—for observing patterns of the life of bears next to my tent. I saw them breed, I knew who was the father and who was the mother of cubs, over many years. I reported on this extensively. But the Academy of Sciences said the research was unorthodox, unacceptable...they warned me to stop living among them...but I knew them. I could read their moods and intentions, their interactions, which bears were in competition, which bears were in exile, *da*? And which ones dominated the group, usually the females. But then that fool came, and messed things up. And then there was the bad incident..." Vladimir took another swig and fell into reflective silence.

"Incident?" Bjorn suggested.

"Yes, the other researcher who came one summer and wanted to live among the bears like I did. He was enthusiastic, but a nervous type. I told him to keep his tent some distance away from mine. He did not react calmly in the presence of bears. And he was a nuisance to me."

"So what happened?"

"Well, he got in the way of my presence and worried the bears. And then one night...it happened."

"What?"

"The bears. Some big grizzly bear came. I don't know if the fool had left food in his tent or what. Anyway, one night a bear forced his way into the tent. This poor man was unprepared and...in the morning when I went over, I saw his tent had collapsed. There was silence all around, no bears in the vicinity. I pulled up a flap of the tent and found the researcher, dead, on his back. More than dead, badly chewed up. His stomach was ripped open and there was blood everywhere. All his things tossed all around. I had to radio to the research centre. That was when they ordered me to leave the site and give up my investigations in the field. 'You were lucky that did not happen to you,' they said. As if it was about luck. I understood the bears. They did not."

"Whew, what a story," Bjorn commented.

"Yes, but perhaps more interesting is my research among the natives of Kamchatka. They are the ones who understand the bears from living with them, not the academicians."

Bjorn could not believe his luck at encountering this Russian character and his knowledge and interest in bears.

"I would love to do bear research," Bjorn offered impulsively.

"What is your interest in this?" asked Vladimir.

"I don't know. I'm just very interested in bears. I'm trying to learn a lot about them. That's one reason I'm visiting Haida Gwaii. And I want to learn something of the language. It may have been my father's language. But I have no knowledge of any Native language, I was raised by white people."

"That is sad. It is hard to be cut off from one's culture and mother tongue. The language is your mother."

Bjorn moved his glass away as Vladimir sought to top it up. "I don't know if you know," Bjorn offered, "there is a lot going on here now—about possible oil tankers passing through this region, past the Great Bear Rainforest. I want to do something about that."

"Yes, I know about the Rainforest. Capitalist polluters. The Soviet Union did not work very well, but Marx and Lenin knew about capitalists and their greed…and your name, Bjorn, you surely know it means bear—who gave it to you?"

"It isn't my Native name, I don't know what my Native name is, that's one of the things that bothers me. I got the name from my adopted family." And Bjorn told Vladimir about his background, his mother's Norwegian background, and his quest for more information about where he came from. And how bears seemed to come into his mind so often.

"Yes, it seems there is much going on with bears here in Canada now, particularly if the Great Bear Rainforest is going to be sacrificed to the big oil companies."

"Yes, that's where I want to help."

"You're an interesting young man, Bjorn. Maybe we can talk more on Haida Gwaii after we arrive, if I can arrange the time. Who knows, I might be able to help you. I am staying at the lodge of a Native friend out of town. I will call him to see if there is place there for you also. He is very friendly to me. I knew his father."

Bjorn beamed. "I really would love to talk to you more about this. I'm concerned about what's happening with the bears. .. And I believe I have some channels of communication with the bears. I need your advice."

Vladimir cast a more searching glance at Bjorn in the face of his new-found insistence. Then they felt the boat shudder as it glanced off the wooden pilings of the pier, pulling into the dock at Skidegate. Bjorn had scarcely realized that they were so close to arrival. Vladimir cast another long look at Bjorn as they disembarked. "Come with me, then," he said.

Chapter 31

Bjorn could not believe his luck in meeting up with Vladimir on the crossing to Haida Gwaii. Vladimir had so much to tell—details, insights and lore for which Bjorn thirsted, all mixed in with this strange personality. Above all Vladimir's understanding of bear psychology fascinated Bjorn. Vladimir seemed to think of bears, not just as inhabiting a place here or there, but as part of a universal vision.

Given the late hour, Bjorn and Vladimir went off to a small hotel in Skidegate. "Tomorrow morning we will take a float plane to a lodge owned by a young Haida man. His father was a good friend of mine, a native Haida naturalist. We met at a conference on bears in Alaska many years ago. I visited him twice here on Haida Gwaii. He passed away last year but his son invited me to visit again. He has a big lodge way down on the south end of Haida Gwaii, visited by many environmentalists. It is near one of the old villages and there are sometimes artists there as well."

"I know you're busy," Bjorn replied. "But I want to hear more about the Natives and the bears on Kamchatka."

"What is your interest in that?"

"I want to understand bears, who they are, what role they play in our lives. It's important to me personally, to my life."

Vladimir seemed surprised at the intensity of Bjorn's expression of interest, but then smiled. "Alright, come along. We can share one of the large rooms. After Soviet days we Russians are used to having to share spaces with many people."

The next day they clambered into a seaplane to ferry them south to an ancient site and to the lodge maintained by Vladimir's friend. Below them were magnificent Pacific seascapes infused with the poetry of the wild, the sea coming off the exposed Pacific side pounding the great boulders, venting its full force direct and unbroken upon this outlier of the North American continent. Many of the beaches, some rocky, some sandy, were suffused with the mists off the powerful surf, here and there creating a brief rainbow effect as the sun broke through intermittently. The smell of salt pervaded the air. It felt as if the land was already in the grips of a long-term project of Nature to gradually pulverize and ultimately reabsorb the land back into the relentless sea.

The force of the waves on the Pacific side was directed against the islands four-square, surging across the long ocean from the massive Asian mainland over several thousand miles away to the west. "It must be a straight shot to Japan across the waters from here," Bjorn commented.

"Not to Japan, my boy, what you feel here comes from Kamchatka, from Russia. Russia is the closest land to these northern Canadian islands."

An hour and a half later they touched down near the site of one of the ancient Haida villages, SGang Gwaay, where many of its traditional totem poles stood, windswept but many still upright, in front of an area where huge traditional long-houses had once been lined up. From there it was only a short Zodiac ride on to a small island crowned by a beautiful large house made of natural wood, strongly suggestive of Native architecture. The owner, Paul, a swarthy man in his forties with an elongated face, salt-and-pepper hair, big hands and a warm smile, came out and hugged Vladimir as an old friend. He shook Bjorn's hand warmly as a friend of Vladimir's, and invited him to stay in the large suite as well. Bjorn was astonished that Vladimir addressed Paul in some language that did not at all sound like Russian. "It is Haida," Vladimir explained. "I have studied the language periodically but my knowledge is not very good. And these ancient Native languages are very difficult to pronounce. I'm interested to see what connections there might be with the languages of eastern Siberia. After all, all these people originally came out of the same area in eastern Siberia and across the land bridge to Alaska and on down. You are closer to Russia here than you think." Vladimir seemed increasingly larger than life.

Bjorn was overwhelmed by the beauty of the house. It consisted of beams and planks all in natural wood, lightened by an expanse of glass that gave the impression of being in a boat at sea. They sat in the great room with its high ceilings, its triangular roof segments fanning out in different directions overhead. Bjorn sat down in a chair made of large ring of black iron from which hung some kind of animal skin, making him feel he was being swallowed up into a nest. Vladimir sat next to Bjorn at one end of a chunky couch also made of skins and natural wood. A fire was burning in a large fireplace in the centre of the room, keeping the general chill at bay.

"Ah, I remember all this so well from earlier years when your father was here, God rest his soul," Vladimir said to Paul. "Are you still working as a naturalist too?" Paul nodded. Paul had anticipated Vladimir's tastes. They sat down to multiple small plates of appetizers—sliced sausages, pickles, cold cuts, various salads of potato, beet, pea and diced carrot with mayonnaise. Vladimir beamed at the sight, as well as at the four bottles of wine, seemingly the only alcohol available. "Russian-style food, Bjorn. We call these *zakusky*—little bites," Vladimir said. He spent some time talking with the host about his father's last years and his work at that time. It had been five years since he and Vladimir had last talked.

Vladimir then turned to bring Bjorn into the conversation as well. "You remember, I was talking about Native peoples yesterday. The Academy of Sciences in Moscow did not appreciate my field work out with the bears, especially after the death of the other researcher." He swallowed a whole tumbler full of wine in three gulps.

"In any case, I spent two years living among the native people on Kamchatka, talking about their stories and myths about the bears. They are a people who truly understand bears. But alas, scientific investigators in the Academy do not appreciate the role of stories and myths. To them they are just idle tales and imaginations, and not verifiable, not "scientific," as they say. They want hard facts and statistics." Vladimir poured himself another glass of wine, gestured the bottle towards Bjorn but Bjorn waved him off.

"But stories tell more about the animals than science does. The stories reflect the knowledge of people who have lived among bears for tens of thousands of years."

"Are there a lot of bears there?" Bjorn asked.

"*Da*, maybe 12,000 bears in Kamchatka, mostly brown bears—what you call grizzly. They are the biggest bears in Asia. But people are coming now all the time to Kamchatka to kill them, to make trophies. It is a scandal, but since the fall of the Soviet Union, things have gotten much worse. The communist regime in Moscow, that your country loved to hate, very well knew how to protect wildlife and had a good budget for rangers and wildlife specialists to protect the animals. Today our capitalist government is very weak, it has no money and cannot afford to pay for wildlife protection."

"Yes," Paul said. "In some ways I am more angry at the Chinese hunters there than I am with the Americans here. I remember when I was in Kamchatka with my father, the Chinese would pay ten thousand dollars to kill a brown bear, just for their—what's it called, bile gland? The Chinese men seem to believe it will give them an iron prick for good sex. And just for this they kill these animals."

"Yes," Vladimir said, "sadly it is difficult now for Kamchatka authorities to resist the money, and they do not have enough people to protect the bears."

Vladimir turned to Bjorn. "So, my dear Canadian friend, you must become serious. You are a rich country with many resources. Russia and Canada are the last great lands rich with open northern spaces and wildlife and resources. We are losing control in our country to capitalists who want to exploit all natural resources, pollute the water, anything for profit. The number of bears has dropped heavily. People are fishing illegally all over Kamchatka, they are making dams to catch the salmon so the fish are not breeding properly and they are not coming back to streams. Bears do not have enough to eat and sometimes now they attack people. Before, they never do this." He poured Paul and himself another glass of wine and stabbed at a slice of salami with his fork.

"Well," Bjorn replied, "I'm studying about how to preserve the Great Bear Rainforest. Many people are also interested in doing it, especially our First Nations. But it is hard to fight against big corporations. And now we have the giant Norwegian fish companies building fish farms on the fish routes in the fjords that are passing disease to the young wild salmon. It really makes me angry to see how our own government here in BC is totally on the side of the fish farm business."

"Ah, you are imitating the mistakes the Soviet Union!"

Bjorn stared out of the great plate glass window which looked out over a rocky inlet and rough beach, trees surrounding the house on three sides. The light outside was fading as the sun slowly sank into the western sea, its last light captured and reflected by each incoming wave and caught on the sparkles of the mists. The recessed lights inside the great room drilled down from the ceiling, leaving them illuminated in a largely dark room. The light of the fireplace cast an uneven flickering light. Bjorn had never been in such a house before in this remarkable natural setting. And the little wine that he had drunk was beginning to take effect, his mind flickering slightly in tune with the fire. He knew he should drink no more. The men watched the fire dance in silence.

"Did you know, Bjorn, there is a conference on bears and their habitats in Juneau two months from now? I am going. You must come. We could continue our discussions there."

"I would love to come," Bjorn replied. "I have only been to one academic conference on bears and it wasn't very good." But he thought back fondly on his heady time with Dawn.

"Well, they are mostly boring, but there are often interesting people there. I invite you."

Paul went into the kitchen and brought out more *zakuski*, including many herring dishes. They ate more in silence.

"You know, Bjorn, what you have here is rare and priceless. Do not forget, Lenin once said, "the capitalists are so greedy that we will sell them the rope to hang themselves." It is all about money now. There are no values left and there is no one who respects the wild nature. I thought I would come to Canada and see the champion of protecting the environment. But frankly I am now disgusted when I come to Canada and see all the damage and loss. You learn nothing from Russia except how your government can try to silence its own scientists. And this bear-hunting? They call it recreation? That is Marxist double-speak. The right word for that is 're-killing.'"

Bjorn felt slightly nervous at the harsh direction of the conversation. It reminded him of the tough language he had heard from the Native Americans in Denver when he was there with Dawn.

Their host got up and came back with a bottle of chilled vodka. "For you, my friends, I have been saving this for last." Vladimir beamed and filled each of their glasses with more vodka. "You are not drinking, my friend." Vladimir looked at Bjorn. "I know you have problems with alcohol. But it makes us uncomfortable when a friend does not participate in the celebration."

"Just a drop. I'm not used to drinking hard liquor," Bjorn replied. His head was spinning, and he didn't know if it was from the alcohol or the flood of new ideas in the conversation. They sat silently again for a few minutes. Bjorn wanted to change the subject and turned to Vladimir. "Can you tell me more about the bears you were studying in Kamchatka?"

"Well, it is not just Kamchatka. We are the only country that has a bear for our national symbol. Bears are smart and wise, they are strong, and cunning. We are proud to identify with bears for our symbol."

Paul brought in still more plates with snacks and set them down in front of them. Bjorn was getting tired and woozy and wondered how long this session might go on into the night.

"You have asked us so many questions, my young friend. But why are you so interested in bears?" Vladimir turned to Bjorn.

"I don't know, I have always been interested, since I was a boy. I first loved to read about them in books. They are powerful. And warm. They seem sympathetic to me, even though they are powerful—even dangerous. I feel drawn to them. For me they symbolize, I don't know, maybe the freedom of the forest, the spirit of nature."

"Ah, those are nice words perhaps, Bjorn. But that is a small view. Bears are bigger than that. Bears are linked to the world, to the cosmos. In Russia it is among our many Siberian peoples we have the deepest understanding of bears. You need to come to Russia to properly understand this. Our peoples worshipped the Bear long before we adopted Christianity."

"Really, Bear worship?" Bjorn asked.

"Until the Christian religion tried to stop it. What a crazy religion! Those weird myths out of the desert about Moses and Jesus and Mary. They are worshiping *people*. People should not be worshipped, it is the power of Nature and its animals—that is the true power we should worship."

Paul nodded vigorously at Vladimir's words. "People who live in cities have completely lost touch with the realities of the world," he said. "That is why our people believe that keeping contact with the world of animals keeps us in touch with true reality, not the empty life of cities and television. We Haida understood this better than most peoples. Just look at our totem poles and carvings of animal spirits. This is what we perceive in the world." He passed the plate around again.

"People are stupid!" Vladimir broke in. "They flatter themselves to think that they are made in God's image! Can you imagine that! Men are newcomers on the face of the earth, why should we worship them, humans who claim to speak for God? But the animals, they are deeply linked to the soil, to creation, long before humans came. And humans, they are the devils, the source of destruction of the world. Could there ever be more clear evidence that we humans are the true devils, the destroyers?"

This kind of talk was more radical than Bjorn had ever heard before, and he was not sure how to deal with it. It was so sweeping in its vision, so disturbing in its condemnation of the world of today. Yet these ideas also unleashed further thoughts in his own mind. He sat in his chair, his brain softening from his periodic little sips of vodka, even as he grew more stimulated from the new ideas entering his head.

As Vladimir tossed back another shot of chilled vodka his face took on a wilder aspect, his eyes reddening. But he remained silent and stared at the fire.

"Let me tell you," Vladimir continued, now with a slight slur. "In the ancient days all northern peoples understood our connection to the power of Nature. When a bear was killed in a hunt, it was important that the bear be made happy, to understand why he was sacrificed. Our world will not operate properly without bears that bring wisdom and stability."

Bjorn felt he was falling asleep in front of the dancing fire but wanted to stay in the discussion. "Many of our First Nations here look to Raven too." Bjorn volunteered. "That is the creature who represents wisdom and creation."

"But this is too limited, Bjorn," Vladimir objected. "A Raven is small, intelligent yes, but he does not inspire fear and awe in us. The Raven is a trickster, you cannot trust him. He interferes with our lives, maybe in important ways. But the Bear is the true sacred symbol of power, of justice, the destroyer of evil."

"Hear hear, to the Bear," Paul said, lifting his glass.

"So, my friend, this is why Russia is happy to take up the image of the bear. *Da, da*, we have our Orthodox church with all their old gray beards and incense and chanting and interminable ceremonies. That is all part of the Christian myth and fantasy we borrowed from the deserts of the Middle East. But Russia is older than the Orthodox Church, Russia is eternal, if we look deep into our roots we recognize our true selves in our bears."

Bjorn was now succumbing to sleep, overwhelmed by this wave of new revelations and perspective and by the alcohol. He smiled inwardly in recognition that his inability to hold his liquor at least proved the reality of his First Nations origins. And he knew his attachment to bears had grown much more profound.

The next day Paul arranged to take Vladimir and Bjorn by boat three hours north to another ancient site of Skedans. The long trip in the black Zodiac exposed them to the elements, bouncing up and down over the white-tipped waves against the overcast skies and pounding Bjorn's bones as the craft rose up and then and dropped down hard into the wave troughs, heightening the sense of distance and isolation. They finally clambered out and up onto a pebbled beach and walked towards the site of the abandoned village. Bjorn felt overwhelmed with awe. "This site was abandoned over one hundred years ago," Paul told them. "That was when smallpox hit the village like a storm, causing virtually all of the villagers to die. The remaining families fled to a few northern villages to maintain the devastated community." The site was overgrown with moss and vegetation, yet the remnants of a few huge totem poles, some leaning, some fallen, gray and weather-beaten with time, still projected their animal spirits of the poles onto the site. The emanations of the past were palpable as they walked around the site in hushed awe. "The spirits are still here," Paul said. "We feel them living among our ancestors who are buried here. The spirits still work to protect us. When we had severe tsunamis here in past years the spirits came to tell us to prepare, to be ready to face the attack from the sea. The spirits watch over us and provide us with the information we need to survive the dangers of Nature which pass by. I have been warned by spirits many times, telling me to be careful about steps in my life, when a situation is safe and when it is not."

"You can communicate with the spirits?" Bjorn asked.

"They communicate with us," Paul replied. "That is how we have been able to survive for so many thousands of years, under their protection."

Bjorn was astonished at hearing him speak casually, matter-of-factly, about communications with creatures both natural and supernatural. "We could not live without them," Paul said.

I am not crazy, Bjorn thought. I know I have also felt such communications from Bears. I know they are watching over me, guiding me in some way that I cannot always understand.

Bjorn stood in silence in the grove of trees, sites of huge old longhouses dug deep into the ground, their massive fallen cedar roof-pieces lying nearby. As they took the long boat ride back to Paul's island house Bjorn felt overwhelmed, vindicated. Here was this important culture lying out one hundred kilometers from the mainland, storm-beaten in the ocean, yet maintaining one of the most vital cultures of any along the coast. They had survived for over ten thousand years, brought low only by white men's disease and their superior fire-power. And his father might have been one of the members of this remarkable people and culture! They lived with these creatures, many of them supposedly part of myth, yet they were real to the people, they had impact on people's lives, they interacted. Bjorn now felt access to a far broader spectrum of reality than he had ever experienced before. Yes, the animals did interact with people and offer knowledge.

"Tell Bjorn about the Haida story of the woman who married a bear," Vladimir prompted Paul that evening.

"We have many stories of bears in our lives," Paul replied. "But this one is well known, and to some other Native peoples along the coast as well."

Bjorn settled back among the pillows and watched as Paul told the story.

"A young woman was out picking blackberries when she slipped in some bear shit. She then cursed the Bear People. Then, as she went home she was carried away by a bear who was angry at her words. And so, after living among the Bear People for many months she fell in love with the bear and married him. She had twin children, both bear cubs. You can see them on some of our totem poles. Later on her own brothers who had been out looking for her for years finally found her. Her bear husband knew her brothers would kill him, but he was willing to sacrifice himself for her and their children."

Bjorn was astonished by the story. A woman marrying a bear! So bears and people could interact on a regular basis, the bears entering into human lives and producing bear children! They could share a world. His own feelings of communication were not just a fantasy.

"So all of our old culture, we're bringing it back," Paul said. "We lost all our stuff, our artifacts, our homes, we were almost wiped out by the white man. But we're making it, we're coming back. We've got all our grannies and aunties coming in to our language centre, and we're recording thousands of hours of stories and tales and legends and lore, before it gets lost, in our own language. Some of it is in English as well. Some people know our stories but can't speak well enough to tell them in Haida."

Bjorn was thrilled by this tale of cultural revival on Haida Gwaii. He was moved by the huge efforts of contemporary Haida to restore their language, arts, and identity. Such a project was doable! Indeed, wasn't restoration of his own identity just what Bjorn's own life was all about now?

Chapter 32

Mason wearied of jockeying for position in front of the cash bar during the happy hour reception at the Goldpark hotel where the conference was being held. He knew he needed something fairly stiff before what he feared might be a dreary opening conference dinner. He wondered whether he really should have come to the conference at all. The hotel was slightly on the seedy side and so many of the conference attendees seemed to be scruffy types, gawky eco nerds and policy wonks. The room lacked buzz. Most people around him were drinking beer. What else could he expect at a conference about bears? A whole bunch of naturalists down in the biological weeds, but probably no big picture people here. Still, it helped to build his credentials, and who knows, he might pick up a useful stray idea here or there.

He glanced at the name card on the lapel of an older man standing right next to him in the crowd pushing up to the cash bar. "Mr. Medvedev. From Russia, I see. I didn't know there were Russians at the conference."

"Vladimir Medvedev," he replied, extending his hand with a hint of a bow. "Yes, of course Russians are here, we probably know more about bears than any other country." He smiled and spread open his palms. "My country is a bear itself after all."

"What an irony we're standing here in Juneau, Alaska, on US soil," Mason observed. "If history had gone a little differently, we could well have been standing here in Juneau, Alaska on Russian soil," Mason went on as they finally got their drinks.

"Ah yes. I would have to say that was one of our bigger blunders back then, selling you Alaska, and at such a cheap price. But our incompetent Tsars were desperate for money, to pay for their losing wars." He took a swallow from his tumbler glass and Mason could tell it wasn't water, the sweet alcoholic smell of vodka was strong on his breath. "But still," Vladimir continued, "we can't complain. We still have a lot of northern ice and snow left for ourselves. And you, sir, your name card says you are from an oil company?"

"Yes, Tundra, we have world-wide interests but I'm especially looking after operations here along the Pacific coast in Canada. And at least Alaska is no longer a confrontation point between Russia and America as it was during the Cold War," Mason added. He grabbed a handful of nuts before offering the dish to Vladimir, who poked around in the bowl with his finger before taking one.

"Yes, we're all glad about that," Vladimir responded. "If the Soviet system still existed I would not likely be here as an independent scholar." He sighed."Indeed, the Soviet system had far too many disadvantages alongside its advantages."

Mason smiled. "Advantages? Pardon my asking, but from a North American perspective, we weren't aware of any advantages. It just seemed to be a harsh, oppressive and backward regime. It couldn't last." Mason was happy to have a little political edge to their conversation amid all these technical biologists and zoologists.

Vladimir was not the least fazed.

"The West of course likes to tell itself that. You all spent too much time spreading negative propaganda about the USSR. Worse, you wanted to believe it all. You were never able to look at our country objectively. Our reality was much more complicated."

"So what would you say was good about it then?" Mason probed, juggling his peanuts in his fist.

"Well, bears for a start. We had great protection program for all our wildlife—strong laws and strong environmental guardians in the forests. That began to come apart after the Soviet state collapsed…you know, capitalism does not always coexist very well with the environment."

"Yes, but with all due respect—may I call you Vladimir?—from what I know, the Soviet system created an environmental horror story itself. You didn't even need capitalism to pollute the country, you did it with good old communism, with centralized oversight and full government powers to prevent it."

Vladimir did not bat an eye. "Ah, yes, that is indeed partly true. Our leadership was often ignorant and obsessed with industrialization to surpass the West. But now, look at your own oil companies. If I may say, you are now producing the dirtiest oil in the world right next door in Canada, and putting the whole region and environment at risk."

Mason stiffened. "I actually happen to know a good bit about that, sir. Yes, there are some risks involved, but we are working with state-of-the-art technology. And we have a strong commitment to the environment as well."

"But which comes first, your profits or the environment?" Vladimir asked with a pixyish expression.

"It's not an either-or-choice, we expect to do both." Mason wondered if he should just terminate the conversation here with this guy, but felt in a feisty mood. Vladimir seemed ready to continue the sparring. "I'm glad, Mr—I'm sorry, what was it? Surrey? It is wonderful that you are rewriting the rules of capitalism and ignoring maximum profit."

"Look, Mr. Medev—I'm sorry if I'm not pronouncing it right—why do you think I'm at this conference on bears? I'm the COO of Tundra oil here. What greater evidence could there be of our commitment— my personal commitment—to producing and shipping oil cleanly? What else would I be doing here?"

"I will leave that question to you to answer, sir."

They sat down at one of the many tables for four in the lounge. Mason thought he recognized a young man approaching the table. "Do you know Bjorn Fisher?" Vladimir asked Mason.

"Ah, actually yes. Bjorn Fisher. Aren't you the young man I spoke to at the end of the public meeting in Bella Bella a month or so ago? You said you were interested in bears? And how Tundra should create a bear study centre? I'm Mason Surrey, you may recall, Tundra's COO," he said, extending his hand. "What brings you to the conference here in Juneau?"

"Bear issues, and the environment in the Great Bear Rainforest."

"And your background again?"

"I'm Canadian, First Nations background, from the Rainforest area."

"So I assume you've been part of the activism against the pipeline, then."

Bjorn was astonished at finding himself at a table next to the COO of Tundra. "Actually no…not so far," Bjorn replied cautiously. "I think it's more complicated than that."

"Well, that's good." Mason smiled. "I don't get to hear that word very much from environmentalists these days. It *is* complicated. Uncertainty in the face of complexity is the sign of an inquiring mind." He smiled.

Bjorn felt emboldened. "The bears are an important symbol of the region. Vladimir here has been helping me learn more about them, not just right here in the Rainforest, but around the whole global Arctic region." Bjorn felt encouraged to press on, while he had Mason's presence. "People think that the oil and pipeline industry doesn't know or care about these environmental issues. But I don't think it has to be that way."

"Well, young man, that's exactly right," said Mason. "That's why I'm here. The bears not only have to be protected, but the company needs to be committed to protection." He smiled broadly at Bjorn and Vladimir. He realized that his time at the table tonight might turn out to be more interesting than he had expected. "Tell me about your background."

"There's not a lot to tell. I was adopted, but like I said, I'm from First Nations background."

"What nation?"

"Heiltsuk and Haida," he affirmed.

"Well, certainly two peoples deeply involved in the environment of the area and its culture. What are you doing now?"

"I was at university earlier. I'm working as a guide in the Rainforest, and I'm studying more bear lore. I want to study some bear biology as well."

"Bjorn is very enthusiastic and committed on this subject I can say," Vladimir offered. "We've been talking about bear lore since I met him two months ago in Haida Gwaii. He says he is interested in coming to Russia to study more about bears." Bjorn didn't recall saying anything like that.

Mason perked up. "Well, you don't have to go to Russia to study bears. We're looking for young First Nations representatives who can help us understand this problem right here. And I've been meaning to get a hold of you, to talk to you more about how to help the First Nations understand the real story about what we at Tundra are doing."

"You know," Vladimir said, "frankly speaking I am uncomfortable in principle with this big corporate project. But I am encouraged that you seem to be seriously interested in bear issues related to it."

"Well, thank you for acknowledging that," Mason nodded. "Yes, we are. So Bjorn, if you have any interest in looking into a job with us on this issue, I'd be happy to talk to you more."

Bjorn struggled to conceal his astonishment. "Yes, I would, I absolutely would. But I wonder what I could do for you?"

"Well, that's to be explored. In principle you could continue your bear studies and develop a more credible voice. You could also help provide some background information on First Nations issues and their concerns over the bears and the Rainforest. Of course, I can't promise you anything right now, but if you seriously want to pursue the issue, send me a note." He handed Bjorn his card.

"Thank you." Bjorn read the card and then stuck it in his wallet.

"Stay in touch, young man…and now, if you'll both excuse me, I need to talk to a few more people here."

As Mason moved off, Vladimir beamed at Bjorn. "Well, my friend, that is a very interesting development."

Bjorn shifted in his seat. "I don't know what to say…I'm not sure I know why I told him I was interested in helping his company."

"Yes, you do, Bjorn," Vladimir smiled. "You do know why you told him that."

That night Bjorn was intrigued as he replayed in his head the new turn of events. He had only casually mentioned to Mason Surrey at the information meeting in Bella Bella that he might be willing to help advise on the project. And it was a project he fundamentally opposed. Yet here the Tundra COO had just offered him an opening for a possible job. He knew it wasn't simply his own charm that had influenced Mason. It was clear that Mason was interested in recruiting First Nations members, especially youthful ones, to promote the project among First Nations peoples—most of whom clearly opposed the project.

But what lay behind Bjorn's own sudden impulse to speak in more moderate terms about the pipeline and tanker project with the Tundra COO? Just to ingratiate himself with Mason? Vladimir had hinted at the benefits of doing so. Even Joseph many months ago had suggested that Bjorn could attain First Nations goals more effectively by working from within the company. But how? There was no way he could sustain such a pose for long. Mason would certainly sense that. But maybe it was possible Mason was actually interested in bears. Could he be influenced?

The next day around lunch time Mason was sitting alone, reading his email. He looked up and spotted Bjorn wandering into the dining room carrying a plate from the food line; he waved him over to his table.

"So, how do you find the conference so far?" Mason asked.

"A little specialized on bear biology, but I'm learning stuff."

"Yeah, there are a lot of zoologist types here. OK, Bjorn, just following up on what you were saying yesterday—tell me in your own words, why do you think there is so much opposition among First Nations to the Tundra Project?"

Bjorn sat down at the table, happy to have a chance to continue his contacts with Mason. "Well, look, it's simple, they're afraid that some catastrophe is bound to take place that will spread tremendous havoc along their coasts. They have lived off these coastal waters for ten thousand years. It could be wiped out in one bad spill."

"Do you personally believe this project automatically spells disaster for the environment?"

"Well, not necessarily…it might, but, well, I don't feel it has to." Bjorn was struggling with his pink-coloured burrito wrap trying to keep its contents from spilling out the bottom.

"Tell me about the bears. What they mean to you."

Bjorn put his burrito down for the moment. "Well, they have a powerful presence. They have been here forever. They came to North America from Russia maybe 30,000 years ago when the two continents were still connected by a land bridge. First Nations people also came across that land bridge, maybe 12,000 years ago. We—the First Nations people—believe bears possess special wisdom, they preside over the environment and defend justice. If they are hurt it suggests that bad things are coming."

"That's quite some role they're supposed to play. Have you actually seen many bears?"

"Yes. And I'm a tourist guide on boat trips to show people bears."

"Hmm, interesting. And a white Kermode bear, a spirit bear, have you seen one?"

Bjorn noted Mason pronounced the word correctly. "Yes," Bjorn lied.

"Where?"

"In the Rainforest, near Bella Bella."

"Is there a centre for the study of these bears in British Columbia right now?"

"No. We need one."

Mason seemed intent on pressing forward. "What do you know about hunting of bears in BC?"

"I think it's unacceptable, a criminal act," Bjorn replied. "All these Americans and other foreigners coming in to kill grizzly bears for trophies. And the BC government lets it happen, year after year."

Mason paused. "Well, what do you think First Nations people would think if Tundra used its political weight to try to put a stop to this killing? To show how serious we are about the environment?"

"I'm sure people would be really impressed, really enthusiastic over that. It's an issue that means a lot to us."

"Hmm, why don't you check around in the next few weeks and see what kind of attitudes you can pick up among the First Nations people here along the coast. I'd be very interested in knowing."

Mason's mind raced ahead as he considered the impact of Tundra buying into the whole of First Nations bear narratives. "Tundra could possibly be instrumental in putting some real money into a bear study centre. And support First Nations art related to bears. Maybe commissioning a totem pole for the company, and some bear images and masks for a centre on bear arts."

Bjorn was surprised that Tundra's COO seemed so willing to talk about these important policy issues with him. But he decided to avoid looking too humble himself. "OK, Mr. Surrey, but you know the poles and the statues aren't meant to be 'art' in a museum, right? They're functional. They do things, they tell stories, they remind us of identities, they call upon certain spirits from nature. They are *supposed* to stand out in the sun and rain and snow, even gradually deteriorate. That's where they are in touch with nature, where they have their power, not inside somewhere. They're not dead. The tradition is a living one."

"Well, you certainly seem to have picked up a good bit about all this. Where have you learned about this mostly?" Mason asked.

"Just being around, it's part of our tradition." He knew he was exaggerating his own knowledge here. "And I've learned a lot from Vladimir Medvedev. He has incredible knowledge of bear lore from Siberia."

"Oh yeah? Tell me about this Medvedev guy. I thought he might be a little flaky."

"No, he's not really. He has an amazing wealth of knowledge. You should talk to him more."

"OK, tonight looks like a slow night at the conference. Maybe if you guys are free for dinner we can continue the discussion."

Bjorn left the conversation walking on air. Here he was talking privately with the COO, and even seemed to have his ear. Events were moving in a direction he could hardly believe. He was sure Vladimir's perspectives could have impact on Mason too.

And Mason found new ideas spinning in his own mind. What if Tundra offered to establish and fund a major bear research centre somewhere in the Rainforest region? And to use its powerful political weight in BC politics to team up with the environmentalists to stop the grizzly hunting in BC? It could be a spectacular coup and would surely win immense amounts of goodwill among First Nations peoples and environmentalists, remove the bad guy image from the company. Mason needed to demonstrate a broad vision of the bear issue to be credible. And this kid Bjorn was attractive, young, idealistic, a useful figure to feature in Tundra's plans for bear research.

Chapter 33

That evening Mason took Bjorn and Vladimir out to one of the better restaurants in Juneau with a view out over the harbour. They were joined by a thin young man whom Mason had also invited along, Evan Muskee, a young American bear scientist from Washington State whom Mason had met during a conference session. "I thought you would all enjoy meeting each other," he commented. "We all like bears."

Vladimir did not shake hands, but bowed stiffly to Evan. As they sat down, he immediately asked the waiter to bring him a double straight vodka, cold, before the others had ordered anything to drink. "Right now, please," he instructed the waiter.

Mason looked at Vladimir with amusement. "I guess it's true what they say about Russians and their vodka," he laughed.

"In a country where life can be cold and rough, we know what to do to stay warm and happy."

"Bjorn tells me you've had a lot to do with bears in your country."

"Yes, I have worked with them all my life. I probably know more about bears' behavior than anyone else."

Mason glanced over at Evan who sat quietly, looking Vladimir over. "Well, OK, that's impressive I guess," Mason said. "What is it that interests you in them?"

The waiter brought the others their drinks, white wine for Mason, beers for Bjorn and Evan.

"Bears are masters of the world, the source of wisdom."

"That's an interesting view," Evan commented, "but it doesn't sound very scientifically based."

"Scientific? This is bigger and more important than mere science. We are talking about ancient forces in the world." He paused, looked at them, and took a long gulp from his glass. "You perhaps are thinking more about bears as you know them from zoos and laboratories." He signaled to the waiter to bring him another.

"No, not just laboratories," Evan replied. "But I'm not sure I'm ready to see anything deeply philosophical in them either," Evan continued. "They're an interesting animal species, among many."

"Then that is your blindness," Vladimir rejoined. "Philosophy, as you call it, or native wisdom, is more profound than just zoological information. It affects our societies, how we see things. Laboratories can't tell us that. For us Russians, bears are sacred. They are our national symbol. But more than that, for many of our aboriginal peoples, especially in northern Siberia, they are an object of worship."

"Perhaps, Vladimir," Mason intervened, "you might tell us a little bit more about why you see bears in a philosophical light."

"Gladly. If you will permit, let me tell you about the bear ceremony that we have in northern Russia. You will learn about how the bear fits into the way of the universe." And, his tongue, limbered up by further shots of vodka, launched him into a story that he seemed close to his heart.

"Let me tell you of my trip, to quite another world in our mixture of peoples on our Russian soil. A trip to a world where bears and humans come together in a bloody ceremony of sacrifice, redemption, and salvation."

Evan maintained a faintly indulgent smile on his face as he listened to Vladimir hold forth.

"I was only a very young man, finding my way in the world of Soviet anthropology. It is in the Russian north, near Lapland, where the people there have worshipped bears for thousands of years. The ceremony was an astonishing thing to watch, but also disturbing. The story may open new doors for you."

Mason exchanged amused glances with Evan, while Bjorn seemed transfixed by Vladimir's presence and passion.

"These people, they call themselves Sami, they are distantly related to Finns and branches of them live all across northern Scandinavia and Russia. The Sami in Russia are very old and very isolated. You know, the Sami say that the bear comes from the heavens. They say he is the son of God in the heavens. He comes down to earth—yes, just like Jesus—to live among us and to be sacrificed and to rise up again into the heavens before his next visit."

"Yes," Evan said, "I have actually heard some of these ancient stories. They are common to many aboriginal peoples."

"Well," Vladimir continued, "you should be aware then that for many of these peoples the bear was so sacred that they do not even dare to speak the word "bear." They choose another word instead to indirectly represent a bear."

"That is like Jews who do not dare to even say the name of God," Mason observed. "They use other words."

"Exactly. And that is why there are so many dozens of words for bear in Russian, and in Finnish languages. Even in Russian we gave up our old word for bear—we now say "medved"—"honey eater.""

"But that's like your name!" exclaimed Bjorn.

"Yes, indeed it is. Isn't that strange that I was born into that family name? It is a common one, but still, it maybe determined my future."

Bjorn thought about the parallel to himself as well.

"So you studied all this in university in Russia?" Evan asked.

"University? No, I traveled to the area, on my own. I lived there for two years. I did field research, not just sitting in libraries and laboratories like so many scientists."

Evan frowned. "Some of us find that academic research can also teach us something as well."

"Well, in any case, I was young, and I remember how in summer the tundra was still lush and green and covered with wild-flowers. A friend from the Anthropological Institute in Leningrad—now, thank God, we call it St. Petersburg again—had brought me to her home village among the aboriginal peoples of eastern Siberia. It was to be one of the major events of my life, the images still deep in my mind."

"How long were you with these people?" asked Mason.

"Two years. I have written a book, the only comprehensive book on the subject...a pity you can't read Russian, it's a major scientific language.

"Anyway," Vladimir continued, "there was a young man in the village, named Bogdan. They told me he had gone into the forest in early spring to stay for several days by himself alone before he returned home to his village. He was especially chosen for the sacred task of finding two bear cubs. He was just a plain village boy, dressed in a brown wool cloak and leather shoes from the village made from the skin of caribou. Some called him naïve or simple-minded but no one could dislike him. Others understood that his skills with bears were a supreme gift, given by God. That is what his name, Bogdan, means in Slavic languages.

"Bogdan showed me a picture taken at that time, when he came out of the woods. He had in his arms two small bear cubs. Their eyes had probably been open only a few days. He set them down on the ground in a large barnyard where they would stay until the following summer. They looked scared, but Bogdan reassured them with calm words and stroked them. He taught the bears how to drink caribou milk from a bowl. He visited them several times a day to increase their familiarity with humans. With time he brought them food from his own table— meat from caribou he had killed for his family. And potatoes and carrots from their own garden.

"He let them out into a larger enclosure where they could play in the fresh air in view of the forest, roll in the grass and then sleep in the sun.

"The people from the village came by often when the bears were playing outside to see them and exclaim over their beauty and to pat them for good luck. They even held their children over the fence to rub their shiny fur."

"You saw all this?" Mason asked.

"*Da, Da*, I was there, taking notes for my book. I talked with the villagers and with Bogdan about this often. Anyway, the cubs grew in size. They had grown fearless of humans. On certain days I saw Bogdan take them out with ropes around their necks to go for a walk around the village so people could see them. The bears would often walk on their back legs, 'just like us,' everyone said, laughing. And people would try to give them treats, for good luck. At night the young bears would go back into their enclosure for safety. You know there are rogue bears around who could sense these bears no longer smelled like the forest, and they would kill them."

"So why were these people doing all this?" Mason asked.

"Well, it was his special mission on behalf of the village. Bogdan was respected and honoured in the village for carrying out this task that was so important to the welfare of the village and its future. The village shaman had especially chosen him. Bogdan was known for his gentle nature and purity of heart and commitment to this sacred contact with the bear world. They called him "he who communicates with bears.""

"Well, if we are in for a long story here," Mason interrupted, "we better order some food first." After the waiter took their order Mason continued. "So, this Bogdan was responsible for bringing up the bears, as you were saying."

"Yes, he treated them with love, he wanted them to be healthy, with good eyes, with no scars from fighting in the forest. They got fat, an image of bear perfection. They always came when Bogdan called them, they knew they would get some treat. Bears may not often bond with humans, but they bonded with Bogdan."

Vladimir was now into his third tumbler of vodka.

"And then, during the following spring months young women came out and danced around the bears, singing songs of the power of the bear. But they never addressed the bears by name. It is improper to give names to these bears because it would make them individual bears. You see, they are not individual bears. They represent the whole of the Bear People in creation."

Vladimir, now flushed, leaned over the table and said, "You will forgive me for mentioning about sex here. But it is important—about the ties between people and the bear world. People in the village, they said the women have a special relationship to the bears. I heard people sometimes say that women give the bear cubs their breasts to suck their milk, that it was an honour."

Evan raised his eyebrows.

Vladimir raised his finger in the air. "Yes, seriously, the women want the bear! In their village stories they say they are happy to fuck with the bears, they joke that the bear is better than their husbands!"

"Well, I really don't think we need to…" Evan began to show clear distaste, but Vladimir plunged on. "I am not inventing these stories! Listen to the tales of the aboriginal peoples. So many stories about children who have a bear father and human mother. So the people also believe young women must stay away from the bears to avoid becoming pregnant…maybe they are attracted to bears' large equipment." He gave Bjorn a wink, who blushed.

"OK, Vladimir," Mason said, "we get the idea. The bears obviously mean a lot in this culture."

"But that's amazing!" Bjorn said. "That is just like here among the First Nations, they all have a story of a woman who went off and married a bear and had children from him."

"Yes, many northern peoples have a legend of a young woman who marries a bear. There is also a myth that when the first woman became a lover of a bear, women were given menstruation in punishment."

Mason laughed. "Vladimir, I don't know what kind of an animal researcher you are, you seem pretty fascinated with all these sexual aspects."

"Perhaps that's enough anthropology for one evening," Evan said, looking around the room.

"No, please listen," Vladimir interjected. "The most important thing of the story comes now. At the end of the second summer is the time of the bear ceremony. Everybody prepared special foods to give to the bears, even pots of honey. The bears were getting very fat. The shaman went to consult the Spirits and then he announced the exact day of the ceremony. When the day came Bogdan and a few selected young men and women dressed in their own embroidered shirts and aprons and all came to the bears' home. They called the bears outside. The bears were so used to being handled that they allowed the women to dress them in shirts and pants made with nature symbols from the forest, especially for the occasion."

"The final feast was ready. Roasted meats and bowls of reindeer milk were brought and placed in front of the bears. When the bears had eaten, the young men and women sang more songs to the bears and danced around them. They told the bears that they are a joy to the people's lives. And they told the bears how they now feel deep sorrow, for the time has come to part with them so the bears may finally travel back up to heaven to be reunited with their Father."

"You saw all this?"

"Yes! I watched as the bears were brought out into the town square where they were surrounded by the townspeople all singing their bear song. Special archers were chosen from the village for the privilege of delivering the bears to heaven from their last moments on this earth. They fitted sharp arrows decorated with special streamers into their bows. They spoke a special prayer and took aim. They fired arrow after arrow into the bears as fast as they could until ninety-nine arrows had been fired! It was painful to watch. The bears staggered and fell, blood running from their mouths. And then they lay silent. The people were silent too. It was a moment of sadness, even grief at what they had done. But they knew they had done what they must do."

"Sounds pretty grisly to me, no pun intended," Mason commented.

"No, this is not about blood. This was a moment of truth and redemption. They knew the bears were now on their way back to their Father in heaven; they will tell their Father what happened in their lives on this earth, how they were loved, respected, well-treated, well-fed, worshipped until the moment came for their journey to the sky to rejoin their Father."

"OK, we get it," Evan said in considerable impatience with Vladimir's long narration, "that's quite a tale. But it belongs in anthropology books or mythology, not science."

"There you are wrong, my dear Evan," Vladimir responded. "What can zoology tell us about the place of the bear in the world, in the cosmos? What does it teach us about the meaning of the bear in peoples' lives?"

"Yes, that's just the point," Evan responded. Bjorn noticed that Evan never addressed Vladimir by name. "Science is not interested in all this mumbo-jumbo about God and spirits and going to heaven. We're interested in how the bears live, mate, survive, how they interact with the environment."

Bjorn was still under the spell of Vladimir's tale. "Well, so after the ceremony, what happened with the bears' bodies?" he asked. "Did they bury them? Burn them?"

"No, the ceremony of honouring the bears means the people must eat the flesh and the blood of the bears whose spirits have gone back to their Father. This is the central moment of the ceremony. The bears have just begun their journey back home. They will only be there for a short time before they return to this world again the following year. It is dangerous for the people if the bears should be angry about their treatment and give a bad report to their Father for then they might not return again. And that would be a disaster for the people because the hunters depend upon them for their lives, food and clothing. And the world needs the bears to bring wisdom and order and justice."

"And the shaman?" Mason asked.

"Here is where the shaman has a major role. He uses a ritual knife to cut up the dead bears by a special procedure. The men save the blood and drink it to give them strength and to share in the common blood with the Bear People. And the meat of the bear is distributed out among all the people, every single one of them in the village must take a piece to eat and celebrate, consuming it over several days."

"Christ," Evan burst in. "This is goddam cave-man stuff! I don't know how come you all in Russia allow all this primitive stuff to go on. Maybe that's what's wrong with your country!" He folded up his napkin and threw it on the table.

"No!" burst out Bjorn. "This is really important!"

"So all right, Vladimir, let's get to the end," Mason urged.

"OK, I finish. But you should pay attention because this is important. The bears' carcasses have to be treated with great honour. No drop of blood must be spilled, not one piece of meat wasted or allowed to fall to the ground. That would dishonour the bears and those making the sacrifice. When the feasting is finally done, the people take all the bones that they have saved, every single one, and make sure that they are all carefully arranged and the clean skeleton put back together again, into the bear shape. Then they take the bears' skulls and carry them up into a high tree where they nail them to the trunk from where the bears will look out. Their eye sockets are deep and wide, able to survey the wide world. The eye sockets reach deep into the back of the skull where insight and wisdom live. This skull and its bones have now become part of the universal bear."

Bjorn was struck now in remembering the lone bear skull he had found by the stream in the forest. Maybe it was there as the result of some ancient bear worship ritual?

"Alright, Mr. Medev, I've heard quite enough of this," Evan said.

"Medvedev," said Mason.

"Sure, whatever. God knows what happens off in these primitive places. Your little anthropological tale may amuse some people. But folklore doesn't make for science. Have you, sir, ever in your life done any hard science on bears? Have you ever been in a laboratory, have you taken DNA samples on bear fur, studied their habitats, their diet, analyzed their feces? Do you have information on the impact of salmon runs on their diet and welfare? Do you know anything about how environmental change is affecting them? That's what a real scientist does, not hanging around in villages watching women have sex with bears and worshipping them up in heaven!"

Vladimir remained silent for a moment, and simply glared at Evan. "You are a typical American scientist, totally materialist, technical, narrow in your views. You look at the world through a tiny microscope. Aboriginal peoples look at the world through a huge lens. They are interested in the big meaning of bears to human life!"

"Yes, that is what science is, Mr. Medev. We're not interested in the grand world and the cosmos, we're interested in how bears live and survive. I'm sorry to say that if that is what passes for science in Russia, no wonder your environment is going to hell."

"OK," Mason said, "let's not get personal about this. They're different perspectives."

Bjorn nodded vigorously, relieved that Mason was not taking Evan's side in this discussion.

"What do you mean, different perspectives!" Evan rejoined. "Mr. Surrey, if you are interested in Tundra setting up some bear research centre, you better be realistic about what you are going to do. Some of us could possibly be interested in coming to a research centre for a sabbatical in the Great Bear Rainforest. But I'm sure as hell not coming if you are going to spend time listening to these so-called scientists and their drunken spiritual mumbo jumbo about bear spirits."

Bjorn had been thrilled by Vladimir's tale. He saw more deeply now that bears did possess grander perspectives, the combined wisdom of hundreds of thousands of years. He was glad Mason showed respect for the story.

Vladimir did not let Evan's remarks go unchallenged. "You are a typical ignorant westerner who knows nothing but so-called "scientific facts." The way we think about our environment, the respect we have for it, the interrelationship of all animals and creatures and what they teach us—that is the science that we need, to keep the world from falling apart." He turned to Mason. "Studying the DNA of bear fur, like this so-called bear specialist wants to do, will teach us nothing about our planet and how we think about our place in it."

"Well, I'm sorry, Mason," Evan said, "but I've had about enough of this bullshit from your guest. You better do some hard thinking before you start setting up your Tundra whatever it is. Thanks for the dinner." And Evan rose and walked away from the table.

"Vladimir, I'm afraid you've broken up the party. Your stories are interesting. But Evan is right, they have nothing to do with science. I'm sorry we had to get into a quarrel here, but you've obviously got a different perspective. Still I do have to say, over the years I have learned that it isn't all just about science either. It's about vision. So anyway, I think you've delivered your message tonight. Let's call it a night. But Bjorn, stay in touch."

Vladimir, without saying anything, departed the dining room on his own.

As Bjorn reviewed the evening in his mind that night, the events unfolded before his own eyes like a tableau, as if he had personally witnessed the details of the village drama himself. The more he thought about it, the more the emotional, psychological, and spiritual impact of the story overwhelmed him.

This was not just about preserving wonderful wild creatures in the forest. It was way bigger than just the Great Bear Rainforest. Bjorn could see how the bears had died for the People, they had gone to Heaven to be with their Father. It was almost like the Bible stories he had heard when he went to church with his family as a boy. *Were the bears like Jesus? Sacrificing themselves for the People? And to come back again? To bring a greater message about how everything is interconnected?*

Would I sacrifice myself?

The next morning, before they went their separate ways at the end of the conference, Bjorn told Vladimir of his feelings. "I want to thank you, you have opened my eyes to a bigger picture."

"Yes, Bjorn, there is a bigger picture. Your First Nations background is a precious legacy. All these aboriginal peoples who crossed out of Eurasia, they had absorbed bear wisdom for tens of thousands of years and brought this wisdom across into North America with them."

"I can see that now," Bjorn responded. "Maybe we are seeing a great struggle—-between the Bear People and the Human People, over where the earth is going."

That night in his hotel room Bjorn suddenly felt overwhelmed with fatigue. He trembled with emotional tension from these new revelations. It wasn't just a matter of helping preserve bears in the Rainforest. It was a much greater struggle in which the future of the world lay in the balance. He now understood he was part of a far older tradition than he had ever dreamed. Heiltsuk or Haida, it did not matter in the face of this great Eurasian First Nations tradition. Maybe he had at last discovered his place.

I am coming. I am closer. You can feel me. You know the evil that threatens our lands and the Bear People.

"I hear you," Bjorn thought. "I will be ready."

Chapter 34

Bjorn was surprised at how quickly Mason Surrey followed up on his interest to stay in touch with him after their conversations at the bear conference in Juneau. He was even more flattered at Mason's proposition that Bjorn accompany him as a guide to some locations in the Great Bear Rainforest in the near future. Mason mentioned he wanted to get a feel for the Rainforest through personal experience, check it out for some iconic scenes, maybe even some shots of bears fishing at the falls in their natural habitat. "Can you plan me a short trip, maybe three days, sort of my first excursion into the area? We can talk about how all this might fit in with the establishment of a bear research centre in the Rainforest."

"Definitely," Bjorn immediately assured him. But Bjorn also had no clear idea about how he would manage this situation.

Mason flew Bjorn to Calgary to discuss the trip and to get Bjorn's suggestions on First Nations' aspects. He detailed to Bjorn more about his thoughts to embrace the Great Bear Rainforest project. "My predecessors all saw the environmentalists as the enemy—"tree huggers" as they called them—people who were working against the interests of the company. This strikes me as a narrow and unenlightened perspective. There is no reason why this can't be a win-win situation here. I hope I can make that clear through sponsorship of a serious bear research centre."

Bjorn was excited to be included in some of Mason's planning ideas and was impressed with Mason's seriousness about the bears. "If the bears are preserved and respected I think a lot of people along the coast could be supportive of Tundra. New emphasis on green tourism, respect for the environment—a lot of our people know there's more of a future in bear tourism than in killing them."

This was the first time Mason had an opportunity to bounce some of this thinking off a younger generation coastal Native and was pleased to see Bjorn's cautious optimism and interest in the idea. He liked Bjorn. He was sincere, idealistic, passionate, qualities he found missing in his own children.

"You know," Mason continued, "I'm just convinced that enlightened energy development does not have to be at war with the environment. Believe me, when I was in Nigeria I saw how badly the local people were exploited, how badly the situation was handled, and how quickly it spun out of control. But here I really think it can be different. And furthermore, Bjorn, I like your strong personal attachment to bears. Vladimir is sort of a crazy old guy, but you know, he does see something here, the cultural symbolism. He has that broader perspective, almost global or mythical view of bears that impressed me, aspects I'd never thought about before. And certainly nobody in our company has a clue about. But still, I've got to sell it to my headquarters in Toronto. And frankly it's a hard sell."

Bjorn had never anticipated that his relationship with the COO could ever evolve in this direction. But as he lay in bed that night at the hotel where he was staying his thoughts began stirring in uncomfortable directions. He felt demons arising in his mind in keeping with the blinking neon cabaret sign across the street, that insinuated shifting pulses of red into his room through the blinds. His thoughts gained velocity, taking possession of his mind, effectively obliterating sleep for much of the night as his brain spun out the potential options of events before him. On the one hand he felt a growing warmth towards Mason, flattered to be the object of his attention and even confidence. He felt that Mason really liked him, took an almost paternal interest in him. Bjorn felt he had already had some influence upon him, and he might even have more down the road.

Mason had offered what for Bjorn was a generous fee of $10,000 to accompany him on the trip. Yet Bjorn could not quite quell the idea that he might be compromising himself on a project that had a lot of downsides as well.

And how had it come to pass that Bjorn, of all people, might now be about to find himself alone working with the Tundra COO in a remote forested wilderness?

The next morning over coffee Bjorn told Mason that he found a lot of appeal in Mason's approach but he wanted a few days to think about it the trip. "Sure," Mason said. "I'm not sure what more there is to think about, but if you want a day or two, get back to me soon please."

"I'll be in touch," Bjorn replied. And he went back to Bella Bella, but not before contacting Vladimir about the whole proposition.

"Fascinating!" Vladimir listened attentively as Bjorn recounted the whole story of his meetings with Mason and the offer he had made to Bjorn to accompany him to the Rainforest.

"Remarkable!" he added, as Bjorn finished his story. "You will go, of course. This is too good a chance to miss."

"You mean to get in closer with Mason and the project?" Bjorn asked.

"Yes, of course…and who knows what might happen in the Rainforest."

Bjorn paused. "What do you mean, 'What might happen'?"

"I'm just pointing out that a great deal of power has just shifted into your hands. You have multiple opportunities, ways to influence Mason."

The cryptic and leading nature of Vladimir's comments disturbed Bjorn. And he felt angry with himself as well, precisely because Vladimir had pinpointed something specific that earlier had only been a dark and vagrant thought in his own mind a few nights earlier.

The next day he pressed Vladimir about the implications of what he had said. "I'm not implying anything," Vladimir said. "I'm only raising possibilities, paths of action for you as you think about your future relationship to this oil project. You could, among other things, ingratiate yourself more deeply with Mason, maybe end up in an influential position within the corporation on bear issues. How many

First Nations young people are in a position to influence a COO of a major corporation?"

"I guess that's true."

"Do you know, by the way, what it means in English when people say someone has gone berserk?"

"Sure, crazy, dangerous, running wild, maybe deranged."

"Yes but do you know the origin of the word? It has to do with bears." Vladimir waited for Bjorn to take the bait.

"What about bears?"

"The word comes from the old Anglo-Saxon language—you know, early German legends, like Beowulf. The old Viking warriors would put on a "bear shirt," it was *ber-sark* in the old Germanic—*sark* meant a shirt. When the warriors put on this shirt, they would acquire all the powers of a bear, and be unstoppable in battle. They would run ferociously and fearlessly at the enemy, knowing the *ber-sark* would protect them against anything, and give them supernatural strength. The enemy was truly afraid when they saw the Viking warriors running at them in bear-skins…and then the Vikings swung their stone axes…"

Bjorn departed that afternoon, his mind buzzing. At one point he contemplated begging off on the trip with Mason entirely. And darker thoughts entered his mind that ended his sleep for the night.

Alone with Mason, deep in the forest? Could he influence him? His stomach crawled as he thought about the implications of the impending trip. How should he act?

"I can't believe this, Bjorn!" Joseph had said when Bjorn had recounted the details of the trip. "It's amazing you've managed to get that close to this guy."

"Yeah, I think he likes me."

"Don't let it flatter you. He's fucking buying you, man, pure and simple. He's the devil. He's here to tempt you with money, with a job, with influence, with power. He's trying to corrupt you. And he seems to be doing a pretty good job of it I might add."

"Well, fuck you, Joseph. He's not totally cynical. I mean, I think he partly wants to do the right thing. I think he really is personally interested in the bears. He has environmental concerns going way back in his life."

"Oh come on, Bjorn. Wise up! He wants to exploit images of cuddly bears to help sell his project. Even if he does put money into a bear centre, what do you think is going to happen to the fucking bears—and salmon and all the other wildlife— when one of these goddam tankers goes down! And mark my words, it will!"

"Maybe I can have some influence over him on all this."

"Influence! Don't be naive! He's a big oil exec. He may love bears to death. But his bottom line is to bring the goddam oil over the mountains to the coast. And then ship it through our Rainforest. Nothing's going to change that."

"Well, I'm confused, Joseph! I don't know what to do!" Bjorn cried.

"Look, you can walk away is one big option. On the other hand…"

"On the other hand what?"

"Well, getting closer to Mason does gives you a lot of options, your chance to figure out what's going on in the company, maybe influence him, change things. Who knows. Just keep your eyes open. Don't let him buy you, man."

In his enthusiasm Bjorn called his mother to give her the news about his planned trip with Mason. "He's the COO Mom, and he wants me to personally accompany him for a short trip into the Rainforest. I can't believe it!"

"Bjorn, that's wonderful. You've really moved ahead in your life. He sounds like a really valuable contact who could change your life."

"Yeah, that's true. Except I worry that maybe I'm compromising my principles, in helping out the one company that could be bringing real damage to the Rainforest."

"Look, you don't have to compromise. Just use this opportunity to give him the best advice you can. I'm sure a savvy COO will understand the environmental aspects of this oil project, you might be doing some real good for the cause. I'm excited for you."

"Thanks, Mom. It is a big opportunity. We'll see what comes of it."

Mason contacted Bjorn by phone two days later. "I hope you are you still up for this trip. I'm really looking forward to it. I'm also thinking I should take along a hunter as well, just for safety in the forest."

"Yeah, I'm definitely up for the trip. But I recommend we not take any armed hunter along with us."

Mason lifted an eyebrow. "Oh? Even for security? Why not?"

"Because you can spook the bears with too many people. And from all you've told me about your project ideas, the last thing you need is to be in a situation where you kill a bear there. And besides, there's a belief, a superstition…"

"What superstition?"

"That you need to encounter the bear on his own terms. Coming in armed, like it just sets up the wrong relationship. All the wrong vibes. It means you're already preparing for a hostile encounter," Bjorn answered quietly.

Mason paused to reflect for another few seconds, contemplating Bjorn's suggestion. "I'd like you to have the full experience," Bjorn said, "and not just a tourist view of the area. To appreciate how magnificent it is."

Oh, the bear came over the mountain, to see what he could see. And the oil spilt into the ocean was all that he could see.

Chapter 35

Nature had never approved of the enterprise but it had bided its time in responding. It lay in wait, gathering its forces for a grand convergence of wind, tide, locale and circumstance to launch its long-planned assault. It patiently tolerated human efforts, and indulged their technological delusions and naive self-confidence and pretenses to mastery of the challenges of navigation through the jagged and labyrinthine coast of the Pacific Northwest. The unbridled waters in all their wild, wayward and untamable complexity simply lay in waiting.

Shipping tar sands oil from a Pacific coast terminal had been a running and bitterly contentious issue on Mason's platter. It was above all a lightning rod for environmental activists. He was assaulted by conflicting expertise from tanker specialists, maritime specialists, weather and oceanic specialists, biologists, chemists, environmentalists, and politicians with dollar signs in their eyes. Mason could master none of these areas of expertise on his own, yet he was called upon to respond to challenges and questions on all of them and orchestrate some kind of response. The problem lay on his mind for months on end. The more he sought to learn more about each of these areas of expertise, the more his original certainties were shaken. He was assured constantly by the experts that studies decisively demonstrated what low levels of risks were involved with the use of modern technology. He also knew enough about "experts," in any field, to entertain doubts in his own mind.

Mason had also grown weary of attempting to defend the project on his home turf. He was invariably cast as the heavy, the grasping capitalist who "didn't give a shit about the environment" as his daughter put it. Nor did it leave him alone in bed at night as he wrestled with his own conscience and sense of judgment. How could he project certitude as COO about the project as long as he entertained personal doubts about the judgment of experts on the potential risks waiting to happen?

And tonight Mason found himself standing alone high on a windswept cliff overlooking one of the great finger fjords of the Rainforest. Though it was dark and wet he had an unobstructed view of the shipping lane channel below. He was buffeted by freezing cold winds that penetrated his light clothing. Dark clouds and swirling mists sometimes swept in around him temporarily blocking clear vision. But now an aperture had suddenly opened beneath him enabling him to witness events down in the storm below. He felt himself suspended in the air almost like a bird with panoptic vision above what he now perceived to be a massive ship's deck. The deck was seized with turmoil—shouting, chaos, fear, agony.

It was the night of the super-tanker. A vessel of three hundred thousand tons, longer than the Empire State Building is high, carrying two million barrels of oil, eight times the amount of oil spilled in the disastrous Exxon Valdez spill in Alaska in 1989. "Well-engineered, seaworthy and safe" were the commercial bywords applied to the vessel; indeed such vessels always are, until tested against the realities of a vengeful sea. And the tanker now groaned under the massive load of the world's dirtiest oil, piped across all of British Columbia to the Pacific coast, some 1800 kilometers from the tar sands of Alberta. And he was witness this night, soaring high, to a ship's encounter with the fullness of unbridled marine fury.

When the moment came, the sound was terrifying, overwhelming, unmistakable, unforgettable—the searing sound of massive forces colliding and grinding together as hundreds of thousands of tons of man-made raw moving steel met unyielding, timeless, immovable rock along the edge of the channel.

The familiar rhythmic pulse of the vast craft's engines turning over in calmer waters suddenly vectored into high whine as engines and their masters desperately sought to avoid, then disengage from the looming reality of the long-feared encounter—human engineering versus Nature: tons of moving steel suddenly immobilized, creaking, groaning, listing in collision with ancient rock. A darkness fell over the wounded leviathan as initial power on ship-board failed; emergency lights flickered on desperately trying to illuminate the dimensions of the cataclysm. More metallic screeching as men tried to disengage their metal creation from Earth's primal rock. But Nature's material mocked naval steel. Plates, engineered never to be torn asunder, yielded meekly to superior force. Human voices bellowed in animal panic, trying to grasp the dimensions of catastrophe.

Meanwhile the inert, black load sloshed within the ship's steel belly in sullen anticipation. It had only been recently that intrusive steel and diamond drills on the earth's surface had probed, plunged, reared, mounted and raped the stone caverns deep below the earth wherein this substance had so long lain. It had been perhaps only weeks since it had been harshly sucked up out of its billion-year lair and discharged out into waiting tanks on the earth's surface; its natural viscosity was dosed with chemical additives to enable it to slip more easily along the thousand kilometers of steel pipe down to the sea. It was then readied for transport onto tankers to haul it long distances for ultimate delivery and ingestion into the maw of industry, yielding up its latent energy to man's purposes.

For the moment, however, the black oil, trapped within humanly-certified impenetrable hulls, awaited its moment of liberation from confinement. The substance readied itself for release back into the natural medium it had once been so familiar with aeons ago: the timeless salt water of the oceans. Geological memory recalled earlier aeons when sea and forms of proto-life cells had commingled on the sea bottom. And then inexorable tectonic plates thrust the ancient subterranean lagoons of the black liquid closer to the earth's surface, still bearing its precious elements of primeval decomposed sea life trapped in underground caverns.

And now the ferocious wrenching apart of the steel plates heralded the black liquid's moment of liberation; its escape from its steel cocoon was now at hand. The cold north Pacific waters eagerly sluiced into the exposed cavity of the dying steel monster, readily facilitating the escape of the black tar bitumen back into its ancient marine environment. But the bitumen had no need to move quickly, the laws of physics were now firmly on its side. The black substance contained enough weight and gravity to maintain its own sinuous, unctuous unstoppable ooze out of man's steel plates and into union with the native sea water.

The massive tanker, the blue whale of the maritime world, had pressed the limits of the structural and navigational boundaries; it now lay mortally wounded, wallowing helplessly in the restless sea, each wave motion opening and reopening the gash in its steel flesh over and over again with each rolling list against the rocks.

The wounded steel beast could no longer withstand the power of the waves as seawater penetrated ever deeper into its body. Soon, with an almost human groan and a bellowing of seawater, oil, steam and air in rapid interchange, the hulk began its final descent, hull now rearing obscenely out of the water, propeller blades impotent, readying itself for the final shuddering slide into the depths.

The drama on the surface that Mason was witnessing, suspended from above and drenched and pummeled in the elements, now shifted to below the waves.

The flow of the black poison was slow but inexorable as the bitumen—silent, seeping, deadly—groped its way along rocky bottom and consigned itself to drift, shift, rise and fall with the cresting waves. Soon it would be able to broadcast its presence along large areas of the coast, to endow rocky outcrops and stony bays with a lustrous and glistening jet black sheen. If it were not such an obscene violation of Nature to find this ancient product of the earth, in virtually its original form, re-mixing with the ocean, the mother element of the globe—it could almost be perceived as beautiful: a stunning jet blackness highlighted against the still untouched white beach—an abstract study of contrasting colours and textures.

Within hours the continually accumulating body of leaking bitumen and toxicity—tens of thousands of swimming pools worth—would float to the surface in all its thick ebony blackness. Over the hours and days it would gradually dilute, spreading through the motion of wind and water to create a thin film of great carrying power, a perceptible sheen vivid to the eye in smoother waters. As dawn rose, the bitumen's dark brooding presence could be noted from the air in differing rainbow hues of spilled petroleum—greens, reds and browns.

The full palette of colours would be vividly evident to birds aloft, even if they failed to grasp its mortal threat. Their feathers, created waterproof, served now as sponges for even the thinnest slick of oil, absorbing weight into their feather-bulk, causing them to lose buoyancy and their thermal insulation against the frigid waters. The black chemical coating would eventually draw them slowly, struggling and helpless, beneath the waves forever.

Few creatures of any kind could sense the danger until it was too late. And where the petroleum had been rocked and tossed, windblown and whipped by the wave motion in shallower inlets, it would take on the character of a thick pudding, what oil specialists euphemistically chose to call "mousse." Much of it would soon sink to probable irrecoverability on the ocean floor where it would work its lethal chemical interactions upon everything it touched for decades to come—affecting sea beds, clams, oysters, crabs, water fowl, and the grand food chain of innumerable fish, mammal, and marine life.

While the great whales may have been protected by their distance from the coast, smaller mammals closer in such as dolphins found their skin coated, the toxic substance ingested through their blow holes and their mouths to eventually poison their bodies.

Small creatures inhabiting sandy beach inlets and coves faced total holocaust as wide habitats were wiped out. The life within living coral reefs too was snuffed out. Eggs and larval organisms attached to rocks, grasses and other spawning grounds were immediately seared, eliminating a generation or more of a given species with incalculable cascading effects upon the food chain over the decades.

The land and the sea knew. The peoples of the land and the sea knew. There is no land, no sea, nothing that humans will ever leave alone as sacred. No bounty of nature is granted protection from the maw of human thirst for energy. Even the magnificence of the Great Bear Rainforest, one of the jewels of our blue planet, seemed to pose no serious barrier to the insatiable process of sucking up, processing, producing, selling and consuming the dirtiest oil on the planet.

The oil spread a cloak of birth defects and death over most life forms, biological damage that moved relentlessly up the food and bio chain. The egg sacs of herring roe in the eel grasses were compromised, creating stillborn eggs by the millions, fish that would not come into being, that would never provide food to larger predators. Those smaller creatures that did survive with traces of petroleum in their bodies proceeded to enter the biological systems of salmon and otters, their predators.

Creatures that fed off the salmon found their supply dwindling, bears and eagles among those most hard hit. Four year cycles of salmon and herring and oolikan migrations were disrupted. And so, quite casually, petroleum entered into the human food chain. Seafood sources such as clams and abalone beds were devastated, then died and their breeding grounds in the sand and muck of the shorelines were poisoned for long years. Indeed, the First Nations living in the area of the massive oil-spill of the Exxon Valdez in 1989 knew how the impact still existed at all levels in the broad area of Prince William Sound in Alaska. As the deaths of the smallest creatures projected their impact all the way up the food chain, it put fishing communities out of business there, creating new social pathologies out of environmental cataclysm.

Mason hung, mind reeling, precariously balanced on the edge of the cliffs overlooking the scene of agony below. Terrified, he was losing his footing. The power of this emotional reality transcended the sheaves of engineering blueprints that made up so much of his waking professional hours. This vision of the black polluted future would never cease haunting his mind. He could not arrest his fall.

Chapter 36

In succeeding days Bjorn still found himself angry both at Vladimir and at himself. At Vladimir for having insinuated a thought into his mind that now haunted him. At himself for feeling some undefined attraction to the idea of taking bold action, having the power to take action, or even the threat of taking action. He also knew any act of violence was almost certainly a foolish, even dangerous idea. He could never get away with harming Mason. He was fairly sure Sam Winters too, would firmly oppose such an idea. While Bjorn believed deeply in the importance of stopping the pipeline and the tankers, he questioned his ability, indeed willingness, to undertake any kind of decisive act. And Mason, furthermore, would certainly be on guard.

Indeed, Bjorn had not yet sorted out his mixture of emotions towards Mason. Tundra's ultimate agenda was for sure negative, even evil in its casual engagement in policies that could ultimately destroy the environment and bears' habitats. Yet Mason seemed to understand the dilemma that Tundra as a company was posing. Mason had furthermore granted Bjorn some dignity in taking Bjorn's ideas seriously. He had even showed respect for Bjorn's First Nations background and had already taken him into his counsels. At times Mason showed signs of an almost fatherly interest towards Bjorn. Was it possible to separate the man from the pipeline project?

These tensions grew within himself, paralyzing him. He called in sick even as his services with the tour groups were needed. He simply had to clarify his mind on this urgent issue. Where was his life going, what did it mean? Was he losing his sanity and balance? Distraught, Bjorn locked himself in his room, perhaps to retreat into his mental forest to evade troubling and intrusive thoughts. As he lay in his bed he closed his eyes and hoped for some calming sleep. But he felt himself adrift. He clutched onto his bed which seemed to be twisting, like lying drunk in bed when the bed itself spins nauseatingly out of control.

Against his will he was being dragged out of bed, out the door and into the forest by a force he could neither identify nor control. This time it was not to the familiar clearing in the forest that usually offered him comfort and solace. He now stood in a darkened forest in a totally unfamiliar place, trembling at his vulnerability, listening, waiting, turning his head slowly in all directions. He sensed the spruce branches waving in his face, though they were more suggestive this time of a barrier, a warning off. It was cold and the light barely illuminated the features of the forest around him.

After a few tense moments of anticipation, nothing emerged. At last he felt an exhaustion overwhelming his body, he could barely stand. He sunk to his knees and rolled over onto his side in a small hollow with some leaves and branches. He sought to insulate himself from the troubling waves of emotions and thoughts cresting over his consciousness. He did not think he could withstand the onslaught upon his mind, his total loss of control, like some bad trip on acid.

At last Bjorn had fallen into something like soothing sleep. He woke up with a start. The surroundings had gained greater clarity now, illuminated by a moon whose brilliance varied at the mercy of clouds drifting across its face. Where was he? What time was it? Why was he here? Could he have slept through the night? He was clearly not at home in his bed. Then he remembered the strong sensations of being drawn into the forest. A large cloud now sharply muted the penetrating rays of the moon. Darkness surrounded him, eliminating his awareness of almost everything. He felt cold, shivering, trembling. He sat up among the leaves and branches, senses on guard. The leaves and twigs felt very uncomfortable on his skin until he was horrified to discover that he was now utterly naked, exposed on the forest floor. His vulnerability and shame terrified him.

Then—it wasn't clear at first but then he smelled it for sure—that unmistakable rank animal gaminess that he knew from before. He looked desperately around but saw nothing. Yet the smell overwhelmed his nostrils, its familiarity driving fear into his heart.

There were sounds of branches and twigs breaking not far from where he lay, some thing or things moving in the darkness, in the underbrush. Then, slowly, in the varying light his eyes adjusted to the darkness. He now thought he recognized the scene from a previous experience. He watched, all senses alert, transfixed, frightened, until there it was. The hulk of the great Bear loomed up over his head, slowly lumbering down towards him, gradually filling his vision. It hissed as he had never heard from a Bear before. Bjorn instinctively crouched down in despair, still naked, pressed into a fetal position of self-protection. And waited.

Yet, within a few minutes the first wave of terror had passed. He recognized he was powerless in the presence of such massive power. He had no choice but to yield to the inevitable. He was now beyond fear, but rather in a sense of suspended consciousness. In one sense he felt no surprise at being here. It was almost as if he somehow belonged here. The Bear grunted lightly and shook its head, as if shaking off some undesirable entity or thought. Then it shuffled ever closer, looking him directly in the eye, with terrifying proximity. Bjorn felt more overwhelmed than threatened by this intense presence. Some unknown medium drew him into a kind of wordless channel of communication, an exchange between two mental presences.

The Bear remained motionless as its huge bulk loomed over his body maintaining its stare, a stare Bjorn knew he could not hold. He could only avert his eyes from its power that broadcast presence and assertion. There was no doubt the Bear had come for him. Though with what purpose was unknown.

Now the Bear advanced right over his body. It lowered its huge muzzle and Bjorn could feel and smell distinctly the coarse hairs and whiskers surrounding its jaws that were moving ever closer. He now experienced a new wave of fear, the prospect of his imminent end. This was something he had not seriously reckoned on, the possibility of a logical denouement that would bring an end at last to his troubled and unfulfilled odyssey. The Bear nudged his naked body, forcing his arms and hands away from his torso to make him straighten out, abandoning the security of the fetal position. Bjorn's face, his neck, his belly, his groin now lay open, fully exposed and vulnerable. Never before had the Bear's presence felt so powerful, so imminent and commanding. He knew his personal will had vanished; his own identity now yielded to the Bear's. He closed his eyes in total resignation.

Later—he had no concept of how much time had passed—he sensed that the Bear had withdrawn slightly. Bjorn wrapped his arms around his curled-up body again to try to restore warmth. He trembled—with cold, yes, but even more from the intensity of experience, drained by some kind of process of communication that had wordlessly transpired.

He understood that he was to follow. He arose, his bare feet sensitive to the rough ground, tripping over branches in the darkness, stubbing his toes on roots, wincing as sharp stones probed the soft soles of his feet, branches scratching his unprotected body. The Bear moved slowly down the far side of the ridge, pausing occasionally to look back at him. Bjorn followed as they descended some distance. Moving was painful and he did not think he could go on much longer walking through the dark forest. His teeth chattered in the cold air.

The sounds of water entered his consciousness. A pool revealed itself in new moonlight, with water falling in the background. The pool itself seemed to contain some deep source of light; its surface shimmered and the bottom of the crystalline pool was clear to the eye. The Bear moved up to the edge of a pool and waded in with all its bulk, looking behind at Bjorn assertively, leaving no doubt that he must follow. Bjorn, already shivering and frail, did not believe he could withstand the cold mountain water. But as he entered the water he found to his surprise that it was comfortable to his body. The Bear moved up to the spot where water was falling in a light stream from above and stood under it. Bjorn too moved in under the waterfall and found to his astonishment that it had the effect of warming his body as he bathed in it.

A few minutes later the Bear led Bjorn out of the pool and proceeded down the slope to a clearing on the other side of the ridge flanked by a sheer rock face to the left that he recognized through its tracings by familiar lichens. To the right Bjorn was immediately confronted by a striking sentinel cedar whose massive twisted trunk rose to nearly fifty feet before the trunk suddenly branched out into broad smooth U-shaped fork of dual columns now running parallel, up another hundred feet, almost as if the tree was torn between two identities, each struggling upwards towards the light. At its base Bjorn perceived a low dark cave mouth, a beckoning opening into a Bear's den.

The opening lay at the base of the massive granite outcrop. The Bear sidled into the hollow opening, becoming quickly enveloped in darkness. Bjorn hesitated, but knew he was moving on command. He approached the entrance and peered into the gloom but saw nothing. Still he stooped and entered the hollow.

Once inside, his eyes quickly adjusted to the darkness as if the space was faintly illuminated. There was the Bear. But Bjorn's nostrils were quickly assailed by an overpowering stench that pervaded the space. It was more than just Bear. Was it Bear scat? Rotting carrion? Or blood? He hardly dared to breathe in the noxious air that nearly caused him to retch. It was the stench of another world that was not his.

Two large shapes then loomed into his range of vision off to the right of the Bear. Looking closely he was unnerved to perceive what were surely three other large grizzly Bears in the back of the cave. They stared at him motionless but with lips drawn back in a hostile look. Bjorn felt deeply his vulnerability once again. He involuntarily held his hands over his groin, and shivered, from the chill of the cave, the overwhelming odour of the enclosure, and the emotional intensity of the encounter.

Bjorn did not know whether his eyes were simply growing accustomed to the light, or whether some sort of source of light was emerging. The rock walls and ceiling of the cave grew clearer. He then noticed high up near the roof of the cave there were a series of skulls, more than a dozen white skulls—clearly those of Bears. Each radiated a faint light out of the eye cavities. They were placed so as to look out, each in a different direction, to all points of the compass, a kind of eerie, all-spectrum sentinel.

The stench of the cave still invaded his senses. He then thought he noted one of its sources: a multitude of bones and decomposing bodies or corpses of unidentifiable creatures or beings extending back deep into the cave. Aspects of death dominated the darker recesses of the cave, while light from the skulls illuminated the foreground.

The Cave is my refuge, the nurturing womb, the home. The Cave contains my mind. To hibernate, is not to sleep. It is to sink into deeper awareness, to gain deeper perspective. To bear witness to events outside the Cave.

On the ground lay several large granite slabs, like benches. On one he noticed a heavy dark skin of some animal. The Bear nodded its head meaningfully towards it. Bjorn advanced and saw that it seemed to be a complete Bear skin. Wordlessly encouraged by the Bear, he bent over and lifted it. It was incredibly heavy, and smelled thickly gamy. A huge Bear's head was still attached to the skin at the top, falling back as if forming a hood. With some effort he slipped the skin over his shoulders and wrapped it around himself, his arms going into some kind of opening under the heavy front limbs of the Bear, complete with its lethal claws. He braced for what he knew would be a cold and slimy inside, but upon putting it on over his exposed body, he felt an instant warmth, a physical and psychological repose and sense of well-being. Bjorn stood waiting until he sensed that he was expected to seat himself on the slab. He did so hesitantly and stared at the Bears. He felt his body continue to warm, soften, as if melting out into the Bear skin. Despite its heavy weight, the robe felt right, even familiar, as if he had worn the skin before, as if it had been made for him.

He saw the Bear's gaze shift to something behind him. He then saw a human figure enter the cave. To his surprise, he quickly recognized that it was Mason, also naked. Mason did not acknowledge Bjorn at all—as if he did not see him. Perhaps the Bear robe had partially disguised Bjorn, but not his face. Mason, with a deeply fearful expression on his face, took a seat on another granite slab. All three Bears now moved to the front and stood, looking directly at Mason who sat in front of them. The Bears looked at each other, moved their heads in some kind of communication, although Bjorn heard no sounds pass between them. The tension among them seemed to rise and clicks and growls arose. They stared at Mason with particular ferocity. Mason sat watching them, shivering from cold, vulnerability, and palpable fear, still quite oblivious to Bjorn's presence. Meanwhile Bjorn's own fear seemed to recede as he sat watching the silent spectacle in front of him that had taken on the feel of a tribunal. And from behind the three Bears a drum beat was audible, the same staccato, unvarying rhythmic beat that arrested the mind, a formality of ceremony, just like the Bear dance he had witnessed at the long house in Bella Bella with Joseph years before.

After what seemed like a long time the first Bear uttered a low growl and a huffing sound that Bjorn knew only too well, raising his fears once again. The Bear approached Mason who had now sunk to his knees, with his head down in a supplicating position, trembling. The Bear reared back and delivered a terrible roar in front of Mason's bowed head. The figure of Mason seemed then to drop, untouched, to the ground where he lay unmoving.

The Bear then sniffed at Mason's still form for a few moments and retreated.

The events struck terror into Bjorn. He was not even sure whether Mason—if it was Mason in the flesh—had even known that Bjorn had been there as the Witness. He couldn't tell whether the figure that looked like Mason was even alive any longer. After a long interval, Bjorn heard the beginning of a song that the Bear seemed to be singing. The song was familiar to him, but he could not at all say from where. The song had sounds that resembled words but he could not understand them. Yet he was sure that the song signified part of a ritual, perhaps the completion of a ritual, of some kind of natural order being restored.

The Bears gradually withdrew back deeper into the grotto leaving Bjorn alone. The drumming sound diminished in intensity and then faded. In the dim light he could no longer make out the body of Mason at all, it seemed to have disappeared. Had Mason died? He seemed not to have been touched. But where was he? Or could a Bear have dragged him away? He had no recollection. The muted illumination from the Bear skulls began to fade like theater lights dropping.

A pervasive numbing exhaustion from the entire encounter crept into his body, overwhelming him. He felt his body, still wrapped in the rank skin, slip down onto the slab. He struggled to no avail to keep his eyes open. He drifted off again, uncertain about what state he was in, where he should go, or what he should now do.

At some later point he remembered a kind of awakening. He could not determine how long he had been asleep. The Bears were not to be seen. Had his body remained there on the slab, or had he been enveloped, absorbed into the skin and spirited away? The skin was gone. He was still naked, but he felt no chill.

How should he understand this event, this series of events? One thing was certain: that here, in this cave, at some point he had been witness to some kind of an act of judgment. And that his own presence there was a kind of investiture, transmitting a message to him in his altered state.

And then, far off in his vision he saw a strange white light. As he struggled to perceive it, it grew closer. He began to recognize a shape. He now saw an older First Nations woman dressed in a Native robe. He immediately knew—without a moment of hesitation he knew—that this was her—the woman for whom he had been searching since childhood. She stood at a distance. Neither of them could make any utterance. But she smiled and waved, and he waved back. She waved again and Bjorn wanted to move forward towards her, but she then seemed to retreat into the darkness. Tears swelled into Bjorn's eyes.

He could not even guess the passage of time that had elapsed, but he found himself back in his bed in his room in Bella Bella. He was consumed with exhaustion, drained of all emotional and intellectual reserves. He felt his chilled body and found that it still bore traces of slime. An exhilaration swept through him despite the horrifying series of images and events that he had just experienced. It was the exhilaration of a certain clarity, a sense of purpose, involvement, mission. He had crossed a kind of threshold, his mind opened in new directions. The experience was now etched into his character.

Chapter 37

I t was unfinished business. Loose ends of a rope that could no longer be left untied and fraying. Bjorn knew of nowhere else to turn at this decisive moment. He had to return to Sam and lay out the unresolved strands of his life. Not without a little reluctance, since Sam had kept him on a partial psychic starvation diet over the months and had more probing questions than answers. Bjorn's mind was awash with conflicting impulses, any of which had serious implications for his course of action, even his destiny. And Sam listened, carefully.

The single harshest reality of Bjorn's own past—the trail to his biological mother—had grown cold. Whatever paper trail had existed had been lost in the mists of time, loss of records, bureaucratic incompetence, absence of reliable eyewitnesses. He would never now come to learn even the basic story of his origins. Most painful of all was recognizing that the search was all one-way—his search for his parents lay unreciprocated. There was no search by someone else to locate their son, no one yearning to embrace him out of the mists of the past. Yet, had he not recently had a vision of his mother—and he had no doubt it was his mother—and she had smiled and waved to him in the Bear cave?

Who am I? I am not of my family who raised me—that's plain as my face. But where is the First Nations connection? The Natives don't see themselves in me. I belong to no clan, much as my heart craves to. Am I just an Indian wannabe, as Joseph's friends accuse me? What does it take to belong, to win acceptance? The Bear channel almost offers me more perspective and direction than anything else I have encountered.

I see the Bear in me, for sure. I feel it—my one unerring instinct. But how do I become part of it? Is Vladimir the bridge to it? Vladimir made clear to me my deeper Native Eurasian roots. The ceremonies

Vladimir spoke of so powerfully to me—is that my ceremony? Do I wish to be sacrificed? Or to sacrifice another? In Siberia they said the Bear was Jesus.

His frustration now struck out in multiple directions, at all the things that weren't right in the world. His mother Claire had expressed concern over his growing anger. But his emotions still remained unfocussed, inchoate. The appropriate outlet was not fully clear. Where did the blame lie? Should he blame his birth parents for having abandoned him, yielding him up with no protection against the harshness of the world? Leaving him with no umbilical to his true world? Or should he blame the arrogant white racists who had presided over a massive operation designed to destroy First Nations as a coherent culture? What Joseph had called "culturicide?" For creating a system that had damaged a generation or more of Native peoples, including his own birth mother? That had separated him from her, and then abandoned him to a well-intentioned white family that could never understand the depths of what drove him? Or should he blame First Nations communities for not accepting him fully when he came back to them? He remembered hearing about new-born penguins that got separated from their mother for some days, so that when they were finally reunited with her they were rejected by her because they no longer smelled like they belonged to her. What did he "smell like" now, and who was it recognizable to? To animal links, to some greater reality?

Why was it that the vast animal and spirit world remained an unknown world to most white people—even to many Indians? But not to him. It was like a particular spectrum of light, or sound, that only certain animals and a few Natives could perceive. Everyone else had been conditioned from an early age to tune out any such spectrums as unreal, unwelcome. Indeed, why should people ever be interested in those worlds and realities if they could neither see, nor hear, nor smell beyond a narrow spectrum? Surely the "real world" is not limited to the specific boundaries of only what humans can and cannot perceive.

Bjorn was now sure that he had achieved some access to that world and its communications. He knew he was not alone in this gift—he had heard how shaman and other healers possessed a range of unusual spiritual gifts. That was why they were shaman—seers, see-ers. And a bitter irony hit him: for all the life of privilege he had possessed in growing up in a white world, this same cultural "advantage" had likely deprived him of an intuitive range of expanded communication with a broader natural world. If he had grown up among First Nations communities might he not have been able to cultivate this gift, been mentored in how to enter into communication with other forms of life on this planet? It was as if he had grown up in a spiritually impoverished ghetto, unaware of a vast other world that existed out there.

How long had it been since his last visit to see Sam? A year? The house remained unchanged to his eye. The same pale blue structure, rickety fence and the gate that you had to lift up before it could swing open. He did see a new wood sculpture in the front yard, portraying three salmon dancing in a ring. It stood next to the older orca carving.

This time the door opened just as he was about to knock. Sam stood in the door frame, again with a faint smile as if he had been expecting him. Inside the house very little had changed. He gestured to Bjorn to take a seat on the bench with the skin draped over it. As usual, he let Bjorn take the initiative in the conversation.

"You asked me several years ago what my story is," Bjorn began. "I think I now know. I have come to see that the way of life of our people is threatened. I believe I have some obligation to try to do something about it. The Great Bear Rainforest is under direct threat from oil companies, especially by oil pipelines and tankers."

Sam smiled, gave a nod of recognition but let Bjorn continue.

"You told me before that I needed to listen. I have listened. I have also come to realize that I have special feelings towards Bears; they somehow communicate with me. They have something to say. Sometimes I feel it may be just one particular Bear speaking to me, but perhaps in the name of all of them. They have told me of their anger at what is happening to the Rainforest."

"They address you with words?"

"Well, maybe not actual real words, I don't know. But they leave a clear message in my mind."

Sam nodded.

"I've learned how this great Rainforest has been known as a sacred place by people here long before the white man. But now that sacredness is violated. Governments and businesses just ignore its sacred character. Their promises to preserve it are meaningless. They are trying to turn it into an industrial highway that will pollute it. Destroyed for Nature, for the Bears and for the people. Something needs to be done."

Sam listened intently to the flow of passion but remained silent until he sensed that Bjorn's immediate outpourings had come to an end. He then said, "Your observations are correct. A sacred trust is being violated."

Encouraged, Bjorn went on. "I feel I have now become an actor. I am no longer just drifting, unrecognized, irrelevant. I have found myself. Others will now know that."

"And what have you found?" Sam said with some interest.

"I have realized there are two different worlds. I think there is a basic struggle unfolding—between Bear People and Human People. It is clear to me that the Bear People have an ancient understanding of our earth and its evolution and its wellbeing. The Human People are blind to it. This is a struggle between right and wrong. The Bear voice tells me that I must act."

Sam paused. "And what kind of action do you propose?"

"That I must stop the people who are doing this."

"Yes, if you are talking about this pipeline project it must be stopped. Indeed, our people are working to block this action. We have extensive plans for legal action in the courts already underway. We are making progress."

Bjorn smiled derisively. "I do not believe that legal action means anything. The system is rigged in favor of industry and government. The people in charge of protecting the forests are working with those who seek to destroy it. The people in charge of protecting the Bears are issuing the licenses to kill them. The people in charge of studying and protecting the fish are working with the industrialized fish farms. The commissions to study environmental impact are working for the energy companies, for Tundra. The government muzzles the scientists who see the truth about what is happening." He paused and looked at Sam. "None of these people care about the sacred land. All they want is to bring their pipelines and tankers through."

Sam nodded, now unsure about where all this was going. "Yes, all correct. So what would you do?"

"A role has been revealed to me. I have gotten to know the COO of Tundra. I have spoken to him on several occasions. He likes me. He seems personally interested in bears. He wants to use them to help promote the image of the corporation. He wants me to help him in this. He wants to set up a bear research centre in the Rainforest. His company is willing to fund it. He even wants to pressure the government to end the hunting of all grizzlies."

Sam raised an inquiring eyebrow.

Bjorn paused. "I think he may be sincere in all this, but he is still doing it for his corporation's image. He is still determined to bring the pipelines and tankers through. He believes that accidents and damage can be avoided through vigilance and technology."

"So what is your relationship to him then?"

"It is almost miraculous that I should have met him and developed a relationship with him. It's like—I don't know—like something almost destined to be. I believe I have somehow been selected for this. And now he's asked me to help him. I think in some ways he almost sees me as a son."

Sam raised his eyebrows. "A bear research centre is one thing. To get him to cancel the pipeline is quite different."

"I think I could persuade him."

Sam smiled. "You would persuade him? Is it realistic that you could change his mind? The head of a big corporation?"

Bjorn glanced at the floor for a moment. "No, I don't think it is realistic. But something must be done."

"And what would that be?"

"I know that I must stop him. Personally."

"Do you mean through violence?"

"I do not know what will be necessary. But persuade him in some way. The message is clear."

Sam paused and fingered his wooden cane, feeling the carved ridges and rings and intertwining vines that ran down its length. "I understand. I share your youthful passion. But I do not think what you are considering would be a wise idea. I do not think that the Creator intends for one life to be taken in place of another life."

Bjorn stared at him silently, fixedly. "I did not say taking a life. But some strong measure."

"Any kind of violence will lead only to further violence. Our peoples have slowly earned the respect of the white man over time. It has taken a long time, and we have been badly treated in the meanwhile. But at last the white man has gained sufficient wisdom to start to see us as responsible curators of Nature, to show respect for Creation. Violence from our side does not show respect for Nature. It damages our own moral position—which has been growing stronger, even with the government."

Bjorn stared silently at Sam, in growing disbelief. Sam kept his eyes fixed upon him until Bjorn dropped his gaze. "What would you have me do?" Bjorn finally asked quietly.

"You should work with our Elders and our people who are fighting this invasion of our sacred lands, the sacred lands of all people. We now have our own Native lawyers and environmental specialists. They possess the wisdom and experience to know how to conduct this fight in the way that is right, avoiding violence and in line with what the Creator makes clear."

"But that method is not working! It is a waste of time! It gets no attention! We are weak in the face of these industrial forces. And furthermore I have..." He paused.

"You have what?"

"I...I have the opportunity to act. The Bear has told me to act." He told Sam of his vision of the Bear cave.

"Have you ever considered that this voice you hear is not really the Bear? That it might be your imagination, your passion and your concern overflowing, creating images, clouding your mind and your judgment?"

Bjorn flared. "It's not my imagination, dammit! I feel this presence, intently. I feel the communication. This has not happened to me just one time, but repeatedly, over several years. The Bears seek action to save this land. Surely you know what the tar sands and pipeline projects mean for us all."

Sam nodded. "I have told you about my son, he works up there in Fort McMurray. We have had a falling out over this. I know the place. It smells of the underworld." He fell silent for a moment and looked at Bjorn again. "But your personal actions will not change the course of events. Only change of heart by all the people, including white people will bring change. Not threats to one individual, however important he may be at the moment. White men surround us like a swarm of hornets. Swatting one does nothing. We are swamped by them."

"I do not think the Bear People shrink from action."

"The Creator did not create the Bear People and Human People to be at war. Both are part of the Creator's creation. There must be balance between them."

"How can you speak of balance!" Bjorn rejoined. "There is no balance! White people have all the money, all the power and control over government and corporations."

"Situations do not remain the same forever. Change is part of the natural order. Our peoples are clearly much stronger now than one hundred years ago. We are changing things slowly. We have gained much greater legal power. But we must move with caution. With respect for all the forces involved. So that they do not turn all their power against us again."

Bjorn grimaced.

Sam looked at him searchingly. "Let me tell you something, Bjorn. Do not think of us as beaten down, oppressed and helpless. That is just a short view, just a snapshot in time, an instant. It represents thinking from a mouse's perspective, one that lacks vision. It is not a reliable guide for action today. After all, our people came here 12,000 years ago. A decade here or there are just grains of sand on a beach."

Bjorn's frustrations grew as he seemed to be failing to communicate to Sam. "OK, but I did not come 12,000 years ago. I am here now, and this is a vital moment in time. It calls for action during my life here and now."

"You are not listening!" Sam snapped. "We have shared the land with a wealth of creatures from whom we are descended and with whom we have lived from the beginning of man's existence here. We shared the grinding isolation of the walls of the Great Ice around us. We shared the liberating age of the melting of the Great Ice. And we shared the ordeal of the Great Flooding when we and the animals needed to seek safety in the high places, when the sacred mountain tops provided refuge that saved our peoples over several generations from perdition in the vast waters around us."

"I know all that!" Bjorn cried. "We're not talking about history, we're talking about now!"

Sam sighed. "Do you really believe that a mere hundred years of setbacks from the white locusts can bring our world to an end? You must adopt the perspective of the Bear that speaks to you. It is the long view from the mountain top. And that is why we must move slowly and with wisdom, not rashly like a snake that strikes out impulsively."

Bjorn fell silent, overcome by disappointment, disillusionment and helplessness. He had been confident that Sam would be strongly supportive of his ideas. They were aimed at a vital cause. They were aimed at the chief enemy. And they flowed from his communications with the Bear People. Fate had arranged for him to achieve a close personal relationship with the COO. Surely if anyone would understand these communications, the larger message, it would be Sam.

How could he ignore all the voices that had been speaking to him? Offering insight? Vladimir, the AIM people, the story about the Siberian peoples and their Bear sacrifice. The Bears' special role in Creation and in communication with the Creator. His experience with the Bear robe in the Bear cave? And Mason? How else could it be that he had met Mason, that Mason had become interested in Bjorn's insights and knowledge? That he was even willing to expose his safety to Bjorn in the forest? This could not all be just a coincidence, an accident. It was predestined.

The tension inside him had risen to the point of explosion. But he would no longer seek to persuade Sam. "I have to think...I must think this over," Bjorn stuttered. He rose from his chair unsteadily, in consternation and confusion. Sam remained in his chair and watched Bjorn closely. He then rose, approached Bjorn and clasped his shoulders. "My son, you must think about what you are doing. You are not serving the cause or our People in this way. You are not serving yourself or the Creator's order. I beg of you to reconsider your ideas. Do not shame us with any threats of violence. Work with the natural order of evolution of things."

Bjorn, uncomfortable, slid out of the embrace. "I will think about what you have said." And with no further comment or farewell he moved towards the door, lifted the handle, stumbled outside and moved off towards the setting sun. He was utterly on his own.

Chapter 38

O pening her post box early one afternoon, Bjorn's mother found among the flyers and bills a letter postmarked Bella Bella, and in Bjorn's handwriting. Bjorn almost never wrote. She opened the letter on the spot.

Dear Mother,

Mother? Why this sudden formalism, when he always called me Mom?

I have been struggling for many months trying to decide in what direction to take my life. I feel many conflicting signals that upset my mind. But I have come to firmly believe that I have a mission to complete in this world. A mission that the Bears have made clear to me.

Don't think that I'm just having hallucinations. I have studied a lot and learned a lot about this whole outrage of the pipelines and, worse, the tankers carrying all this poison through the sacred lands and waters of the Great Bear Rainforest, and the total indifference to the environment by big corporations. I know I must act, it is my moral obligation. Who knows, it may be my intended purpose in life, starting when you gave me the name Bjorn. Maybe you already sensed something about me then that took me years to understand while growing up.

I think you know that, by some fate, I have a personal relationship with the COO of Tundra Oil. We have talked. He believes my insights into Bears are important. He wants to try to help by establishing a bear research centre in the Rainforest. He likes me, almost treats me as a son. But he is still determined to go on with the pipeline and tanker project. I now have an opportunity to do something.

I want to thank you for all you have done for me. It has been hard growing up trying to learn about my real First Nations identity, and having no knowledge about my origins. I know I have made life difficult for you and my family. But somehow I now feel I am finding my way back to my origins and carrying out the will of the Rainforest, whatever that may be.

You have always stood by me and supported me, and that has meant a lot to me. My search for my roots, as you know, has nothing to do with rejecting you. I will always be grateful to you for your raising me and caring about me. Maybe you helped set me on this path, even without fully knowing it.

I hope you will understand how important my destiny is.

Thank you. I will always love you.

Your son,

Bjorn

A chill passed through her body, a bolt of fear. This was a farewell letter if she ever saw one. She had no idea what Bjorn had in his mind to do, but it seemed to reflect some kind of decisive turning point in his life. And it was clearly directly linked to the COO of Tundra.

Her mind swam with various courses of action as she tried to get through to Bjorn. She received no response from his cell phone. She then thought of Sam Winters. He might know more about where Bjorn was and what his plans were. He might even help her to intervene. But intervene to what end?

Or should she try to contact the COO of Tundra directly? She didn't even know his name. She feared that passing along vague anxieties and suspicions to the COO would seriously damage Bjorn's own future with him. After all, the letter was not clear as to what an "opportunity to act" could mean. She had only the vaguest sense of what Bjorn's relationship with the COO was.

She immediately booked tickets on the morning flight up to Bella Bella to try to locate Bjorn. She had no telephone for Sam Winters and knew of no other way to reach him except to go directly to his house, if she could remember how to find it.

She arrived in Bella Bella around noon the next day and got a room in a small hotel. It was a darkish day, no rain as yet, but low hanging clouds were limiting visibility into the deeper inlets. She called Bjorn's number repeatedly but there was still no response. She went to the rooming house where she remembered he was staying. The young woman there told her she had not seen Bjorn for several days. "But he's often away," she added. Claire left a note telling him she was in town and for him to contact her immediately by phone.

She went on to to try to find Sam Winters's house as best she could. She worried that she might appear foolish to him, a distraught mother flying up to this small coastal town in a panic about her son. But she had no alternative. She finally came to the house where she recognized the sculpture in the yard, maneuvered the stuck gate and proceeded to knock on the unvarnished wooden door. She must have waited nearly one minute before she heard someone come to the door. Sam Winters opened it and registered no surprise. He gestured for her to come in.

"You may remember me, I'm Bjorn's mother, we met maybe a year ago here." Sam nodded in recognition. She wondered whether it would be presumptuous to address him as Sam, but "Mr. Winters" seemed too formal. He gestured for her to take a seat on the same skin-covered bench where Bjorn sat on his visits.

"I'm sure you are surprised to see me here now," she volunteered.

"No," he replied, but offered nothing more for the moment.

"I received a letter yesterday from Bjorn that upset me very much. His state of mind seems confused. He speaks of how bad things are in relation to the pipeline project. He says he has a relationship with the COO of the Tundra Corporation. He talks about the urgency of carrying out some act or mission that he doesn't identify. I'm just sick with worry, I'm afraid he may be in some mentally unstable frame of mind and might do something foolish."

"Do you have the letter?" Sam asked. She dug in her handbag and handed it over to him. She wondered about sharing the intensely personal nature of the letter with him, but at this point she had nothing to hide from him.

Sam pulled out a drawer from a small table by his chair and extracted a pair of old horn-rimmed reading glasses. He read the letter over slowly, seemingly twice.

He nodded. "This letter is a cause for concern."

"Do you know where Bjorn is now?"

Sam shook his head.

"Do you think he is still alright? Has something happened to him, to change him?"

"I'm not aware of what his thinking is at this point. The last time I saw him was less than a week ago. He was agitated. But I don't know whether anything has happened to him since then."

"Do you know what kind of mission he is talking about?"

He considered the question for a moment. "No, not specifically. But I fear he could be about to take some unwise action." "

"Like what?"

"As he told you in this letter, he is deeply disturbed about the whole pipeline and tanker project. I believe he is trying to plan a trip into the Rainforest with the COO." He paused. "Possibly to take action against him."

She paused, not quite sure of how to respond. "To persuade, protest? Threaten him? Her voice faltered. "To hurt him?"

"Possibly. He believes that bears are telling him to commit an act of resistance against the pipeline company."

She nodded. "Yes, I know. Bjorn has always felt a special bond towards bears. Ever since he was a boy. He told me about communications he believes he has with the bears, messages about the environment. But I had never heard him talking about doing anything violent before."

"I believe that may be now so," Sam replied.

"Well, did he tell you anything about that? Did you say anything to try to discourage him?" An edge of impatience crept into her voice, but she did not want to offend Sam. He was the one vital link to Bjorn.

Sam leaned forward. "I will tell you what I know. Just five days ago he asked to see me. I had not seen him for maybe a year. He had changed. He wasn't talking so much any more about his concerns about his identity or his search for his Native mother. Instead he was very emotional about the environment, the pipeline and tankers through the Rainforest."

He paused. She waited impatiently for him to resume the account.

"Bjorn was very passionate about carrying out some kind of action. Acting on behalf of the bears." Again a pause.

"Well, couldn't you say anything to discourage him? To stop him? Unless you agree with him on this."

"Please understand, Mrs. Fisher, that I am not just a passive observer. I told him clearly I disapproved of using violence. I told him the Elders of our people would not share his thinking, it violates our traditional ways. I said there were legal channels the Native people here are already using skillfully to stop the tankers. This is a process that has been unfolding for a long time. It is bigger than any one person. It will take some time and patience to resolve. But there is movement. Bjorn did not want to hear my views. He left quite angry, I believe."

She sighed heavily. "Well, if you could not persuade him, I doubt if I can. But we must do something."

"I fear his mind is clouded, closed. I do not understand exactly the nature of the messages that he believes he is receiving from the Bear People. But he spoke of visions."

"Well, doesn't this suggest that he might now be mentally unstable?"

Sam closed his eyes. "I cannot enter Bjorn's mind. He may possess different perceptions. There are worlds in this Creation that not everyone is able to perceive. Each creature perceives the limits of reality differently. A worm's reality is not a bird's. A bear's reality is not an eagle's. Our own human reality has its own limitations. But each of those worlds is still real."

Claire felt irritated at Sam's vague philosophizing about animals and visions. "What were his visions?"

"Mrs. Fisher, I cannot say outright that he is not in touch with some profound messages, from life forces in other worlds."

"But you're not saying that you think it's OK for him to receive messages to commit violence, even murder?"

"I don't know that he has been specifically directed to commit violence or what kind of violence. But certainly he has powerful feelings about the destruction that is being carried out on this earth, and on our Rainforest. He is convinced it is his obligation to use his powers to try to prevent this. Many of us here also believe the tanker project must be prevented. But it should not have to include violence. But Bjorn may be interpreting his 'mission' that way."

They considered the situation in silence for some moments. Claire could hear children shouting outside the house.

"Do you know anybody else here who might know of Bjorn's whereabouts, or how to contact him?"

"One person."

"Well, who?" she said impatiently.

"There is a boatman about Bjorn's age who knows him well. His name is Joseph. If you ask at the Coho Restaurant they can probably tell you where Joseph is."

"Yes, I know Joseph. I have met him before. I don't think he is particularly fond of me as Bjorn's white adoptive mother. But I'll try to talk to him again. Otherwise I just don't know what to do, how to stop this." Her voice quavered. "And I certainly don't want to bring the police into the situation just because I'm worried about what might happen. If I go to the authorities and start talking about Bjorn's possibly killing someone, it will create a huge issue. It will ruin Bjorn's job and future forever, and all maybe based on nothing more than my fears or guesses. I don't want to do that to him."

Sam nodded. "Yes, I agree you must try to locate him. If he will listen to you."

"Sir, I am on good terms with my son. But," she bit her lip, "he has a lot of deeper, even darker thoughts that he doesn't always share."

"Have you tried contacting the adventure company where he serves as a guide?"

"No, I don't have any information about them at all."

"Joseph will know. I know this is a difficult situation. I wish I could help you more. If you can leave me some way to contact you I will inform you if I should learn anything." Sam sighed. "Let me tell you that I like Bjorn. He is an intense and committed young man. I would be sorry to see him destroy his life, or another's. Violence is not a course of action our Elders will support."

"I will contact you if I hear of anything where you could help. And thank you for listening to me. And for your advice and knowledge."

Sam nodded and saw her to the door, and watched as she crossed the yard and worked at lifting up the gate to go out, following in Bjorn's footsteps.

Through The Coho, Claire managed to track down Joseph. He was coming off work and was tired. He was angry about news of recent political negotiations between the Heiltsuk and the provincial capital in Victoria about the tankers. He was surprised to see Claire again, small, intense, tracking him down at his table at the canteen.

"Joseph? You may remember me. I'm Claire, Bjorn's mother," she announced and immediately sat down at his table. With little preamble she launched into her concerns about Bjorn's state of mind and whereabouts. "I think he's getting too intensely involved in this pipeline and tanker issue. I fear his state of mind is confused. And he could get involved in some act of violence."

Joseph reflected for a moment. "Well, with all due respect, I'm glad he's getting involved. It wasn't your fault, but it's only been here in Bella Bella that he's begun to really learn about First Nations issues. About the stuff that has been going down here for over a hundred years."

"Look, yes, Bjorn has talked to me a lot about these injustices. I'm really sorry about them. But that doesn't mean Bjorn should do something foolish."

"Foolish? Like what?"

"I don't know any details, but I understand he's developed a relationship with the COO of Tundra."

"Yeah, I heard something about that. He thinks he has an opportunity to get some sense into him on the tankers."

"Yes, but what do you mean 'get some sense into him?'"

"Look, Mrs. Fisher, if he has a chance to influence the COO, I think that's all to the good. And I don't think of Bjorn as a violent kind of guy."

Sensing some of the same elements of hostility from Joseph as before, she despaired of getting much help from him.

"Joseph, I don't want to argue with you. Can you just tell me how I might find him?"

"If he's not at the rooming house, and Sam doesn't know where he is, I'd check with his job at the Adventure Tours."

"Alright," she said, rising from the table. "But would you please let me know if you hear anything from him? I'd be grateful." She wrote her cell phone number down on a napkin.

"Sure thing."

Claire contacted Adventure Tours. "He hasn't been in for several days," the manager said. "We'd like to know where he is too. He's screwed up a lot of our tour scheduling by not being here. He didn't say a thing about not coming in. If you see him, you better tell him his job is hanging by a thread."

She had run out of ideas and was beginning to feel frantic. Her last resort might be to contact the Tundra COO directly, and try to learn what was going on. But she had no idea what she would tell him even if she did get through to him.

She finally found a Calgary number for Tundra. "May I ask the nature of your business with Mr. Surrey?" the receptionist asked.

"Just tell him that this is Bjorn Fisher's mother calling and that she's concerned about locating Bjorn. Maybe he can get back in touch with me."

"Can you be any more specific?"

"No, it's a personal matter."

"I'll pass it along. What number can he reach you at?"

She received a call back that evening. "Just a minute, I'm putting you through to Mr. Surrey."

"Hello, Mrs. Fisher? I believe you were trying to get a hold of me?"

"Yes, I'm sorry to disturb you, but I'm worried about Bjorn and I can't reach him."

"Any particular reason?"

"No, well, it's just that I can't locate him, and he's been rather silent lately. I'm not sure how healthy his state of mind is, whether he might be depressed or something. He's been talking a lot more about contacts he feels he has with bears as well."

"Well, yes, I have heard him talk about that. I know he feels close connections with bears. We have talked a lot about the welfare of bears in the Rainforest area. Bjorn is an interesting, passionate young man. I wouldn't worry about him. I'll be seeing him very shortly."

She didn't know how to explore this further, and she certainly didn't want to jeopardize Bjorn's ties with this important business leader. "I haven't been able to reach him for some time now. I wonder if you could just tell him to contact his mother as soon as he can?"

"Certainly."

"And may I ask, I'd heard that Bjorn might be planning some kind of trip with you?"

"As a matter of fact, yes. We're both interested in the possibility of establishing a centre for bear studies in the Rainforest, that Tundra might sponsor. We're going to take an exploratory trip together into the Rainforest, day after tomorrow as a matter of fact."

"And Bjorn seems in good spirits? No problems?"

"No, Mrs. Fisher, no problems. Anything I should be aware of?"

This was the question she had been dreading. She decided she would not plant seeds of suspicion in Surrey's mind. "No, not really. As long as he seems well and in good spirits, and thinking intelligently about the bear project."

"Well, thank you for the call, Mrs. Fisher. I'll tell Bjorn you called. I'm sure he'll get back to you. Any urgency?"

"Yes—well, no— I just wanted to be sure everything is alright with him."

"I understand. A mother's concern. I'll pass it along."

Surrey hung up, leaving Claire acutely disturbed. She had exhausted all avenues. She didn't know what more she could do except hope for contact from Bjorn. She knew Bjorn had a temper, and could act recklessly. He had spoken rashly to Sam, and had sent her a disturbing letter. But did that constitute grounds for a damaging intervention? And intervention against what? Her fears ran loose.

Chapter 39

Mason's eyes began to blur, weary from examining the detailed images on his laptop. It was huge, this Great Bear Rainforest, and despite studying the various physical and satellite maps of the area, found himself still confused at locating places on the sheer expanse of the land. Its landscape was nearly empty of people and settlements, while inlets and fjords rent the landmass, complicating efforts to get a clear bearing on specific locations.

Mason's stark and chilling vision of a dying supertanker had imposed upon him a new and emotionally vivid sense of the maze of waterways—and the stakes involved—more than any analysis of the scientific physical maps. He had not yet quite located the spot on the map where Bjorn had said they were headed. Broken Ridge Lake was where they intended to fly in by float plane and then hike on to Black Falls. The search for these precise spots in a vast swath of wilderness intensified his sense of entering into true remoteness.

While he was excited at the prospect of the trip, Mason's state of mind still entertained slight misgivings. The trek would be physically demanding, certainly a little uncomfortable for him given that he was not a regular woodsman nor was he in trim hiking shape. But at least the trip was short; only for a few days and then he would be back. Yet he acknowledged to himself that if the trip were to be called off tomorrow, he might even feel a slight sense of relief. Wilderness challenges presented less allure to him at this stage in his life but he knew the trip was a commitment he could not avoid.

Melanie watched him from her side of bed as he sat down on his side and issued a brief sigh. "Mason, don't tell me you're losing enthusiasm for your big bear trip tomorrow." Melanie's slightly glib manner of the past many months often peaked at bedtime, perhaps filling in the interstices of waning intimacy between them.

Mason shrugged. "No, it's not the trip. I'm just unhappy about where all this is going."

"You mean about yourself? Or Tundra? Or about us?"

"Of course it's about us, you're planning to leave. Of course I care."

"Isn't it a little late to be thinking about this now? We've been moving towards this for some time. I just don't think things are working out anymore between us. You're moving in another direction, consumed with your work, especially this whole Bear Rainforest project. You're more distant. And I feel increasingly isolated and alone in my life. Even your family just doesn't seem to mean that much to you anymore."

He turned to look at her. "Melanie, you know that's not true, that's not what I want. I do care a lot about the family. And I care a lot about you leaving."

The emotion in his voice seemed to catch her unawares. "Well, I'm afraid you haven't really shown it—or to the kids either. You're in some separate place most of the time, in your head, or off somewhere. Maybe a few months separation will make things clearer to both of us."

Mason let the remark go. But a few moments later he circled back. "I guess I do have this slightly uncomfortable feeling about the trip," he said, pulling off his undershirt.

"Oh?"

"Yeah. I don't know, the more I think about it, I guess it's maybe a little strange going off with Bjorn, just the two of us. I don't really know him that well. I mean, I like his enthusiasm for the project, and he's had some experience as a guide with tourists in the Rainforest, but..."

"But what?" Melanie put down her magazine for a moment, waiting for Mason to expand.

"He's a real tree-hugger. With all these mystical ideas about the forest and bears. I know I'll get a lot out of seeing his perspective first hand. And I do feel some sympathy about where he's coming from. His search for his roots and all. I like him personally."

Mason crawled into bed and stared up at the patterns in the ceiling. "And I am committed to the project. I think it's incredibly creative for Tundra to adopt the Bear Centre idea. It makes a great selling point to

First Nations communities. And it's a worthy cause. I just hope I can sell the hard-headed types back in the home office in Toronto." He reached over to turn the light off on his side of the bed. "I would love the experience of seeing a Kermode bear as well. It would personally be thrilling—and it's a natural as a symbol for Tundra and a research centre."

"Well, I wish you luck with it. I'm sure the trip will be worthwhile…and take bear spray." Melanie leaned over and turned off her light.

"When are you planning on moving out then?" he asked in the dark.

"I don't know, I'll have to see. Maybe at the end of the month."

"I wish you weren't leaving." He put out his hand across the covers, but she didn't reciprocate.

"This isn't easy for me either, you know," she said.

"Maybe we can talk about it some more after I get back at the end of the week."

"Mason, we've been over this a lot. I just don't think the basic facts on the ground are going to change that much. A break from each other for a few months might help us."

He sighed and closed his eyes, but was unable to banish the spectres that inhabited the wee hours of the night. His mind kept reviewing his challenges both at home and at work. And he had not been able to totally suppress those recurring flashes from his disturbing tanker vision.

And then there was Bjorn. He sometimes struck Mason as a murky figure, enigmatic and not always reassuring. He seemed elusive, unrooted. A floater, a loner, not really tied to any community despite his First Nations roots. Mason wasn't sure he fully understood where Bjorn was coming from in the end, or even where his heart lay. He seemed genuinely keen on playing a significant role in helping bridge the gap between Tundra and First Nations. He was clearly enthused at the idea of a Rainforest Bear Study Centre. Mason liked his enthusiasm. But Bjorn cut an unlikely figure for a slot in the corporate structure over the longer run.

And what was it about bears with Bjorn anyway? Some kind of love, or worship, or mystical attachment? He seemed somehow in thrall to them, speaking of them as his totem animal. This trip might help him get a better take on Bjorn, on how well he might fit in over the longer term.

And there was Vladimir with these weird mystical interests in the whole bear thing who Bjorn had been hanging out with. Vladimir's overall agenda also seemed rather unclear. Mason had to admit he'd also found Vladimir fascinating. His invocation of bears in native myth and custom was striking, even disturbing in opening up new perspectives. Indeed, Vladimir was right, bears should be more than mere subjects of biological and zoological research. This broader vision appealed to the non-scientist, to the cultural streak in Mason's own thinking.

Mason worried about how arduous the trip would to be. Wilderness meant wildness. There was no question he needed to develop a better personal feel for the significance of wilderness, the sense of being alone in it. It was exciting to think that this was exactly what so many of the spirit quests of Native youth were about. Enforced isolation by oneself, vulnerable, naked and empty-handed in the wilderness, having to come to terms with raw Nature and the terrors of one's own thoughts and imagination. What were his own deepest thoughts? His own terrors?

Mason had heard psychologists speak on the power of silence in healing—Nature as a form of therapy. It wasn't all just touchy-feely tree-hugging. Even corporate retreats had adopted some of these ideas as a way to stimulate more harmonious work relationships among the staff. The impact of the wilderness could change a person. Daily reference points dropped away. Symbols of power and hierarchical status from the real world suddenly cast out the window. The forest was a leveler, it changed the criterion of leadership. The ability to exercise good practical judgment, to master the wilderness environment—these skills didn't come automatically with executive rank. Out in the wild you had to prove yourself to others for them to have any confidence in you. Or else you had to reveal to subordinates your own lack of competence in forest survival. Indeed, Mason knew many executives who feared corporate wilderness expeditions for that very reason: their authority stopped at the forest's edge. How could rank matter in the forest? He worried Bjorn might think less of him if he showed physical weakness. And he had to admit to himself that he was still a little nervous about the reality of bears in wilderness situations.

Mason could have hired some old local Indian guide to take them out, but he felt that sharing the spiritual connection that Bjorn talked about was also important. Bjorn grasped the mythical, the ethical, as well as the commercial symbolism of a Tundra Bear Centre. And he was young. Youth represented a powerful symbol of the forward-looking vision that Mason sought for Tundra. Mason was above all determined to destroy the caricature that the damn Greens and tree-huggers were always trying to hang around his neck—as if he were some kind of ruthless exploiter of Mother Nature. The environmentalists sold him short and that angered him. It had even infected his relationship with his family. He would surprise them all with his progressive views and policies.

Only the first comforting light of rational dawn finally began to dispel his darker spirits. He slipped out of bed in the early light even before his alarm went off. He quietly dressed, avoiding disturbing Melanie. Frame pack in hand, he stepped outside into the cool air of dawn in the distant sky and set out for the airport. He slipped the pack over his shoulders, its weight to be his companion for the next four days. It was a new experience for him to carry a frame pack—heavier than he expected—but it somehow lent his trip greater authenticity.

He had an early flight from Calgary over to Prince Rupert, the main port and terminal in northern BC that faced out into the Pacific and to the distant mists of Haida Gwaii. He would meet Bjorn in Prince Rupert. One hour later, as his plane sat on the runway, he watched pink suffuse the horizon in the early morning light. He tried to channel his mind into meditative mode, to take things one step at a time, to put premonitions aside, to yield to the present experience as it unfolded.

Bjorn's night was equally caught up in swirling indecision among conflicting courses of thought and action. The sheets of insomnia curling around his body brought vividly to mind the vestments of Bear skin he had donned in the cave. First Nations understood how fine the line could be between dream states and reality. It was in that trembling gap between sleep and wakefulness that the real transmission between the two worlds took place.

What was that Bear skin robe? A new identity? A mission now literally enveloping him? A shroud? He could even now recall the intense animal muskiness of another form of life actually penetrating his own—the weight, the *responsibility* of the skin upon his frame. His mind could no longer evade the authoritative impact of these images from the Bear cave. He had received another message there—this one clear, vital, unambiguous, and decisive.

For all his connection and empathy with Mason as a person he now knew there could be no compromising with Tundra's planned assault upon the land and its creatures. The Bears supremely understood the ultimate cost. No matter how well-intentioned, no matter how creatively crafted these corporate efforts were to invoke and promote the Bear image and their welfare, in the end it all came down only to clever compromise. The consequences of those corporate policies would serve neither the land nor its creatures. They would demean the worthiness of human stewardship over this sacred trust, this hallowed legacy of Nature that was the Rainforest.

But how far did his mission extend? He had not yet perceived the exact course of action. Or perhaps it had not yet been revealed to him. Tomorrow might tell. In only a few hours Bjorn would be launched on his inexorable journey. He sensed his destiny was now in the hands of outside forces that he could not yet fully understand. Or indeed, if this trip with Mason was actually even meant to be the decisive moment in Bjorn's confrontation with Tundra. Would he receive any clearer signal? Even Sam Winters had lacked the vision, or the will, to clarify his mission.

Mason spotted Bjorn emerging from his flight from Vancouver into Prince Rupert airport. He waved to him from his table in front of a coffee bar at the far side of the waiting room. He perceived Bjorn to be in a subdued state of mind. Mason had chartered a small plane to fly them from Prince Rupert down to a float plane facility outside of Bella Bella, less than a one hour's flying time. They would stop in the facility overnight there and the next morning take a small float plane to the landing spot on Broken Ridge Lake. "You're not carrying much baggage," Mason commented to Bjorn, looking at his small frame pack.

"No, a lot of baggage is just baggage. I feel freer in the forests when I go light. For this trip I don't need a lot. Your frame pack is bigger than you need to haul around with you," he said, glancing at Mason's large pack resting against the wall.

Bjorn sat down at the table with Mason and hauled out a metal water-bottle with a bear logo on it from his pack.

"By the way, your mother called me yesterday," Mason commented. "Did you know she's been trying to locate you?"

"My mother? She did? What did she say?"

"She was just trying to find you. She said she was worried that you seemed uncertain about future plans and she couldn't reach you. She asked that you call her as soon as you have a chance. I think she said she was in Bella Bella."

"Bella Bella? OK, when I get back I'll call her. She's always worried about me."

"Well, it's nice sometimes to have someone worried about you. I wouldn't mind it," Mason commented.

They waited in the lounge without much talk. Mason looked at his watch, then got up and went over to the charter desk. The operator told him they had had to delay the flight for one hour, there was a problem with the steering controls that needed fixing. One hour stretched into three. Mason found his general level of anxiety rising and fumed that they might not get to their lodge before dark. Late in the afternoon they were finally summoned to the small four-man aircraft for take-off. It would still remain light enough outside for the whole flight. "Might get some weather on the way in, though," the pilot commented. They strapped on their seat belts and hoped to avoid a rough ride.

The small plane took off, offering great darkening vistas out over the Pacific as they flew south and gradually inland. "Boy, it sure is utter wilderness down there," Mason said, looking out the window. "All that rainforest, it's endless. Just like the maps—no sign of any settlements, roads, nothing."

"Well, that's good, keeps the area preserved."

"Still, I wouldn't want to get lost down there either."

"I wouldn't worry." Bjorn mostly remained silent during the flight. As they travelled south, the sky grew overcast and darker as they descended to their destination. As they approached the camp area near Bella Bella the small craft began to bounce alarmingly, lurching to the left and right in response to growing lateral gusts. "It would be a hell of an irony to get killed on a flight just getting into a place like this," Mason said, and then immediately regretted betraying this sign of weakness to Bjorn.

"We are fated to die when we are fated to die," Bjorn said. "Worrying about the aircraft won't change anything."

Mason chose not to pursue that line of thought. For one moment he checked in the seat pocket to locate the barf bag, in the hopes he wouldn't need it. And with the darkness he had renewed doubts about the whole expedition. Wasn't this a little crazy? Or worse, had it truly been necessary? What was he really trying to prove, and to whom? Who would know whether the COO had personally traveled to the heart of the Great Bear Rainforest or not? Or whether he had personally seen a Kermode bear? And the predicted rain for the next day would make it a lot less pleasant.

He probably should have brought somebody else more upbeat and talkative along for company and moral support. He regretted having let Bjorn talk him into such a lean, stripped-down expedition. In the end, you really only learn about a man when you travel with him.

A triple bounce and a sharp swerve to the left accompanied the landing in the wind and rain, but the pilot maintained control. It reminded Mason of some of the wilder flights he had taken around the Niger Delta; in Nigeria the dangers were less from the crazy bush pilots and the flying environment than from the ugly political scene on the ground when they deplaned. At least that factor was not present here. They climbed down from the craft and walked a hundred yards to a small lodge maintained mainly for hikers where they would await a smaller float plane in the morning to insert them into the heart of the forest. They swallowed down a few rudimentary cold sandwiches from the self-serve canteen. "It's going to be a long day tomorrow," Mason said as they headed off to sleep early.

"Yes, it will," Bjorn replied.

Chapter 40

Mason awoke at five am, the early morning light already filtering in through the trees. Shit, it was raining, but no surprise, it just made the day a bit grayer. The rain beating on the roof created a shroud of isolating white noise. Out of habit he picked up his cell phone left out on the side table, but quickly put it down again, determined to resist the compulsive tentacles of the outside world. Dammit, let his staff take care of things. No umbilical, at least while he was here. Except for his family. He might want to call his son and daughter back home in Calgary. I'm out here, guys, in the Rainforest, for real. I told you I'd make it. You'd love it here. And I do care about keeping this place preserved. Next time you should come along with me.

But his kids might not be convinced. Mason could hear his daughter's sarcastic rejoinder. "Blood money" she had once called the Bear Centre project—it was just environmental exploitation, she'd said, shipping all that black poison like black diamonds through sacred lands and waters. It would take more than one junket by him to the Great Bear Rainforest to convince them that their dad had a green side to his soul.

He looked at his watch. Still half an hour before he and Bjorn would sit down and get a bite to eat before catching their float plane out. Mason wished that Bjorn was more congenial, especially on a trip like this. He had seemed morose yesterday. He actually could have been a good man to sit down with over a bottle of whiskey, shoot the breeze on Bjorn's own background—First Nations, bear lore—and Mason's tales from Ogoniland. Trouble was, Bjorn didn't drink any more. Mason at this stage in his life was by now slightly uncomfortable with men who didn't drink, at least socially. He felt it was some kind of smug statement. Or by Bjorn perhaps a rebuke, a suggestion of weakness on Mason's part, a subtle assertion of Bjorn's moral superiority. Or more likely it just might be a hint that Bjorn's own mental state was simply delicate; that he didn't trust the dislocating effects of alcohol upon his personality. He noted Bjorn's mother had spoken of concerns about whether Bjorn might be depressed.

But no, he knew Bjorn wasn't actually straight-laced, he was honest about the whole thing, he admitted he couldn't hold his liquor. Still Mason felt a bit more of a distance between them, especially out here in the wilderness, no longer Mason's turf. Maybe being here together in the forest might loosen Bjorn up. Mason had in any case brought along his whisky flask for psychological fortification.

He had hoped Bjorn would share his wealth of bear lore out while on the trail—it would surely be more profound than the usual stuff of grizzled old hunters blathering on about the one that got away. Clearly Bjorn had developed deeper insights into the role of bears in native cultures around the world. He could be the perfect First Nations rep for Tundra if he played his cards right, able to project a sincere, youthful, knowledgeable, passionate, and credible image.

By six am Bjorn still hadn't shown up in the canteen. Mason went and knocked on his door. No immediate response. He knocked again, more loudly. Bjorn stumbled to the door and opened it. "What's the matter, Bjorn? How come you aren't up?" Mason asked. Bjorn retreated back into his room. "Sorry. I overslept."

Mason eyed him critically. "Christ, Bjorn, you look really bleary. You been drinking?"

Bjorn flinched. "No! You know I don't drink anymore."

"Well, whatever, let's get something quick to eat in the canteen and then get our asses in gear. Plane should be ready to go shortly. You told me we had a fair distance to hike today after the float plane drops us off."

"Right...but the forest will wait."

Mason found this comment a bit off from the potential enthusiasm he was expecting. Especially since Mason was feeling even less comfortable with their expedition plan now that they were here. The soggy weather outside was further disheartening, although he knew it was very much part of the rainforest experience. And it could blow over in a few hours. The actual details of the hiking and camping schedule he had left to Bjorn. For Mason the preeminent task was to get a first-hand feel for the forest—the Great Bear Rainforest—to which his own future and that of the company was going to merge. He was determined to experience it personally—not on some guided tour, not with some subservient staff or glib forest pros, but in direct contact with the raw forest experience. He also hoped to get a few good pictures of the area, and of bears if possible at the place they caught salmon, and even of himself in the forest. He had brought along his Canon Powershot, a good quality point-and-shoot camera for maximum simplicity.

After a plastic-tasting cold bacon and egg sandwich out of a cooler, a glazed donut and bitter machine coffee, they went out to the landing zone at the nearby dock to rendezvous with the pilot of the float plane. They soon heard the whine of the engines and saw the plane drop down through the mists onto the black surface of the lake. The propeller whirred softly as the craft drew gently up to the dock. "Mason? Hey, I'm Paul, just throw your packs into the bin in the back. We're headed for Broken Ridge Lake, right? Visibility isn't too bad, should have you there in about twenty minutes."

Mason and Bjorn secured themselves in their narrow seats, slipped on headphones for communication over the engine noise, and the plane roared down the lake, skimming low over the water for a long way before slowly lifting off and rising up over the trees in a north-east direction, mists still drifting intermittently over the forest below. They exchanged a few comments with the pilot over various landmarks. About twenty minutes out the pilot pointed to a lake ahead of them. They circled and quickly dropped down onto the small lake. The props reverberated in reverse feathering as they braked, shattering the pristine silence of the lake. They pulled up to a rough pier that lay in front of a primitive camping hut. "So I'll see you guys back here in four days, right? That's Thursday, at four pm?" Paul asked. Mason nodded. "Call me on my cell if there's any problem. Signal can be spotty, depending on where you are. Try to call from an elevated spot." And then the float plane turned around, roared back down the lake and lifted off, leaving them together in the silence of the forest.

Mason was relieved that the drizzle had now let up, though the lake and surrounding area were still flecked with drifting curtains of mist and clouds that shifted in the wind, alternately revealing and then concealing the mountainous surroundings. *This is it,* Mason thought, *this is the real thing.* They donned their packs and Bjorn took the lead, heading off along a slightly rough but well-defined trail. Mason was intent on trying to absorb the setting, the smells, the sounds, the mood, the experience, even while trying to maintain the pace that Bjorn set. The power of the setting was enough for him right now; he didn't feel like engaging in a lot of talk either as they walked along. Nor was Bjorn at all talkative. Mason knew that some noise of human passage would of course be wise so as not to surprise bears or other wild animals. Bjorn responded tersely to Mason's few questions and exhibited a fairly cool and taciturn manner that irritated Mason. He had expected greater cordiality, shared camaraderie on the trail of adventure together. Maybe this kid really was less communicative than he had expected, raising questions about how good he would be with handling people, either at a Bear Centre or in forest guiding situations.

They proceeded in relative silence for some time through the forest with occasional rest and water stops. "Spot anything?" Mason asked.

"Saw what looked like a deer or two farther off. Don't see much signs of a bear presence right around here right now, but pretty surely we'll see more when we get nearer to the river."

Mason was having to work a bit to keep up with Bjorn's pace; his breath grew faster and his pack now seemed heavier. He had brought too much. Although he felt physically strong, he was at least twenty-five years older than Bjorn, less physically fit, and probably more tired than normal from insufficient sleep and trip and family concerns over the past two days. He did not yet feel psychologically at ease out here in the forest wilderness yet either.

After another half-hour Mason felt the need to stop again, but didn't want to reveal any weakness or tiredness. Bjorn looked at him as if he were lagging. Eventually they did stop again, and sat on top of a fuzzy green nurse log lying on the ground just off the path and drank from their canteens. Bjorn sometimes looked askance at Mason in ways that struck him as peculiar.

"Something bothering you?" Mason asked.

"What would be bothering me?" Bjorn replied. "You're the one who's facing uncertain new ventures out here."

Bjorn's comment bordered on surly and Mason turned to stare at him. "Just what uncertain new ventures are you talking about?" Mason asked.

"Nothing. Just you're the one who's looking at plans to harm this forest, not me."

'What the hell are you talking about Bjorn?" Mason snapped. "I thought you saw some promise in this, some cooperation on preserving the Rainforest, and bears."

Bjorn looked at Mason with an expression that he hadn't seen before. "I just mean that a big bear study project may not make up for what the tankers are going to do."

Mason did not want to get into an argument with Bjorn at this point; he had never actually talked tankers with Bjorn before, only bears. Bjorn's line of comment now seemed unexpectedly negative, at odds with his more forthcoming attitudes of recent weeks. This was a new side of Bjorn; Mason feared perhaps he had previously misread him and regretted he hadn't plumbed Bjorn's personality more before setting off on a trip with him.

The forest was quiet, a slight breeze waving the fronds of the cedars. There were few distinctive landmarks along the way, just a winding through emerald thickets, spruce, cedar, ferns, nurse logs. Only occasionally did the forest canopy open up into a clearing revealing the grandness of the rainforest setting. They climbed steadily at a significant pace for about half an hour to the point where Mason finally called for a rest break. He almost had the sense that Bjorn was deliberately pushing, testing Mason's fitness. After a while they then emerged out onto a high open knoll revealing the kind of panorama Mason had hoped for. To the west there were high mountains, separated by ravines and saddles among the peaks where remnants of glaciers lay. There was no rain now, although far off they could see signs of a storm in the distant mountains. The green facade of the mountains nearby were punctuated by various high waterfalls plunging down the face in streams of froth, to rendezvous with other streams to form the rivers that fed on down into the many pristine lakes. Mason took a number of photos but did not ask Bjorn to take one to include him. They then approached a smaller waterfall in front of them of some twenty metres drop. Mason always enjoyed selecting out a constellation of drops on the edges of the unbroken flow of water as they broke loose before the plunge, individuating into separate clusters for the long fall. He would simply track them on the way down with his eyes as their individual existences ultimately vanished again as they merged into the swirling pool at the base. He saw it as a metaphor of life's short passage, one that separates us out into individuals for a brief period in the flow of time until we all merge again into the great collective at the end.

Although they had been hiking mainly on lower ground, they had gained some elevation early on in one fairly steep ascent. They emerged out onto an escarpment that took away Mason's breath. Wildflowers populated the clearing—avalanche lily, mountain heather, white rhododendron. From the lookout point they could now see the azure water of some of the lakes below them, and the tufts of green islands of vegetation lying between the shifting meanderings of slow-running rivers that snaked their way across the flat green wetlands to ultimately flow into the top of distant fjords and finally out to sea. Mason took a few more photos. He had never encountered on his own such vast stretches of unspoiled beauty quite like this. He felt confirmed in his determination to associate Tundra directly with ideas of preservation and conservation. The two concepts must not run in contradiction. He wanted to respond to the scene, to speak of its inspirational character. But Bjorn's taciturn and distant manner discouraged expression of Mason's more expansive feelings.

They descended from the open lookout area and Bjorn eventually turned off left onto a smaller side trail marked by a small white blaze on a tree. "None of this seems very well marked. How come we're leaving the main trail?" Mason asked.

"This main trail's more regularly used by hikers," Bjorn replied. "Probably too much human smell. Can either attract or repel bears. We don't want to do either. And this way is shorter to our destination."

"There certainly doesn't seem to be anybody else out here at all right now," Mason commented. He grew discomfited with their departure from the better marked trail and onto a less smooth trail. "You're sure you know where you're going?"

"Don't worry."

As they paused for a water break again Mason asked, "Are there supposed to be more bears in the direction of the river?"

"In this whole vicinity where the streams flow down there should be a number. It's good fishing territory. Should mean the presence of bears."

"What should we be doing about them?"

"They know we're here. We mainly want to avoid challenging them."

"Why won't they feel challenged by us at the fishing spots?"

"Because they'll be concentrating on fishing, not us."

"But you do have the bear spray if we need it, right?"

"Don't worry."

They stopped again after an hour at Mason's request, sat on a rock and ate some trail food overlooking a stream. At last the sun broke through the mists that were now lifting off from the forest. As the sun's rays came through the trees Mason's spirits rose. He drew sustenance from his presence in the new environment around him, feeling more in tune with his surroundings. He took a few more photos just to record some of the many impressions that he wished to retain from the rainforest, possibly to be revisited.

They proceeded downwards along a path that now demanded greater attention, more careful footwork, as there were more roots and stones on the trail to be avoided.

By mid-afternoon Mason was feeling quite tired. "Maybe we should call it a day soon."

Bjorn shrugged. "One place is more or less as good as another for our purposes," he replied. "There are few real camping spots around here anyway. We just want a place with a little clearing, maybe some fire stones. Sheltered from winds, not too far from a stream."

They eventually found a place with a crude ring of stones left by some previous campers. Bjorn set up a small camping tripod stove to boil some water for a freeze-dried boeuf bourguignon stew. "Doesn't seem much like forest food if you ask me," Mason commented.

"You want to catch something to eat out here?" Bjorn asked.

They chewed on their freeze dried dinner in tin bowls in relative silence.

"You really think we might be able to spot a white Spirit Bear?" Mason asked.

"There's a decent chance. Maybe one out of ten bears in this area is white."

"Some kind of recessive gene, isn't it?"

"Don't know the exact biology, but local people on this coast believe that when Raven created the world, one out of ten bears were made white—remnants of the glaciers that surrounded them thousands of years ago."

Mason was pleased to see that the subject of bears seemed to bring some greater spark to Bjorn's mood.

"And the white Kermodes are actually a form of black bear, right?"

"Right. But naturalists have found that white bears actually catch up to thirty percent more salmon in the streams in the daytime than black ones. They claim it's because the fish don't see the white bears as clearly as the black ones when they are jumping up over the rocks and falls. That's when the bears often grab them, right in the air."

"Is that really true?"

"Sure, because at night when the bears' colour is harder for the salmon to see, the catch rate between the white and black evens out to about the same."

"Are there grizzlies together in the same place with the black bears?"

"No, not so much. The black bears like to avoid the grizzlies, they don't get along and a black bear wouldn't come out of an encounter with a grizzly very well."

"Would a grizzly actually eat a black bear?"

"Sure, especially cubs, easy prey."

They both fell silent for a while, listening to the forest. "How are you feeling?" Bjorn asked, turning and staring straight at Mason with a slightly challenging expression.

Mason didn't like the undertone. "I'm OK, why shouldn't I be? It's a huge new experience and something I've got to do. I want to feel it for myself."

"You will," Bjorn responded. Mason shot him an inquiring glance.

After eating they ensured their small supply of food was hoisted up over a branch some distance away from their campsite, something Mason recalled from his boyhood camping with his father in the Rockies that always invoked bears. He pulled out his flask of whiskey. "Helps me get to sleep," he said. He extended the flask over to Bjorn who waved it off.

"So how does being out here make you feel about your whole project now?" Bjorn asked.

"Much the same. I'm still convinced that Tundra, doing it right, can responsibly deliver energy while preserving the environment."

"You still believe that, then?"

"Of course I do. I wouldn't be here if I didn't. I thought you believed it as well."

Bjorn was silent, and then smiled and said, "I'd hoped you'd change your mind. I think it's a fantasy."

Mason turned to him sharply. "What do you mean, fantasy? I thought you were excited about the project, the Bear Centre and other plans."

"You haven't rethought the whole deal of the tankers then, after seeing all this magnificent land here—that's threatened?"

"No I don't need to rethink it. It's at the heart of my project, my vision. Energy plus environmental commitment. I still believe I can do it."

Bjorn's face darkened. "Mason, it's a sell-out in the end. Oil is a dirty business, it's evil. You can't just pretty it all up with white bears."

Mason sat up straight and stared at Bjorn, barely suppressing his anger. "You get me all the fucking way out here in the goddam woods to tell me that?"

"I never said anything different. I just said I'd help you to come out here. And here we are."

Mason was troubled at the explicit and decisive shift in Bjorn's views and the perceptibly new, darker tone in Bjorn's speech. He stared hard at him.

"Alright, then. I suggest we call a halt to this whole damn trip. You're not the partner I thought you were, not the partner I want. I want to go back in the morning. I'll find someone else interested in joining the project." Mason's fought to keep his voice from wavering with emotion.

"Don't you want to follow this trip to the end?"

Mason's antennae were now on full alert. "What do you mean, 'end?' Are you threatening me?"

Bjorn shrugged, remained silent for some period. "I mean, to finding the bears. But let's talk about it in the morning when it's light. Things may all be clearer by then."

Mason was considerably unnerved now by these last exchanges. He was shocked at Bjorn's sudden open repudiation of the project. He detected a clear new element of belligerence in Bjorn's tone. Any trust he had once had in Bjorn now vanished. He cursed himself for having allowed himself to come out here in the wilderness with this untried and untested young man, now clearly some kind of zealot, maybe even unstable. He felt a new layer of fear as he looked across at Bjorn, who in the fading light seemed to be watching him strangely. How had Bjorn's character transformed itself so sharply over the course of the last week or two?

Mason took several more good swigs of whiskey to calm his nerves and overcome his anger and disappointment. He resolved to stay awake during the night as much as possible as a safety precaution. They pulled out their sleeping bags and unrolled them, Mason deliberately placing his on the other side of the fire-pit from Bjorn. He dug in his backpack and surreptitiously pulled out his all-purpose knife to keep close at hand inside his bedroll. During the night Mason remained tense, alert to sounds in the forest or any signs of motion on Bjorn's part. The whiskey however had had its effect and before Mason realized it he found himself suddenly awake in the early light of dawn, chilled, aching, feeling his face drawn from lack of solid sleep. He quickly looked over at Bjorn who was awake. He was staring at Mason.

"You didn't even sleep?" Mason asked.

"Someone had to watch for bears," Bjorn replied.

"OK, I want to go back now in any case. Our trip is over."

"We can swing by some different falls on the way back and see if we can find something. It's on the way."

Mason thought. He was already at Bjorn's mercy out here. He might as well go on by the falls on the way back. There would still be time to get back to the lake pick-up point. The pilot wasn't supposed to be back in any case until the day after tomorrow, unless they called soon to move the pickup date forward to today. Mason would place the call shortly. Meanwhile he would be on guard against Bjorn. He felt distinctly apprehensive, as though he could not get out of the forest any too soon. Getting away from exactly what he wasn't sure, but he didn't want to dwell further on negative scenarios. Nonetheless he felt entrapped. He knew he needed Bjorn's guidance to get back to the lake pickup point. He was unnerved to think that he had to spend even that much time more in the forest with him.

"Alright, we'll go on past the other falls on the way, then I want to head straight back. I'm calling the pilot to make a pickup at the lake today."

"Your decision."

Mason picked up his cell to call the number the pilot had given them. No signal. "Why is there no goddam signal up here at this higher altitude? There was at the drop-off point lower down." His voice betrayed almost a hint of panic as he hurled his phone to the ground in bitter frustration.

"Maybe if you get back to the lake you'll get a signal."

"*If* I get back? What in hell do you mean?"

"I mean it's not very sure what our plans are now."

"Goddam it Bjorn, stop playing around with me! I once had some confidence that you were interested in being part of this project. It's now clear you're the one who's backed out. And I'm very disappointed."

"And I thought I had some confidence in you to do the right thing. I now see that is a mistake."

"What do you mean, 'do the right thing?' I've always been very straightforward about my plans here."

"Mason, it's a folly. I understand it now, it's very plain. The Bear World is at war with the Human World."

Mason stopped and stared at him, dumbfounded. "Jesus, Bjorn, just what does that mean? What kind of war? What are you trying to tell me?"

"Nothing that shouldn't be clear by now. The Bears sense the destruction that you are planning."

"What kind of psychic bear bullshit is this?"

Bjorn hesitated in the face of the challenge from Mason. "I hadn't been sure yet. It wasn't all clear to me earlier. But now it is."

"OK, forget the falls," Mason said. "I want to go straight back to the lake."

"Let's take this small side trail, it's a short cut back to the main trail," Bjorn stated. Mason knew he had little option other than to follow Bjorn's knowledge of the trail routes. They walked for another hour, Mason keeping a close watch on Bjorn from behind. The ground here in this area of deciduous trees was damp with decaying leaves underfoot. Mason suddenly tripped on a root under the leaves, lost his balance under the weight of his pack and fell heavily to his side. "Shit, my ankle!" he cried. "I've twisted my fucking ankle!" He tried to get up and winced when he put any weight on it. "I think I've torn a ligament."

Mason's nerves were trembling on high alert. He did not know how he was even going to be able to hobble back to the lake with his burning and torn ankle. He lay against a tree trunk and pulled out his flask again. Despite the pain and his nerves he found himself fighting sleep. He felt beset with confusion, uncertainty and fear, near the point of tears of bitterness and frustration at his helplessness, his naiveté at what he thought he might accomplish. A sense of resignation, even fatalism, slowly insinuated itself into his mind.

Bjorn was now fully in command of the situation. The pain and the size of Mason's swelling ankle was growing. Mason twisted out of his backpack so he could move his body more easily but found he still could not put enough weight on the ankle to stand. All bets, all speculations on what was going to happen now were beyond knowing. The reality was right here, right now.

Bjorn moved over towards Mason and bent down. "Let me help you."

"Stay the hell away from me!"

"You need help in walking."

"Just give me a minute. I'll manage."

"Who knows, we may yet be able to see bears," Bjorn commented. Mason thought of challenging Bjorn angrily on the way he was being played. But he felt bone tired, psychologically exhausted, drained. The whiskey at least warmed his bones and he could no longer stop himself from drifting off into even a few moments of fleeting half-sleep.

Bjorn began now to look around the place more intently. Suddenly he knew. This place was deeply familiar, the details of the setting unmistakably recognizable. The clearing. The left side flanked by a sheer rock face distinctively traced by patterns of lichens yellow, green and orange. And there on the right the striking sentinel cedar whose massive twisted base rose to nearly fifty feet before the trunk suddenly branched out into broad smooth U-shaped fork of dual columns running parallel up another hundred feet. And there, at its base beckoned the low dark cave mouth. There was no mistaking the place. It all made sense now. The signals were now fully clear. Let it unfold.

They rested on a rock outcropping soft with moss, Mason half lying on his side in pain, keeping all weight off his ankle.

"You're in trouble, Mason. I don't know what we can do with you, to get you back. We better stay here a while," Bjorn said. He felt some concern for Mason's welfare but the messages told him that events were now totally beyond their control. Things would unwind in a clear inexorable sequence.

Chapter 41

The quiet of the forest was broken only by a raucous, prolonged cawing of a raven. Mason was startled out of his doze by the sound of loud crackling of bushes not far off, like the sound of a large creature moving through the underbrush. He looked around in panic, for support from Bjorn, and in urgent need of the bear spray. But where was Bjorn? He was not in sight. Mason now saw in full clarity how terribly wrong the situation had turned. He realized a turning point was truly at hand—wilder, fiercer, less comprehensible than he ever could have understood. He felt a rush of helpless terror—strangely mixed with outrage, strangely followed by a sense that he could struggle no longer, a yielding to inevitability.

Mason turned his head to look up in time to see Bjorn advancing upon him, grasping a heavy piece of a broken-off branch raised over his head. Mason tried to rise to his feet, stumbled in pain back towards a tree trunk, losing his balance and falling into a half-kneeling position. He saw Bjorn was ready to swing. Mason put up his arm to fend off the imminent blow aimed at his head. The heavy piece of wood struck Mason's extended upper arm with a resounding crack and fell to his side, now immobilized in shooting pain. He turned his face up towards Bjorn. "What in hell do you think you are, Bjorn?" he groaned, half in anger, half piteously. Mason rolled over onto the ground again, stunned, desperately seeking to get to his feet, to fend off any further attack from Bjorn. But he could barely manage to maintain full consciousness from the pain in both his upper arm and his ankle as he fell again heavily to the ground.

Bjorn lowered the heavy piece of wood to the ground, breathing heavily and looking at Mason. Yet, as if the blow he had delivered had also been a shock that brought Bjorn to his senses, he suddenly found his own emotions shifting, oscillating between confusion, horror and determination. He suddenly recognized Mason as a half noble, half pathetic figure, but for whom he now felt a surge of emotion, anger, pity and sadness. But there was only one path. A deep staccato drumming sound penetrated Bjorn's consciousness, a trance-like beat almost as part of a formal ceremony whose source was unknown. Conflicted, he stepped back, uncertain about where the momentum of events was going.

A crackling sound in the underbrush to the side distracted their attention. Bjorn retreated back from Mason, eyes now focused on the underbrush.

The Bear slowly emerged and paused. It glanced first at Bjorn, then at Mason on the ground. It remained silent and motionless for the moment, except for a heavy breathing sound. Then it made deep snuffling sounds in its throat, sticking its tongue rapidly in and out like a snake sampling the air. Bjorn recognized the sign.

Mason struggled to collect his awareness only to look up and perceive the Bear, its massive size over him. "No!" he cried, "the bear spray!" He tried to struggle to his knees before the Bear's bulk was upon him. It rose up on its back legs and then swung its massive paw striking Mason with full force on the side of his head. Mason felt a devastating crunch in the base of his skull and fell to the ground.

The Bear paused, fell forward onto all fours again and moved to the body. It sniffed it intently. All the while Bjorn watched in awe, confusion, terror, even pity. He had not known whether the Bear might actually make an appearance in this his fateful forest expedition with Mason. He wondered what exact role he himself was now intended to play in this unfolding scene. This act of justice served lay far beyond Bjorn's own control or understanding. It was no longer just about Bjorn and his anger at Mason or even the threat to the environment. Things had moved to a higher plane of confrontation.

Shock, but no longer surprise, now surged through Bjorn's mind. Certainly, this was the order of things that had to come, as they must be. However it would play out, Mason and Bjorn were joint actors within the grander calculus of natural justice. A final act in a drama long scripted.

The Bear continued to grunt, snuffle and nudge Mason's body in an act of identification, investigation, ascertainment. Bjorn could only look on in fear, gripped by the power and awe of the moment, this confrontation with some kind of great animal force at work in this world of men. It was the biggest Bear he had ever seen. Then the Bear swung its attention away from Mason, its great heavy head turned around to fix Bjorn in its eyes, its nostrils working on its square, almost pig-like snout. Its intense odour pervaded the scene.

Bjorn remained in a crouch, paralyzed. Should he cower in submission? Or attempt to interact with this presence? Or try to flee? Could he in some way signal his understanding, indeed his act of commission in what had just taken place on the forest floor? Was it a mission that he had just now fulfilled in bringing Mason out here? Or was it a larger purpose whose full extent had not yet been fully revealed to him? He knew he should not, indeed could not make any attempt to withdraw from the scene. To pull out the bear spray would be a patent intervention, a rejection of this course of destiny. He could not grasp whether there was even any imperative for him to flee. He struggled to grasp the Bear's intent, as if he could tune in to some shared wavelength but he could not discern it. He suddenly remembered Ears's reassurances from his childhood, *I will always be with you till the end.*

The Bear sat with its prey for long minutes, taking stock, as if in some kind of communication with it. It then lay down beside Mason's inert body for a few minutes. The Bear rose again and moved alongside Mason's body. It began to sniff more vigorously around the form. Finally it raised its long muscled arm and with two strokes of its massive claws ripped away the clothing over the belly of the man before him. Bjorn watched in horror as the few layers of clothing were raked away, shreds lying torn around the now exposed midriff. The Bear gave an exploratory lick, and then slowly sunk its teeth into the white belly, penetrating the resistant skin. Then, shaking its great head, it tore the flesh away, ripping a gaping wound in the abdomen.

There was no hurry. The Bear took its time in its explorations as if savoring the significance of the ritual. Its muzzle grew stained with red as it delicately and deliberately probed the innards of the torso before it, lapping at the vital juices of outflow. It seemed to find what it was looking for and began to yank out the desirable parts, the liver and kidneys. It chewed quietly, emitting small grunts and snuffling sounds, occasionally pausing to look around to ensure that it had its prey all to itself.

Half an hour had passed as the Bear continued its explorations and its ruminations within the body cavity. Then, first glancing at Bjorn, then looking around, it withdrew, seemingly satisfied for the moment. It clearly had not settled down to gorge itself at length upon the lifeless cadaver. It seemed rather to have accomplished something, fulfilled a ritual. It sat back on its haunches to contemplate.

The Bear lay with the corpse for many hours, occasionally going over to it and grunting quietly. But strangely it ate no more. The symbolic pieces had been devoured. This was not a simple exercise in feeding. A greater act had taken place. Nor did the Bear drag the body off into the underbrush to hide it for later feeding as would be normal. Instead, in the full light of midday, it moved away, leaving the body behind it. At least for now. The Bear shuffled off at a slow pace, swaying through the underbrush and evaporating into the witnessing forest.

It seemed as if long hours passed. Bjorn had lost all sense of time and still felt half paralyzed with fear, awe, wracked with confusion about what his role was, had been, what he should now do. Time passed until he grew aware that dusk was approaching. He knew he could not depart through the underbrush or even find the trail in the darkness. At some point he must have fallen asleep close to the killing site, oblivious, through emotional exhaustion and shock, of where he was.

Early in the morning the dawn light again began filtering through the morning mist, awakening Bjorn. The power and horror of the blood scene of the day before surged back into his mind. The Bear was gone. Its work had been done.

Bjorn stood up and walked over to the site where Mason's mutilated body lay. He now surveyed the mangled corpse, still feeling strangely torn by emotion. He sat with the corpse for some minutes, almost as if in meditation, perhaps in sadness, perhaps even in a kind of perverse fellowship, aware of the significance of what had taken place. He realized that this man had placed trust in him, had taken him under his wing, had shared some of his aspirations for a program that might help the Bears. He had in some way almost become a father figure to Bjorn. But Bjorn had learned that it could not be, that Mason's mission was ultimately quite incompatible with his own, with that of the natural order of things. His experience in the Bear cave left no doubt of how the Bears perceived the situation and the act of justice that must occur. The overwhelming power of the moment drained him, almost as a relief. He burst into bitter sobs. These events were not even truly of his volition, but were simply the way the story had to end.

Bjorn on sudden impulse leaned over and reached down to grasp Mason's body under the arms. He lifted and dragged it up against the large moss-covered tree with the twisted dual U-shaped trunks reaching to the sky. The blood from the gaping torso was congealing. He could see that only a few key organs had been ripped out. He paused for long minutes. Then, driven by an uncontrollable impulse, Bjorn reached deep into the body cavity and located the heart. It required some energy to rip it loose with both his bare hands, almost unconscious of the grisly task he was performing. He examined the organ, the very heart of Mason. Bjorn hesitated, then placed the heart back into the cavity of Mason's torso. Half in astonishment, Bjorn examined his own hands and wrists, turning them over front and back, now soaked deep red with Mason's blood. He reflected, then found himself raising his fingers to his mouth. He licked some of the gore off his hands with his tongue.

No other part of the lower trunk of Mason's body was exposed. His head betrayed only a deep slashing gash on the side of the skull where the bear had struck with lethal force. The neck was oddly twisted, lolling unnaturally to the side. Mason's right arm too was strangely twisted where Bjorn had struck him with the bludgeon. Bjorn gently propped the body more securely back against the tree and crossed the arms over its lap, head leaning back against the trunk in a more proper pose, eyes dimmed in death. Propped up, Mason's body appeared to be surveying the forest scene, but the gore of the open torso in full display left little doubt of animal intervention. Mason's face was without scratch and seemed strangely serene.

Bjorn drew a deep breath. He bowed his head for a few moments in an act of acknowledgment. He began to hum a few notes lightly, slowly trying to recover some sounds from his memory. He then broke forth into a more complete rhythmic song, in words that he did not fully understand, but that were linked to his experience with Bears. The song brought warmth to his heart and he felt at peace for the first time in a long time in his troubled quest.

Bjorn remained in contemplation of the scene for what felt like several hours. He then began to consider how he was going to get back to the rendezvous point and how he would relate the story about Mason's end.

A light breeze picked up, gently transporting the morning mists of the forest into motion, as if forces were engaged in some kind of encircling movement around them, overriding the stillness. A few boughs of cedar around him moved gently, lending a new living dynamic to the moment and the scene.

Then he heard it.

The great Bear had returned. Bjorn remained transfixed, motionless, perplexed as to whether this was part of the same scenario in tandem with the Bear. Had the Bear come back again for Mason? To work over the carcass? The Bear went over to Mason's body, licked around the torn flesh of the abdomen, then looked away to focus his stare upon Bjorn. Bjorn did not move. The Bear continued to stare, emitting a snuffling noise, bobbing its head, its meaning unclear. Bjorn had not known whether the Bear was even going to appear at all again during his time in the forest with Mason. Or whether it would drag Mason's body away. Judgment had been served after all. Mason was dead.

The forest seemed to fall silent except for the cawing of a raven. The other sounds of birds, of swaying branches and rasping limbs were now strangely absent. And then Bjorn began to realize that perhaps the drama was not over. Perhaps he had misread the true character of his relationship to the Bears. He was certain he had understood their outrage at the threat to the environment, to the Rainforest from Tundra's cynical plans—indeed in a broader sense, to the whole planet. Yet a dawning sense of fear swept over him as he realized he himself might be more of a part of this overwhelming cosmic drama of retribution than he had anticipated. His fate was unknowable, out of his hands, beyond his own human reckoning. Perhaps he had fulfilled his mission, at least vis-a-vis Mason. But could he escape involvement in the grander scheme? Should he show gratefulness, relief, signs of solidarity and at-one-ness with the Bear? He knelt, almost supplicating, watching as the great Bear seemed settled into a moment of contemplation, considering its options and the nature of its mission, its great head swaying.

The Bear then turned its attention towards him once again. Its huge form advanced, not in a charge, but with a determined sway, with certitude of mission.

Unable to grasp the new scene, Bjorn stumbled back and then pulled his knees up into a fetal position of supplication in the face of such intense power. His bowels turned to water. And then in a flash of awareness, fear gave way to resignation, followed by submission. The justice of the scene was beyond his ability to grasp or forfend. This final ritual clearly now involved himself every bit as much as it had Mason. Rituals as elemental as those of the natives of the Siberian North. The moment had come. The Bear lowered its head, quickly encompassed Bjorn's neck in its huge jaws, lifted and shook once or twice vigorously, instantly snapping all life out of Bjorn.

The great Bear then fell back down upon its forepaws, surveying the situation. Tension seemed to drain from its hulk. The encounter, whatever its purpose, however constructed, seemed to be over. It lowered its head and snuffled Bjorn's form before it. It nudged his body with its nose, rolling it here and there in a half-exploratory fashion. It then rose on its hind legs again, looking around as if to survey the forest scene, noting that the forest was the sole witness to the act. It then seized Bjorn's foot and dragged his lifeless body off into the underbrush, moving deeper into the wilderness, ever farther away from the direction of the camp, away from the trail that led to the lake rendezvous point, away from the flight back to the ranger's office, away from the entrance to the Great Bear Rainforest, away from Mason's office at Tundra oil, and away from Bella Bella, the locus of Bjorn's quest.

I am but one particle of dust in the cosmos, cast into the void by some primal eternal force. I am the seed of something greater. Particles dance and merge to form a substance of cosmic significance, the seed of eternal justice.

I assume my full shape, a powerful brown shape. I experience tens of thousands of generations in my wanderings from North Asia into the New World, across the land bridge that guided us across the continents. Eventually I will assume human form, as we are transformed in the dance. And in the end the dance will reveal me. Justice will prevail.

Chapter 42

Over the days the distant events far off in the rainforest revealed themselves slowly but inexorably, overwhelming Claire Fisher. She was waiting in frustrated and anxious anticipation, having exhausted her earlier avenues to locate Bjorn's present whereabouts. As the silence grew prolonged her fears solidified. While some plausible explanation could conceivably exist accounting for Bjorn's disturbing silence and absence, her heart told her there was scant hope.

Bella Bella was another existence for her. It resonated with Bjorn's presence over several years, with his recent life, and with the culture he aspired to be part of. It submitted her to the disturbing experience of being an outsider, alone in a predominantly Native community. Yet even as she felt emotionally distraught, the warmth of people on the streets and in daily encounters were a salve. She walked the streets at length, sought out the cultural centre and shyly sought permission to visit artists' workshops. She found herself craving contacts with First Nations culture, to greet new ways of life that might stand in for her missing son, a special living connection to Bjorn himself in this time of anxiety. They could perhaps offer a few tentative keys to his state of mind and his heart.

Sensing now it was almost surely in vain, each day she nonetheless repeatedly put in calls to Bjorn on his cell phone, hoping to penetrate to whatever locale or state of mind he was in. She kept visiting his rooming house to see if they had received word. As much as she craved advice and wisdom, she did not feel it was appropriate to press Sam Winters again. He had told her he would contact her if he received more information. She checked in again with Joseph once or twice again, but he too had heard nothing.

Then that Saturday, in response to Claire's several previous visits, the local RCMP contacted her directly. "Mrs. Fisher? We have some partial information that I'm afraid it is not very encouraging. The body of Mason Surrey has been recovered in the forest. So far it seems likely he was the victim of a bear attack. We have no specific news about Bjorn yet but the search continues."

A gradual picture of events now began to take on unwanted shape in Claire's mind. Indeed, the moment she had first heard that the COO was missing, the details settled into coherence in her mind. This was obviously what Bjorn had been referring to when he had spoken of "his opportunity to do something." Clearly Mason Surrey's death had to be directly traceable to Bjorn in some fashion, although she would not share her deepest fears with the RCMP. The events in the forest could not have been mere accident. She could scarcely imagine the unfolding of the awful scenario in her mind's eye.

By now she had to intellectually accept what her heart had immediately signaled earlier—that Bjorn was dead. It was just a matter of time before his death would be confirmed. Only the exact circumstances and manner of his death remained shrouded. If there had been any doubt before, his letter to her had been an early and unmistakable farewell message.

Bjorn's words to her in his last conversations, as well as Sam Winter's revelations, had opened her mind to consider a now credible reality—that the bears had in some way exerted influence upon Bjorn's mind. He had spoken with certainty that he would be the instrument of the bears' will. But even Bjorn could not know the full implications of what the "bears' will" could be.

By Sunday afternoon the RCMP contacted her again. "Mrs. Fisher? I am very sorry to have to report that we have located Bjorn's body, some half a kilometer distant from Surrey's. All indications are that he too was the victim of a bear attack." She went in to the station for more information the next morning. The officer was gentle and sympathetic, but suggested, off the record, that there were a few disturbing anomalies that they needed to investigate. "We thought initially it was a straightforward bear attack. But we found Surrey's mutilated body propped up in a sitting position against the back of a tree. We're puzzled about how this could have happened. Bjorn, for whatever reason, would most likely have been the only person who could have left him seated against the tree, after the attack. Can you think of any reason why your son might have left him there in that position? Unless Surrey had crawled there by himself which is highly unlikely, given his devastating mortal wounds. But maybe you can tell us, was Bjorn on good terms with Surrey? Was there any bad blood between them? Signs of a quarrel?"

Claire did not know how to respond to these probing questions but sought to deflect any suspicions from Bjorn. "As far as I know they were on very good terms. They were interested in taking this trip into the Rainforest together. I know Bjorn believed he could serve as an advisor to Surrey on First Nations views and to discuss the creation of a possible bear research centre." She repressed any expression of her presentiments of violence.

The following day she received an even more chilling piece of information. The RCMP had discovered a human heart—almost surely Mason's—lying loose and unattached within Mason's body cavity. Why it was simply detached from the body and left alone was unclear, although theoretically a bear could have done it. But the RCMP also mentioned that there were remains of dried blood all over both hands and wrists of Bjorn. The blood almost surely belonged to Mason since Bjorn's death had not involved loss of blood. Why would Bjorn have so much of Mason's blood on both hands? Claire sickened at the thought, and her mind moved in terrifying directions as she tried to fathom the sequence of events that could have unfolded with such an appalling result. Had this been some kind of weird ritual sacrifice? Was Bjorn capable of such a grisly act? One more comforting possibility was that he had tried to stanch the flow of blood out of Mason's chest wound.

The RCMP brought Bjorn's body back the following day. Pending further investigation and the coroner's full report, the RCMP remained reluctant to discuss any further suppositions about possible foul play. But Claire privately could no longer remain in denial to herself about what Bjorn had done.

"I'm sorry, Mrs. Fisher, I know it's terribly painful, but I'm going to have to ask you to come in to identify Bjorn Fisher's remains." *Remains.* What layers of meaning resided in that word. Dread filled her entrance into the morgue as the smell of formaldehyde invaded her nostrils. The drawer was pulled out, as she gazed on in cold fear. As soon as they pulled the sheet back off Bjorn's face she quickly made positive identification. His face mercifully appeared calm. When she forced herself to inquire, the officer admitted that only his neck and none of the rest of his body had been disfigured. Mason Surrey's body, however had been grossly disfigured and disemboweled, and had been flown to Calgary for identification and delivery to his family.

The worst that could happen had now happened. The dimensions of the events were now on full display. Claire wondered whether there were any more terrible revelations yet to come. What more could there be? She knew her task now was to come to terms with the events, to absorb them, and to learn to understand the trajectory of Bjorn's life.

The next morning she encountered Joseph on the street. The news traveled rapidly in a small town where many knew about Bjorn and his quest for his roots. "My condolences, Mrs. Fisher. I'm really very sad to hear all this. Bjorn was a good man. He was a good friend. He cared about his heritage and the environment to the very end." He did not mention his assumption that Bjorn had taken the fateful action against Surrey. Nonetheless, Claire assumed from Joseph's bitter tone in their earlier discussions about First Nations and the Rainforest that Joseph supported Bjorn's views. And Joseph, uncomfortable, showed little desire to prolong his contact with her. "I'm sorry," he repeated, "I liked Bjorn," he said as they parted.

Claire indeed had wanted to talk about Bjorn at greater length with Joseph, to gain any precious new insight into who her son had really been in the eyes of the outside world. She had of course raised him over long years, but parental insights invariably differ markedly from the way a friend and contemporary of Bjorn would see him. She now craved that privileged insight, but there were few sources remaining who could offer those heart-warming insights or revealing anecdotes to fill in her portrait of her lost son's life.

She felt an urgent desire to seek out Sam Winters again, to gain his view of these final revelations. She took the path back to his house in the afternoon, but he was not home. In the early evening he was still not there. She wondered where he could have gone. The sad task of taking Bjorn's body back to Vancouver still lay ahead of her, and she had little reason to prolong her stay in Bella Bella. She tried Sam's house again at noon the following day and did find him home. As he let her in, they exchanged sad smiles as he nodded to her in deepened acknowledgment of their joint concern and pain.

"I am truly sorry for the loss of your son, Mrs. Fisher," Sam offered.

"Thank you. I guess what I had feared—maybe what we both feared— came to pass."

"Yes. This is an ugly event. But I feel especially sorry for Bjorn. He was a promising and passionate young man. But he slipped from the right path. He let himself be taken over by crude political emotions that were not helpful."

She bit her lip and nodded. "I don't really know how to ask this, but…what about the bears? You know how he was convinced he was in touch with them. I know we talked about this once before. But how do you interpret that now? Was he just a confused and angry young man?"

Sam paused for a moment. "Bjorn believed that he had real communication with the Bear People. He talked about it often to me."

"And you believe it?"

"I do. But what kind of exact impulses, visions and messages Bjorn received cannot be known to any outside person. Each of us draws different messages from the world around us. You cannot tell me what my reality is, or I you. Each creature perceives reality differently and yet they are all pieces of a greater truth, a greater whole."

"Yes, but you do believe there were messages?"

"Messages? We each receive different messages in our understanding of things. What is more important is what we actually choose to do about those messages. In the end I believe that Bjorn did what he truly believed he had to do, in his own mind."

"Are you saying that you approve, then, of his action?"

"No, I do not approve. But we do not know the details either. Let me tell you, Mrs. Fisher, in our Native beliefs it is not an appropriate action for our people to kill another human, whatever the cause, even in the name of protecting the environment. That is important to us. You should know that I went to see the RCMP about this matter the day before yesterday after I received the first reports about the death of Mr. Surrey. I simply could not remain silent about what I knew about Bjorn's state of mind. These matters are linked directly to the investigation.

"But I hope you didn't directly implicate Bjorn."

"Mrs. Fisher, please understand, this issue affects our community directly. I cannot remain silent. I have also spoken with many of the Elders of this community in the past two days. They do not know a lot about Bjorn, but I do. Bjorn's birth mother may or may not have actually been from this community. But whatever his roots, what is important is that this killing does not represent what First Nations people in this region believe is right. Murder and violence go against the principles of the Creator. It is a rejection of the wisdom and reflection of our People."

"Did Bjorn know of your concerns, and of the Elders?"

"Yes. I made that fully clear to him—that such violence violates the spirit of the tradition he was searching for. Worse, what he did solved nothing, and may have made things worse."

Claire felt still unsatisfied with her understanding. "But, do you think you might have been able to change Bjorn's interpretation of the messages he believed he was receiving?"

Sam sighed. "If we had had more time, I believe my views and the views of our Elders might have influenced Bjorn, maybe addressed his concerns more clearly and prevented his tragic act. But in the final analysis we can never know what forces brought him together with Mason Surrey in such a destructive way."

"But yet you believe the bears counseled violence?"

Sam looked with some compassion at Claire. He shook his head. "We cannot always choose what we will be a conduit for in this life. Sometimes we are instruments of forces that we cannot fully identify."

Claire for the first time felt the gates of emotion open wide as the full reality of sadness and loss overwhelmed her. She felt that this man understood Bjorn better than perhaps anyone, understood the depth of his feelings and even showed sympathy for Bjorn's dogged belief in the reality of his communications with Nature. She did not fully grasp the dimensions of everything Sam had said, but she found his richer perspective strangely comforting, it gave her license to permit her emotions to flow in front of him. Sam did not appear discomfited by Claire's tears. He merely nodded and sat expectantly for many minutes until she recovered her composure. He then rose and touched her gently on the shoulder.

"Bjorn's story will be talked about for a long time, Mrs. Fisher, among white people as well as Native peoples. And among environmentalists. Who knows, maybe this act of violence will bring new attention to the issues of our coastline and our animals. And our world. Bjorn came to understand the threat to our natural order. But he acted with fire in his heart instead of light."

Claire felt overwhelmed at their exchange, at the new dimensions of thinking about reality that it opened up to her, at the possibility that "myth" had actually led Bjorn to understand deeper realities. She mourned him and she mourned his impulsiveness. His wrong action in the name of a broader vision.

"I thank you for your help, Sam." Her voice trembled. "And for your help to Bjorn over the past years. You have let me understand a little more deeply what my son has experienced." She moved unsteadily to the door.

"In the end we should honour Bjorn not for his act, but for his passion, concern, and understanding of the damage to our land. I shall remember him," Sam said.

"Thank you. That means a lot to me. My experience with my son is still far from over."

As she lifted open the gate and went out Claire decided to go for a long walk around through the town on her way back to her lodgings. She felt drained, unsure even of what level of existence she was operating on. But rather than closing this sad chapter in her life, she felt as if a new door was opening. She felt an unexpected thirst to absorb more deeply the life of Bella Bella around her. She was surprised, initially even a little disturbed, to find a small element of pride creeping into her grief, pride that her son had been driven by a passionate commitment to a just and worthy cause—however flawed his judgment.

She understood and drew comfort from Sam's conviction that Bjorn had indeed received some form of communication from the bears over the years. And that such communications were invariably personal and subjective—but took meaningful form in Bjorn's mind. The signs had perhaps been there from his boyhood.

Claire knew she would never understand exactly what had taken place in the forest that day. But she could see the deeper roots, how he had come back from meeting radical environmentalists in the US, his first exposure to those passionately and dangerously committed to the environment, who had been willing to risk their own lives and the lives of others in the name of this cause. She found a new understanding for similar cases of First Nations protests and demonstrations in Canada to protect the environment and sacred lands from industrial corporations.

She realized she would not abandon the struggle that Bjorn had joined. She would deepen her knowledge about how First Nations understood the relationship and responsibility of humankind towards Nature and Creation. She would salve the pain in her heart through peaceful actions to help protect the Great Bear Rainforest. To help bring about reconciliation between First Nations communities and non-Natives.

She now knew there was no pressing need for her to rush back to Vancouver. Her emotional vulnerability opened up within her a new emotional receptivity to the character of life in Bella Bella, to the profusion of animal life expressed in Native art around her: the magnificently arched bodies of the carved orcas, the hierarchy of creatures inhabiting totem poles, each one telling a different piece of the story of the pole. The carved masks that provided direct links to other creatures and to other worlds and psychological states—states to which most humans remained insensitive or blind. To the existence of a broader world outside normal human awareness and experience that needed to be sought out.

Tears came to her eyes as she experienced a need to absorb and understand the ubiquitous salmon images around her. She found herself newly moved by the mystery of the salmon cycle of life and death in fulfillment of their purpose. As if Bjorn in some way had been through a cycle—but to give birth to what?

She encountered Joseph again in the streets of the town several days later. "You're still here," he observed. "I thought you were going back."

"No," she replied, "I want to find Bjorn in this place."

Joseph began to feel the first touch of compassion for this woman who really did seem to want to understand. "I'd be happy to take you out on my boat sometime and show you some of the places that meant something to Bjorn." Claire gratefully accepted this offer and Joseph's gesture of reconciliation. She knew now that these waters were the place where Bjorn's final remains must rest.

Over the days she felt Bjorn growing closer to her. She had to help validate his life by reaching out to absorb at least a few modest elements of his insights and the world in which he lived.

And she resolved to travel to Calgary to meet Melanie Surrey, whose husband had been killed by Claire's own son in a blind dance of conflicting idealisms and visions.

Author's Note

This novel is a work of fiction. None of the main characters of the novel or their interactions represent actual individuals, situations or events. Nonetheless, a few events of the novel do partially reflect actual political, social, and environmental situations in North America and especially in British Columbia. Discussion and portrayal of the activities of the American Indian Movement and the Animal Liberation Front are based on open source materials, as are the controversies and politics surrounding bear hunting, pipelines and oil tankers on BC land and waters. The agonies and controversies over oil exploitation in Ogoniland, Nigeria are also based on public historical record.

In dealing with First Nations tradition, beliefs and concerns I have tried to represent them in good faith as best I can; inevitably they may fall short of accurate portrayal in the minds of some, for which I apologize. Naturally, in the end I alone am responsible for the entire content of the book.

I am aware of the pitfalls of a non-Native writer writing about First Nations, or about any other cultural minority, especially those who have been exposed to the withering power of dominant white culture. There are indeed legitimate grounds for concern about "white appropriation," "cultural appropriation," or even exploitation of Native cultures in the past and present.

On the other hand I believe the world will be a much poorer place if all of us as human beings are not able to concern ourselves, write about, or reveal the exploitation and problems that all minorities encounter. These huge social failures and shortcomings on the part of the dominant culture will not be alleviated any faster if only Native writers can bring them to public attention. The history of the world is about cultural domination the world over as well as about efforts, even within the dominant cultures, to change things.

Acknowledgments

I thank George A. Fowler, translator of numerous Chinese and Indonesian novels, for his constant encouragement along the way and for his creative suggestions in shaping the novel.

I thank my sister Meredith Ann Fuller, a fine writer in her own right, for her patient reading of the manuscript in an early form and for offering many valuable suggestions and fixes on the draft.

Special thanks to Judy Dunn who has been keenly interested in the whole project from early on and offered many suggestions and insights along the way into the material, especially as relates to her knowledge of First Nations life, and the identity crises of youth.

I thank Adrian Juric for his constant interest and encouragement in the themes of the novel.

Thanks to Meg Fellowes for early comments and suggestions for further readings in the field of First Nations experience; and to the many members of the Squamish Environmental Society who helped educate me over the years on many key environmental issues in BC.

And to Thor and Dorte Froslev who have tirelessly fought for environmental issues in BC through the remarkable institution of their Brackendale Art Gallery, and for their work for the protection of Bald Eagles; they provide a constant source of inspiration.

And to John Buchanan, the premier and tireless environmental "amateur", pioneer and muckraker of the environmental cause in Howe Sound and Squamish who has taught me much over the years.

And to the Squamish Nation whose celebrations, ceremonies and artistic presence have enriched my insight and life and given me the privilege of living in the same community with them.

And to so many other Squamish environmental activists, too numerous to mention, who have helped inspire and educate me over the years.

Above all I offer thanks and deep appreciation to my skilled and savvy editor, Rebecca Wood Barrett whose editorial eye, enriched by her screen play expertise, suggested painful but necessary cuts in exposition as well as offering many valuable suggestions on plot, character and dramatic settings. The novel would not be what it is today without her efforts.

As for myself, I have been reading books, studies and novels for more than twenty five years on Native Americans and First Nations, as well as many other aboriginal cultures in Latin America—far too many of them to name. But for this novel I wish to especially note a short list of books from which I have particularly received help and/or inspiration. The list regrettably cannot be comprehensive and I have surely overlooked some key books.

Sherman Alexie, *Reservation Blues*

Judith Berman, *Bear Daughter*

Fergus M. Bordewich, *Killing the White Man's Indian*

Joseph Boyden, *Three Day Road; Through Black Spruce*

Robert Bringhurst, *A Story as Sharp as a Knife*

Ann Cameron, *Daughter of Copper Woman*

Roger Caras, *Monarch of Deadman Bay*

Marion Engel, *bear*

Suzanne Fournier and Ernie Crey, *Stolen From Our Embrace*

Christie Harris, *Raven's Cry*

Nick Jans, *The Grizzly Maze*

Cliff Kopas, *Bella Coola*

Peter Knudson and David Suzuki, *Wisdom of the Elders*

Arno Kopecki, *The Oil Man and the Sea*

Lee Maracle, *Bobbi Lee, Indian Rebel; Sun Dogs*

Ian McAllister, *Great Bear Wild*

Megan Felicity Moody and Tony J. Pitcher: *Eulachon (Thaleichthys pacificus): Past and Present*

Robert J. Muckle, *The First Nations of British Columbia*

Seattle Native Art Museum, *The Spirit Within*

John G. Neihardt, *Black Elk Speaks*

Jamie Sams and David Carson, *Medicine Cards*

James Gart Shelton, *Bear Attacks, the Deadly Truth*

Paul Shepard, Barry Sanders, *The Sacred Paw*

Hillary Stewart, *Looking at Totem Poles*

Hyemehyohsts Storm, *Seven Arrows*

Timothy Treadwell, *Among Grizzlies*

John Vaillant, *The Golden Spruce*

Richard Wagamese, *One Story, One Song; Medicine Walk*

Pamela Whittaker, *Kwakiutl Legends*

Personal trips to Bella Bella and Haida Gwaii have also been invaluable.

89074911R00231

Made in the USA
Columbia, SC
17 February 2018